Adventurer, you whose weight is borne by your winged soul! The mystical world of Theldesia is home to dragons and giants, magical beasts, and demihumans. Fragrant green winds blow across this new yet ancient land that opens before you like a blank page. Fill it with your life.

LOG HORIZON
7 THE GOLD OF THE KUNIE

MAMARE TOUNO ILLUSTRATION BY **KAZUHIRO HARA**

YEN ON

NEW YORK

184

▶**CHAPTER 5**
CONSIDERATION OF FRIENDSHIP

▶**CHAPTER 4**
GUILD MASTER

142

CONTENTS

▼ CHARACTER INTRODUCTIONS

KINJO

▶ SEASONED YOUNG LEADER

LI GAN

▶ GEEKY PERSON-OF-THE-EARTH LORE MASTER

NAOTSUGU

▶ PANTIES WARRIOR

A TRUSTY GUARDIAN AND SHIROE'S GOOD FRIEND, NAOTSUGU IS A CHEERFUL, TOUGH YOUNG GUY AND FORMER DEBAUCHERY TEA PARTY MEMBER. HE TOOK A TEMPORARY HIATUS FROM ELDER TALES, ONLY TO GET TRAPPED IN THE GAME WORLD ON THE DAY HE RETURNED.

THE SUCCESSOR TO THE TITLE "SAGE OF MIRAL LAKE," WHICH APPEARED IN THE OFFICIAL *ELDER TALES* GAME SETTING. FOR A PERSON OF THE EARTH, HE'S HIGHLY EDUCATED, VERY KNOWLEDGEABLE, AND WELL-INFORMED ABOUT ALL SORTS OF THINGS.

THE YOUNG LEADER OF THE KUNIE CLAN, WHICH PROVIDES MANY SERVICES THAT ARE VITAL TO ADVENTURERS, SUCH AS THE BANK. A TOUGH CUSTOMER WHOSE POKER FACE DURING NEGOTIATIONS AMAZES EVEN SHIROE.

▼ PLOT

EVER SINCE AKIBA'S LIBRA FESTIVAL, AKATSUKI HAD BEEN TROUBLED.

ALTHOUGH SHE WAS CONFIDENT THAT SHE WAS A SKILLED ASSASSIN, SINCE SHE HAD AVOIDED HUMAN RELATIONSHIPS AND HAD NO RAID EXPERIENCE, SHE COULDN'T CALL HERSELF SUPER-TOP-CLASS. IN CONSEQUENCE, SHE WAS DESPERATELY SEARCHING FOR A WAY TO ACQUIRE A MYSTERY, A NEW SPECIAL SKILL CALLED OVERSKILL BY SOME.

JUST THEN, SOMETHING WHICH SHOULD HAVE BEEN IMPOSSIBLE IN AKIBA OCCURRED: A MURDER. BECAUSE SHIROE WAS AWAY, AKATSUKI DESPERATELY HURRIED TO INVESTIGATE THE INCIDENT, AND WHILE BATTLING THE MURDERER, SHE EXPERIENCED DEATH FOR THE FIRST TIME. AT AN OCEAN IN THE SPACE BETWEEN LIFE AND DEATH, AKATSUKI WAS REUNITED WITH SHIROE. THIS WAS THE TRIGGER SHE NEEDED TO RID HERSELF OF HER HESITATION.

WHEN AKATSUKI REVIVED IN THE TEMPLE, MANY PEOPLE FROM AKIBA WERE THERE, WORRYING ABOUT HER. ALTHOUGH SHE HAD BEEN BAD AT DEALING WITH PEOPLE, SHE DIDN'T RUN, AND FOR THE FIRST TIME, SHE SINCERELY ASKED FOR THEIR HELP.

MASSACHU — WILLI

▶MITHRIL EYES

FIELD BATTLE COMMANDER AND GUILD MASTER OF SILVER SWORD, AN ELITE COMBAT GUILD. ALTHOUGH INVITED TO THE CONFERENCE HELD TO ESTABLISH THE ROUND TABLE COUNCIL, HE SHOWED NO INTEREST IN AKIBA'S SELF-GOVERNMENT AND LEFT PARTWAY THROUGH.

DEMII

▶THUG WHO'S VIOLENT AND PROUD OF IT

A MONK AND THE LEADER OF THE BRIGANTEERS, THE GUILD THAT CAME VERY CLOSE TO RULING SUSUKINO THROUGH TERROR. HE'S HAD IT OUT FOR SHIROE EVER SINCE SHIROE BEAT HIM LIKE A RUG.

TETOR

▶SELF-PROCLAIMED GALACTIC IDOL

THE CUTEST CLERIC IN THE UNIVERSE. A GALACTIC IDOL (WIDE-RANGE TRAVELING ENTERTAINER) WHO PACKS LOVE, COURAGE, HOPE, AN APPETITE, A MISCHIEVOUS HEART, AND A TRIUMPHANT FACE INTO A SLIM BODY, AND WHO'S INTENT ON PROSELYTIZING.

AS A RESULT, AKATSUKI MASTERED SHADOW LURK, A MYSTERY THAT WAS HERS ALONE, AND SHE MANAGED TO DEFEAT THE MURDERER BY WORKING TOGETHER WITH MANY OTHER COMPANIONS.

WHEN SHE DID, IN ADDITION TO ACQUIRING A MYSTERY, SHE GAINED HER FIRST FRIENDS.

CHAPTER. 1

SHIROE OF THE NORTH

▶ LEVEL: **94**

▶ SUBCLASS: BORDERLAND PATROLMAN

▶ MYSTERY: UNOPENED EYE, SHINING SHIELD

▶ HP: **14750**

▶ MP: **7325**

▶ ITEM 1:

[ARMOR OF SILVER OATH]

WHITE FULL-BODY ARMOR WITH A DULL SHEEN, MADE OF MAGIC STEEL AND OTHER MATERIALS QUARRIED FROM MOUNTAINS. IT HAS DEFENSE CAPABILITIES BORDERING ON FANTASY-CLASS, SUCH AS COMPENSATING FOR AGGRO AND COLD RESISTANCE. A PROTOTYPE THE ARTISANS OF AKIBA CONCENTRATED ALL THEIR SKILLS TO MAKE,

▶ ITEM 2:

[GUARD OF LIONHEART]

A BIG, FANTASY-CLASS SHIELD WITH THE SOUL OF A LION WHO TURNED ITS FANGS ON THE GODS SEALED INSIDE IT. IT CAN REDUCE MOVEMENT SPEED OF NEARBY ENEMIES. SHIROE RECALLS IT USED TO BE CALLED "LION'S GREAT SHIELD," BUT ITS ABILITIES HAVE INCREASED AS WELL, AND THERE ARE MANY MYSTERIES ABOUT IT.

▶ ITEM 3:

[GRIFFIN TANDEM SEAT]

A TWO-PERSON GRIFFIN SADDLE, INVENTED BY THE ARTISANS OF AKIBA. IT ISN'T A PARTICULARLY POWERFUL ITEM, BUT NAOTSUGU THINKS IT'S A GEM WORTH BRAGGING ABOUT. HE'S TRIED SEATING A VARIETY OF PEOPLE BEHIND HIM, BUT MARIELLE IN PARTICULAR GOT ALL EXCITED, AND THAT WAS ROUGH.

\<Chalk\>
Used to draw marks
in dungeons.

▶ 1

Pale crimson Foxfire illuminated a magnificent room.

Unlike the Bug Lights that were prevalent in Akiba, the flames were delicate, and their weak light didn't reach the corners of the big space. The intensity of the wavering glow fluctuated, creating shadows here and there.

The spacious room, which looked deserted, had but one master.

A woman with black hair was curled up in the shadows, with a blanket wrapped around her like a cloak.

Nothing in there was shabby.

The room was outfitted with luxurious furniture. A sofa decorated with Japanese brocade. Silk damask wall hangings, a canopy bed, a table of limestone. However, none of the furniture seemed to have been used and loved in anyone's everyday life. The atmosphere it gave off was inorganic and distant, as if the furnishings were there simply because they had been ordered to be.

As usual, lying as if hiding in the shadows of those furnishings, Nureha was passing the night without a wink of sleep.

A waterfall of bundled papers spilled from a small, round table, spreading into her field of vision. They appeared to be documents; there were letters written on them, with red marks like scattered flowers. On closer inspection, the marks seemed to be wine stains.

Nureha strained her eyes, taking in the dimly illuminated scene.

There was no way she could read such tiny, precise letters in such a dark space. And besides, she was already battling the illusions that arose from the darkness, both on the page and in the room beyond.

Various things appeared from the shadows. Most were white, indistinct human shapes.

Even the outlines of the figures were vague. They whispered and giggled to each other in hushed voices Nureha couldn't hear well, shooting glances her way. Weighing, taunting looks reached her from the nebulous, smoky shadows.

She clenched her fists, which had grown cold, and glared at them.

Sometimes, more tangible, fat, nausea-inducing arms appeared. They would would grab Nureha's hair, trying to drag her toward the white shadows.

Nureha gave a low, threatening growl, like a wild animal. She already knew that if she did, the shadows would disappear.

She spent a long time that way, bottling up her ears to silence the voices that seemed to curse her.

The entire guild hall, with its sixteen luxurious rooms, had been set up as her private chambers. Aside from Nureha, there were fewer than ten people who could enter it. At this hour, late at night, no one would come here except the People of the Earth ladies-in-waiting who were on night duty.

In the midst of this empty darkness, Nureha spent endless nights.

She was physically exhausted, though she didn't remember having accomplished much of anything. Cold blood circulated through her four limbs, which were as heavy as sandbags, and the world was so gloomy it could have been underwater.

This was nothing particularly unusual. It had been this way for ages.

Gaining an Adventurer body hadn't changed the isolation of Nureha's nights.

She held a hand up in front of her eyes.

Her fingers were slender, white, and smooth, like some exquisitely fashioned object.

Gleaming, pale pink nails were attached to this lithe, bewitching work of art.

Then came fine, delicate skin. The rolling outline of her arm, which held no sense of warmth, still evoked ample softness.

A bitter, irrepressible delight mixed with the darkness, which held nothing but hatred and rejection.

Nureha herself saw no great value in this body, but she was well aware that it drove others mad. It was a debauched joy, which that knowledge brought her. She moved her white fingers, more alluring than their former, real-world counterparts, stroking the darkness.

Her sweet, husky voice; her floral scent; her body, bound only by the pretense of clothing—all were objects of desire for others. At that thought, a sticky, unclean delight welled up inside Nureha.

The white shadows laughed shortly, taunting her from the documents that were their territory, but she responded with a contemptuous look. The white shadows gave accusatory moans, but the wind seemed to have changed: The Nureha who had been enduring agony up until a moment ago was gone.

Curled up in her blanket, she purred, deep in her throat.

Even she thought it was a sinister sound.

If the young heads of the administrative families had been there, or Loreil, the leader of the imperial guards, or no, even Zeldus or Nakalnad, or anyone else, she probably wouldn't have made a harsh, creaking sound like this. Captivating others with a coaxing voice that seemed to be coated in honey was routine for Nureha. It was what she'd done up till now, and what she would no doubt continue to do.

She thought it was senseless.

She thought it was ridiculous.

Still, the more she thought these things, the funnier it was to see hoards of people running this way and that, sometimes fighting, sometimes grieving, cursing each other, and quarreling so they could boast of their own supremacy, all from desire for senseless, ridiculous Nureha.

The people who'd scorned her and accused her of being evil now showed such attachment that they'd throw away their fortunes or their lives at a single, coaxing word from her. This was both her weapon and her armor on these long nights. The only thing that made her forget the pain that tormented her, even temporarily, was the madness of the people who fought over her.

Only the ludicrous figures of the people who worshiped Nureha as if she were gold or jewels—worthless as she was—warmed her, healed her, and set her tingling sweetly.

For while she was watching them, she was able to feel pleasant. Most of all, only the trivial, ridiculous performances of the people who danced around her made her certain that this world was just as worthless as she was.

Remembering the warnings of the white-faced Adventurers who'd pleaded with her brought a faint smile to her lips.

This world isn't a game. We have to fight to survive here.

Nureha was aware that her smile was a grim one.

What foolish things to say. Rubbish. What was the point of saying that now? Nureha thought they might as well have been talking in their sleep. The boy Adventurer who'd once said those words to her was now working away as a member of Plant Hwyaden, offering up his life every day. When he'd spoken of fighting to survive, had he meant finding employment in a guild and becoming a worker bee?

Ridiculous.

A few hours after the Catastrophe had occurred, Nureha had stripped the few Adventurers who'd approached her of all their possessions: their money, their food, and even their weapons and defensive gear. It had been easy. They'd been panicking, and they'd blindly believed even the most preposterous lie.

Several days later, their devotion had given her a hint regarding a new world. They'd stopped thinking due to the magnitude of the shock, and when Nureha obligingly took command, they obeyed her every word. She had organized them, encouraged them with kind words that made them forget their anxiety, and in a few weeks, she'd become one of the wealthiest Adventurers in Minami.

Then, one month after the Catastrophe, having obtained her Overskill, she acquired Minami's guard system.

The coup d'état had been over before anyone knew it was happening. Having obtained the greatest military might possible, with that power behind her, Nureha negotiated with the People of the Earth nobles and administrators and acquired even greater wealth. Once she'd come that far, it had been easy to gain control of the Temple.

Yes.

It had been easy.

The fight for survival the boy had warned her about several months after the Catastrophe, as if he were telling her the secrets of this world—that was all it had amounted to.

It was so dull no one could have objected to calling it imbecilic.

The boy's extreme innocence had actually made her hate him.

This world is not a game. When she'd heard the words, Nureha had been able to smile from the bottom of her heart. She was grateful for that terribly childish statement. If people were this naïve in the face of an unprecedented disaster, then the world was a hunting ground full of defenseless sheep indulging in afternoon naps.

The boy's expression had been desperate, and she'd felt a small temptation to dash the black contents of her heart all over him, but she'd firmly maintained the attitude of a forlorn older sister. She knew that was the mask he wanted.

However, inside, she was filled with the nearly irresistible impulse to laugh.

She knew that. She'd known it for ages.

In the first place, Nureha had never played.

She'd never thought of *Elder Tales* as a game, as leisure recreation. Not even once.

Even when *Elder Tales* had been an MMORPG—a game, as far as most players were concerned—to Nureha it had been a harsh battle-field, something necessary for her survival.

Unless you kept bleeding, unless you kept screaming, you'd be forgotten.

Being forgotten meant being erased from the world.

Unless you were someone who meant something to somebody, unless you were wanted, unless you were treasured, you might as well be dead. Or rather, it was even worse than being dead.

After all, death was silence and nirvana and an ending, but living as worthless, insignificant rubbish that nobody liked wasn't an end. Living as an inferior breed that no one needed meant that all the hells there were would continue endlessly.

In order to attract interest, Nureha had trained hard enough to draw blood. Her entire life up to the present had been a fight for survival: an attempt to make herself liked, to make herself wanted. There hadn't been one single game.

Nureha knew hell. She knew the miserable loneliness that seemed to sear her to the core.

No matter how painful the effort, it had been far better than being ignored. When her training finally bore fruit and she was able to gain favor with the slightest word or gesture, Nureha threw that favor to the ground as if it were trash.

To her, this was revenge. It was a ceremony to show them that to her, their favor was absolutely worthless. The eyes of the players who were well-disposed to Nureha were dulled by greed, and jeering at their destruction brought her an indescribable exultation.

We have to fight to survive here.

It was a line out of a farce.

Why? Because that line made it sound like they hadn't had to fight to survive in their former world.

That might actually have been the case. For that boy, at least. Maybe he'd been very lucky, had lived in a meadow of flowers. Along with the impulse to laugh, that thought made black hatred well up inside her.

From what Nureha knew, every moment was a fight for survival. In that respect, there was absolutely no difference between their former world and this one.

Decipher the systems, search out the weak points, make them get careless, toy with them, make them trust you, betray them, steal their share—that was the fundamental structure of the world. If he was making an intentional resolution to do that, he was much too far behind the times.

She understood very well why it had been easy to unify Minami.

Nureha had always meant to steal it. Of the tens of thousands of players who had been exiled to this world, she alone had lived it as if it were reality from the very beginning. To her, that had been routine.

She had simply lived as she had when *Elder Tales* had been a game: She had clung to goodwill, fostered attachment, and scattered love and discord. She had merely demanded her own share, as usual. That was why she was the beloved center of Plant Hwyaden. This world had chosen Nureha. She had achieved happiness. She had won everything!

With the sound of the sigh she slowly expelled filling her ears, she glared at the shadows with hatred.

She'd been chosen, so why was she so full of pain? She shivered, hugging her own tail like a body pillow.

Why did she have to curl up like a wounded animal, holding her breath, just getting through the night?

Nureha clenched her teeth, and the fox ears on her head quivered.

She looked up. At the other end of her gaze, the door opened as if a rectangle of light had been cut out, and a maid appeared.

"Lady Nureha."

"......"

Nureha looked away, openly ignoring her. It was Indicus, the maid in charge of Plant Hwyaden's practical affairs. She was Nureha's confidante, but she wasn't of interest. The woman was almost a sort of curse that clung to Nureha.

"Not using your bed again, I see."

"..."

Nureha looked up at Indicus, who was turned into a shadow by the light behind her.

The maid's normal expression was a frozen mask, but she wore a big smile now. That smile was never directed at anyone but Nureha, and whenever she saw it, she felt as if her stomach was spasming. That smile had the same smell as the arms that reached out from the darkness of her bedroom, no matter how many times she cut them off, no matter how many times she cleansed herself. It clung to her, stickily, sludge she couldn't completely wipe away.

"Were you thinking of Shiroe?"

"......"

Nureha glared at her, steadily.

However, unlike those vague white shadows, Indicus wasn't frightened, and she didn't fade.

With a sharp smile like a crescent moon, she glided closer, bending down and putting her face close to Nureha.

The scent of cold steel drifted from the maid, causing Nureha to bite her lip. It was a smell that wouldn't have suited most women—the hint of a well-maintained blade.

"Were you?"

"Don't talk about him."

She thrust those words at Indicus, brimming with irritation and anger, but they didn't seem to reach her. It was always like this. Indicus had never accepted any of the wishes Nureha asked of her, with one exception—and it was an exception she'd traded everything for.

"What did I tell you? I did, you know. He's no good. You can talk to him, but nothing will come of it. He can't connect to anything. He's always been like that. He isn't a player. He's merely static with advanced abilities. Do you understand? Lady Nureha?"

Nureha's vision was beginning to blur with pain and fear.

"That's a man you can never have. He's just a traitor, but he's bright. You could probably say he's scrupulous. He recognizes it, you know. The stink of the gutter."

Even though she'd been expecting them, had been prepared for them, Indicus's words hurt Nureha like a blow to the stomach. The memories she'd desperately pushed into the darkness materialized like countless ghosts, trying to drag her back to that familiar hell.

This was the true form of the indistinct murmurs, the things the white shadows whispered.

The past Nureha had shed back on Earth, the memories she'd erased.

"My dear girl, do you really think anyone would touch you? Dirty, sordid, shabby, beggar you? You're filthy with lies. There's nothing the least bit real about you. A closer look at what's 'real' about you just reveals a stench worse than rotten sewage. You, who always wore a faint, sickening smile and gazed over here hungrily."

A mad terror rose again.

A plastic school lunch plate. Soup with garbage mixed into it. Memories of biting her lip in a cramped locker, hoping no one would find her. Memories of having her belongings hidden and having to walk over winter asphalt with bare feet, of falling into a restless sleep in the shadow of the bushes, so that even her family wouldn't find her. All sorts of recollections of defeat.

"Please understand. No human as disgusting as yourself should be conceited enough to think they could connect with someone else… Don't you see? I'm the only one who'd associate with a woman as filthy as you."

The urge to vomit was rising in her throat, and she desperately pushed it down.

She managed to bite it back.

It was sheer luck.

To keep her from registering that weakness, Nureha frantically opened her eyes wide. Indicus had described her accurately. She knew all that without being told. She was more aware of her dingy, disgusting self than anyone.

However, knowing herself was completely different from having someone else point it out to her.

"You're a very convenient princess to gaze upon from a distance."

Nureha glared at her, but Indicus's fingers twisted her ear.

"So. Lady. Nureha. We can't have you going to Akiba. A little self-awareness, please. This place, Plant Hwyaden, isn't your salon anymore. You'll gather lots of puppets and build your castle, and this time, I'll obtain the whole Yamato server. Remember, Lady Nureha? That was the promise, wasn't it?"

Nureha's wish. Nureha's request.

A dream on which she'd wagered everything, so that she'd never have to go back there.

No matter what she had to do—and she meant that literally—no matter *what* she had to do, Nureha never, ever wanted to repeat the experiences of her past. That was why she'd joined forces with Indicus. Plant Hwyaden was Nureha's castle. It was a castle that never slept, filled with countless lights and soft compliments.

"You're going to make a place for yourself to belong, aren't you?"

Keeping up appearances so that Indicus wouldn't see her weakness, Nureha nodded desperately.

"That's right. It's about to begin, you know. The Ten-Seat Council."

Indicus seemed to have lost interest in Nureha. Nureha didn't attend all Ten-Seat Councils; she wasn't interested in guild administration in the first place.

"Because you're the princess, yes. I'll tell everyone for you, Nureha. After all, you are Plant Hwyaden's precious, precious guild master."

Leaving words of sympathy behind her as a parting gift, Indicus's footsteps receded.

In the midst of the curse from her past and self-loathing that made her writhe, Nureha hugged her sides, folding in on herself, and shrank, becoming ever so small.

Her hands and feet were so cold they hurt, as though her metabolism had dropped. The blanket she'd wrapped around herself was heavy, and it didn't bring her any warmth.

Her pulse fluctuated violently, and the world sank into darkness before her eyes, as if she were anemic.

All that rose up were terrible recollections and memories of humiliation, and their ghosts tried to drag Nureha back to Earth. The evil spirits attacked her whenever Indicus gave the order, and she had to keep fighting them all alone.

However, the corners of her lips held a very faint smile.

Don't you see? I'm the only one who'd contract with a woman as filthy as you.

Not true.

That wasn't true now.

It had been only a verbal promise; you couldn't call it a contract. It might have been nothing more than an exchange, nearly a jest, said only in passing between the two, but right now, Nureha had one other promise in addition to her contract with Indicus.

Because it's probably more in line with your wish to have me as an enemy than an ally.

The parting words spoken by the young man Indicus had given up on. They shielded Nureha, if only ever so slightly.

In the distance, a low, metallic sound rang out, announcing that it was nine o'clock.

The hands of the clock advanced slowly, as if they were sticky, and the night still seemed to stretch on forever. Even with very little sleep, Adventurer bodies could function without much trouble. That advantage was also the prison chain that trapped Nureha in the night. She went through repeated cycles of light dozing followed by sudden, terrified awakenings.

In this room, where her customary nocturnal battle would continue… *Someday, for sure.* Forming the shape of these words—words she'd never once spoken, words like a prayer—with silent lips, Nureha drifted into a shallow sleep.

▶2

The room, in which several men and women were assembled, had a curious design.

Pillars with carved drapes adorned the walls, finely patterned vases spilled over with fresh flowers, and even the tables and chairs were inlaid with gold. All of it was barely of note though, in comparison to the magnetic vitality of the people gathered in the room.

There were the eight council members, each of them exceptional, along with their attendants.

"Where's Indicus?"

The question had come from a man with glasses and neat clothes that made him look like a bureaucrat.

"She's with the princess. She'll probably be back soon. Don't worry about it, Zeldus," a woman in a military uniform answered.

"The designated time was when the moon rose. It's well past that," the man named Zeldus huffed.

"The princess is the same as ever."

"Those two should just get married already."

A young voice that exuded arrogance and a musing voice chimed in as well, one after the other.

The room was shaped like a gradual staircase; the height of each step was about four centimeters. Though it was really more like a series of low landings than stairs. On each landing, an individual's unique space had been set up.

Many had sofas or leather-upholstered chairs, and some of the landings were equipped with desks or small bookshelves. All together, there were ten seats and ten different levels. The arches that opened in each of the room's four walls had also been built at different heights, and the structure seemed to promote coming and going, so it was likely that these levels indicated the rank of the person who occupied them. It was as if the room's odd construction showed their relationships just as they were.

Kazuhiko sat in a low chair, hugging his favorite katana, while looking around the room. This gathering was the Ten-Seat Council. It was an assembly of the people in charge of Minami's administration, and in practical terms, it was also the core council of Plant Hwyaden.

Participants in the Ten-Seat Council were called Ten-Seats, after the name of the council, or Seat Officers.

At present, two of the Ten-Seats had yet to arrive: Nureha, guild master of Plant Hwyaden; and Indicus, who had gone to fetch her.

Indicus would probably appear soon, but there was no telling about Nureha. She was capricious and seemed uninterested in the trivialities of the day-to-day running of the guild, and she almost never attended councils like this one. Now that Plant Hwyaden was established and had become an enormous organization, the decisions of Nureha—its founder and leader—weren't needed on a daily basis. The members were used to her absence.

This Ten-Seat Council meeting was a regular one. Kazuhiko hadn't heard that there were any special topics for discussion.

However, that didn't mean he could let his guard down.

The relationships among the Seat Officers were complex and delicate. Plant Hwyaden had been established by assimilating all the Adventurers in Western Yamato, which meant its foundation was unique to begin with. It had a completely different essence compared to the guilds of the former *Elder Tales* MMO, where players who got along with each other formed groups so that they could play together. The objective of this enormous organization, which had been formed by swallowing up many preexisting guilds, was mutual aid and cooperation in order to survive in this strange world that resembled *Elder Tales*. In other words, the goal of creating Plant Hwyaden had been the intersection of interests.

It was a single guild that espoused perfect equality, but its internal politics bristled with disparate factions. For people who knew a certain amount about Plant Hwyaden, this was common knowledge.

But this wasn't all that was unique about its history.

In order to establish this enormous guild, the first thing Nureha had done was twist the guard organization around her little finger. The guards of Minami were a lower branch of the House of Saimiya. In other words, since its establishment, the organization of Plant Hwyaden had been deeply involved with the People of the Earth.

As such, Nureha, as Hwyaden's guild master and as the "State Councilor of the West," had gained rank and power.

Meanwhile, the Senate, which had joined the House of Saimiya in controlling Western Yamato, had showed a great interest in Plant Hwyaden and was eager to assimilate it.

Currently, one could say that the town of Minami was in a state of balance in which many forces—each of Plant Hwyaden's internal factions, alongside the People of the Earth's House of Saimiya and Minami's Senate—struggled with each other.

Kazuhiko was part of one of these forces.

The security organization Miburo—the original name of the famous historical Shinsengumi forces—was a department of Plant Hwyaden that protected the peace in Minami and cracked down on corruption and fraud.

However, in practice, it was Kazuhiko's private army.

Kazuhiko and some of his like-minded colleagues had banded together to halt the corruption plaguing Minami as much as possible, and had ended up becoming one of Plant Hwyaden's internal factions. Their power wasn't among the greatest in Minami, but because they had some influence, they were allowed a chair on the Ten-Seat Council.

Two guards in short, black, formal Japanese overcoats known as *haori* stood behind Kazuhiko. Many of the Ten-Seats attended the council with similar guards in tow.

Of course the guards meant nothing at the council, but this sort of posturing was necessary in order to maintain the faction equilibrium.

Squinting his eyes, Kazuhiko glanced at the highest position in the room—the First Seat.

On the top level was an elegant, feminine, elaborately worked throne that looked as if it might have been brought back from fairyland.

The seat's mistress was currently absent. It was the place where Nureha, guild master of Plant Hwyaden, was meant to sit.

On the level below it were a tea server and silver trolley, and a brusque stool that showed no signs of use. It was currently unoccupied, but practically speaking, it was the second seat in charge of this council: the seat occupied by the maid Indicus.

Those two hadn't yet appeared, but once Indicus arrived, no doubt the council would begin.

The third landing was wide, with a utilitarian chair and an enormous work desk that took up both sides. At that work desk, a stubborn, cruel-looking, bespectacled young man was silently drafting figures and written instructions. Sometimes he would look up and eject a trenchant comment from his sardonic mouth. It was the third seat, the Adventurer Zeldus, nicknamed "the Watchtower."

He was the man in charge of Plant Hwyaden's development and finances. The Iron Chancellor.

On the level just below his, a female soldier relaxed, leaning against her backrest, with a liquor bottle set directly on the floor. This was the Fourth Seat, "the General Who Dominated the East"—Mizufa Trude. She was the strongest general in the Senate, and the greatest commander within the Holy Empire of Westlande's People of the Earth army.

"The days are boring without the scent of blood. I feel like I'm going to rot. We've got all the time there is. If it means I can go to war, I'll wait as long as they like, even if the moon sets on us."

The woman was past thirty and beautiful, but rather than the dauntlessness of a soldier, there was a marked sense of criminal cruelty about her. She was sitting in a dissipated way, with her arms spread wide, occupying the center of a sofa meant for two people.

"Didn't you come here just to drink fine liquor, Lander?"

Lander: a slang word for a Person of the Earth.

The jab had come from a big Adventurer seated in a leather-upholstered chair on the next level down. The Fifth Seat: Nakalnad, "the General Who Conquered the South." He was wearing rough armor reminiscent of construction equipment, as if to point out that he was a Guardian.

The words had been insulting, but Mizufa agreed with a generous "You've got that right."

"Pretty nice life, hmm?" Nakalnad raised the cup he'd drained; his expression was bitter. A maid as unobtrusive as a stain on the wall approached like a ghost and poured him fresh liquor.

These two were the center of the military, and they were in charge of Plant Hwyaden's foreign campaigns.

They led, respectively, the People of the Earth military corps and the Adventurer army.

The common opinion among the Adventurers who attended this council was that Mizufa's seat order was higher out of consideration for the Senate, since the military might Nakalnad actually commanded was several times greater. In the days of the old Yamato server, Nakalnad had been the guild master of Howling, the strongest guild in the Kansai area. Glimpses of Plant Hwyaden's internal politics showed through here as well.

"I'm sleepy. Why do we meet at night? Seriously."

The Sixth Seat stretched ostentatiously. Quon, the "Singer of Prophecies."

"Night's not the only time you're sleepy."

Zeldus's voice came down from the higher level; he hadn't looked up from his documents. Quon wore casual clothes—a shirt and jeans—that would have been right at home on a street corner on Earth. The only fantasy-style item was the warm-looking cloak he'd wrapped himself up in.

"I'm keeping an ear out for a GM Call," he protested.

At his words, several of the participants gave small, wry smiles.

This young man, Quon, didn't technically have the ability or the desire to hold a seat on the council. It was just that during the *Elder Tales* era, he had been a game master on the administrative side. Game masters were administrative employees who had avatars just like Adventurers, participated in the game world, and dealt with any trouble that came up there. In simple terms, they were a type of troubleshooter.

Having been a Fushimi Online Entertainment employee, he had detailed knowledge of the circumstances and information on the administrative side. Since he'd gotten pulled into the Catastrophe when he was logged in from his own home computer instead of the dedicated mainframe at the FOE offices, most of his game master abilities had been sealed, but even so, it was possible that he'd be able to help clear up situations. That was why he held one of the ten seats.

GM Call, or "Call from Beyond," was one of the game master abilities Quon still held. It enabled him to receive pop-up notices with information regarding administrative events that occurred on the Yamato server. He could also receive a summons from FOE, but if they believed what he said, there had been no contact since the Catastrophe, and the only events that had occurred were timed or triggered types.

"So you're saying your connection to the higher world is fading, eh?"

The old man in the Eighth Seat, one down from Kazuhiko, teased with a chuckle.

"Man, shut *up*. It was the Council's decision to monitor calls, remember?"

At Quon's sulky attitude, the old man cackled. He seemed jolly, but his eyes were blunt with cruelty. The Eighth Seat, Jared Gan, "the Great Wizard of Miral Lake." He was an authority on magic and history who represented the People of the Earth. Along with Zeldus, his knowledge and magic abilities were being focused into the development of new technologies.

"The princess…won't be joining us tonight either, hmm?"

As Loreil Dawn, Ninth Seat and leader of the imperial guards, muttered this, Indicus entered. She was a beautiful, intelligent woman dressed in a maid's uniform. Her footsteps sounded like someone striking rock, and with that sound as its opening bell, the Ten-Seat Council commenced.

"Let me begin tonight's Ten-Seat Council. For the first topic of the day, we will hear a report on urban welfare."

Indicus began the council abruptly, without prelude. This topic was always the first one she chose. Holding his breath as if he were diving underwater, Kazuhiko tried to keep his heart cool and collected.

The town of Minami was peaceful and wealthy.

However, it was built on the invisible exploitation of the People of the Earth. At present, there were approximately ten thousand Adventurers living in Minami, and three times that many People of the Earth. There were many restaurants and inns run by People of the Earth, but the majority of them were Servants.

Servants were People of the Earth hired to look after Adventurers. There was demand from Adventurers, since this freed them from having to do odd jobs, and People of the Earth welcomed the positions as lucrative employment. On the other hand, it was true that it was a hotbed for a variety of trouble. Minami's prosperity was built on all sorts of hidden warps and stains.

Quite apart from Kazuhiko's thoughts, the council went on.

Currently, the government of Minami's biggest program involved issuing guild passes.

Adventurers affiliated with Plant Hwyaden and People of the Earth living in Minami were able to receive guild passes issued by the Plant Hwyaden staff office. Passes came in several different ranks, and those who held them could use restaurants and inns that corresponded to that rank completely free of charge. This meant there would no longer be any need for Plant Hwyaden members to walk around with cash. In addition, since the passes would not be purchased, but loaned for free—although they would need to be renewed every three months—it was believed that they would make great contributions to Minami's development.

As he listened to the splendid report, Kazuhiko renewed his determination.

It was likely that there would be even bigger trouble, and lots of it, from this point on.

He could understand the advantages of the guild pass system. There was great significance in the fact that they guaranteed lifestyles on a certain level for Adventurers who avoided fighting monsters. In addition, Plant Hwyaden would probably be able to implement more meaningful policies, such as purchase management for materials. However, it was the People of the Earth who'd be sacrificed in the process. Miburo existed to preserve justice in the city. That meant protecting the weak. Kazuhiko and the others were fighting to relieve the wretchedness of the People of the Earth, which many Adventurers pretended not to see.

Before he knew it, the council had gone from a report on an investigation of raid zones to the situation in Nakasu, and then continued to current conditions in Akiba.

"Akiba's sent an army to the northeast, then?"

"That seems to be the case," Nakalnad answered to Indicus. "It's made up of five legions, led by 'Berserker' Krusty. 'Black Sword,' 'the

Hatter,' and 'the Old Winged Dragon' are with them. The report's from 'Number One.'"

Although the shape its efforts took was different from Minami's, Akiba also seemed to be taking great pains over its relationship with the People of the Earth.

In contrast to Minami, which had made connections with the existing local leaders in the House of Saimiya, Akiba's Council seemed to have chosen to coexist with the League of Free Cities, the People of the Earth organization that governed the area north of the Kanto region. Most of the Ten-Seat Council members felt that that decision had made the difference in Akiba's and Minami's speed of reform.

Minami had stabilized far more rapidly than Akiba, and it was producing superior results on all fronts, including lifestyle services and the development of new technology. For Adventurers trapped in this other world, nothing was more important than everyday stability, and Minami was in the process of acquiring it. This was good fortune for the Adventurers who lived there.

"'Machiavelli-with-Glasses' is gone, too."

Pushing his eye mask up, the Tenth Seat tossed those words to his fellows.

It was the laid-back voice of the "Transforming Jester," who sat in a tropical-style resort chair made of a wooden frame and sailcloth. He had been snoozing peacefully until just a moment ago, but now the council was silent, as if it was holding its breath.

"'Machiavelli-with-Glasses' is gone, too." There was no telling how the Tenth Seat had interpreted the silence, but he repeated himself. "I don't know whether he went along on the northeastern expedition, but it looks as though he's made himself scarce."

The man, who wore a smile that looked a bit too dangerous to call mischievous, was a skinny Summoner, dressed in a rough mantle with ragged edges. A former companion who'd raced across Yamato with the organization known as the Debauchery Tea Party. KR.

From the very lowest level, the grinning KR looked up at his former companion, Kazuhiko, and still higher, at the maid.

"Well? What'll you do, Indicus? It looks like the 'static' that doesn't go according to your calculations has taken off running yet again..."

Shutting the thick wooden door, Naotsugu brushed the snow off himself.

Outside, it wasn't what he would have called a blizzard, but snow danced in the mountain wind. Although it should have been early afternoon, the thick storm clouds made it gloomy, and the temperature was low.

He was wearing cold-resistant equipment, so he hadn't frozen out in the blizzard, but his legs had bogged down beyond belief. Naotsugu was a Guardian, and he was wearing full-body metal armor. Technically, he shouldn't have been able to move around in snow at all in that sort of equipment. The fact that he'd managed to patrol in weather like this was due entirely to his Adventurer's physical abilities.

"Naotsugu?"

"Yeah, I'm back."

Shiroe spoke to him from the depths of the lodge, and Naotsugu answered.

He loosened his belt and took off his gauntlets. The gauntlets were the latest prototype-class item, created by artisans, and they hadn't existed in the days of *Elder Tales*. They were more versatile than the ones level-90 Naotsugu had acquired on a raid, and while he used them all the time, since they were a handmade item that was more recent than the Catastrophe, Naotsugu couldn't equip them or take them off from the menu.

Finally removing the weighty items—whose mass made them seem more like a type of weapon than gauntlets—he tossed his other equipment into his Magic Bag, piece by piece. What appeared from under his rough armor was three-quarter-length indoor wear. It was a casual look, no different from what he would've worn on Earth.

It certainly was a freezing mountain winter outside, but whoever had built this lodge had understood the region's seasons well. The log walls were double layered, and there seemed to be straw stuffed between them.

In combination with the thick tapestries, this kept the room at a fairly pleasant temperature.

Naotsugu peeled off his bulky mountain-climbing socks and shoved his toes into slippers. People told him that wanting to take off his socks the minute he got home was an old-guy thing, but he'd been that way ever since he was a kid, and he wished they'd get off his case about it.

"How was it?"

"Nothing wrong. The snow is zipping around and the wind is blowing hard."

"It doesn't look like it'll stop even if we cry."

"Short Stuff's the only one who'd cry."

"There you go again, talking like that just because Akatsuki's not here…"

In Japanese terms, the room was about ten tatami mats in size.

The fireplace blazed red, and Shiroe, who was camped out on a thick rug, had lots of notes and maps spread around him. Even at a quick glance, there seemed to be at least several dozen. Naotsugu recognized some of them; in particular, there was the map of the nearby area. Densely covered with notes and memos written in red ink, it was a summary of the reports he'd made over the past week.

Although the lodge was warm and comfortable inside, it had been a week since they'd left their friends in Akiba. Naotsugu looked around the area, feeling worn out.

"Where's the little old guy?"

"He isn't that old. I think he's probably around thirty."

"He laughs like an old guy, though."

Without looking at Naotsugu, Shiroe—who'd traded his trademark coat for indoor wear—began carefully stacking the nearby memos on top of one another.

"Want some help?"

"No, it's fine. This won't take long."

"Oh, okay."

He was probably concentrating.

So as not to bother Shiroe, Naotsugu sat down on the fur rug.

"……"

"……"

Shiroe took out a thick notebook, setting it next to the stacked memos, and began drawing up some sort of document. In this world, there were no computers or word processors. Shiroe had muttered that organizing information was rough, but even then, when Naotsugu tried to help him, he turned him down. He'd always been stubborn.

Probably ever since we first met, Naotsugu thought.

Right after he'd joined the Debauchery Tea Party, the idea of grabbing something to eat in real life had come up. Since it was an online game, this was only natural, but the Tea Party members lived all over Japan. As a result, it was really impossible to get everyone together for a dinner party. However, even so, five of them who lived in the Kanto region had met up in the real.

The first time he'd met Shiroe, he'd been drinking pu-erh tea.

When Naotsugu had said, *That's oolong tea, right?* Shiroe had explained the difference to him. That explanation had gone on for thirty minutes, and had ultimately extended to the political situation in Taiwan and speculation in tea leaves. The "vital fall" had occurred in the EU at about that time, and even university students hadn't been able to stay unconcerned about the topic.

Naotsugu and Shiroe's friendship had begun at that offline meeting.

At the time, they were both university students, and the fact that they lived at a distance that could be covered by a one-hour bike ride if they wanted to hang out was key. Friends outside school were valuable. He'd often taken the stay-at-home Shiroe along as he wandered around town.

He couldn't count the times they'd been yanked around by Kanami's whims.

It was so bad that, when she'd said, *We're going to a fish paste factory in Odawara*, he'd seriously thought about punching her. Even so, when they actually did go, it had been fun, and the all-important fish paste had been shockingly tasty. Naotsugu thought that Kanami's personal magnetism, or maybe her sense about things like that, had been really something.

…And so Naotsugu and Shiroe had known each other for a long time.

He was used to kicking his legs out and relaxing beside a silent Shiroe like this. It was something he'd done a lot when he was a student, and he did it all the time at the guild house.

The heat from the fireplace made it to his toes, which had been buried in a snowfield. The stinging tingle gradually eased, and the warmth returned.

Naotsugu twisted around, rummaging through his Magic Bag, and took out a metal canteen and cups.

The liquid he poured out was mog milk. The drink, which had mashed mog fruit in it, was similar to banana milk on Earth.

When he held one out with a "Hrn," Shiroe replied with a "Mmm" and took it without looking up. They both sipped the faintly sweet mog milk in silence. Friends were like this with each other. Energetic, witty conversation was formal behavior.

"Locked-up-on-a-snowy-mountain-with-Shiro-and-some-old-guy city."

Even so, Naotsugu muttered vaguely, not out of spite, but because he was bored.

"What, Naotsugu? Lonely?"

"Yeah, kinda. For a resort, this place is super empty."

"It is pretty rural."

Shiroe's response left Naotsugu flabbergasted.

This lodge was a closed zone, but the snowy mountain it sat on was in a field zone that was roughly sixty kilometers per side. Naotsugu had been the only Adventurer in that field zone. Before he'd entered the lodge a few minutes ago, he'd checked using the Frontier Inspector in-zone list, so he was sure about that. You didn't call an area like that "rural." It was a trackless waste. What Naotsugu wanted to say was that on the Yamato server, Tearstone was a land-locked desert island.

"Where are you from again, Shiro?"

"Tokyo, almost."

At that brief answer, Naotsugu heaved a deep sigh. This was the problem with Tokyo natives. They couldn't tell the difference between rural areas where people actually lived and the back end of nowheresville.

Disgusted, he dropped his head into his hands—he was already resting on his elbows—and rolled around.

About ten days ago, Shiroe had asked him to stay behind and hold the fort. He'd said he was leaving Akiba for a while, and had asked if he'd take care of Log Horizon. Naotsugu had turned him down in one second flat, and here he was.

He hadn't heard where Shiroe planned to go or what he was planning to do, but Naotsugu thought it was probably to do something tiresome. It also wasn't something that was needed in general, but Shiroe thought it was necessary. Naotsugu had known right away, just from seeing his face.

If it had been something that everyone would understand was necessary right away, Shiroe wouldn't have hesitated to ask someone else to handle it. There would be no hesitation over everyone doing something that was necessary for everyone. He was attempting to do this on his own because it would be hard to persuade people of its necessity.

He'd thought this had improved since the Crescent Burger incident, but apparently one or two opportunities weren't enough to completely cure inborn temperament.

Man, he's stubborn, Naotsugu thought, but then thought better of it, deciding that this was patent Shiroe as well.

If Shiroe had a bad habit, there were tons of things about him that were good enough to cancel it out. The problem was that Shiroe himself didn't know this, and this smart-yet-dense friend of his needed to travel with a kickstarter who'd give him hell. Naotsugu prided himself on the fact that, as his old friend, he was suited for the job.

Besides, whenever Shiroe pushed himself like this, the view afterward was fantastic.

If they were on their way to see a view like that, he wasn't going to surrender his spot to anybody.

"Think you could tell me why we're shut away in a locked room on a snowy mountain? It's about time for that."

"We aren't shut away. We're just holing up."

"Shiro, you're-never-gonna-be-popular-that-way city."

"I mean it's peaceful. You really don't get it, do you?"

The problem was that, in Shiroe's case, he was more than half serious.

"…We're holed up here because I don't want our location known. It's fine now, but considering what's ahead, I'd rather not tip our hand."

Having finished verbally horsing around, Shiroe began to explain, quietly, bit by bit.

"For the moment, our objective is money. In short, we're fund-raising. To that end, I need to persuade a certain person."

"That old guy?"

Naotsugu remembered their traveling companion. The small elf Person of the Earth scholar was holed up in the next room... Literally.

"No, not him. Li Gan is involved in this maneuver. I brought him along so that he could help with the persuasion. What I say may not be enough to get them to trust us. He may not look it, but he's famous."

"He really doesn't look famous."

"Even if he's the Sage of Miral Lake?"

Oh, is that *what he is?* At Shiroe's words, Naotsugu was convinced.

The Sage of Miral Lake had been a well-known NPC in the *Elder Tales* MMORPG. That said, Naotsugu had never seen him on a game screen. He was a sage that was mentioned in legends and rumors in the game. He had made an appearance in the backstory for the Nine Great Gaols of Halos, a raid they would speed-run during their Tea Party days.

"So he actually exists?"

"Yes, he does. He does indeed."

"Why are we fund-raising way out in the mountains, anyway? If you need money, couldn't you just borrow it from the Round Table Council?"

"Mm." Sitting cross-legged, Shiroe hemmed, frowning. "It's a pretty large amount," he said with a sigh.

Naotsugu felt a headache coming on.

He really couldn't trust that *pretty* in this case. Shiroe had looked slightly calmer last time, when he'd been planning to buy up what was now Akiba's guild center.

"About how much, exactly?"

"In all, about eighty trillion or so."

It was ridiculous. An absolutely ludicrous sum.

According to the math, that amount was over ten thousand times more than all the money held by all the Adventurers on the Yamato server. It was the sort of amount they wouldn't be able to scrape up from all the Adventurers in the *world*, let alone on the Yamato server; the sort of amount that probably didn't exist in the first place.

Naotsugu looked at Shiroe, his mouth hanging open. Shiroe's brow was furrowed, and he was groaning to himself.

However, on seeing Shiroe groan, Naotsugu understood. Shiroe wasn't doing this as a joke or on a whim. He thought that amount was necessary, no matter what.

"...Got any ideas about who to ask?"

"The whole amount wouldn't be possible, so we'll split it over several installments, take it little by little."

Although it's a fact that no matter how we split it up, it isn't an amount that could ever be "little by little"... Shiroe gave a troubled smile.

"Well, no help for that. Gimme a bit more info. Tell me about this strategy you've thought up."

"There's no strategy. We'll wing it, get down on our knees and beg. We'll just persuade them."

"Persuade who? How?"

When they'd gotten that far in their conversation, sipping their mog milk, the door to the next room opened and a man in a robe appeared.

"Shiroe. It seems our guest has arrived."

The People of the Earth magician, who had shifty eyes and an entertained expression, giggled, then thumped Naotsugu on the shoulder. For a Person of the Earth, he showed an unusual lack of reserve. Naotsugu was rather taken aback by his attitude, but Li Gan spoke to him as though nothing had happened.

"Do watch, Naotsugu. No explanations are necessary: Shiroe's negotiations are about to begin. This is going to be amazing. These negotiations may actually be battle-class, or even national-defense-class magic."

What did "national-defense-class" mean? Naotsugu's question was cut off before he finished asking it.

Someone had knocked at the door of the lodge.

Not twenty minutes ago, there had been no Adventurers within a ten-kilometer radius. Did that mean the visitor was a Person of the Earth? ...But were People of the Earth even able to travel this far into the snowbound Tearstone Mountains?

As Shiroe and Li Gan watched, Naotsugu took his sword from his Magic Bag and warily approached the door.

▶4

"Shiro. Company."

Even before Naotsugu's announcement, Shiroe had crammed his maps and documents into his Magic Bag.

He'd anticipated that they would have a visitor, and a table and tea service had been set up in the room with the fireplace.

Is that how it's turned out... Shiroe thought, at the sight of Naotsugu's perplexed expression as his friend returned from the door. The visitor who followed at his heels wasn't one Shiroe had expected, but it wasn't an individual he'd never considered, either.

"This way, please."

Shiroe felt a bit bad about ignoring Naotsugu, but welcoming their visitor took priority just now. He gestured to a sturdy oak chair.

"Climbing snowy mountains is quite taxing."

As he spoke, the young man with violet eyes—Kinjo of the Kunie—brushed at the shoulders of his formal outfit with its stand-up collar, although there wasn't a single snowflake on it, and sat down.

"May I say it's been quite some time since we last spoke?"

"It has, and you may."

At Kinjo's response, Shiroe fell silent. Inwardly, he heaved a deep sigh, thinking that the situation was growing increasingly difficult.

Shiroe had been waiting in this cabin in the mountains, far from civilization, in order to negotiate with the Kunie clan. He'd had several reasons for traveling all the way into the Ouu Mountains, but one was that this area was close to the assumed location of the Kunie clan's headquarters.

...This is rather, erm...

Shiroe felt that, frankly, this was a problem.

To begin with, he'd anticipated that negotiating with the Kunie clan would be difficult.

At first, all Shiroe had known about this mysterious clan was that they ran the bank. The bank was one of the convenient functions available to *Elder Tales* players, a service that provided storage for items and cash. Once deposited in the bank, these things could be withdrawn from any bank in Yamato, not just from the specific branch that had accepted them.

The Kunie clan had a transference technique that was different from the Call of Home spell and the intercity gates the Adventurers used, and banking wasn't the only service they provided.

A home delivery service that carried letters and parcels from one individual to another, a bazaar service that made it possible to buy and sell all sorts of items… They handled a wide variety of things. The guard systems established in most towns were also administered by the Kunie clan.

The *Elder Tales* players—or, after the Catastrophe, the Adventurers—took the existence of these services for granted. They seemed to be part of the public infrastructure. When, during the establishment of the Round Table Council, Shiroe had said that the Adventurers couldn't live without the support of the People of the Earth, he'd had this clan in mind.

Of course, at the time, he hadn't known that these services were provided by the mysterious Kunie clan.

After the formation of the Round Table Council, the Council—and mainly Shiroe—had attempted to contact the Kunie clan. They'd managed it rather easily, and that was when he'd made the acquaintance of Kinjo, the person in charge of activities in Akiba. However, they hadn't been able to advance beyond that point.

They'd learned that the Kunie clan provided a variety of services in the region of Yamato. They'd also learned that these services were indispensible to the Adventurers. They'd managed to formally greet Kinjo, the Kunie representative in Akiba… But that was as far as they'd gotten.

Kinjo hadn't openly ignored them or shown clear animosity, but he'd rejected all of Shiroe's probes with his serene smile and eloquent tongue.

In any case, as Shiroe had thought previously, while the Adventurers couldn't live without the People of the Earth, the People of the Earth would probably manage to get by without the Adventurers. In this world where brutal monsters reigned, they might not be able to prosper they way they would have on Earth proper, but even so, if they used noncombat zones and magic technology, they'd be able to survive. The Kunie clan was a prime example.

Even if the Adventurers disappeared, the Kunie clan wouldn't fall. That, more than anything else, meant the cards available for Shiroe to negotiate with were extremely limited.

Even so, Shiroe had continued to gather information in an attempt to acquire ammunition of some sort, and the person he'd dealt with had been Kinjo, who lived in Akiba. No doubt this young man who gave the impression of a seasoned veteran had picked up on Shiroe's intent; he'd kept intel on the Kunie clan inaccessible. The clan's organization and actual abilities, their hidden knowledge, their headquarters, ideas, objectives—any and all information.

Shiroe had gotten most of the knowledge he currently had regarding the Kunie clan from Li Gan, rather than Kinjo.

"This is Li Gan. The Sage. Do you know of him?"

"Yes, of course. It's a pleasure to meet you. I am Kinjo, and I serve as the contact for the Kunie clan."

"Charmed, charmed. To think I'd have the privilege of meeting a member of the Kunie..."

Li Gan waved a hand in response to Kinjo's greeting, answering with a smile.

Kinjo also smiled, thinly.

"This is quite the unusual day, isn't it? I've managed to encounter both Master Shiroe of Log Horizon, the great mage of the Debauchery Tea Party and representative of the Adventurers, and Master Li Gan, the Sage of Miral Lake. It is an honor to have been invited to participate in this historic occasion, Master Shiroe. There are few in the history of the Kunie who have been privileged to such glory. No doubt even my great predecessors never dreamed such a day would come."

Kinjo's response troubled Shiroe.

Kinjo certainly wasn't hostile to Shiroe and the other Adventurers. He wasn't silent, and it wasn't that he didn't understand what they said. He simply refused to disclose information he didn't wish revealed, and he camouflaged even that refusal with this sort of theatrical verbosity.

Shiroe felt like sighing over the coming negotiations. He'd personally sent a request to the Kunie clan of Akiba—in other words, through Kinjo—and had asked to speak to a responsible person in the clan, but he'd never imagined that the man himself would come all this way into the mountains of Ouu.

At that point, a different possibility occurred to Shiroe. However, even during the few moments he spent examining it, the terribly cheerful Li Gan had continued conversing with their guest.

"Your presence has made this splendid occasion even more miraculous. The Kunie... They are a mysterious clan. A clan that supports the countries of Yamato from the shadows, the organization that preserves wisdom of the ancient civilization that once wielded enormous magical power. And you, Master Kinjo, are their leader. I can't tell you how that raises my expectations."

"Your expectations?"

"Yes. Master Shiroe here is a veritable jack-in-the-box, you see."

"Oho. Is he, then!"

I wish you wouldn't give me impossible setups.

Shiroe glanced at Li Gan, saturating the look with that emotion, but the man's familiar, gaunt face wore a smile brimming with curiosity.

It wasn't that he hadn't noticed. Even if Shiroe was in trouble, this droll People of the Earth sage simply didn't intend to save him.

"Um, ah..."

"Heh-heh-heh-heh."

Glaring at Li Gan, who was chuckling, Shiroe began the negotiations.

"Kinjo, the request I'd like to make was outlined in my letter."

"To arrange for funds, you mean? For a loan?"

It was trivial.

He was asking for money.

"That's right. I'm glad we've managed to understand each other so quickly."

"Yes. That's saved some trouble, hasn't it?"

"I'm much obliged."

Shiroe would have preferred to hold these negotiations in Akiba. Now, with Krusty and the other major members of the Round Table Council off conquering Seventh Fall, the town of Akiba was quite vulnerable, and Shiroe himself had a premonition of trouble as well. Since Soujirou had stayed there, he thought things would work out somehow, no matter what happened, but even so, he hadn't wanted to leave.

He'd come here because Kinjo hadn't let him make that proposal.

It wasn't that Kinjo had turned him down. It was more accurate to say he'd been evasive, letting any requests get lost in light conversation, and had left the matter unsettled. Shiroe was only a university student, and when it came to the art of negotiation, he couldn't win against a professional.

The fact that Kinjo had easily moved on to the main topic this time was unexpected, but it was also welcome.

"No, no, it isn't anything to bother yourself about. Saving trouble. That's very important. To the Kunie clan, it's very important indeed."

"I see…"

"You came here because you knew of the Kunie village, correct?"

"That's right. I heard about it from Li Gan."

"Oho. So Miral Lake had a record like that… I seem to have underestimated him slightly."

"I thought it would be good form."

Shiroe frowned a little as he responded.

It hadn't been about good form at all.

It had been one of the cards he'd played after learning that the Kunie clan headquarters was in this region, information obtained from his research of old documents with Li Gan. The statement that they knew the location of their headquarters was, essentially, intimidation. This made Shiroe uncomfortable. He didn't reject the method, and he didn't intend to hesitate, but that didn't mean he was doing it happily.

During the Round Table Council affair, he'd been irritated.

He'd wanted to yell *Enough already!* at the big guilds, who were just sitting by idly and eying the problem, and so he simply hadn't worried about whether this way of doing things was a threat or intimidation.

However, the Kunie clan was only carrying out its duty, just as it had always done.

"As it is a request from you, Master Shiroe of the Round Table Council, we would dearly love to accommodate it, but I'm afraid we are unable to do so."

"Why is that?"

"Because it would violate a contract that has been in effect since the time of our progenitor."

At that answer, Shiroe sighed.

He'd known from the beginning that these negotiations would be difficult. It was why he'd asked Li Gan for assistance, and why he'd looked into a variety of things beforehand. There wasn't a single recorded instance of the Kunie clan's bank providing funds to an external party, either through investment or through financing. All they did was pay out money that had been deposited with them. That was it.

Shiroe remembered the chats he'd had with Kinjo in Akiba. Capital-to-asset ratios, credit limits, trust—to Shiroe and the others, these were common banking terms, but they hadn't gotten through to Kinjo. Of course, when Shiroe had explained them to him, he'd understood what the words meant, but that was all.

The facility known as the bank in Akiba wasn't similar to the institutions they'd had on Earth. That was the conclusion Shiroe and the others had reached. As a facility, it would have been more accurate to call it a depository with a transfer service; the goal of the organization wasn't finance.

…In that case, something was odd.

Say he conceded that there was no bank in this world. It was still unnatural that there was no moneylending. Shiroe wasn't an expert, so he didn't know all that much about it, but although banks were one thing, the history of moneylending was a long one. He thought he remembered hearing that they'd had it in Rome, and as a country, Rome had existed since before 1 AD. This world was styled after the Middle Ages. If it didn't have moneylending, its economic development was too rudimentary.

When he'd asked Li Gan about this, he'd only looked mystified, and Shiroe hadn't been able to get a clear answer out of him. According to Elissa, a Person of the Earth, it seemed as though aristocrats sometimes made loans to lower-ranking nobles and citizens of their domains, but it was rare, and no similar lending or borrowing was seen among the common people.

As a result, merchants didn't have much influence in this world. Most buying and selling took place between nobles, and merchants were no more than intermediaries and carriers. There were also some People of the Earth who seemed to be half noble and half merchant.

In addition, royals and the nobility weren't the source of trust in the currency here.

In the first place, the rulers—in the form of the royals and aristocrats—didn't mint the currency. It was "found" when monsters were defeated. The more monsters that were subjugated, the more currency came into circulation in the markets; in other words, the money supply increased. Apparently, the system on Earth in which nations backed trust in currency didn't apply here.

In that case, where was the trust?

In universality.

There was one single currency in circulation in this world. It had denominations—gold coins, half coins, and quarter coins—but no name. Unlike Earth, where yen, dollars, and euros existed side by side, there was only one currency, and so there was no need to differentiate it with a name. The coins were simply called "money," "gold," or "gold coins." What was more, Shiroe guessed that they were shared not just on the Yamato server but on all servers: In other words, throughout the entire world of *Elder Tales*.

In short, the faith that the coins they possessed wouldn't turn to worthless rubbish one day stemmed not from nations' might and influence but from the fact that no other currency existed. It might be a more secure value retention system than the one on Earth, where currency could lose its value because one issuing country had fallen. Even if Eastal, the League of Free Cities, or the Ancient Dynasty of Westlande fell, it wouldn't damage the circulation value of coins acquired in Maihama.

Of course, there was the fact that the coins themselves had the value of precious metal, but didn't processing them require the skills of a Blacksmith? To Shiroe, the trust in the currency seemed to stem mainly from their universality.

Then there was the issue of the Kunie clan's banks as well. Even if they were essentially no more than depositories, their defensive capabilities were the real thing. Once deposited with them, money was protected by absolute security. Many banks were in independent zones, and they were usually fortified with guards. In addition, banks had technology that could identify unknown individuals, and money deposited at one branch could be instantly withdrawn from another branch. They even had a function that could settle accounts, including market and zone maintenance fees. They provided a very convenient, advanced system, but it was applied only to coins.

The fact that the system was so very convenient and autonomous seemed to be the reason the rulers didn't mint their own separate currencies.

"When you defeat a monster, it's possible to get coins, isn't it, Kinjo?"
"Yes, that's right."
Shiroe pressed toward the crux of the matter.
"You can also get several hundred gold coins from treasure chests in dungeons."
"A feat due entirely to the valor of the Adventurers."
"If it isn't possible to get financing from the Kunie clan, what about getting coins from whoever distributes them in those places, before they actually distribute them?"

▶ 5

Li Gan was excited.

He was here because he'd been invited by Shiroe of Log Horizon, with whom he'd formed a friendship at the Ancient Court of Eternal Ice. The excitement that event had caused Li Gan was the same as if a storm had come and changed the previous weather completely.

The Sage thought highly of the young man beside him, whose gaze was so intense it obscured both the past and the future. In the library, Li Gan had spoken with feverish enthusiasm of the World Fraction, the fruit of his lifelong research. This man, who'd grasped its background and prospects in a single night, was an unparalleled great magician.

Li Gan studied Shiroe's profile so intently it was as if he'd forgotten to breathe.

This young man, who called himself Shiroe of Log Horizon, was an Adventurer whose profession was magic. Adventurers were strong. Their abilities were overwhelmingly higher than those of the People of the Earth. Adventurers, this other strain of humanity, were geniuses in everything they did: not only as warriors, but as scouts, healers, and magicians.

However, as far as Li Gan was concerned, that didn't mean that all high-ranking Adventurers were worthy of being called great magicians. Adventurers had formidable abilities, but for the most part, they were too specialized toward combat. For a magician who used knowledge to peer into the depths of this world, competence with combat magic was really only a digression.

Shiroe was one of the few magicians among the Adventurers who was different, and a great magician at that.

Li Gan believed that in this world, there were four paths to ultimate knowledge.

Each path was independent, and they never touched each other.

In feudal Yamato, technology and knowledge were things that had to be concealed. Acquired knowledge was transmitted quietly, as secret teachings, and in many cases it never left the group in which it was handed down.

One path could be found in the People of the Earth academics, to which Li Gan himself belonged.

In the sense of being able to openly devote oneself to study, that meant the magic academy of Tsukuba, and in terms of hiding in the shadows and preserving knowledge, it was Miral Lake. As the Sage of Miral Lake, Li Gan was the guardian of Miral Lake, "the Lake of Forgotten Books." The latest in a line of scholars that went into battle against the principles of this world.

The second was probably the Adventurers. Li Gan and the other sages of Miral Lake had always thought that Adventurers had magic and knowledge that was completely different from that of the People of the Earth. Although enormously powerful, the magic they used was the same as that of the People of the Earth. However, for a long time, they had wondered whether their knowledge might not have a different source.

Did the Adventurers isolate a portion of their own souls in some other world? That had been a suggestion for research, and at this point, Li Gan was certain of it. On top of that, there was the possibility that that other world was connected to the Age of Myth. By now, it was nearly common knowledge for Li Gan and the magicians of Tsukuba that the various miracles and inventions that the Adventurers had presented since the Catastrophe were related to those supertechnologies. They called these "science" or "heritage."

The third was the abilities used by the Ancients. Like the Adventurers, they were a tribe of heroes that was beyond the common sense of the People of the Earth. Although they were of the exact same races as the People of the Earth—humans, elves, dwarves, half alvs, felinoids, wolf-fangs, foxtails, and ritians—the Ancients and Adventurers surpassed their upper limits with ease.

The Ancients had also handed traditions down in secret since time immemorial, and it was said that these existed within secret societies known as knight brigades, which protected regions all over the world.

The fourth and final path was the Kunie clan.

Much about them was mysterious, and even Li Gan could only guess at the full picture. They were definitely People of the Earth, but they weren't affiliated with Yamato's academic organization in Tsukuba or with Miral Lake. It was said that they handed down techniques from the ancient alv civilization, and that the sphere of their influence stretched not only throughout Yamato but to the continent as well.

In the sense that they accumulated the knowledge of antiquity and handed it down to the present, they resembled Miral Lake, but they didn't spread that knowledge. The greatest difference between them and the People of the Earth academics at Tsukuba and Miral Lake was their closed nature. Not only did they not have wide contact with the People of the Earth, they did not conduct research. They were a clan that lacked curiosity and disliked contact.

Miral Lake's policy was to gather all sorts of information, and in the past, the sage had made dozens of attempts to contact the Kunie clan. However, there was no record of any sage ever having succeeded in exchanging research information.

Now, one member of the Kunie clan was seated at the same table with Li Gan and Shiroe of Log Horizon. Li Gan's excitement was only natural.

Shiroe's remark seemed to have badly shaken the leader of the Kunie clan.

Kinjo gulped, looking startled. Then, as if to conceal it, he put on an expressionless mask and fell silent. This lasted for quite some time.

"Do you think that's possible, Master Shiroe?"

When Kinjo finally replied, Shiroe's response was to glance at Li Gan and draw his chin in slightly.

Apparently it was his turn. Praying that his leaping heart would calm itself, Li Gan began to speak.

"The prospect of which Master Shiroe speaks is something no one has ever considered before. Now that I think of it, it's true that it seems to be one of the mysteries of this world. It's a viewpoint that complements the Spirit Theory. Monsters reincarnate repeatedly. However, souls aside, where does the money come from? There must be some sort of system that issues money to the monsters. And, if it is possible to obtain a new perspective like that, Miral Lake has a vast number of books. Yes, we went over all of them. Books of all kinds."

Li Gan pushed up the amethyst circlet he wore and scratched at his forehead, as he always did. The circlet was a magic item that had the marvelous effect of endowing him with improved memory and insight, but it was still a metal circlet. It hadn't been long since Li Gan had inherited it from his predecessor, and he wasn't used to it yet.

However, without this magic circlet, he probably wouldn't have been able to accomplish this investigation in such a short time. And, even if he had the circlet, without the books his predecessors had collected and left behind, he was sure he wouldn't have been able to acquire even the slightest clue.

"In the books, we discovered the village of the Kunie that Master Shiroe mentioned. That, and the gold the Kunie possess."

"……"

Kinjo's face remained expressionless.

Li Gan simply inquired. He had done so for a long time now. Those who belonged to Miral Lake collected knowledge. What they gained as a result of their endless collection were new questions. The answer to those questions was new knowledge. They went into the struggle against the resulting questions prepared to die, and the cycle repeated.

"In the very deepest part of the Depths of Palm, the books said, there is a vast vortex of gold. A winding river exists, where money that has appeared from the void vanishes into the void again, and then flows on to a forgotten subterranean garden. Hades first raised his army of the dead out of the desire to obtain this gold. That is found in the traditions as well. The Sage of Miral Lake took part in its defense, fifteen generations ago, and he set a seal on the Depths of Palm."

This sort of assistance wasn't all that unusual for the Sages of Miral Lake.

In the process of collecting all sorts of knowledge, the Sages obtained a variety of magic articles. Some were cursed and some were not, but most were extraordinarily dangerous if used incorrectly. The people—mostly nobles—who brought them to the sage wanted them to be sealed safely at Miral Lake.

Being able to grant these requests raised Miral Lake's reputation and helped to increase the amount of knowledge the sages could gain. Even without that, having items no one else had in their care meant they had more material for research. Miral Lake had a very practical reason for researching the art of sealing. In addition, this art could be used not only to keep objects in custody, but to seal off places and areas.

"On a past adventure, the Nine Great Gaols of Halos, I acquired the Key of Eternal Darkness. This item was created by the Sage of Miral Lake, wasn't it?"

Li Gan nodded in response to Shiroe's words, letting him take the floor.

"This key qualified us to challenge the Nine Great Gaols of Halos. That zone was sealed by the…I'm not sure how many generations back, but a previous Miral Lake sage. There are several dangerous, sealed zones. We confirmed this matter as well."

At Shiroe's words, a shiver ran down Li Gan's spine.

In the first place, Li Gan was a lore master, and his combat-type magic was extremely weak. His training wasn't so poor he'd lose to a band of knights in the service of some petty lord, but that was only against People of the Earth, and his skills couldn't compare to those of the Adventurers.

Even so, guarded by Shiroe and his friend Naotsugu, Li Gan had gone into the depths of the dungeon.

This was because all that was written in the records of Miral Lake was "I was asked to set a seal, and did so," and there had been no mention of a method for releasing the seal or details regarding items. When they went to the site, they'd found an enormous bronze door that was over ten meters tall; it actually had been sealed, but the method was in the secret arts of Miral Lake, and they'd learned that it wouldn't be all that hard to unseal it.

He hadn't understood what Shiroe had meant by the term "unimplemented zone," but in their investigation of the materials, they'd learned that countless sealed doors like this one existed all over Yamato. Not all of them had been sealed by Miral Lake, but for one reason or another, entering these regions and facilities was currently forbidden.

"Then you mean to obtain money from this vortex of gold?"

"Yes."

"And you believe the vortex has some connection to the Kunie."

"That's right."

As Kinjo questioned Shiroe, he finally seemed to have regained his mental composure.

"...In that case, wouldn't taking gold from it be stealing? Does the Round Table Council intend to plunder?"

He responded with a question, and his voice was cold.

However, with that, it was clear.

There really was that much gold in the vortex under the Depths of Palm. The place was also connected to the Kunie clan. They'd gleaned hints of this from the materials, but they hadn't been certain. It could have been completely unrelated to the Kunie. Li Gan had discussed it with Shiroe and had shared this possibility, but Shiroe had insisted, and he'd listened and contacted the Kunie clan.

One of their questions had been answered.

The Kunie clan was connected to the secret of the Spirit Theory in some way.

They weren't positive yet, but Kinjo's reaction had begun to prove it. The secret of the Kunie reached into the depths of the creation of the world. That conviction delighted Li Gan so much that he wanted to dance a little jig. The Spirit Theory was the greatest thing in his research. At this point, he would have liked to pour a toast with the wine he wasn't allowed to drink.

However, Shiroe's voice was pained.

"That's why we called you. We don't want to antagonize the Kunie clan. The Kunie are important. Even when it comes to using the money we acquire, unless we entrust future affairs to your people, we won't be able to make plans."

"How, or rather, on what, do you intend to use it, Master Shiroe?"

"If I explain that, is there a possibility of securing your cooperation?"

"There is not. Our progenitor's orders, you see."

"…Kinjo."

Before Li Gan's eyes, Shiroe's lips tightened as though he were enduring something. Even so, he seemed to be desperately trying to connect a thin thread.

"Kinjo. It isn't that we don't understand your progenitor's order. We understand it only in the way of Adventurers, but we know it is a rule that stretches back to the Age of Myth. We have no intention of telling you to break it. We don't want to compel you to do something forbidden. However, for that very reason, we want you to search the outer bounds of that rule."

"……"

"That's right. In the Catastrophe, the rules changed. We're in a new era. It hasn't stopped, either. I'm sure this is—"

Kinjo had closed his eyes. He looked like a steel statue.

Shiroe's persuasion didn't seem to have reached his heart.

Li Gan's delight soon began to fade as well, like the sun going behind clouds. He didn't know what was happening here in front of him. Since birth, he'd studied only magic theory and phenomenology, and something he didn't really understand was breaking. Put into words, it would probably be the negotiations. However, for someone like Li Gan, it felt as though he could *hear* something breaking, something that was too valuable to be expressed with the word *negotiations*.

Three of the world's four wisdoms were gathered here, and this was the best they could do?

In spite of himself, Li Gan clenched his hands into fists.

The atmosphere in the living room was dazed.

As Shiroe added dry firewood to the orange flames of the fireplace, Naotsugu watched his rounded back. The table had been cleared away, and two sleeping bags were laid out.

It was the interior of the mountain lodge, after the negotiations with Kinjo had fallen through.

That's a pretty dejected-looking back, Naotsugu thought.

Such was Shiroe.

He'd put the poker in and was adjusting the position of the firewood. He was probably tending the fire with extra care because they'd be going to sleep after this, but he also looked as if he was at his wits' end and was aimlessly stirring the fire around.

Naotsugu guessed he was probably thinking difficult things about the failed negotiations, over and over. He'd watched the discussion from the sidelines up until a short while ago, and even to him, Shiroe had seemed hard-pressed. Even more so than he'd been on the day the Round Table Council was established.

"Hey, Shiro."

"Hmm?"

"That's enough. Come stick your feet in your sleeping bag."

"Okay."

Restlessly, Shiroe moved to his sleeping bag, then sat down on top of it, cross-legged. That put him in the same position as Naotsugu.

On Earth, because the fiber materials were excellent, most sleeping bags had been thin and lightweight. However, in this world, high-performance insulating material hadn't been developed the way it had on Earth, and so in general, sleeping bags were made of felted wool that had been sewn together. They weren't as good at keeping out the cold as their counterparts on Earth, but since they were thick, they were pretty comfortable to sleep on. Combined with a rug with long piles, they made perfect places to sit.

"Want some, Shiro?"

He showed him a mug of hot wine. Shiroe sniffed, as though he was smelling the air, then turned him down: "No, I'm good."

He should just have some, Naotsugu thought, but he didn't press him.

To Naotsugu, it seemed as though on nights like this, you needed to drink some booze and sleep spread-eagled, but Shiroe wasn't the type. He knew that, even if he left him alone, Shiroe would find his rhythm again. There was no need to force him to go along with anything.

"So, that was a total bust."

"Yeah."

As he answered, Shiroe's expression was troubled.

In terms of results, Naotsugu thought it probably hadn't been a loss. He didn't know the details, but Shiroe needed a vast amount of cash. It wasn't the sort of sum they could collect from the Adventurers. If he wanted to pull together an amount like that, the places he could get it from and the methods he could use would naturally be limited.

After hearing what he'd discussed with Kinjo of the Kunie clan, Naotsugu had begun to see the general picture.

Shiroe was trying to use the settings from the days when *Elder Tales* had been a game.

When Adventurers defeated monsters, they got the coins the monsters had possessed. If the monster was humanoid and intelligent, the type that would have tools and treasures, this was only to be expected, but Adventurers won coins even when this wasn't the case. Even if it was a Wild Dog, a Large Boar, or some other animal, for example.

There was technically no reason for this. *Elder Tales* was a game, and the monsters dropped coins because the game was designed so that players could defeat monsters and use the assets they obtained to grow stronger. In other words, it happened for the convenience of the game.

However, if convenience was the only priority, the game would lose any semblance of reality, and it wouldn't be as interesting. To that end, a variety of background information had been added. The explanation this time—"Actually, a powerful magical device from antiquity gives coins to the monsters' souls as they're reborn"—was one of them.

It was a ridiculous idea. However, since monsters did in fact drop coins, there had to be some sort of cause, and it had appeared before their very eyes as fact. Shiroe probably knew this, and had attempted to use it.

And, Naotsugu thought, it had worked.

In that case, let us meet there. At "the winding river where money that has appeared from the void vanishes into the void again, in the forgotten subterranean garden."

However, in order to reach it, no doubt you'll need many brave warriors. The Kunie clan's answer will depend on how you and the others manage to reach the deepest spring, Master Shiroe, and the results of your challenge.

Those had been the last words Kinjo, leader of the Kunie, had said to them.

They'd been fighting words, spoken in response to a challenge.

Shiroe had ascertained that there was a vast amount of coins in an uncharted zone deep underground. He'd gathered evidence, gone to the site itself to reconnoiter, and even confirmed that they could release the seal and enter the area.

Then he'd confronted the Kunie, its probable owners, with that fact.

At that point in time, Shiroe's plan had already succeeded. Put in plainer terms, Naotsugu thought, Shiroe hadn't even needed to talk to the Kunie clan in the first place.

There was a subterranean zone, the treasure they were after was there, and they even had a way to get in, so all they had to do was go there and get the money. Then they'd have won an enormous fortune.

Well, that means Shiro's probably bummed about something else.

When he thought about what that might be, the answer was automatically clear.

This problematic friend of his had wanted to talk with the Kunie clan, even if it hadn't been necessary.

There's no strategy. We'll wing it, get down on our knees and beg. We'll just persuade them.

That was what Shiroe had said before the meeting.

At the time, Naotsugu had suspected his friend was only *saying* he had no strategy, out of his own unique brand of humility, but he really hadn't had a plan. *What a clumsy guy.* In spite of himself, Naotsugu laughed a little.

In order to achieve an objective, Shiroe would work out absolutely any kind of plan and make thorough preparations. Even this time, he must have taken a lot of time to set things up. Naotsugu had gone along when they reconnoitered the very lowest area of the Depths of Palm, and from what Li Gan had said, they'd been preparing for that for quite some time. Some of what he'd been researching in his office until late at night, every night, had been in preparation for today's discussion.

Shiroe had prepared that thoroughly in order to acquire the money he was after, and it had borne fruit in the shape of the Kunie clan's promise. They simply had to enter the new underground zone, then get the money.

However, he'd had a hope that lay beyond that.

When Shiroe wanted to become friends with someone, he didn't work out a strategy. He stopped saying anything that wasn't so straightforward that one couldn't help but wonder if he was an idiot. Shiroe hadn't wanted to force his way in and steal the gold, he hadn't wanted to catch the Kunie clan off guard, and he hadn't wanted to lie. In other words, that meant he'd wanted to make friends, and he was at a loss because *that* had failed.

Because Naotsugu knew this, "That was a total bust" was all he could say to his friend.

"And anyway, what was that speech a minute ago? That wasn't like you, Shiro."

"Wasn't it?"

"Those were some serious weasel words. There was nothing citified about it. You couldn't even tack *city* onto it."

"It was, huh…"

Naotsugu was irritated and was reproaching Shiroe. However, the response was a very absentminded affirmation.

"That's seriously cold. I thought we were friends," Shiroe said. Naotsugu heaved a big sigh.

In the first place, it was only natural that the day's negotiations had failed.

The Kunie clan had always been terribly tight-lipped, refusing to talk about themselves at all, and Shiroe hadn't said a word about his all-important objective for acquiring the assets, or about his hopes that the other party would give their consent as well. Both sides had been much too secretive.

With a relationship like that, of course persuasion wouldn't go well. Even Naotsugu, who was in his first year as a working adult and had been assigned to a job in sales, could understand that easily.

If it had simply been selling a kilo of pepper wholesale for ¥2,450 according to the same deal they'd had for ages, it would have been easy. All they would have had to do was take the order, deliver the product, and send the bill, just as they'd always done for this particular customer. However, if they were proposing a new product or establishing a lasting, long-term contract, things were different. They had to know the other party's circumstances very well. They also had to communicate their own circumstances to them. They couldn't be selfish; they had to fit the hopes of both parties together, as accurately as possible. That was the premise, and the rest was sincerity. When trying to convince the other party, it was only natural to attempt to meet them halfway.

That was why these negotiations, in which both parties had hidden too many of their cards, had been bound to fail.

Not only that, but their hand had been hidden from Naotsugu as well.

Naotsugu didn't know what Shiroe wanted to do with this money once he got it.

He didn't know why he was in such a hurry, either.

He thought that was really cold.

"What are you thinking now, Shiro?"

"……"

"It's not over yet, so c'mon, tell me what's eating you. Spit it out."

What's eating me, what's eating me. Shiroe thought it as if it were some sort of spell. Then he flopped down onto his back and went on, groaning.

"Naotsugu, listen…"

"Yeah?"

"Kinjo said, 'In order to reach it, no doubt you'll need many brave warriors,' didn't he?"

"Yeah."

Naotsugu gave a noncommittal answer, wondering what in the world Shiroe was talking about. They already knew where they were going to get the money, so the problem had to be improving their relationship with the Kunie clan. Hadn't that been what this was about? As Naotsugu racked his brains, Shiroe continued:

"No matter how you look at it, he was announcing a raid, wasn't he? I mean, it really can't be anything else. I'm in pretty deep trouble."

"Why?"

"We don't have the people."

"Huh?"

He had no idea what Shiroe was getting at, since Naotsugu himself had anticipated a raid. In the first place, in *Elder Tales*, when a dungeon meant to be captured by an ordinary party had a mysterious door in its depths, there was a good possibility that it was a raid zone. However, even if that was the case, they should stand a good chance of beating it. Adventurers were immortal, and the Round Table Council (Shiroe) had sufficient manpower. It might take time, but that was all.

"Almost all the guilds on the Round Table Council are being monitored. The current situation is so fluid that a little push is all it would take, and it isn't possible to get rid of those monitors. I want to keep Minami from noticing us for just a little longer."

Shiroe's answer left Naotsugu dumbfounded.

He didn't want to use the Round Table Council's manpower. He didn't want Minami to notice what he was doing. He wouldn't reveal his ultimate goal. Just how many restrictions did he plan to play under? Naotsugu's mouth hung open, and he couldn't close it. On top of that, there was probably a time limit, too. Well, if he didn't want Minami to know, he couldn't afford to take too long. That must have been why he'd stolen quietly out of Akiba, Naotsugu realized. After all, everyone except for the Log Horizon members probably thought Shiroe was at the guild hall, doing his job. The idea of getting things done before they were discovered was already a time limit in and of itself.

"Are you a total masochist, Shiro?"

Shiroe, still lying down, denied Naotsugu's mutter. "Not at all," he said. "Every day, I think about how I'd love to take it as easy as possible."

Naotsugu was thoroughly appalled, but those words probably hadn't been a lie. He knew that.

Shiroe really did think that way. He'd been like that when he was in the Debauchery Tea Party, too. In order to reach their goals, he'd always tried to point out the shortest method with the best chances. When that method looked troublesome and roundabout, it was because the problem itself was serpentine and difficult.

The path that looked winding and troublesome and roundabout was the shortest course. The strategies Shiroe came up with always felt like that.

Once Naotsugu's friend settled on an objective, he never compromised it.

…Even when he loaded himself down with this much trouble as a result.

About half that trouble isn't even necessary. I bet Shiro's worrying too much, and if he'd just let it all hang out, there'd be lots of people who'd help him.

"Well, I guess there's no help for it, then."

Naotsugu gave a response that was completely different from what he was thinking.

In the end, Shiroe was a guy who understood a lot of things. He also wasn't the type to lose sight of what was important. Besides, even if he *did* end up doing that, Naotsugu would just whack him upside the head.

Shiroe seemed to be in some kind of hurry, but even so, in the midst of that impatience, in order to convince himself, he needed time to roll around. Naotsugu thought all guys were like that, not just Shiroe. He had enough memories of working too hard on his own and causing trouble for the people around him that just remembering made him go beet red. Still, Shiroe thought that sort of thing was necessary.

It was necessary for everybody, and it was even more necessary for Shiroe.

The people around him seemed to have decided to think of him as a schemer and a resourceful guy, but Naotsugu thought Shiroe was actually a pretty clumsy type. Clumsy Shiroe needed a lot of time for hard battles.

During those times, he just had to be there with him.

He didn't have to worry: Shiroe would probably put out unstinting effort he could feel satisfied with. That was the type of guy Naotsugu's friend was. No matter what he was doing, he was incapable of cutting corners.

"There's no help for it. Let's pull together enough members for a raid. No worries. It'll work out."

"Will it...?" Shiroe responded.

"Sure it will," Naotsugu told him cheerfully, kicking him hard. *There's no development we can't recover from*, Naotsugu thought, but he just grinned at him, without putting it into words.

Besides, he was sure Shiroe would find that dawn.

On Tea Party adventures, that had been the condition for victory. Naotsugu decided to look forward to seeing that view.

In the course of his long friendship with Shiroe, this wasn't an unusual night.

CHAPTER.
2
PALM AGAIN

▶ NAME: DEMIQUAS

▶ LEVEL: **93**

▶ RACE: **HUMAN**

▶ CLASS: **MONK**

▶ HP: **16385**

▶ MP: **4627**

▶ ITEM 1:

[WYVERN LEG GUARDS]

A SUPERB ARTICLE CREATED BY POURING RARE MATERIAL FROM WYVERNS INTO HIS FAVORITE LEG ARMOR. THE WING AND TAIL DECORATIONS WERE ADDED LATER, AND THEY EXTEND THE RANGE OF HIS WYVERN KICK.

▶ ITEM 2:

[GAUNTLET OF GREED]

A HIGH-LEVEL REWARD FROM A PAST PVP TOURNAMENT. NOT HIGH IN DEFENSE, BUT HAS THE SOUL STEALING ABILITY, WHICH RECOVERS HP WHEN DEALING DAMAGE, AND INCREASES THE MONEY DROPPED BY MONSTERS.

▶ ITEM 3:

[CAT-SHAPED PUNCHING BAG]

A PUNCHING BAG WITH CAT EARS, CREATED BY GATHERING FURS FROM SHADOW-RUNNING WILDCATS THAT LIVE ON AN ISLAND FAR TO THE SOUTH. IT AUTOMATICALLY EVADES. LATELY, DEMIQUAS HAS ACQUIRED A WOMAN'S SHADOW, BUT HE HASN'T FORGOTTEN GETTING BEATEN BY NYANTA. HE'S CURRENTLY PERFORMING TEST KICKS ON IT.

<HARP>
ONE OF THE OLDEST INSTRUMENTS
THERE IS. IF YOU CARRY ONE
UNDER YOUR ARM, IT'LL MAKE
YOU POPULAR.

Raids were cooperative battles, fought by a number of Adventurers that exceeded the normal party limit of six. They were end content that players had energetically participated in since the days when *Elder Tales* had been a game, and of the many quests in the game, a majority of the greatest ones were raids.

Although they were lumped together under the single term *raid*, there were several different kinds. They were primarily classified by the number of people they required, with the largest—composed of ninety-six members—known as a legion raid. Though, even when you totaled all the level brackets in all areas of the Yamato server, there weren't many quests that required legion raids.

The most common, and the type said to condense the real pleasure of raids, were full raids, which combined four six-member parties. This type of raid, which required a total of twenty-four participants, was the main way to gain fame and glory on the server. Back when *Elder Tales* had still been a game, they had been a hot in-game news item every weekend, in combination with predictions and announcements regarding which major guilds would produce what sort of results.

The Debauchery Tea Party, to which Shiroe had belonged in the past, had been a group that actively sought out full raids. Even if they had no hope of matching the major guilds in legion raids—which required more than a hundred participants if you included reserve personnel—full raids were definitely gala occasions where they could win attention and popularity on the server.

Although this was generally misunderstood, what was necessary on raids wasn't powerful equipment.

If it had been necessary to have equipment and special-skill ranks of the sort one could only acquire on raids to participate in a raid for the first time, no players could ever have played end content. No matter how hard the quest, it had been designed to be an accessible game. If there were no users who could play it, no one would know why the operating company had bothered to provide that content.

Because they were something players aspired to, they had to be difficult, but they couldn't be impossible to clear. Designing raid content required a sort of fine-tuned sense and experience to find that balance.

What made for good raid content?

Back when *Elder Tales* had been a game, a message from the game creators known as the Designers' Letter had included the following words:

Content that lets you and your friends grow together.

Shiroe thought it meant exactly that.

Raids were difficult content that a group with certain equipment and strength at a certain time could conquer by training repeatedly. In this case, *training* could mean analyzing the mechanism of the raid content, or investigating the enemies' special characteristics, or even proposing appropriate strategies, and then, in the end, mastering the teamwork needed to implement that strategy.

Of course, game character performance was important. If you had that, you could force your way through raid content. However, if you did, sooner or later, raid content that required high performance would trip you up. At times like that, what you needed was connections between humans that went beyond equipment and special skill ranks: you needed members who were on the same page.

In other words, if you were going to make a serious attempt at high-difficulty raid content, you needed companions you could call true allies. Mastering teamwork took time. If you plunged into a tough battle with a motley collection of Adventurers, everything from human relations to the level of difficulty required could deteriorate.

When that happened, communities like guilds could collapse in the blink of an eye.

That made this all the more painful for Shiroe.

During the operation to recapture Zantleaf, he'd picked up all sorts of acquaintances. The Catastrophe and the Round Table Council had brought even a veteran *Elder Tales* player like Shiroe a wider range of acquaintances than ever before. However, he couldn't use his telechat contact network now. Recruiting D.D.D., the Knights of the Black Sword, or the West Wind Brigade—major guilds that specialized in breaking through raid content—would probably have given him the best shot at success, but it was best to assume that all of Akiba's major forces were under surveillance by Plant Hwyaden and one other group... Or rather, Shiroe had confirmed that they were. It wouldn't be possible to mobilize those forces.

Of course, there were individual Adventurers who were skilled as well. However, since raids were content designed for groups, it was vital to become skilled *as a group*. An organization cobbled together on the spot would magnify the risk. If this had been the sort of situation where they could gradually solidify their relationships, that would have been all right, but he wanted to finish up this mission quickly. When he thought about it that way, he was hesitant to set up a new organization.

If the Debauchery Tea Party had been around, Shiroe thought, he wouldn't have had a problem. That group of daredevils would have eagerly signed on for any raid at all. He could practically see Nurukan or Tuli whooping and breaking into a run. This would have been the perfect mission for Kanami's friends, who saw every sort of hardship as nothing more than a chance to stand out... And yet.

"Understood. Sure."

For that reason, at that unexpectedly easy response, Shiroe heaved a sigh of relief.

The silver-haired man in front of him had accepted his request immediately.

This was Susukino, one of just five player towns in Yamato. The town was located where Sapporo, Hokkaido, would have been in the real world. A large tavern in the heart of Susukino was currently serving as the Silver Sword guild hall.

The high-ceilinged building felt open and airy, and the damp air one expected on hearing the word *tavern* wasn't there. On a long, wooden seat that was more of a bench than a sofa, "Mithril Eyes" William Massachusetts, an elf who wore his hair tied back, turned sharp eyes on Shiroe.

"Thank you very much. —Are you sure you don't need to hear the details, though?"

"You'll tell me even if I don't ask."

Facing the guild master of Silver Sword, Shiroe mentally organized the things he needed to say. At any rate, for the moment, he had accepted. Now he had to give him a detailed explanation and ensure that cooperation.

When he remembered the gathering held in order to organize the Round Table Council, it was clear that William was very short-tempered. Explaining the situation at length was probably not a good idea. In order to divide the work, he'd split up with Naotsugu and come to the Silver Sword headquarters. He wanted to bring back good results.

"The target is a new raid zone connected to the deepest part of the Depths of Palm. We've gone in and investigated. It's restricted to a full raid. Enemy levels start at 89. We're the ones who discovered it. We've released the seal through a quest. We believe the difficulty will be extremely high."

"Hmm."

After the conversation with Kinjo, Shiroe's group had gone down to the deepest part of the Depths of Palm again and explored beyond the seal. The seal itself was still in effect, but they'd overwritten it so that any people with permission from Li Gan could go beyond the great door, then they had investigated. As a result, and as expected, they'd confirmed that a raid zone lay inside.

The interior was a high-ceilinged ancient ruin. In other words, the image of the Depths of Palm continued in this area, farther underground. The subterranean space, lit by luminescent crystals, was a mysterious facility composed of vertical shafts, arches, and countless temples, all linked together.

The enemies they'd spotted at a distance had been jellylike monsters the color of yellow ocher. This sort of amorphous monster was found in underground facilities that had been sealed. Their level was 89. In terms of level alone, Shiroe's group would have been more than capable of defeating them, but the monsters' rank was full raid; in other words, it had been assumed that twenty-four level-89 Adventurers would fight them together. Shiroe and the others had retreated without fighting a single battle.

In addition, as Shiroe had predicted, the zone seemed to have entry restrictions. Only groups of up to twenty-four Adventurers would be able to enter. This meant it wouldn't be possible to conquer it through numbers and sheer force alone.

William seemed to be considering Shiroe's brief report; the corners of his lips were warped. He was probably pulling lots of information from Shiroe's nearly minimal words. Any veteran Adventurer who was used to raids would do that much.

"What types of enemies are there? Estimates are fine."

"The ones we saw were slime-type monsters. They were five meters or more in diameter. From this point on, I'm inferring, but from the shape of the facility and from tradition, I think there might be giants and mystical beasts. Large monsters."

"Giants, huh?"

A huge variety of monsters made appearances in *Elder Tales*. It was probably safe to say that there was every kind the production company could imagine. However, these monsters fell into several categories. Some examples were the sahuagins and goblins Shiroe and the others had fought on the Zantleaf Peninsula. Other famous ones were the Skeletons and, the ultimate mystical beasts, dragons. One of these categories was "Giant." As you'd expect from the name, these were enormous, humanoid monsters. They were relatively popular on the Arc-Shaped Archipelago Yamato, and they lived mainly to the north of the Kanto region. There were various kinds, such as Cyclops and Frost Giants, but they all boasted high HP and attack power, while their agility was low. Contrary to the common concept of giants, high-level Giants used powerful magic attacks. Compared to Dire Beasts and Treants, they could be considered tough enemies.

"Handy. We're based in Susukino, so we're used to those," William said.

Shiroe nodded in agreement. This was actually one of the reasons he'd decided to scout Silver Sword. The Ezzo Empire—Hokkaido in the real world—was on the front line of the People of the Earth's war with the Giants. After leaving Akiba, Silver Sword had relocated its headquarters to Susukino, which had abundant Giant subjugation raid content. Shiroe had come to call on Silver Sword because he'd known they were one of the few organizations that would be able to carry out this mission.

"That doesn't mean there's no problem, though."

William went on, wearing the same obstinate expression.

"Silver Sword is currently open, but we're not doing business. We're short on people."

"Huh?"

"I mean that we have members who couldn't keep up with the raids. There are guys who don't want to fight in raids anymore, although they're still with the guild, and there are others who've settled down in Susukino."

William's answer was a harsh one.

"In other words, they're retired. They could probably handle a lukewarm raid, but they can't manage the hottest raids anymore. This one is going to be the toughest there is. We boosted our levels to 95, but I doubt that'll make it an easy win. I'll be lucky if I manage to bring twenty people."

"Is it…because of the memories?"

At Shiroe's question, about the terror of losing memories, William shook his head.

"The stuff about losing memories is all just hot air. We don't believe stories like that. And they're not scared. Not of the monsters, anyway."

"Then why?"

Shiroe didn't get it.

He could understand being afraid. Resurrection from death might be a fact, but the idea of your own death brought a visceral terror with it. The pain itself was diluted. When you'd lost most of your HP, the discomfort was still no worse than sore muscles. Even at the very instant of death, it probably wasn't anything you couldn't tolerate. However, seeing an actual steel sword sprouting from your own chest shattered an Adventurer's self-control. The sight of being torn apart by the claws of magical beasts and having your entrails devoured was no joke. Death had a unique terror all its own.

Even major raid guilds like D.D.D. and the Knights of the Black Sword had stopped attempting the very hardest raids after the Catastrophe. In the first place, the difficulty of battle had risen following the Catastrophe. Many Adventurers pointed out the fact that, even with ordinary parties, the low visibility and the difficulty of monitoring statuses meant that the level of the monsters they could defeat had fallen from what it had been in the days of *Elder Tales*. It was probably only natural that the difficulty of the raids targeted by the big guilds was set low.

…And so if he'd said he was short on raid members because their fear of death was strong, I'd understand, but…

"Why?"

"Shiroe…uh. Mister Shiroe."

"Just 'Shiroe' is fine."

"Right. Shiroe, how many times have you died since then?"

Guessing that *then* probably meant "the Catastrophe," Shiroe answered, "Not once."

At that, William's cross-looking face twisted in bewilderment, and he looked away. William seemed more perplexed than irritated before responding.

"I can't explain it to guys who don't understand it."

"……"

"When you die, you understand stuff. All sorts of stuff. Like how you suck at this, or how you're stingy or boring. If you die a hundred times, you see it a hundred times. That hurts, and they can't keep it up."

As William bit his lip, he looked young.

Shiroe watched the young raid master, who was harboring frustration that he couldn't vent on anything. There was something Shiroe needed to understand there, but the moment he spent desperately thinking about it seemed to pass in the blink of an eye.

There was a noise like an explosion, and when he turned, a man he recognized was bearing down on him, his face filled with rage.

►2

Meanwhile, Naotsugu and Li Gan were wandering around that same Susukino.

It was December, and the midwinter town was frosted silver under a high blue sky. The two of them walked through the wide streets, headed to restaurants and plazas, on their way to gather raid members from sources other than the one Shiroe had tapped.

In *Elder Tales*, if you looked at a person steadily, their name, main class, and level would be displayed on your HUD. In addition, there were all sorts of other elements when scouting members, such as which guild they were affiliated with and their equipment, manner, and way of speaking. Shiroe said that conducting a raid by hiring individual Adventurers would be difficult, but the Tea Party had originally been made up of individual Adventurers, too. Naotsugu thought that, ultimately, it would be all right to just follow his instincts, and so he was roaming around town, acting separately from Shiroe.

"Are we recruiting companions?"

"Yep."

Naotsugu responded to the round-shouldered Lore Master who was walking the streets of Susukino beside him.

"I doubt we'll get twenty of 'em right off the bat, but I'd like to find some likely-looking ones."

"Will it go so well? This gathering of warriors for a decisive battle?"

"When it's gonna go well, it'll do that."

Giving an evasive answer, Naotsugu looked around the area restlessly. Compared to what it had been like the last time he'd been here, the town seemed to have grown quite peaceful. It was no longer the ruined Susukino where Adventurers had eyed each other suspiciously.

Silver Sword must have significantly improved the environment. In fact…he'd heard something about that in the news he'd gotten through Shiroe. The guild had left Akiba and come to this northern town in search of a raid environment, and it seemed to have had enormous influence. Susukino's public order had collapsed, and it had been on the verge of becoming a city of violence, but Silver Sword had saved it. Although the group wasn't affiliated with Akiba's Round Table Council, its scale and strength were such that for a time, it had been selected as one of those twelve guilds. Their training was on a whole different level from the hoodlums who'd swaggered around Susukino as if they'd owned the place. Even if both were level 90, Silver Sword was a military group that drilled properly.

Naotsugu had heard from Shiroe that simply having a first-class combat guild in Susukino had vastly improved conditions.

A grandmotherly Person of the Earth wearing a fur coat and cylindrical hat walked by with a child, holding a big paper bag. The bag probably held groceries. Her expression was peaceful, and the child seemed to be having fun, so their situation probably wasn't a bad one. They walked quickly because of the cold.

A look at this avenue showed that the places where people walked had been cleared, and about fifteen centimeters of snow remained on either side. It was cold, but to Naotsugu, the scene seemed like a gentle one, relatively well harmonized.

Sparkling icicles hung from the eaves, and the town was like a work of art, decorated with crystal.

Once they'd passed through the residential district, where there were lots of People of the Earth, the avenue grew wider; it was apparently an artery that led to the center of Susukino. Just as when he'd come here before, the abandoned buildings looked rough, like fortresses, but to Naotsugu, they seemed to blend much better with the scenery now than they had during the adventure in May. That might have been because, rather than being built to intimidate as their appearance suggested, these snow-country buildings were intended to shut out the cold.

"You ever been to Susukino, mister?"

"I've visited a few times."

"We'll probably have to stay here for a bit, y'know."

"Yes, I'm prepared for that. When you explore the depths, I'd only hold you back."

There was a little regret in Li Gan's response.

In a zone designed for parties, the monsters that appeared would be the sort meant to be defeated by five or six Adventurers. For Naotsugu and Shiroe, whose levels were far different from Li Gan's, it was possible to explore while protecting the sage. However, it definitely depended on the difficulty of the situation: they'd guarded him while investigating the Depths of Palm, but in a raid zone meant to be challenged by twenty-four high-level Adventurers, the battles would be severely violent. As they'd discussed beforehand, Li Gan would wait in Susukino for Naotsugu and the others to return.

"You look like that bums you out."

"Well, a little. It is the secret of the Kunie clan, after all. All the information one could see and hear there is truly worth a fortune."

"We'll bring you back as many stories as possible, all right?" Naotsugu told him.

"No, no, don't trouble yourselves. This, too, is the role of the Sage of Miral Lake. Besides, there are lots of unusual things in this city as well. It's being developed by the Adventurers even as we speak. While you and the others proceed with your conquest, I think I'll spend my time learning about Susukino. Just thinking about what sort of new things are being created in this northern country is terribly thrilling."

As he spoke, Li Gan looked around, smiling.

He really must be bursting with curiosity. Naotsugu was using polite speech with him, just in case, but the guy looked as if he might be about his age; he seemed a bit like a science-minded grad student who spent all his time in the lab. To Naotsugu, who wasn't shy with strangers, he seemed like an interesting guy, the sort he could have a good, frank conversation with. He also thought he understood why Shiroe hit it off with him.

"Yeah, that's true. There's lots of good stuff in Susukino, too."

"You're right. I may take this opportunity to investigate your intercity gates—"

"Dbweh!"

Abruptly, a voice interrupted their conversation.

When they reflexively looked toward it, they saw someone's upper body stuck into a huge bank of snow that had been piled up beside a cottage-style house. From the looks of the indisposed person's position, if they had fallen to get there, they must have done it with serious flair. They were stuck diagonally into the huge pile of snow, and Naotsugu couldn't see their face. All that protruded was a slim, well-shaped derriere in hot pants.

"Nice panties!"

Naotsugu grinned and flashed a big thumbs-up.

The line from the small hips to the ivory thighs was fantastic.

"I'm compelled to agree with you there."

On seeing Li Gan smiling next to him, Naotsugu thought, *Oh yeah, I can totally be friends with this guy.* He was a scholastic type, like Shiroe, but if he was able to join in without hesitation at times like this, he was probably more of a guy's guy than Shiroe was.

Li Gan gave Naotsugu an intellectual response:

"That said, although I'm not well versed in the customs of the Adventurers, aren't those generally referred to as 'low-rise hot pants'? In other words, isn't it unsuitable to eulogize them as 'panties' in the truest sense of the word?"

"Nah, it's fine. I'd feel bad about leaving 'em out, wouldn't you? If they've got panties in their heart, then they're panties."

"Well said."

"Help me!"

A figure burst violently out of the pile of snow and regained its feet, directing a protest at the two of them. Its head had been stuck very deeply, to the point where it seemed to have fallen off the roof rather than simply fallen over, but the only sign was that the tip of its adorable nose seemed to be a bit red. Adventurer toughness was at work here as well.

"Sorry, sorry city."

"We saw a very callipygian posterior, so we simply..."

The two didn't seem at all apologetic, and the small shadow howled as if it meant to bite them.

"If a gorgeous girl like me scars up her face, it'll damage all the guys who are crazy about her!"

Naotsugu gazed at the self-proclaimed victim, who came up only to his chest.

She was petite and cute. Her overall silhouette was slim, and she wore a blouse and vest, hot pants that made her pure white legs look longer, a necktie, and knee socks that accentuated the dazzling area between their cuffs and the hem of her pants. The way her outfit looked like some sort of uniform on the top but left as little to the imagination as possible on the bottom was terrific.

It was a style that would have made any guy's heart beat faster, even if he didn't want it to. As a matter of fact, Naotsugu's cheeks were growing hot. Just a little, because he felt guilty about it. However, the expression under the coquettish little top hat betrayed it all.

It was the proudest, happiest, smuggest face Naotsugu had ever seen—in other words, an expression of sheer triumph. The expression was splendidly radiant, so cute that it would be devastating for any watching guys, and it looked as though the girl herself really believed in what she'd said.

Cute.

She certainly was cute.

As frustrating as it was, if he'd said she wasn't cute, he would have been lying.

However, Naotsugu thought that saying it would "damage the guys who were crazy about her" had been a blatant exaggeration. He thought it, but he kept it to himself, thinking that only an ogre would hit a girl with a comeback like that when she was smiling with such lustrous, jellylike lips.

"I'd say that's a blatant exaggeration, wouldn't you?"

Li Gan the ogre didn't keep it to himself.

Li Gan's stock just went up again.

Naotsugu couldn't have been more impressed.

"*Uuu...* You can't bring me down."

"Ah, she's back."

Li Gan kept teasing the girl, who'd staggered but recovered. He looked entertained. At his easygoing comeback, the girl's face went red and she got mad.

The fact that she still wore a vaguely cheerful, proud expression, even then, might have meant she was a bit lacking in grace for a beautiful girl. However, that seemed to be part of her unique charm as well.

She had an expressive face, and as the girl herself said, she certainly did seem attractive.

"Hmm... Yeah, you're cute, but you look so smug about it that I-really-don't-want-to-*say*-you're-cute city... If I'm taking this, that, and the other thing into consideration and making a general call, or actually, obviously, in terms of both volume and panties, Miss Mari wins! In-other-words city!"

"Huh?"

Naotsugu, who'd crossed his arms, had let the words slip out by accident, but fortunately neither the girl nor Li Gan seemed to have caught on. Waving his hands to camouflage where he'd been looking, Naotsugu took a towel out of his belongings and tossed it to the girl.

She was dressed lightly, and she didn't seem to have a magic bag.

"Hrrn, all right. I'm kind to my fans, you see."

Without hesitation, she used the towel to brush the snow away. She seemed clumsy, and there was some snow left on the brim of the little top hat. Removing it with his fingertips, Naotsugu looked at the girl's status display.

"Tetora, huh?"

"Call me Tetora-ra-rah!"

Her expression was resolute, and it left Naotsugu nonplussed. Her level was 94. The same as his. Apparently she was an Adventurer, with lots of real combat experience, who'd fought repeated battles even after the Catastrophe. Her guild was Light Indigo. Her class was Cleric.

"All right, this guy seems easier to win over."

"Stuff like that has zero effect if you say it yourself."

Even as Naotsugu retorted, Tetora latched on to his left hand with catlike agility, practically hanging from it.

"Really? No effect? None? Don't I have a hug effect?"

Her question was delivered with the boastful, self-important expression that seemed to be her default. *No effect!* It would have been easy to deny her that way, but at that point, his lamentable male nature came into play: Even though he knew he was just being teased, having a beautiful girl clinging to his arm in a companionable way felt pretty good. Tetora even smelled sweet, like oranges.

"Luh, luh, lemme go!"

"Ha-haaa. No can do, Mister Naotsugu."

She must have read his status at some point. In this world, it was only natural for people to know each others' names, even when they first met.

"I love nuzzling flustered, panicking guys. Parenthetically, I hate *being* nuzzled, so keep that in mind!"

"I *said*! Let! Me! *Go!*"

Tetora had twisted away, slipping around behind Naotsugu's back, then climbed up to his shoulders, clinging to his neck. Possibly due to her Adventurer agility, he didn't even feel her weight all that much.

As Tetora hugged Naotsugu's head and giggled, she was truly as cute as she'd declared herself to be.

Due to corrections from the system, beautiful men and women weren't unusual in *Elder Tales*, but that was true only for appearance, and it couldn't camouflage the atmosphere the actual person gave off. Tetora was radiating a showy, cheerful atmosphere, and in terms of standing out, she was far and away the best of all the Adventurers Naotsugu had ever seen.

"You look like a tree-climbing pika."

"This skeleton guy is pretty harsh, isn't he?!"

"Skeleton…?"

Li Gan seemed entertained by Tetora's response.

"This is a major incident. You should have saved me, you know? If a lovely girl like me scraped my nose, my fans would cry. And really, the mere fact that I made such a spectacle of myself back there could end my life as an idol."

"Yeah, the upside-down panties."

"They're not panties! They're hot pants!"

Li Gan was keeping up with her. He seemed to have instantly registered the scandal the girl was concerned about, and was attacking her weak point.

"'Hot'… Warm pants… Oh… In other words, you wet yourself a bit, due to the shock?"

"A-a-as if I'd ever wet myself!!"

"And the truth is…?"

"Stomachs get cold in the snow country, and everyone knows a cold stomach means diarrh—"

"That's what I *thought* it was—"

"Wait! What are you making me say, you rascally skeleton?!"

While Tetora—who clung to him as if she were hugging him—and Li Gan squabbled, Naotsugu was at his wit's end. He raised both his big hands, caught Tetora's sides, and lowered her lightly to the ground. He'd felt Li Gan's eyes on him.

The meaning had gotten through to him right away. In short, he was asking, *Why not invite this girl?*

With the raid in mind, Naotsugu looked Tetora over.

In raids, Clerics were frontline healers. They were expected to recover the main tank while relying on their heavy armor. To that end, they had the advantage of being able to use the heaviest equipment of the three recovery classes.

Further, of all twelve classes, they were one of the three classes allowed to wear full-body metal armor, along with Guardian (Naotsugu's class) and Samurai (Soujirou's class). They were also able to equip shields, and of the twelve classes, in terms of equipment, their defensive abilities were second only to Guardians.

Clerics' duty was to rely on this equipment while using recovery spells to support the main tank's HP from the front line. Since the main tank was the first to take monster attacks, it had the roughest position in violent raid battles. Naturally, in addition to sword and ax strikes, those attacks also included wide-range spells like Dragon Breath.

These attacks were aimed at the main tank, but since they were ranged attacks and Clerics were so close, they often got pulled in. Of course, they were that close to begin with because they were able to use more powerful recovery spells that way, but even then, the front line was a terrifying place. Clerics ended up having to bear great responsibility without flinching from the risk, and in *Elder Tales*, they were sometimes called the staunchest defenders.

When he took another look at Tetora's equipment, it seemed very light.

Of course, it was possible that Tetora's current equipment was meant for wearing around town instead of for combat, and he couldn't really count on that judgment. Shiroe might have been able to tell what sort of magical abilities lurked in the chic vest she had equipped, but that was a stunt Naotsugu couldn't pull off. His conclusion was, in the end, that he simply didn't know. Her level was perfect, and when it came to raids, he wanted an excellent healer badly enough to kill for it.

However, because the situation was what it was, he felt hesitant about taking a girl to a battlefield where her life would be in danger.

"Well, when you're as splendid a girl as I am, you just give off pheromones no matter what's going on."

As Tetora spoke, she puffed out her chest and wore an expression that seemed to say, *Goodness gracious, what a pain.*

Apparently she'd misinterpreted Naotsugu's scrutiny. This wasn't at all what Naotsugu wanted to hear, but Tetora had planted her hands on her hips and was rapping away cheerfully: *Pheromones, phero-mones, no help for that, I saw through that, hm-hm-hmmm.* Although there was no telling what she was happy about, she tried to glom on to Naotsugu again, proudly, and he couldn't let his guard down. For his part, Naotsugu desperately tried to peel her away.

"I don't think it was pheromones that came out of that projecting posterior of yours. I think it was probably wind."

Li Gan, who had a finger to his chin and looked pensive, punctured Tetora's attitude with a single strike.

"Wha?!"

"Wha?"

A look of intense sorrow came onto Tetora's face, and immediately afterward, her knees nearly buckled. Forcing herself to regain her footing, even so, she stuck to her guns:

"Idols do *not* break wind!"

"Do they pee?"

"No!"

Naotsugu had made the comeback on reflex, but Tetora picked it up deftly. Her timing was impeccable.

"Okay, you pass."

"Huh?"

"You pass—Listen, this is sudden, but…"

Just as he'd told Li Gan, in the end, it was about instinct.

Besides, Naotsugu had picked up a nostalgic air about Tetora. It resembled his companions who'd just sprinted ahead, even though they hadn't been looking for victory.

That was how Naotsugu managed to recruit a new raid member.

▶ **3**

"So you had the guts to show your face here again, huh, Shiroe of Log Horizon?!"

When Shiroe turned, he saw Demiquas, whose entire body seemed to be radiating anger.

Behind him was a fallen table he'd apparently kicked over; food was splattered across the floor. The members of Silver Sword were looking at Demiquas—in other words, at the table where their leader William and his guest Shiroe were—with dangerous expressions.

This zone was located within the city of Susukino, and naturally, it was a noncombat area.

As a result, no guild members had drawn their weapons. One of them spoke to a frightened Person of the Earth: "We're fine here. Go in back and take a break."

At those words, Shiroe smiled slightly. *They're a good guild*, he'd thought.

However, the enraged Demiquas didn't seem to have taken it that way.

"As laid-back as ever, ain'tcha!"

"It's been a long time, Democracy."

The big, well-muscled man looked exactly as he had half a year ago. His equipment had been significantly updated, but his thick, bare, log-like arms and bloodshot eyes hadn't changed. This world really did bear a marked resemblance to *Elder Tales*: Even though time had passed, there was no change in his appearance. To Shiroe, the discovery felt both natural and disappointing.

This encounter hadn't been unanticipated. When they'd decided to head for Susukino, the first thing Naotsugu had worried about had been running into Demiquas and his guild, the Briganteers. When Shiroe had rescued Serara of the Crescent Moon League right after the Catastrophe, he'd come into conflict with the Briganteers in Susukino. They'd been ruling the town with violence at the time, and they were the ones he'd rescued Serara from. In this world, where settling matters through combat lacked the deterrent of death, the victory Shiroe's group had scored against them might not have had any influence on the situation in general. However, even so, they'd succeeded in rescuing Serara, and it wasn't hard to imagine that since the others had been relying on violence, they'd hurt their self-esteem.

"Step outside, Shiroe!"

Demiquas pounded the massive oak table with a fist like a chunk of iron.

Apparently Naotsugu's prediction had been correct. It had been a completely natural prediction, and it would have been hard for it to be wrong, but Demiquas hadn't forgotten the incident from half a year ago, and he probably wasn't just going to let it go.

"What do you plan to do outside?"

Shiroe knew the answer to this with absolute certainty, but he asked anyway.

He knew what Demiquas wanted, but even so, he couldn't just skip all the steps in the middle. It was a conventional exchange of taunts. This was a grudge Shiroe had created in the past, so he couldn't run from it. Now, when he was right in the middle of negotiations to recruit raid members, he had to avoid showing weakness in front of William.

"Which do you like better, Hamburg steak or mincemeat cutlet?"

"I like tofu."

"That's great. Nice and soft. I'll pound you to a pulp, so get outside!"

"Shut up, Demi."

However, William interrupted bluntly.

"That guy's my guest."

"What the hell do I care?! William, he— My—"

"You lost, didn't you?"

"—!"

"You lost. And quit picking fights."

"But!"

"I'll crush you again, Demiquas."

William issued the warning in a bitterly cold voice.

Shiroe pushed his glasses up with a fingertip, thinking. He'd known about the circumstances in Susukino through reports. That half a year ago, the confusion after Shiroe's group had left Susukino had contin-ued. That after the Round Table Council had been established, they'd put together several caravans between Akiba and Susukino, and had finished rescuing the people who'd been left behind in the city. After that, Silver Sword had moved their headquarters to this northern country, and while Susukino's current atmosphere was slightly barba-rous, it had settled down into a frontier player town.

Susukino had been a lawless city, crowded with combat guilds, but because Silver Sword—a group that had pulled off some of the top raids on the server—had moved in, public order had returned, even if it was rather unsteady. William's group was a guild whose power was right on the heels of D.D.D. and the Knights of the Black Sword on the Yamato Server, and although they hadn't actively dominated the town, they hadn't tolerated any insolent boasting from amateurs. To William and the others, anyone who got violent as a group, especially with People of the Earth—whose combat power was clearly inferior to that of Adventurers—was a despicable coward. They wouldn't let anyone like that talk about *Elder Tales* or combat.

Shiroe had just witnessed a real-life example from that report.

Six ears were sticking up over the kitchen counter. Felinoid People of the Earth had poked their heads up partway so that their eyes hovered just above the counter, and they were watching the situation on the floor. Those eyes did seem to hold the feeling that this was a bit of a problem, but there was no fear in them.

Silver Sword must have won the trust of the People of the Earth here in Susukino. Susukino was on the front line of the struggle with the Giants, and ever since the days of *Elder Tales*, it had been a frontier town where tough guys gathered. This time around, that might have influenced things in a positive way.

They probably felt safer now, when Silver Sword—who were disciplined, even if they were a surly combat group—were here as the town's guardians, than they had when the Briganteers and other scoundrels had swaggered around as if they owned the place.

Finding himself the target of William's cutting words, Demiquas ground his teeth. He glared at Shiroe with a curse in his eyes and enough force to run him through.

"In the first place, friend, you couldn't win against Shiroe."

"Hey, I've picked up a few raid items since then."

True, when he looked, he saw that the Wyvern Leg Guards that Demiquas had equipped seemed to have been drastically modified. In addition, various pieces of his equipment looked well used, showing that over the past six months, he'd participated in several raids. Not only that, but they couldn't have been low-level raids. The King of Beasts' Armor was a found item in the Master of Tenvictory Plateau, a field raid for level-90 players. If he'd done that after the Catastrophe, it meant he'd succeeded at a challenge difficult enough to deserve praise.

"Thinking you could win with equipment is the reason you couldn't beat Shiroe."

"~~~!!"

Demiquas radiated inarticulate murderous intent. In contrast, William's laid-back attitude didn't flicker. Shiroe didn't know what kind of relationship had been built between the two of them, but he could imagine it. No doubt they'd gotten into a contest of strength and had clarified their respective positions in the hierarchy. William had won a victory so overwhelming that Demiquas was left with no choice but to fall silent.

"And then, and then, the Briganteers lost half their members. Well, you can't blame them, you know. He got completely shredded by a swordfighting cat who wasn't even in a guild. That obviously made the foundations shaky. On top of that, the craptastic Rondarg got poached by the West."

"Hey, self-proclaimed idol. It's okay for you to say 'crap'?"

"You mustn't say 'crap.' It will destroy your popularity."

"Hah! I-I didn't say it. I'd never say 'crap.' It would pollute my mouth."

"Planning to be one of those anything-for-attention idols, are you?"

"I'm an orthodox, beautiful, galactic idol! I'm so outer space I'd make the *Voyager* jealous!"

"That sounds kinda lonely. Never mind that, what's Demiquas up to?"

"I'm not lonely!! Demi-Demi is Silver Sword's junior member henchman, and so are the Briganteers. And now Susukino's peaceful. I'm not lonely, all right? Well, about half of it's because Demi-Demi's bride is an excellent person. And also, I'm not lonely."

These cheerful, thoughtless voices reached the table where Shiroe, William, and Demiquas stood in the midst of searing tension. The voices grew louder and louder, probably because they were walking this way. However, apparently, they didn't have the sense to lower their voices.

Demiquas's face went red, and tensed with something that wasn't anger.

"Seriously?! A bride?! What-the-heck city!!"

"He's a married man, is he? Lucky fellow."

"No, they're not married, or rather, he refuses to admit it, but according to my information network—the People of the Earth—his guild house is neat as a pin, his sheets are laundered crisp, and three meals get fixed every day, and his guild members are gaga over her. It sounds like he got himself adopted by a People of the Earth noblewoman."

"Huh...?"

"He kidnapped this Person of the Earth, thinking he'd turn her into a servant, but she took care of him and he went all soft, The End. I swear, it's like some ero-game development. Oh, but Mister Naotsugu? Don't you want me to take care of you? Dweh-heh-heh. I'll help you out. I may not look it, but I *am* an idol, you know."

"Whatever, just get down, you counterfeit idol!!"

Shiroe heard a cute voice laughing—"Gweh-heh-heh!"—in a tone that wasn't cute at all.

Inconveniently, the other two voices were male, and he recognized them.

"So anyway, thanks to that, Demi-Demi's really mellowed out lately... Oh. There he is, even."

That instant, without any lead-up at all, Demiquas flew through the air. Wyvern Kick. The flying kick, which included a glide of about five meters, was a prominent Monk special attack skill. He'd probably activated the skill just by twisting his torso, without using the menu, and he'd done it at a speed that was beyond comparison with what it had been six months ago.

The attack had been made without any preparatory motions, but in a move so quick it was almost impossible to see, Naotsugu rammed it with the shield he'd had ready. The light, clear, high sound was probably proof that Demiquas's attack hadn't been a serious one. This was a noncombat zone, so if he had been, the Kunie clan guards would have appeared. Naotsugu also hadn't blocked it in earnest. He'd just held his shield up over his shoulder, blandly.

However, the attack's direct target, the slim girl who'd been hugging Naotsugu's neck, seemed to have been overawed. Her trembling mouth hung open, and she clung to Naotsugu desperately, like a bear cub.

The trio that had come in through the door consisted of Naotsugu,

Li Gan, and a Cleric. They'd probably gotten information on Demiquas, who was very likely to be hostile to Shiroe, and had come to meet up with him. However, their timing had been rotten, and Demiquas himself had overheard them chatting as they swapped information.

They probably hadn't meant anything by it, but the content of their conversation had infuriated Demiquas. Shiroe had to admit that that was only natural. If people talked about something like that in public, let alone revealed things like those while he was in the middle of picking a fight, it was only to be expected. He did think that unleashing a kick in retaliation had been going too far, but if the other guy was Naotsugu, there was nothing to worry about. He was used to getting kicked during his bouts with Akatsuki. Even in Akiba, it was safe to call this particular Guardian an expert in taking flying kicks and flying knee kicks. Considering that his defense rate against Akatsuki was about 50 percent, Akatsuki's kicks might be on par with those of a professional Monk in real life.

"He *kicked*?!"

"Way to take advantage of the confusion: Where are you putting your hands?! Don't cling! Quit leaning on me!"

"Dammit, Tetora. What're you shooting your mouth off for?"

Thanks to their conversation, which completely failed to mesh, the situation got even more chaotic.

Apparently, the Cleric that was hanging on to Naotsugu's neck for dear life was called Tetora—a cute name. On checking her level and guild, it all became clear to Shiroe: Naotsugu had probably brought her back for the raid. If they recruited another helper or two, plus himself and Naotsugu, they'd manage to pull a full raid together somehow. Just when Shiroe was about to breathe a sigh of relief, William spoke, an entertained smile on his lips:

"Perfect timing. Add that healer and Demi, and we'll have enough people. You saw how hot-blooded he is. He can settle his score with Shiroe during the raid. Hah!"

At his sardonic laugh, Shiroe felt the mood he'd had up until a moment ago fly to pieces.

The raid to explore the deepest part of the Depths of Palm looked set to bring Shiroe unending worry and trouble.

▶ 4

The preparations for their departure went forward without a hitch.

Most Adventurer property was kept in their rooms or guild halls, in the rented safe-deposit boxes at the bank, or in their own luggage. It was common sense for veteran Adventurers in this world to have several weight-reduction bags, also known as Magic Bags. It wasn't at all unusual to carry around with you consumable items and equipment you'd need on an adventure, just as they were.

On top of that, Silver Sword was a guild that specialized in raids. For its elite members, their daily routine *was* combat. After William gave the order, they were fully prepared by evening.

In this post-Catastrophe world, the time they experienced seemed to be twelve times as long as it had been when *Elder Tales* was a game. In addition, now that they couldn't make free use of the Fairy Rings, traveling long distances took a shocking amount of time. In order to reach the Depths of Palm from Susukino, they would have to cross the Laiport Strait. Shiroe, Naotsugu, and Li Gan had flown across the strait on griffins, but that didn't seem possible with a group of twenty-four.

As a raid guild that had participated in the struggle for supremacy on the Yamato server, Silver Sword had many members with flying mounts, but not everyone had them. It sounded as if they would have been able to find enough if they'd strained themselves, but William simply decided to travel overland. Shiroe went along with that decision.

Silver Sword was William's guild, and he was best suited to take command.

Shiroe and Naotsugu understood this logic very well, so they'd placed themselves under his leadership. The ones who grumbled about this and that were Demiquas and Tetora. Possibly because his pride got in the way, Demiquas didn't seem able to get by without complaining, and for her part, Tetora plagued Naotsugu with remarks like "I want to become a *flying* idol."

Good grief. She's really taken a shine to him, Shiroe thought.

For Naotsugu, all sorts of springtimes were probably on their way.

If they were going overland, there was only one route: They'd go through the tunnel that ran under the Laiport Strait. As was usual in *Elder Tales*, this underground tunnel, Z539, was a dungeon. However, for a twenty-four-member full-raid unit whose members' average level was 93, it was no threat at all. In the first place, anyone who was level 40 could get through this particular dungeon as a solo player.

Led by William, the raid unit was currently advancing through this dungeon.

In *Elder Tales*, the basic unit of group combat was the party, or in other words, six people. This sort of party formed the foundation of twenty-four-member full raids as well. Full raids were composed of four squads of six members each, put together, and at times like this, the parties were referred to by numbers One through Four.

There was infinite variety in raids, and no single correct configuration existed. However, in general, the basic pattern was for the First party to be built to be outstanding at defense, and for the Second to emphasize balance so that it could act as a mobile unit. Since the main duty of the Third and Fourth parties was attacking, their members were chosen with an emphasis on firepower.

You could say that organizing parties was the first tough problem in raids.

The basic idea when putting them together was the members' classes. For example, the warrior in the First party—in other words, the main tank—would have to draw attacks from the strongest monsters to themselves at all times, throughout the entire raid. To that end, they needed the highest possible defense abilities, high-level HP, and the ability to attract monsters' aggro with the strongest taunts. The only class to fulfill all these requirements was Guardian. Samurai was another potential candidate, but when you took the presence or absence of shield equipment into consideration, Guardians were more stable.

However, this was just a general theory.

When the participating Samurai had a higher level than the

Guardian, or when the quality of their equipment was better, this wasn't necessarily true. In addition, the personalities of the Adventurer acting as the main tank had an even greater influence than their equipment or level. Since tanks were at the very center of raids and had to take enemy attacks for an extended period, the position carried a heavy burden. Techniques were necessary, of course, but so were strength of will and bonds with the defender's companions. Even among Guardians, there were Adventurers whose minds tended to focus on attacking, and who didn't like guiding or protecting their compatriots. Those were better suited to being in command, or to being active in the Third or Fourth attacking parties, than to being tanks.

In short, organizing parties that would participate in a raid was a difficult puzzle in which you couldn't discover the best combinations unless you carefully considered not only class and level, but the personalities of all the participants. The weak points and actions varied depending on the monster you were fighting, and when you considered countermeasures for those as well, there were innumerable answers. It was a tough problem that had worried commanders for twenty years.

Shiroe guessed that this was the reason William had chosen to travel overland: so that he could grasp the personalities and habits of the new members and refer to that information when forming the actual parties.

I doubt this is going to help him much, though.

Shiroe, who'd thought this, had been put in charge of the Second party.

Its members were:

Shiroe the Enchanter.

Naotsugu the Guardian.

Tetora the Cleric.

Voinen, a Druid.

Federico, a Swashbuckler.

Demiquas the Monk.

Voinen and Federico were Silver Sword veterans, and they'd given Shiroe a much friendlier welcome than he'd expected.

The problem, naturally, was Demiquas. Every time a battle began, he leapt out faster than anyone else in the party, crushing monsters as if venting his anger on them. The monsters' average levels were between 30 and 40. Demiquas was level 93, and the fact that he could tear through them like rice paper was only to be expected. However, you couldn't see either personality or teamwork that way.

Shiroe had spoken to him a few times, attempting to reprimand him, but Demiquas only gave short, threatening responses, and it wasn't possible to have a conversation.

"There's no point in rushing things."

As Voinen spoke to him, he wore an amiable expression.

"It would be nice if we managed to finish up before the year's out."

In a way, Voinen's thought was only natural.

In the first place, raids weren't the sort of problem you could break through in a day once you'd tackled them. Even in his recollections of the *Elder Tales* days, there had been countless normal (albeit raid-rank) monsters and between five and ten boss monsters to a single raid zone. If they weren't careful, even normal monsters could wipe them out. With boss monsters, usually a party would feel out their abilities while getting annihilated dozens of times, then finally find a way through to win.

When they got wiped out in raid zones, they wouldn't be sent back to the Temple in a player town. They'd revive at the entrance to the zone. The zone entrance functioned as the same sort of resurrection area as the Temple.

Even if they got annihilated, they could tackle the zone again from the entrance, but the number of attempts would probably be a large one. Thinking it would take about a month was valid.

As if to support Voinen's remark, on William's instructions, Shiroe had laid in more than a month's worth of provisions and consumables. Not content with this, cautious Shiroe had stuffed his Magic Bag to its limit with a variety of materials and tools, and as a result, they'd probably be able to hole up in the zone they were capturing for about two months.

That would be convenient in terms of giving their watchers the slip as well, he thought. Susukino was remote and sparsely populated, but it was still a player town. It was likely that they'd be noticed. If it was possible for them to lie low in an undiscovered zone, that would probably be safer. Shiroe didn't know exactly how far they could rely on that, but…

All that said, he didn't want to take a lot of time.

Even if they were holed up somewhere, the longer it took, the greater the danger of an information leak. In the first place, if Shiroe's prediction was correct, their watchers weren't the sort who could be shaken by simply switching zones. Nyanta and Akatsuki were creating an alibi for him back in Akiba, but even then, he didn't know how well it would work. As a result, he wanted to settle this as quickly as possible.

In the midst of Shiroe's anxiety, he noticed traces of loneliness within himself.

"That's odd," he murmured, scratching his cheek with his index finger.

He'd only spent six months there, but he missed his guild home, nestled in that ancient tree. He wanted to be in the dining room with the fragrant wood flooring Michitaka had made for them, listening to everyone's cheerful voices. He wanted to drink roasted green tea on the veranda, out in the gentle wind, as he watched the evening sun. For that to happen, he had to make this mission a success. He was a guild master now, Shiroe thought, psyching himself up.

"Wow?!"

When Shiroe glanced in the direction of the weird cry, Tetora was looking at him, her eyes round.

"What, what's up?"

"Shiroe smiled! He was smiling to himself; I saw him!"

"Well, yeah, he smiles."

"Really?! I'd never seen it before…"

The perpetrators of this incredibly rude dialogue were Naotsugu and Tetora.

"Shiro's, y'know… He's moody, see."

"Oh. I see… Poor Shiroe. Want to see my panties?"

"You're an idol. You can't show him those willingly."

"I wouldn't *show* him. I just asked. I was only curious. If I were going to show them, I'd pretend it was an unavoidable accident. Then I'd report whoever saw them."

"You really are the worst idol ever."

"Oh, *stop*. Naotsugu. Even if you fall for me all over again, I can never belong to just one person, you know."

Their combination, which left no room for anyone else to get a word in, startled Shiroe. Before his very eyes, Naotsugu barked, "I'm not falling for you" at Tetora, and Tetora clung to Naotsugu, saying, "Only a tsundere would say something that cold. I'm going to climb you."

They really must have hit it off.

As he watched, even Shiroe forgot his annoyance at the rude words and began to feel oddly entertained. Come to think of it, it was only the second day since they'd met. It was only natural that she hadn't seen him smile; they knew practically nothing about each other.

Tetora, who'd apparently proceeded to say something that made Naotsugu mad, broke into a run, and the man took off after her. Shiroe didn't attempt to stop them. Those two would probably be able to take down any monster they ran into in the dungeon with no trouble, and in any case, Demiquas had taken care of all the ones nearby.

Even so, Shiroe did wave at them and call, "Be careful." From behind him, a voice spoke: "You people are seriously confident, aren't you."

William was fully equipped, and he carried an enormous bow on his back. He came up alongside Shiroe, gazing ahead of them with a sharp expression.

"They're not confident so much as easygoing," Shiroe answered.

At those words, William seemed to smile wryly.

Over the past few days, he'd come to understand that William's sharp, wary expression didn't actually reflect what he felt inside. The expression was his default, and it didn't mean he was in a particularly bad mood. His small, ironic smile had no deeper meaning, either. It was just William's usual face.

A good raid commander had to grasp his members' personalities and the direction they wanted to go. If he didn't, he wouldn't be able to determine their party formation or disseminate orders properly.

Meanwhile, the members of a raid also gradually got to know the raid commander who led them. If they just obeyed their commander's orders, there was no point. They had to understand what the orders meant and the intent behind them, and then, for the first time, they'd gain the speed of response that was necessary to teamwork.

Shiroe, who'd been entrusted with the leadership of the Second party, had consciously attempted to grasp William's character, and as he did so, he'd learned that William thought about his guild members and those around him far more than anyone could have imagined from his habitually cross expression.

In a way, that was only natural. If William didn't have abilities on that level, he never would have been able to command Silver Sword, a combat guild that showed up on the server rankings.

"He looks the same as always."

The fact that William's gaze was turned toward the big man who was destroying a monster made the meaning of those vague words clear. True, in terms of the Second party's teamwork, Demiquas was the only one out of step.

"That's what I'm worried about."

Shiroe felt apologetic, and the emotion showed through a little in his words. However, William smiled fearlessly, stroked his thin chin with his left hand as if pinching it, and squinted his sharp eyes as though there was a wry smile in them.

"Still, he came to raid, too. He'll learn. Even I and the other knuckleheads learned. If you don't learn, you really can't go any further."

Several pieces were missing from William's words, and Shiroe wasn't yet able to understand what he meant.

▶ 5

Three weeks had passed, and the party was in the middle of their capture.

Their plans to aim for a month had crumbled easily, and the future had grown less and less clear. Even after three weeks, they'd only managed to defeat two bosses. They didn't even have a grasp of the entire zone.

The party's atmosphere grew harsher and more fatigued.

"Damn yooooooooou!"

Inwardly cursing at Demiquas, who was doing the howling, Voinen desperately cast Heartbeat Healing. It set Demiquas's HP to recover incrementally for twenty seconds. The green-and-orange pulse that surrounded the big warrior was the spell's effect.

Demiquas went from a rush—his specialty—to pounding the ochre-colored slime creature with middle-guard jabs.

Lightning Straight. The full-force attack, which he'd leaned far forward to launch, punched through the mud-like enemy with incredible ease. However, Voinen came very close to screaming, *That won't work!*

Demiquas's attack pierced the Orc Jelly's body, scattering it with a sticky sound. The substance, which had splattered all over, gave off a foul stench and began to dissolve. White smoke was rising even from Demiquas, the one who'd launched the attack. Orc Jellies had powerfully acidic bodies, and attacking them at close range did great damage to the attacker as well. In spite of this, the enormous slime, which was over five meters, didn't seem to be bothered all that much.

"What did I tell you?!"

Voinen began running toward his companion. The hot-blooded idiot's charge had taken him outside the twenty-meter range in which recovery spells were effective. Heartbeat Healing, which he'd cast on Demiquas before, was continuing to recover his health, but it was nowhere near enough. Unless he maintained his HP by combining Instant Recovery and Small Recovery, Demiquas would go down again.

Demiquas always fouled up their teamwork this way, and Voinen was irritated with him.

From the drainage outlets on their right and left, new Orc Jellies appeared with weighty sounds.

It was a melee.

There were twenty-four members in this raid unit, led by William, whom Voinen followed. It was composed of four parties, but only the First and Second had defensive capabilities above a certain level. Because the First party was specialized toward defense and holding the enemy in place, it had to draw lots of Jellies on the frontline.

The Third and Fourth parties were in charge of firepower, and their mission was to exterminate enemies. Their makeup emphasized defeating monsters, but their defensive abilities weren't all that high. Their role was to swiftly dispatch the monsters the First party had attracted.

That meant the role of the Second party, the one Voinen was part of, was to act as a mobile force.

When more monsters appeared than the First party was able to hold back, their mission was to divide them up and immobilize them. When many enemies had launched a surprise attack on the raid unit, they had to protect the "softer" Third and Fourth parties from them.

As you'd expect, the star of the raid was the First party, which faced off against the biggest, strongest enemies without giving an inch, but the Second held a tactically important position that required resourceful decisions and immediate responses. Unless all members understood the role their own party had to play, coordinated teamwork was difficult.

They were being pursued by monsters that had ambushed them from both sides.

The First party was projecting out onto the front line, which made it hard for them to turn back. Demiquas had gotten impatient with the slow-moving battle, and had charged their way, but encountering enemy reinforcements at that moment in time was highly dangerous. The enemy reinforcements had appeared on either side of the Third and Fourth parties, or in other words, the defenseless rear guard. The spellcasters, who had been performing long-range attacks, were particularly lightly equipped. If attacked, they'd go down easily.

Hey, you're in no shape to talk about other people!!

As far as Voinen was concerned, he was running after Demiquas, who'd gotten too far ahead.

Conscious of his feet, which seemed to be striking the ground much too slowly, he kept a wary eye on the translucent, dirty, gelatinous walls.

This might be bad. Just as Voinen thought it, a mass of silver charged in from his right.

"Anchor Howl!"

With enough spirit to set his eardrums buzzing, the Guardian drew one of the Orc Jellies. It was Naotsugu, who was also from the Second party. Voinen had heard that the guild he was from was famous but small, and he was impressed for the umpteenth time. From his actions, Naotsugu was far more accustomed to raids than Voinen had expected.

The monster, its repulsive body quivering, seemed to have locked on to the newcomer. Naotsugu held his shield up defensively; he probably understood that if he actively went on the attack, he'd get hit with an acid counterstrike, and the damage would increase. In terms of technique, the way he cleverly used taunting skills and his shield to keep the damage down might have been even better than Dinclon, the fellow Guardian who was Silver Sword's full-time tank.

The Jelly that had come up on the left, as if to catch Naotsugu in a pincer attack, stretched upward like swelling mochi, then stopped moving.

He didn't even have to hear Astral Hypno's sharp chant to recognize the Enchanters' hypnotic spell. A monster targeted by it would stop moving entirely, although for only about twenty seconds. Naturally, since it was "hypnosis," inflicting even a little damage would undo the status and let it start attacking again, but even so, being able to cut down on the number of enemies participating in a battle was an enormous help. Since this was a raid zone, the monsters that appeared were all beefed-up, large-scale enemies bent on confrontation, and the time they spent hypnotized was reduced to about four seconds. However, with even four seconds, it was easy to sprint past a stretched-out monster and reach the front line.

"Enemy reinforcements; requesting support! Orc Jellies, direction of travel: eight o'clock!!"

The voice of Shiroe, who'd cast the hypnosis spell, rang out.

Obeying that call, the Third and Fourth attack parties changed their targets. The first to connect was Commander William's Rapid Shot. Crystal arrows glittered like falling stars, opening fist-sized holes in the gigantic Orc Jelly's side. Then an unbroken rain of flame, ice, and lightning magic attacks poured down.

Without exception, raid monsters had stupendous HP. Even under concentrated attacks from ten people, it took a long time to finish one off. Naturally, the Orc Jelly that Shiroe had stopped in its tracks became active again, but in that four seconds, it was quite possible for a Guardian to store up aggro.

Voinen saw a lightly equipped Cleric bounding around.

The healer, whose name was Tetora or something like that, also had more combat experience than her appearance suggested. Her guild was Light Indigo, an insubstantial outfit he'd never heard of, but she seemed to have adapted to the raid in a week. Her equipment was light, in contradiction of the generally observed formula for Clerics, who were able to equip full-body armor. However, he sensed an uncommon instinct in the way she understood this and contrived ways to move around that didn't expose her weak points.

Tetora darted in and out with short, quick movements, again and again, scattering Reactive Heal around. Then, when the Orc Jelly contracted, compressing itself, she took advantage of the motion to hide behind Naotsugu. This was a player technique that used the Guardian's powerful defense as a fortress to protect the other player from raid monsters' powerful ranged attacks.

"Naotsugu, are you okay?"

"Just fine. Bring it on, slime city!"

"Woohoo! You're so cool, Naotsugu!"

"Hey, you just used me as a shield!"

"I'll recover you, so sacrifice yourself for me again!"

Those two were noisy every time, and Voinen laughed in spite of himself. Shiroe and his two companions hadn't lost a bit of their toughness. It was really something.

A strange light shone down from the zone's high ceiling—probably some sort of magic light or luminescent mushroom. Thanks to that, even though this was a dungeon, the faint glow meant it wasn't hard to see their surroundings. When they were exploring, they had the assistance of their Bug Lights as well.

However, even so, they were several hundred meters underground. Now that they'd entered Abyssal Shaft—the raid zone under the very lowest level of the Depths of Palm—even at the smallest estimate, there were several hundred million tons of dirt, sand, and bedrock over their heads. For Adventurers, who were former ordinary students and average adults, this was significant pressure.

In addition, when they were exploring like this, the complicated structure and the drainage outlets meant they never knew when they'd be ambushed, which added even more stress. The capture situation wasn't going very well, either.

It wasn't that they were slacking. This zone was simply more difficult than Voinen had anticipated.

They spent from eight to ten hours a day fighting ten-odd monster battles, give or take a few. That was the best they could do. Every battle was a hard one, and it took time for them to prepare themselves again. The range they'd explored wasn't expanding much, either.

Even so, the three who'd joined up temporarily didn't seem the least bit discouraged.

This, even though the members of Silver Sword, top elites led by William, were feeling quite a lot of tension. Compared to ordinary Adventurers, these three add-ons were displaying activity that went far beyond competent. But it seemed to stem from their personalities, rather than their levels, special skills, or equipment.

"Here I go. I'm going. If you fall in love with me, I'm really sorry."

"Whatever, just do it."

"Tee-hee. All right, here it comes! In response to everyone's requests... Please listen! Aurora Heal!!"

Rainbow light danced wildly, and the wounds of their companions over a wide range in the surrounding area began to recover. The Orc Jellies' ranged attacks pulled in not just the targeted tank but all the attackers who were close enough to launch close-range strikes with swords and axes. His comrade Federico's HP was down to about half. Of course, it was Voinen and the other healers' job to heal them if they could, but in terms of their role, they really had to prioritize the Warrior who was taking all the monsters' attacks directly.

In order to fill the hole Voinen had left when he ran after Demiquas to provide support, Tetora had used a big skill that took a long time to chant.

"Yessss! Aren't I smart and cute and just totally perfect?!"

"Yeah, yeah. Your attitude blows, but thanks for the heal! Hiyah!"

"Concentrate your attacks! Avoid making close-range attacks!"

Shiroe sent a support spell at Tetora. At the same time, Federico, who'd been freshly healed, returned to the front line.

Despite the fact that the voices behind him still sounded like they were enjoying themselves, Voinen was desperately casting recovery spells one after another.

Apparently, these Orc Jellies were pretty bad opponents for the Weapon Attackers and Warriors. Each time they were hit at close range, spray flew, inflicting damage that was almost like a counter-strike. The abnormal statuses and ranged attacks that resulted from their powerful Acid Smoke were threats as well. Just one of them would have been bad enough, but when four or five of them attacked at once, as they were doing now, it was really hard to cope.

"Demiquas, get back!"

"Over mooks like these?!"

As he shouted, Demiquas retreated with Phantom Step. Pungent white smoke was rising thickly from both his arms. The damage to his weapons had to be enormous as well.

"Dammit, hurry up and heal me!"

"You don't have to holler. I can hear you just fine."

Voinen began to chant Heal. Demiquas didn't have much HP left; if he made another charge like this, he'd be unable to fight in no time flat. He'd probably retreated because he understood that, but Voinen didn't appreciate his cursing and irritated attitude.

Demiquas probably hadn't liked his response. Demiquas glared with ferocious eyes and spat, "If you're hearing me, then get the lead out!"

Voinen sighed. *Good grief.*

True, Demiquas was a pain in the neck.

As a member of the same party, he wished someone would do something about him.

If Voinen charged around all on his own the way Demiquas did, the healing work would utterly break down. And yet, since he rushed ahead without a thought for the ranges of Voinen's spells, their formation got dragged around, and it set them up for tough spots like these.

Understandably, the guy had died a lot. Because there were always Recovery classes in the area during raids with lots of people, when someone died in combat, it was possible to resurrect them right away. To Voinen and other raid-guild Adventurers, it was something insignificant, like passing out, but even so, while you were dead, you couldn't do anything. From the perspective of fighting power, dying meant nothing less than lowering the performance of the entire raid unit.

Lately, as you'd expect, he'd learned, and he'd retreat like this before he died, but in terms of efficiency, Voinen couldn't approve of this, either. While he was waiting for recovery, the First party was supporting the vanguard. That First party increased their output to make up for the hole left by Demiquas's retreat.

In other words, the man's selfish charges were being shored up by the goodwill and support of those around him. If that broke off, these grandstand plays could easily pull down the entire unit and destroy it.

Still... Voinen thought as he ran alongside Demiquas. Voinen had layered on Healing Wind and Heartbeat Healing, and Demiquas was returning to the front line as if he were a beast released from a chain.

Viewed fairly, Demiquas was still extraordinary.

Their exploration had lasted three weeks, and they'd been deep underground the whole time. They'd fought harsh battles one after another, day after day. They'd never actually been annihilated, but the individual participants had probably died more than ten times each.

When ordinary people were put in a situation like this, it was perfectly natural for them to get stressed and take it out on the people around them. It was far stranger for Shiroe and the others from Log Horizon to be able to stay cheerful under these extreme circumstances.

Voinen thought of himself as an elite, particularly when it came to raids.

He followed *the* William. He was aware that he was a veteran of hell.

It wasn't just Voinen. All the members of Silver Sword thought this way. They prided themselves on being the toughest on the server.

However, even Silver Sword—a guild that specialized in raids, a guild that had boasted of being the strongest—had been reduced to about forty people, 20 percent of its pre-Catastrophe core members. There were also some who, although still on the register, had withdrawn from the front lines of raids.

At present, particularly when the Adventurers were challenging a zone whose level matched their own, raids were simply that hard.

As proof, D.D.D., who'd bragged about being the top guild on the server, was playing around with the combat level-50 goblin conquest at Seventh Fall.

Voinen and the others thought this was hilarious. The idea of all those level 90s lining up for a level-50 zone... They should call themselves a large-scale-play guild, not a raid guild.

However, precisely because he had that pride, he couldn't completely write Demiquas off. The big Monk was dumb, and he didn't understand teamwork. Since he never listened, he caused trouble for everyone around him. His attitude couldn't have been worse. He had almost none of the stuff it took to conduct the joint operations known as raids.

...But he wasn't a coward.

In the thick of a level-90 raid, end content that even D.D.D. had backed away from, in the midst of raging death and violence, this insolent Monk never stopped moving. He didn't hesitate to make contact with monsters. His eyes never flinched away.

Voinen knew this had roots in Demiquas's envy of Shiroe and Silver Sword. Even so, this wasn't the sort of terror that could be overcome with that alone. How could you possibly confront clumps of slime that were several times taller than you were, and magical beasts who devoured your own limbs before your very eyes, on the strength of your pride alone?

With no help for it, Voinen cast protective spells on himself and Demiquas.

The situation was bad.

Their exploration was making no progress. This was probably the toughest battleground on the server, one that was gradually wearing away even Silver Sword's stoicism. However, he couldn't leave this rowdy man to die. For now, he just ran, in order to fulfill the heart's desire of every healer: to prevent damage.

▶ **6**

William, who had the trust of the Silver Sword members, was suffering.

They'd finished fighting for the day. In a camp that was too full-scale to call temporary, he tossed away a sheaf of papers detailing the results of their exploration to date, kicked back so far in his sailcloth chair that he nearly fell over, and stretched.

"This ain't good."

"No, it isn't."

Shiroe of Log Horizon was there with him. This bespectacled young man drew maps so beautiful that William's couldn't begin to compare. William sat with his legs carelessly apart in a wide-open stance, rocking his chair, and sighed. Even he could tell Shiro's eyebrows were drawn together.

"About how many more do you think we've got?"

"Let's see..."

Shiroe ran a fingertip across a particularly large, illustrated map.

"Three. No, four."

This was the number of estimated boss enemies for the zone.

There were many different types of raids, and this zone was a typical "explorable" raid dungeon—one that had a set map that wasn't randomly redrawn every time you entered it. The content in raid dungeons resembled the content of ordinary dungeons, only expanded and reinforced, made over to suit the larger groups associated with raids.

The dungeon zone was larger than the ones designed for small parties; it had many passages and small rooms, and sometimes there were traps and riddles. There were impressive great halls and caverns at strategic points in that dungeon, and, to protect those strategic points, powerful raid bosses.

All raid enemies were targets meant to be subjugated by a raid unit. In terms of this zone, since it had been designed to be attempted with twenty-four people, if they'd tried to challenge it with the manpower of a six-person party, they would simply have gotten kicked to pieces. It was bad enough that, even if they went in as a full raid, there was the possibility that they'd be defeated if they got careless. However, with normal raid monsters, Silver Sword was able to steadily continue their exploration. Even up to this point, they'd kept gradually filling in the zone map.

The problem was the raid bosses. Defeating them would require different tactics from the ones used for normal monsters.

In this zone, they'd managed to subjugate Vandemie of the First Garden and Elreida of the Fifth Garden. In addition to being powerful, both had had special abilities, and they'd been compelled to fight complicated battles.

"That's rough."

"Yes, and the battles with the previous two were pretty acrobatic."

Raid boss battles always were.

If all they did was get powerful players together and challenge them, it was hard to even fight a decent battle, let alone win.

They hadn't been quite annihilated in either fight, but that only meant there had been no single moment when everyone was dead. They'd retreated more than twenty times, in the sense that of the twenty-four members, several survivors had taken to their heels and resurrected the others in a safe area. Including the resurrections during combat, the members had been rendered unable to fight a considerable number of times.

Of course, they'd been rewarded in a few ways. They'd obtained lots of high-ranking materials of the sort that could only be acquired on raids, such as Primordial Mud, Variable Hide and Star-Iron Sheet Metal, from the Orc Jellies, Mutant Griffs, Venom Hydrangeas and Minotaur Marauders that appeared along the way. These were drop items that could be used as material by Adventurers with artisan-type abilities when they made items. As material, they resulted in extremely high-performance items, and they were so valuable there was no telling what sort of prices they'd bring.

In addition, they'd gotten a total of seven powerful fantasy-class equip items from Vandemie of the First Garden and Elreida of the Fifth Garden.

This sort of equipment had always served as huge motivation for the major raid guilds that competed to be first on the server. In particular, the items they'd acquired this time were all types they'd never seen before. In terms of performance, they were natural extensions of past fantasy-class items, but to Silver Sword, it was more than enough of a military achievement to broadcast.

Shiroe poured steaming coffee from a rough, twenty-centimeter kettle.

As he gazed at it, William calculated the remaining days.

"Ten days…probably isn't gonna happen."

"…"

What was worrying William was the issue of supplies.

Each time they fought, the Adventurers' equipment wore down a little. When they died, it took more damage than usual, and it couldn't be restored with a resurrection spell. It took constant repairs to keep equipment in proper shape.

Naturally, this was common sense in *Elder Tales*, and William had included it in his calculations. On explorable raids like this one, it was an issue that people had been worrying about since the *Elder Tales* era. Their raid unit included Blacksmiths, Armorsmiths, Tailors, Woodworkers, and more. All major guilds knew that you were supposed to conduct repairs in the spaces between battles.

However, in order to do that, you needed materials that could be used to make those repairs. Under the circumstances, without fully equipped workshops, they went through the components used in repairs at a furious rate. On top of that, the materials used to repair the equipment owned by members of a top-class combat guild like Silver Sword—in other words, fantasy-class items—were fantasy-class themselves.

It wasn't just repairing damaged equipment. The same went for the Crystal Comets William used. These arrows paid out explosive damage, and they were fine articles made by top artisans using fantasy-class materials. Since they were consumables, it was possible to make approximately five hundred of them from the material item, Divine Rainbow Crystal. However, when it came to a series of battles like this one, even five hundred was a trivial amount. Of the nearly ten thousand Crystal Comets he'd prepared, he'd already used more than two thousand. This could be said for all consumable items, including potions, balms, charms, and scrolls.

In short, raids formed their own unique cycle.

In order to maintain the equipment acquired in raids, you needed materials acquired in raids, and through them, you gained the right to challenge more difficult raids. If you succeeded at a more difficult challenge, you got equipment whose performance was even higher. However, in order to maintain it, you had to keep attempting very difficult battles.

In order to balance this cycle, stable, historic raid guilds would regularly conduct raids in which they could procure good materials, even if the difficulty level wasn't all that high, to replenish their supplies. However, after the Catastrophe, with the Fairy Rings not functioning correctly, it was hard to make the circuit of the raid zones that were scattered across the world. Even if that had been possible, Silver Sword was an active combat guild. The decision to compromise and go to a tepid zone for the sake of replenishing supplies was repellent to them.

William had spent the time since the Catastrophe in a whirlwind of activity.

He didn't regret it, but even so, it had led to his disgorging the vast amount of material items and supplies that he'd stored up earlier. As long as they had full-raid-class numbers, William prided himself that they were the strongest combat group on the server. However, the state of their coffers was terrible.

"I have some material I pulled together in Akiba as well."

"About how long do you think it'll last?"

"Even if we add that, twenty days."

Shiroe's response was also hard to take. From what he'd heard, Log Horizon was a weak guild with just eight members. The fact that a place that tiny had enough to supply Silver Sword's unit of top elites for twenty days was astonishing all by itself, but even so, it wasn't enough to get them through the situation. It had taken them three weeks and a lot of trouble to defeat two bosses. It would be hard to do twice that much and defeat four bosses in twenty days. From past experience, bosses got stronger the farther they went.

There was one other thing William was worried about.

The cause lay in the young man in front of him.

Shiroe, who was looking down silently as if to hide his expression, was keeping a lot of secrets.

To begin with, this zone was unnatural.

Vandemie of the First Garden.

Elreida of the Fifth Garden.

William hadn't seen the other bosses, but he could guess their names. They were probably Mezalaclau of the Second Garden, Ibra Habra of the Third Garden, and Tartaulga of the Fourth Garden.

The bosses who guarded this zone had the same names and forms as the nightmare superintendents of the Nine Great Gaols of Halos. Of course, they weren't exactly the same. In the Gaols of Halos—raid content that had been provided with the Sacred Heart expansion pack—they had been called Vandemie of the First Prison and Elreida of the Fifth Prison. They were raid bosses in the shape of a winged serpent and a forgotten white horse. These had reappeared, with their names and shapes slightly changed. Naturally, they were powerful, and their past capture methods had been consigned to oblivion.

In games, reusing character data wasn't unusual. This zone was just one of many examples. There must be some kind of background there…assuming this world was a game.

He didn't know whether Shiroe was hiding something, or whether he was unable to say it.

In any case, he was in no position to criticize other people.

That was William's honest feeling on the matter.

He didn't think they were wrong. Not about having left Akiba, and not about having gone on all those raids in the North. He didn't think they were wrong, but Silver Sword *had* put too much distance between itself and a variety of voices. People couldn't move forward by correctness alone. William hadn't wanted to know that. He'd wanted to think that simply screaming "We're the strongest" would be enough. He'd thought that if his friends got cold feet, all he'd have to do to rid them of their unease was raise his voice.

However, he'd realized that in some cases, it wasn't enough.

In the end, maybe William *had* been wrong, and he just didn't want to admit it.

…Wrong to turn down Shiroe's invitation and reject the Round Table Council outright that day.

William wanted to talk about this with Shiroe.

However, right now Shiroe seemed to be harboring some big secret—although William had no idea what it might be—and looked like he was suffering. William wasn't mature enough to go down on his knees and ask for the answer to his own doubt when Shiroe was like this, and he had no desire to become that sort of adult.

He felt like making fun of himself for his childish pride. He also felt like turning defiant about it: *What's wrong with that? It's fine the way it is!*

The conditions of their stores were gradually growing worse, and they were fighting a raid deep underground, where there was nowhere to run. What could he say to his companions from Silver Sword, who were following him through these deteriorating circumstances? He was a game junkie, and the only thing in his entire life that he'd ever put serious effort into was *Elder Tales*. What could he possibly offer them?

William thought he was nothing. All he had was empty bravado.

A child, swinging around that bravado—his one and only weapon—and putting on a bold front. That was him. However, if he had just one weapon, it was only natural for him to use it. As a gamer, William understood that.

"What do you think, Shiroe?"

"About what?"

At that question, William scratched his head roughly.

He couldn't answer a question like that.

In other words, William needed a chance, too: Either to challenge, or to surrender.

To prove who he was, and who he wanted to be. Was there any difference between Demiquas, who lost his way and picked fights with everything he saw, and Silver Sword?

And that chance was right in front of him, in the midst of the battle. William had decided this himself.

For that reason, even if it hurt, the only thing to do was keep going.

CHAPTER.

3

THE CHANGING BATTLEFIELD

► LEVEL: **93**

► RACE: **HUMAN**

► CLASS: **CLERIC**

► HP: **11387**

► MP: **9731**

► ITEM 1:

[SEVEN'S SHOOTING STAR]

A SECRET-CLASS ACCESSORY DESIGNED WITH A RAINBOW-COLORED SHOOTING-STAR MOTIF. BEFORE THE CATASTROPHE, IT HAD AN EFFECT THAT MADE THE FUNCTION OF DISPLAYING "!" AND "?" MARKS IN MIDAIR MORE SHOWY AND LUXURIOUS, WITH TETORA MATCHING THE EFFECT TO HER OWN ACTIONS, MAKING THE MOST OF IT.

► ITEM 2:

[RESONANT JEWEL ROD]

A SECRET-CLASS ROD. WHEN EQUIPPED, IT ADDS AN ECHO TO YOUR VOICE, AND IF YOU WAVE IT, MAGIC NOTES FLY AROUND. IT'S PERFECT FOR LIVE EVENTS, BUT IT HAS AN ABILITY THAT INSTEAD OF JUST COPYING THE USER'S VOICE, IT COPIES SPELLS THEMSELVES ON VERY RARE OCCASSIONS, AND ITS COMBAT PERFORMANCE ISNT BAD EITHER.

► ITEM 3:

[TWINKLE STAR VEST]

A SPLENDID FANTASY-CLASS VEST THAT SHINES LIKE THE NIGHT SKY, WITH STAR-SHAPED BUTTONS. ITS GLOSSY MATERIAL REFLECTS THE LIGHT. BECAUSE ITS SPARKLING EFFECT REINFORCES RECOVERY SPELLS IN RESPONSE TO GREATER NUMBERS, TETORA USES IT ALL THE TIME.

<Pepper>
A seasoning.
Has a pungent flavor

"This ain't good," Naotsugu muttered.

He was wiping the grime off Armor of Silver Oath and Guard of Lionheart with a rag he'd taken out of his pack. All the equipment had been rinsed off with a shower from an Undine that a Summoner had brought to life a minute ago. Some monsters' body fluids damaged equipment; after a battle, it was vital to wash it well.

"What 'ain't good,' Naotsugu?"

Tetora was right next to him, stooping low to wash her fancy baton.

They were both members of the Second party, and lately they often acted as a team. Demiquas was temperamental and always on his own, while Voinen and Federico were members of Silver Sword; they often sent messages to and worked with other teams. Shiroe had settled into the position of adviser or counselor for this full raid, and he was always being called out by William.

That meant that, by necessity, Naotsugu often ended up with Tetora.

"Could it be that the bloodstains won't come out no matter how much you wash them? Is it a curse?"

"Y'know, for someone who calls herself an idol, you say some pretty graphic stuff."

"Charismatic individuals like me are very popular just as we are. Because we're cute."

"Is-that-right city."

The day's exploration wasn't over yet. It was past noon, so they'd taken a break and were getting ready to eat. They were cleaning their equipment, in part because it needed cleaning, but at least half because they were bored.

"I wasn't talking about the equipment."

"I see. Was I on your mind, perhaps?"

"That'd be a no."

Naotsugu denied it bluntly.

If he had to say whether he liked her or hated her, Naotsugu thought that Tetora would have to go in the "like" category.

Talking to her was just plain easy, and it never made him tired. He thought she was one of the good guys, especially when they were having stupid conversations like this one. Conversations when they just horsed around and didn't use their brains at all were, in a way, pure refreshment. Naotsugu thought that dumb stuff had great healing properties. It wasn't because of his interests that he tried to get a laugh by saying "panties" all the time.

"You don't look very cheerful. Want to see my panties?"

"Nope."

"I wonder if I should have gone with a miniskirt instead of hot pants."

"You get away from there, you hear?"

"No, if anything, I'm going to tease you tenaciously."

Keh-heh-heh-heh. Tetora cuddled up to Naotsugu with her usual triumphant smile, a smile that made it look as if she were plotting something. Naotsugu promptly tore her away with a "Gah, get off, yech." Despite what he'd just said, having her play with him like this was a problem. Tetora was small, and with her agility and flexibility, she leapt right in close to him before he knew it. He couldn't strike back with force, so he was constantly losing the initiative.

Tetora was aware of Naotsugu's hesitation when she came to tease him. In other words, it was harassment. It was spiteful. The fact that she knew she was cute made it vicious.

"That's generally how it is, you know. Seeing panties would make you happy, wouldn't it?"

"Uh...huh?"

She'd said the words so naturally that Naotsugu wasn't able to find a good retort.

"You'd think, 'Ah man! Today's my lucky day,' and things like that, wouldn't you? When they belong to a girl as cute as I am, I think it would probably put you in the mood to work hard all day, or to high-five the gods."

Tetora's tone wasn't especially teasing. She was speaking genuinely, and surface aside, Naotsugu was forced to agree with her. He thought she'd probably nailed it. Although, of course, he didn't let it show.

"Yeah, but seriously, kid—"

"I understand those feelings better than anyone! I really must be a natural-born idol! Go ahead and let your heart flutter!"

As Naotsugu watched Tetora say this, snorting and looking proud of herself, he thought, *This one's a big shot.* Setting all the other little details aside, this healer with the triumphant face had a really fantastic smile.

That was a big virtue. Naotsugu firmly believed that smiling was one of the best presents a girl could give to the people around her.

But when Tetora messed with him this way, he remembered Marielle.

The smile was what did it.

And it was frequent. However, even when Tetora wasn't there, he recalled Marielle quite a bit.

It definitely wasn't because he wanted that soft, squishy, oppressive feeling that showed up when he did so, but he *did* think that was a problem all on its own.

If this had been the old Earth, things would have been easier. Naotsugu had landed a steady job, and his life had just settled down. He'd even been without a girlfriend for quite a long time, so there wouldn't have been any obstacles. Life as an Adventurer was fun and seemed worthwhile, but it also felt too unstable to think about "that sort of thing." Adventuring was a situation that was constantly out of his control. And yet, Marielle's feelings were important, too.

They say it isn't good to take too much time, either, Naotsugu thought, and scratched his cheek.

"Waaaaaaugh! That's not it!"

"Agh?! Why d'you yell all of a sudden?!"

Tetora, who'd been creeping up on Naotsugu again, was startled, and she banged her small rump on the ruin's cold stone floor. Naotsugu waved his hands to gloss things over: "That's not it, it's not like that. I'm sorry, though." He lent her a hand and helped her up.

As if to hide what he'd been thinking, Naotsugu muttered, "Some lives are just like that, eh?"

"Naotsugu, you look like a grade-school kid who told his gorgeous teacher he liked her on his test, then got busted when his classmates saw it."

"What's with that weirdly specific comment?!"

"Dweh-heh-heh-heh. And? Something got you down?"

Tetora's expression seemed to say, *I'm not letting you get away,* but as far as Naotsugu was concerned, having her pursue that topic was a huge help. As a result, he went along with her misunderstanding.

"Yeah, actually, it's about Shiro." He pulled a particularly sour expression.

Tetora's triumphant face shone even brighter. It probably meant, *That's just like me! I asked a critical question! I'm so smart!* As Tetora puffed out her chest for absolutely no reason, she looked incredibly dumb.

…Well. Naotsugu couldn't just let Tetora soothe him like this.

It was true that something was on his mind, but he wasn't sure how to talk about it.

"Hey. Food."

Federico had approached just then, and he held boxlike dishes out to them. They were filled with generous helpings of brown stew and asparagus. Since Naotsugu had been thinking, he was a bit late in noticing, but Tetora immediately accepted hers with a beaming smile and a "Thank you, Federico!"

As befitted someone who called herself an idol, Tetora was popular. The raid members had accepted her in no time and made a pet of her. She even seemed to have a few actual fans.

As proof, a smile appeared on Federico's bearded face as well, and he said, "Nah, it's fine." From the way he'd handed them their portions and gone away, he seemed as if he might be a lot easier to get along with than his appearance suggested. He was probably going to deliver Demiquas's and Voinen's portions as well. The pair from Silver Sword willingly took on odd jobs like this. *You really can't trust advance reviews*, Naotsugu thought.

"Let's hurry and eat, Naotsugu. Then you're going to tell me what's bothering you."

"Yeah."

Answering vaguely, Naotsugu looked around for a good place to sit.

They were in one of the countless small rooms in the Abyssal Shaft zone. The room was "small" only in comparison to the scale of the dungeon; it was actually about fifteen meters square, a space roughly the size of a smallish gymnasium, cut into a rectangle. There were carvings on the enormous pillars, although they weren't ornate, and it had the atmosphere of some kind of palace or religious building. Its high, barrel-shaped ceiling gave off a faint light.

There had been tons of rooms that looked like this space in the surrounding area. In the hours since they'd begun their exploration that day, they'd made an exhaustive search of those compartments, and had continued to exterminate any monsters that appeared.

The pair sat down, using a granite pillar that had crumbled just the right way as a bench.

"Thanks for the food."

"Thanks for the foooood!"

Astonishingly large chunks of meat peeked out of the stew they'd been given. As he stuffed his face with it, Naotsugu brooded. This was pretty hard to explain. It was a fact that Shiroe was at the heart of the problem, but the bit about things being "bothersome" was just a feeling.

If he extracted the issue simply, it was that Shiroe seemed to be suffering somehow.

However, the guy known as Shiroe was a natural worrier, and he tended to take on a lot of things and be hard-pressed to keep up with his work. Possibly because of that, to people besides Naotsugu, apparently Shiroe always looked slightly troubled and pained.

Naotsugu didn't think that was true, however.

Even if his expression looked pinched, Shiroe was entertained by all sorts of things, and he often cut corners and slacked off. He even sulked and went to sleep at his desk fairly frequently.

Still, to the multitudes that weren't close to him, Shiroe always seemed to be dealing with a tough problem, and his weakness was that even when he really was having trouble, no one understood. Shiroe was always hemming and groaning to himself, but even so, in the end, he generally solved the problem, and so it was hard to register his limits, the things he really couldn't do anything about all by himself. It was even harder to explain this to other people.

After all, even Naotsugu couldn't explain how to tell what sort of stern expression was only a pose, and what sort of expression meant he was actually in trouble. Naotsugu knew…but only vaguely.

Right now, Shiroe was probably suffering a lot more than he appeared to be.

However, even that was only a hazy feeling.

He couldn't explain it.

"See, Shiro's…" Slowly, Naotsugu began to speak. "He sort of looks like he's maybe in trouble."

"'Maybe'?"

"Yeah."

"Then let's go save him. Okay?"

Tetora, who'd skewered a piece of asparagus with her fork, made a snap decision.

Don't say it like it's easy 'cos it ain't, Naotsugu huffed.

"People call that four-eyes 'Machiavelli' and other stuff, but he's not crafty so much as he's a show-off. He's thinking, 'Is it all right for me to call for help? Is it okay for me to do a job like this?' Stuff like that."

"I see. At heart, he's a hermit."

"Yeah, he's a hermit. There's no denying that."

"He needs an idol!"

"I'm pretty sure he's okay there."

"Then why did he come all the way out to this hole in the ground in the middle of nowhere?"

Naotsugu almost answered, *Because he needs money, duh,* but then he realized that that wouldn't be an answer at all. Shiroe wasn't the type who found happiness in accumulating money so he could stare at it. Money was a tool to use for some other purpose. It had been that way during the Crescent Moon incident, too. That prompted the question, *In that case, what's he going to use it on this time?* but come to think of it, Naotsugu didn't know the answer to that.

During the Round Table Council affair, it had been used to buy up the zone that housed the bank. However, obtaining the bank hadn't been Shiroe's objective, either. He'd only needed a weapon, in order to get the Adventurers of Akiba to the negotiating table.

What would he use the money for when he got it? What did he intend to do by using it that way? Now that he thought about it, Naotsugu hadn't heard about any of that from Shiroe. Shiroe was a close friend, and he could trust him even without knowing. However, when he had to explain it to a third party—Tetora—it was a problem.

Reason, reason…hm…

Naotsugu racked his brains, and then the words came to him, like a divine revelation.

"I'm just guessing, but I think it's to protect his house."

"His house?"

"I'm not talking about an actual, physical building. I mean the place he lives."

"In other words, his guild?"

"I don't think it's just the guild. I don't really know, but…"

Chewing on a piece of bread he'd soaked in his stew, Naotsugu kept talking, saying things as they came to him.

"If we're going to live, we need food and a roof over our heads, stuff like that. Then we need people. No matter what, we need a place where we can be with the people we're close to. In the old world, that was probably family, and in this world, it's the people in our groups and our guilds."

Over the past six months, Naotsugu had watched Marielle and the Crescent Moon League.

A place where everyone could feel at ease. A place where they woke up, did their jobs, had dinner, made a racket together, and told each other *We made it through another day. Good night!*

The importance of it, and its warmth, and the kind smiles that supported it.

"But see, even things like that need a place to belong."

"Huh?"

Tetora didn't get it, and Naotsugu kept talking, as if he was trying to persuade her. He was pulling things even he didn't know from some place deep inside himself.

"It's like a house for our houses. In other words, it's Akiba. You can't just have your own guild, all by itself, in an empty world. Because, see, it's linked to all sorts of other stuff. Even guilds need a place to belong. Duties, and companion guilds… It's connected to other places like those, and I don't really know how to put it, but we've got to take care of things like that."

That was probably the case.

It was also likely the reason that Shiroe had spoken so desperately during the establishment of the Round Table Council.

"Towns are like huge houses. If the town isn't happy, none of the guilds in it can be happy. All the people that live in those houses will be unhappy, too. Shiroe's the type who'd go head-to-head with the town or something even bigger to protect his own small house."

"A home, huh…"

When Naotsugu looked at Tetora, worried about whether his explanation had gotten through to her, he saw an expression he hadn't expected. It was her usual smile: triumphant, self-important, kind, and strong.

"Protecting the place where you belong is important. For wolves like us, it's the most important thing there is. If you're expecting that much from Shiroe, he's an amazing person. —Even greater than I'd heard. I don't know what we should do about our guild, either."

"Light Indigo isn't doing so great? I haven't heard much about that guild; did you lose lots of people after the Catastrophe or something?"

"No, it's not like that. And anyway, in terms of your explanation, Light Indigo isn't a guild or a house. It's more like a waiting room, or a workplace."

"What's that supposed to mean? Is it an idol training school or something?" Naotsugu asked, confused.

However, Tetora said, "Thanks for the food!" and clapped her hands together over the square dish, then grinned and poked Naotsugu's cheek.

"It's pretty much an idol training school. We're all idols who protect the places everyone's hearts call home. I knew coming with you was the right decision! No wonder my charisma sensor went off. Even without the Light Indigo business, I'll stick with you until the very end of this raid, absolutely!"

Naotsugu didn't really understand Tetora's proud smile, so all he could say was, "Yeah, please do."

▶ **2**

"Dwehchoo!"

"My, my. That wasn't a very ladylike sneeze, was it."

"My nose itched like crazy."

At a table in a warm dining room, Henrietta chided Marielle.

Marielle looked around, wondering if cold air had blown in from somewhere, but the Crescent Moon League's dining room was the very picture of peace.

They'd requested a dining room where everyone in the guild could eat together, and the room was spacious and high ceilinged. The Crescent Moon League was a genuine midsized guild now, with more than forty members, and it was hard to fit numbers like that inside. Even so, they'd managed to get two tables that seated sixteen people each, and if they brought all their chairs in, everyone fit.

At mealtimes, this room was filled with noise and bustle, but now, early in the evening, it held only Marielle, the guild master, and Henrietta, her right-hand woman. The atmosphere was tranquil.

Ever since the Catastrophe, life in Akiba had been eventful.

There had been many painful things, and many things that had made them so happy they'd wanted to dance. Through all sorts of events, around the time of the Libra Festival, it had seemed as though the town had slowly remembered what it was supposed to be. It wasn't like the dazzling smiles that had been seen right after the establishment of the Round Table Council. However, the people who walked around town had begun to look as though they were savoring the happiness and abundance of being able to relax and live stable lives every day.

Winter here was colder than it had been in their old world, but in the town of Akiba, time was passing peacefully, predominantly.

It was the same for Marielle.

Over these six months, she'd been trying hard to act like a guild master, but lately she'd been able to take it easy. It had begun when Henrietta said, "If you frown like that all the time, you'll turn into a prickly middle-aged woman, you know." Marielle couldn't forget how, in the instant she'd been lectured, her guild family had looked away from her and giggled a little. She hadn't felt it herself, but she must have been too tense.

She'd have to give it some thought and do better. Marielle gave a soft sigh.

Henrietta, the person who'd delivered the lecture, also seemed to have relaxed a bit recently.

Asuka was helping her manage the accounts, apparently. Since she was involved with duties for the Round Table Council as well, she was gone quite frequently, but she did have enough time to slow down and spend the evenings like this.

The two old friends took sips of cocoa out of thick mugs, which they held closely, to warm their palms.

"……? ……?"

"Oh, Nanami? What is it?"

Henrietta spoke to the little girl who'd looked in through the door, then come trotting over. The girl made a slight detour around Henrietta, then hesitantly peeked up over the edge of the table, looking around.

The girl had joined the guild just recently, and she was still terribly shy.

Henrietta—one of the causes of that shyness—had lowered her eyes and was pretending to coolly drink her cocoa, but Marielle noticed that the corners of her lips were twitching.

The day Nanami had come to the guild, Henrietta had launched into a wild, joyous dance, tumbled the little girl around with the force of a large coin-laundry dryer, and dressed her up in so many outfits that counting had gotten tiresome after thirty. Nanami had finally burst into tears, the Assassin Hien had objected fiercely, and since then, Marielle's friend had refrained from doting on her too much.

However, even if Henrietta had repented, the experience had probably been rather horrific for Nanami, a Person of the Earth. At times like this, she tended to keep her distance.

"Wanna sit on my lap?"

Marielle put an arm around Nanami's waist and scooped her up onto her knees.

Now Nanami, who was still very young, was able to see over the entire table.

Since it had been built to seat sixteen, the table was both wide and long. Spread across it was Marielle's carving knife, the woodworking tools she'd been using, and some fine-grained maple scrap wood; a rough income and expenditures estimate, which Henrietta had been calculating at her leisure; cocoa for two; and cloth sacks. For safety's sake, Henrietta returned the carving knife to its bag. Marielle was grateful to Henrietta, who always covered for her smoothly, even when she was silent.

Nanami's eyes were wide with curiosity, and she was fidgeting. Marielle put an arm around her, pulling her rump closer, and felt herself smile involuntarily. She couldn't have said exactly what it was, or how, but all sorts of things had seemed very precious to her just then.

Illuminated by soft magic light, the dining room was warm and calm. Part of the kitchen was visible through a large aperture, and inside, two Chefs were busily making preparations for dinner. When they listened carefully, they could hear voices conversing, moving down the corridor, greetings from companions who'd returned from outdoors, and the cheerful responses that came back.

Nanami smelled like fresh laundry. Marielle probably did, too. To Mari, this seemed a bit like a family bond.

"Would you like some cocoa? Or were you looking for Hien?"

Henrietta held a mug out to Nanami, tilting her head. Nanami flinched, looked up at her face, looked at the cocoa, then looked at Henrietta again. The little girl turned back, as if asking what she should do. Marielle smiled at her: "Go on, take it."

Nanami set her hands on the mug, carefully so as not to spill any, and took it. It was big for her, and it was all she could do to use both hands and drink cautiously.

"!"

Apparently the sweetness had been a shock.

Nanami froze, looking startled.

To the Adventurers, this girl was as naïve as could be; everything she saw fascinated her, and she seemed to want to learn so badly she could hardly stand it. This entertained the guild members, and they made a pet of her and had her try all sorts of things. However, Nanami herself seemed to like Hien—the first person she'd met—the best. When he wasn't there, she turned timid and fidgety, and her eyes were always searching for her reliable "big brother."

Nanami sniffed at the cocoa, seeing what it smelled like. Then, seeming to have decided she liked it, she held the cup as if it were a treasure and kept drinking.

I hope she relaxes like this, slowly, little by little, Marielle thought, taking care not to let Nanami slip off her lap.

Nanami, who'd been drinking eagerly, abruptly went still.

When she peeked in, sensing trouble, only a mouthful of the cocoa remained.

Nanami was probably thinking, *I drank it all by myself! What should I do? It was Henrietta's!!* or something of the sort; she went awkward and began acting suspiciously, and Marielle smiled at her.

"You don't have to worry. Umeko won't get mad about somethin' like that."

"I will get angry about being called Umeko, however."

At that bone-chilling comment, Marielle made an exaggerated show of fear. Nanami was adorable as she looked back and forth, timidly comparing their expressions, and the two of them burst out laughing. That exchange made Marielle certain that Henrietta felt the same warmth she did, and the idea made her far too happy.

We're a good guild, aren't we?

She was proud of that.

"Man, is it *cold* out there!"

Although what it had said hadn't been anything like a homecoming greeting, at the sound of the cheerful voice, Nanami straightened like a clockwork doll and looked around.

"That sounds like Hien. I imagine he's in the entrance hall."

Failing to register Henrietta's casual attempt at earning points, Nanami nodded with a grateful expression, then hopped down from Marielle's lap. She hugged Marielle, who was smiling at her, then went off in the direction of the entrance hall on slightly unsteady feet.

"Honestly!"

"What's the matter?"

"That Hien is so popular. I'm a bit jealous."

"You say that, but it's all 'cos you spooked her with that horror show of yours, Umeko."

"Ma-riiii…"

The two of them giggled together.

Being able to tease her old friend like this made Marielle unbearably happy.

"—In that case, that sneeze a short while ago must have been Master Naotsugu."

"Dwah?!"

"…However, that world was short-lived."

Her friend, who'd been smiling in harmony with her just a moment ago, now wore a mean smirk and plunged into a cross-examination.

"Was it Master Naotsugu? Was Master Naotsugu talking about you?"

"How on earth would *I* know?!"

This might be a world of magic, but it wasn't so magical that you could instantly sense things like that.

"I see. I'll check with him via telechat, then."

This clever maneuver, which seemed to blaspheme fantasy, left Marielle with her back against the wall.

Going to this friend of hers for advice on romance might just have been a mistake. Marielle thought she'd regretted it more than a hundred times by now. Henrietta really was a capable worker, and she fielded a vast amount of work every day, but she had interests to match, and the ones at the head of the list were dressing up little girls and tormenting Mari. She was a mother-in-law. It was scary.

"Eeeeep! Spare me!"

"Why?"

Don't ask me "why," I can't do *that!* Marielle muttered the words to herself. She had no idea what expression to wear; she averted her eyes, but even so, in a spirit of resistance, she kneaded her fingertips together.

"'Cos..."

"Yes?"

"We only telechat once a day, at twenty-one hundred, after dinner."

"......"

Henrietta accepted the words Marielle had let fall, and there was a silence, as though she was digesting them. Then she responded with a stupefied "Huh?"

"Huh?!"

"I-I'm not sayin' it twice!" Marielle retorted.

Henrietta wore an unusual expression: Her mouth hung open so far it was nearly square.

"I mean, he's on a raid, y'know? He's in the middle of a real tough job! It's life or death, only we don't die! Still, listen, I know Naotsugu's fightin' with everythin' he has, and Shiro's probably thinkin' like crazy, and I can't bother them. So I promised I'd only telechat at night, when they've got their camp set up—"

Henrietta, who was pressing her fingertips to her temples and seemed to be suffering through a headache, sighed.

What a rude friend. Apparently Marielle's consideration wasn't getting through to her.

"That wasn't what I was asking about. Or rather, I suppose it may have been... So you telechat every day?"

"Right."

Marielle didn't really understand, but she nodded.

"I tell him about what Akiba's like, and what Akatsuki's been up to. Come to think of it, I told him about Nanami yesterday. Remember I made her a new smock? I talked about that. And about how we went to buy rubber boots together, and how Hien and li'l Nanami danced in the entrance hall. I told him about that new tandoori chicken, too. We both kept sayin' how we wanted to eat it together. Naotsugu's a big guy, so I bet he could eat three of 'em, y'know? Maybe even four, since they're spicy! Then we talked about how lassi was good, too, and how we really did want to go out to eat together, and we just went on for so long... Say, Henrietta, you thought the tandoori was yummy, too, right?"

"Um."

Henrietta stood. She looked as though she might have heartburn.

"What's wrong?"

"I'm going to run a delivery over to the Production Guild Liaison Committee before dinner."

"Oh."

"If this goes on, I'll be so full I won't have room for dinner. Honestly, Mari, you're so... What's the word...?"

Henrietta's shoulders slumped, and she left the dining room with an armful of files. Marielle waved, watching her friend go. Lately, this had been routine at the Crescent Moon League.

Even though Marielle wasn't aware of it, a white victory star had appeared on the Sumo Wrestling score chart in Henrietta's mind.

The outcome of this battle for the star had been a contest just as fierce as the raid.

▶ 3

Just as the scout team had reported, a dull, dark purple suit of armor knelt, perfectly still, in the center of an enormous, bowl-shaped coliseum. When they'd measured from a distance of more than a hundred meters using a Gunner's Lock-On Sight, its height seemed to be about sixteen meters. It was probably a golem or a type of giant.

Raid bosses' detection ranges were wide, but they were also unique. In this case, it was likely that the battle would begin when William and the others entered the coliseum.

The enemy was Ruseato of the Seventh Garden.

To William, this enemy had the same form as Ruseato of the Seventh Prison, whom he'd fought many times in the Nine Great Gaols of Halos. Its characteristics would probably be the same, even if its abilities and tactics were stronger. According to the scout team's reconnaissance force, Ruseato of the Seventh Garden seemed to have White

Knight and Black Knight modes as well. He remembered it being a difficult boss who switched between the two sets of abilities as it attacked.

William raised his hand to the level of his shoulder.

That alone was enough to focus the raid members' eyes on him.

They'd had a briefing session beforehand. The scout party had charged and died many times over, and even as they did so, they'd brought back valuable information. Even Shiroe of Log Horizon had admitted that, with the tactics they'd built through combining this information, they had a 50 percent chance of victory. For a first battle, that wasn't a bad figure at all.

He felt heat swelling at his back.

Grabbing that chance, William brought his arm straight down.

Obeying the order, the unit flooded into the room like a river that had burst forth. With the First party in the lead, they plunged down through the grayish-white spectator seats.

They slid down the ruined, crumbled walls, surging forward, forward.

In general terms, the range of a monster's attacks was proportionate to its size.

Goblins were only about 140 centimeters tall; bare-handed, their attack range was just a couple dozen centimeters, and even if kicks and spears were included in the calculations, it was no more than a meter or so. However, if it was a troll two meters tall, you needed to figure that the range of the club it swung around was about three meters. From the size of the enormous raid boss in front of them, they had to assume that its attack range was fairly large.

At Shiroe's suggestion, the Silver Sword group had spent the past few days training to gauge ten-, fifteen-, and twenty-meter standard points implicitly. Thanks to that, they wouldn't misjudge distances with this giant enemy.

However, even that wouldn't come until after they'd launched the first attack. First they had to get into the enemy's attack range; then the vanguard would reach the front line, and the fragile spellcasters and long-range attackers would have to be posted in a safe area beyond the outer edge. They'd need to change their attack positions constantly, but their strategy used the difference between the enemy's range and their own. Unless they made expert use of tactics that involved taking up positions in a blind spot, the rear guard wouldn't be able to last through the raid boss's attack. Each attack was simply that powerful.

Running at the head of the muddy torrent, Dinclon charged into the twenty-meter range as if he meant to split it open. As though life had suddenly been breathed into it, Ruseato of the Seventh Garden stood. Its visor looked like mechanical armor, and the crimson light that seeped through its gaps ran down like water as the monster raised its enormous halberd. He saw Dinclon, shield at the ready, grit his teeth and prepare for the impact. His efforts paid off, and the Silver Sword Guardian, reinforced by heavy armor, blocked the raid boss's first attack.

The damage was slight, about 10 percent of his total HP.

Still, that didn't mean the enemy's attack power was low. Purification Barrier, which had been cast on Dinclon before the battle began, was a damage interception spell. Cast by a high-level Kannagi, the spell had negated about 4,500 points of damage that should have been taken by the target. In other words, even after that had been negated, he'd taken damage. If the barrier spell hadn't been there, he would have lost more than 30 percent of his HP to that single attack.

It was fearsome offensive power.

However, even that had been factored in. The damage obstruction, which had been canceled, was recast immediately.

Dinclon, the Guardian at the head of the First party, was the leading edge of the unit. In terms of arrows, he was the hardest possible arrowhead. The steel Warrior, who'd had a series of recovery spells cast on him, reached the feet of Ruseato of the Seventh Garden and used the special aggro skills Anchor Howl and Taunting Shout in rapid succession.

This marked the beginning of the battle.

"Begin the assault!"

From the Third party, William sent the message to the entire group.

With support songs from Bards, varicolored magic and projectile attacks rained down on the raid boss. In a raid like this one, it was hard to tell, but a terrific number of weakening effects were layered over Ruseato now. This was another reason for incorporating all twelve classes into the full raid. Save for a few exceptions, the same weakening effect couldn't be layered over itself, but a many-sided net cast by a variety of classes displayed its effect on powerful enemies.

The fusillade of attacks clouded their field of vision for a moment, and heavy explosions seemed to rock the earth.

Ruseato had swung its great steel weapon as if to gouge out ten meters around itself. The attack had killed two members and left several who had been engaged in close combat near death.

The attack was so brutal that even Dinclon lost half his HP.

However, the Silver Sword battle lines didn't collapse.

The unique Kannagi resurrection spell, Soul-Calling Prayer, teleported the dead to the feet of the caster and revived them. In addition to this convenient spell, which simultaneously evacuated the members to a safe distance and resurrected them, a Summoner who'd summoned a Carbuncle chanted Phantasmal Heal. This HP recovery spell, an oddity among the Magic Attack classes, didn't measure up to a recovery spell from the usual classes, but it did more than enough to lighten their burden.

Recovery classes besides the Kannagi prioritized recovering wounded members. While this was going on, Dinclon didn't retreat a single step under Ruseato's attacks.

The powerful attack that had mowed down the surrounding area a few moments ago had probably been one of the raid boss's certain-kill attacks.

That attack had been branded on the eyes of the Silver Sword members. A shabby Summoner who stood next to William, holding an adorable, fluffy Carbuncle by the scruff of its neck, began to count in a steely, determined voice. As that voice rang out, everyone listened to it.

Without exception, raid bosses' enormous attacks had conditions.

One major condition was—to use the vocabulary of the Adventurer-players—Recast Time. Powerful attacks couldn't be unleashed back-to-back. Each skill had its own cool-down period. There was no telling whether that time would be ten seconds or thirty, but the cool-down time itself had to exist.

As they'd discussed beforehand, the Summoner was counting in order to measure it. Of course he kept up his magic attacks, and he didn't neglect his response to the combat situation.

In the days when *Elder Tales* had been a game, they could just leave this sort of count to an external program, or—if handled in a low-tech way—to a stopwatch hung beside the monitor. Raid bosses' every action had been analyzed by the millisecond from reference videos of recorded play, had been compared against the logs, and everything about it—attack damage, attribute, range, interval, motion, penetration rate, critical rate—had been laid bare.

Raiders had shared that information through cloud services, discussed it in chat rooms, and gone on the attack with the latest, most efficient techniques.

"Eighteen, nineteen, twenty, twenty-one…"

A hoarse yet firm tenor voice overlapped with the sound of swords, the ring of clashing steel, and the noise of the thunder and flame attacks that raced through the air.

The members each focused their five senses, desperately buckling down in an attempt not to miss anything that voice said, and not to lose sight of the enemy before them.

In this world, where everything had been swallowed up by chaos, Silver Sword had continued to fight, and had rebuilt tactics as primitive and awkward as this one.

It might have been possible to call it the ruined state of a once-powerful guild.

That count was crude and undignified, yet it held a prayer that greedily hungered for victory.

When the count, delivered in an unamplified voice, reached twenty-six, Ruseato of the Seventh Garden raised its great steel halberd. The fearsome attack of a few moments before was on its way.

However, William's companions showed no fear.

The Assassins and Swashbucklers leapt through space.

The Bards and Druids sprang back, putting distance between them.

The Clerics cast defense-boosting status buffs in rapid succession on the warriors who'd chosen to tough it out.

Handling the second attack like this was splendid.

After the roaring blast had passed through, the attack had not caused any deaths.

Some players had lost most of their HP, true, but the recovery unit's spells were already healing the damage.

They'd skillfully dodged one of the enemy's attacks.

The corners of William's lips rose ferociously.

That wasn't all: The raid boss, whose very armor looked like a blade, had to be hiding all sorts of twisted attack methods. After all, it hadn't even changed its shape yet.

Still, this wasn't bad. Even as he thought that things were going fairly well so far, William fired arrows.

Before he was aware of it, his throat had sent up a savage yell: "More damage! Get the lead out, speed up and chip away at him!"

He fired an astonishing number of arrows.

As if prepared to dash themselves to pieces, the offensive ranks struck with their swords or unleashed flame, pulling Ruseato into ranged spells colored with light and darkness.

William knew. Without exception, boss monsters that appeared in raid zones had vast HP. The amount was overwhelming. Dinclon, a level-94 Guardian in an ultra-top-class raid guild like Silver Sword, had a bit under eighteen thousand HP, and raid boss monsters had HP that ranged from one thousand to ten thousand times that much.

Say Ruseato of the Seventh Garden's HP had been shown on a meter. If it had been, they could have seen this, but although the offensive ranks were dealing out attacks without a pause, the reduction was truly miniscule. It was such a gradual fall that, on a meter, it probably wouldn't have been visible to the naked eye. Still, keeping it up was the only way to defeat a boss.

"Careful, watch its feet!"

A sharp voice spoke. It belonged to Federico the Swashbuckler.

Abruptly, Ruseato of the Seventh Garden began to move sluggishly, and a black substance that wasn't quite a mist or a liquid flooded from under its feet. The substance moved, undulating, spreading rapidly, immersing the floor of the arena.

"Damage detected, attribute: Poison! Action—No, it's a move obstruction! Attack speed and force both down!"

Dinclon's report reached his ears. When he looked, something like a black, viscous liquid was wrapping around Dinclon's plate boots and tugging at them, emitting faint lightning.

For a moment, William hesitated.

There was damage, but it was very slight.

The flickering lightning was an attack that had been repelled by damage interception. The fact that lights as small as that were appearing one after another, and that the barriers hadn't been breached, was proof that the damage was trivial. He could tell that it wasn't inflicting serious damage even on the close-range attack members, whose defense was lower than Dinclon's.

A special attack that only inflicted slight damage, and which hindered movement—the instant William sensed danger, Ruseato of the Seventh Garden began to walk, its footsteps heavy.

Dinclon used multiple Anchor Howls, trying to stop it from moving, but they were negated. With a bursting effect unlike the usual one, they rolled off the surface of Ruseato's armor.

A low-damage range binding attack.

Realizing the intent behind it, William screamed:

"Range interception! Range recovery!"

As if his yell had thrown a switch, the unit moved.

A barrier that looked like a translucent dome; faintly shining defense spells; the thin orange layer that indicated Reactive Heal… And yet a single attack blew them all away. Ruseato's metal body, which had begun to lay waste, was more a weapon than a monster. An enormous construction machine was bounding around with the agility of a cat. It brandished its halberd as if licking the ground with it, attempting to cut down Silver Sword like it was no more than reeds, or sheaves of straw.

Still. Even so.

More than half their members were left.

And, even as it quailed from the pain, a voice that refused to retreat was continuing to count.

"First healer, maintain the front line! Second party, fall back, resurrect and restore, Third and Fourth reduce the damage seventy percent; prioritize restoration!"

Deep in his throat, as if he couldn't quite hold it back, William laughed.

When he licked upward, the stuff that had dripped down the side of his nose tasted like blood.

It was like concentrated iron. It was the taste of the raid William wanted.

The enemy was strong, just as they'd anticipated, beyond what they'd predicted.

And William's group was still standing.

The fight had only just begun.

▶**4**

Demiquas, who'd retreated ten meters in one move with Phantom Step, squeezed a blazing hot sigh from his lungs as he recovered his own HP with Resilience.

The battle had fallen into an infuriating deadlock.

Gritting his molars as if meaning to shatter them, he focused intently on the enemy.

They had to inflict damage on Ruseato of the Seventh Garden as they parried its brutality, all while its armor was deep purple. That was just as their advance intel had said, and it had gone fairly well. Demiquas and the other close-range attackers had landed blow after blow on Ruseato's obstinate armor, whaling on it and putting cracks in it.

However, when those cracks had sketched a pattern like tree branches all over Ruseato's body, it had shed the armor as if it was peeling a boiled egg.

What had emerged was a Ruseato as white as a hospital ceiling.

The armor that had been stripped from that bleached figure melted into the shadows at its feet, then stretched up, creating shadow warriors. The deformed warriors had thin, featureless silhouettes and held giant war scythes at the ready. Since they were entirely black, they looked like two-dimensional shadow-pictures.

The white Ruseato unleashed beams of light, and Demiquas evaded them.

Compared to what had come before it, it was a limp, weak attack.

And now, thanks to his self-recovery, he was ready to charge again.

Having spotted a good opportunity, Silver Sword launched repeated wave attacks, but the shadow warriors blocked them. Compared to Ruseato, both their range and their attack power were nothing. However, there were too many of them to ignore. Even now, there were already more than ten.

The unit dodged Ruseato's careless attacks, gradually taking down the shadow warriors as they did so.

Dinclon, the main tank, really couldn't handle this many enemies on his own. Five warriors, including that foul Naotsugu, had to draw them off.

The shadow warriors surged in, like insects drawn by the scent of nectar.

Demiquas took aim at the pack with Wyvern Kick.

This flying, gliding kick had a field of fire of about fifteen meters forward, and it could be used both to move and to attack. It was Demiquas's greatest forte, his *absolut Geheimnis*. If he unleashed this attack, Demiquas would land right where the enemy was thickest in a single bound. As a general rule, this was a bad move. Ruseato was a high-level raid boss, and it was hard to avoid his attacks, so if he shook off his healer and other reinforcements, Demiquas would be in a dangerous position. However, the black shadows in front of him were raid enemies, not bosses. To Demiquas, a martial artist, enemies that waved around big weapons like that were easy to take on.

With a piercing fighting yell, Demiquas became a deep green meteor.

He crossed the coliseum almost as if he were coasting through the air on a snowboard, crashed into the chest of a shadow warrior, and slammed a Tiger Echo Fist into its body, which left it looking like it had been pierced by a cannonball.

Leaving an echo vibrating in his ears, the raid mob brought its scythe down as a parting gift. Demiquas repelled the attack by a bare minimum with Back Hand, then, squaring off slightly by raising his right knee until it almost touched his chest, he lashed out with Shadowless Kick.

The enemy flew apart pitifully, like a dropped watermelon.

However, since one shadow warrior had been defeated, Ruseato absorbed the darkness that had been generated, and it seemed to have recovered some HP.

In other words, this was why they were taking one step back for each step forward.

White Ruseato recovered its own health.

The shadow warriors were catalysts for the process, and they also bought it time. Apparently, Ruseato's white reincarnation recovered strength over a set period of time so that it could attack again. Then its armor would be dyed black once more, and it would unleash powerful attacks, moving tirelessly, as though it had just begun to fight.

Outlasting that hurricane certainly wasn't impossible, but that was assuming Ruseato was their only opponent. If the shadow warriors stayed, the vanguard, who'd lost the greater part of its HP to Black Ruseato, would fall to those great scythes.

Healers supported the health of the raid unit. However, both the Kannagis' barriers and the Clerics' Reactive Heals had tolerance limits.

It was nearly all they could do to fight Ruseato of the Seventh Garden by itself.

They couldn't afford to leave the mobs alive. That said, when they defeated them, they recovered Ruseato. For a short while, there had been twenty shadow warriors, and thanks to that, the unit had been pushed to the brink of collapse.

Infuriatingly, the one to find a way out of that situation had been Shiroe.

Black Ruseato generates a number of shadow warriors equal to the number of people who had inflicted damage on it.

At that discovery, Silver Sword had rallied.

They left the attacking to powerful attackers, while the healers and weaker members refrained. When they did, when Ruseato transformed into its white incarnation, they were able to decrease the number of shadow warriors it generated to ten or so.

Shiroe the coward, who did nothing but give orders from the rear, was someone Demiquas meant to avenge himself on, someone he'd never forgive. He'd shattered Demiquas's pride, had even destroyed the Briganteers organization he'd worked so hard to build. If only those three hadn't come to Susukino, Demiquas and the others could have slowly acclimated themselves to this world. If only that Shiroe hadn't come…

He could forgive the cat-headed swordsman. The swashbuckler had blocked Demiquas's path and swung his swords. However, from beginning to end, the coward among them hadn't even looked at Demiquas.

The man didn't even seem to remember his name.

Demiquas could clearly remember Shiroe's expression when he'd reappeared in Susukino. When the man had seen Demiquas, he hadn't looked troubled. That was fine. Shiroe was probably strong; Demiquas had seen that on this raid. In that case, at the very least, he could have sneered or looked contemptuous.

However, the only emotion he'd seen in the damned Enchanter's expression had been the thought, *What a pain.*

Demiquas slammed the rage he couldn't abide into a shadow warrior.

Lightning Straight came back at him, as if to run him through.

He evaded that attack with Phantom Step, kicked it upward with Aerial Rave, then landed a Wyvern Kick in its wide-open side. As it blew away, he slammed another Wyvern Kick into its back.

Shiroe saw Demiquas as no more of an opponent than that.

As if he could go without killing Shiroe! The thought was like flame, and it burned him to the core. Someday, he swore, he'd bring such pain down on Shiroe's head that he'd regret he'd ever been born into this world.

However, now wasn't the time.

Frustrating as it was, he didn't have the ability right now. At this point, even he had to admit it. This Shiroe guy was tough. It was true for his equipment, too, but even his techniques outstripped Demiquas's.

When Demiquas had joined this raid, at first, he'd been planning on attacking Shiroe from behind. He'd laid monsters out as practice. He'd thought that had raised his spirits: His body had been a lot lighter than usual. Demiquas's fists had vanquished the monsters, just as they were tearing apart shadow warriors now.

He'd thought he'd gotten used to the atmosphere of the raid, but then he'd noticed a small sword icon spinning around his wrist. The unfamiliar icon was Shiroe's Keen Edge… That was all it was: Demiquas had only been in high spirits from that guy's reinforcement spell. When he looked for proof, he found it in spades. Haste, which had linked up attacks more quickly than usual; True Guide, which had let him break through the defense of attacks at higher levels than normal.

Just like now.

A shadow warrior that had approached to cut Demiquas down raised its great scythe.

There was still half a second of bind time left for Wyvern Kick. Demiquas should have taken the attack by a hair, but it didn't happen.

Shiroe's support was so subtle that, if this had been the very beginning of the zone capture, he wouldn't have noticed it. What had he called it, Mind Shock? It was a spell that used the shock wave from an impact to make a monster's consciousness go dim. The monsters he normally went up against would have been one thing, but it was only able to stun the raid monsters that appeared in this zone for a second at most. However, that one second was enough for Demiquas: He got out of the enemy's attack range with Monkey Step, turned back, and unleashed a big spin kick, Dragon Tail Swing, as though he were sweeping over the surface of water.

Demiquas's full-power charges and devastation all fell within the parameters of Shiroe's estimates.

That escape and the subsequent spin kick had looked like Demiquas's fierce combat, but Shiroe had merely let him perform them.

Of course, the guy didn't have Demiquas's attack power or martial arts.

All he'd done was cause a little distraction and use a measly reinforcement spell. There was no way he'd be able to take down a powerful monster with makeshift trickery like that.

However, what mattered was the fact that Shiroe had guessed what Demiquas was about to do, and had been able to help him without his catching on. Shiroe was predicting Demiquas's actions perfectly. Demiquas had expanded his skills enough on this raid to know what that meant.

Someday, I'll slaughter him.

When I do, I'll do it in front of everybody.
I'll smash that pasty face and make him drown in tears of remorse.
I'll get a fantasy-class on this raid—
Boost my level, polish my techniques—

Demiquas bounded around, destroying one enemy after another.

His class, Monk, was a Warrior class that had both attack power and the ability to keep fighting. Although he didn't have as much offensive power as the Weapon Attack classes, his HP and ability to handle abnormal statuses were incomparably high. That meant he could charge into the midst of the enemy and survive, and it also meant he could stand his ground, even in the raid boss's attack range, and keep right on attacking. Demiquas kept on shoving, kicking, mowing down, and attacking to the very limits of his techniques, moving as his blazing body dictated.

Yet the battle progressed with painful slowness.

When they were temporarily cornered, William's feverish commands managed to get them on their feet again. The frontline defenders and healers, keeping the enemy weakened: If this vertical line was functioning properly, they wouldn't be wiped out easily. Then they simply had to eliminate the shadow warriors and chip away at Ruseato's HP, suiting their actions to the combat situation.

It took time, of course. During that long time, countless decisions were made, and they all had to be dealt with calmly, deliberately, without error, and promptly. This series of actions was all there was to raids.

Demiquas was heat.

Demiquas was flame.

He evaded the attacks of the enemy in front of him, pierced them, destroyed them.

He leapt at Black Ruseato, brandishing fists of thunder as if to shatter its armor.

His mind gradually emptied until he was simply immersed in the fight, propelled by erupting heat. No more thoughts of when he had been in rotten Susukino; no more thoughts of the day he'd fought Nyanta. Demiquas thought of nothing and became one with the battle.

As a result, he didn't realized that the situation had changed until he heard a scream go up behind him.

It would have been harsh to blame Demiquas. Even for experienced raid members, it had been far too sudden. The enormous iron grates set in the eastern and western sides of the coliseum had opened completely. From the dark gaping holes, Tartaulga'of the Fourth Garden, a frost giant with white eyes and frozen whiskers, and Ibra Habra of the Third Garden, a fiery serpent like a living, writhing corona, appeared.

No sooner had the monsters taken half a step into the coliseum than they unleashed storms of ice and flame from either side. Their target was the Fourth party, which had been concentrating all its attacks on Ruseato. The party was annihilated in an instant, and the side effects alone did massive damage to the rest of the unit.

At the preposterous sight, Demiquas felt an disturbing fluid rush into his mouth from his innards.

This was too much.

Demiquas and the others were fighting Ruseato of the Seventh Garden right now.

Wait your turns, he thought.

They'd fought Ruseato and kept exterminating his kin, the shadow warriors. When the balance had tipped ever so slightly and the enemy's numbers increased just a little, Demiquas's group had been in danger of being wiped out.

Just when things had started to go smoothly. Even though that path had been no more than a faint possibility, like stepping onto thin ice.

Now, at this point, here came two bosses whose ranks equaled Ruseato's.

Even Demiquas could tell, very clearly.

They couldn't win.

This wasn't about tactics or strategy.

The difference in fighting power was so overwhelming it destroyed trivial little tricks like those. In order to fight these three at the same time, they would have needed a legion raid with ninety-six people, not a full raid of twenty-four.

Deep in his ears, he heard a flat voice he'd heard somewhere before. *This world isn't a game anymore. That's finished. Your time is over.*

The realization came to him, then: *Just the way Adventurers put together strategies, the monsters left their posts to concentrate their power.*

If Demiquas had been a guardian of the dungeon, this would have been an obvious tactic, the first one he came up with.

Combine their strength and exterminate the Adventurers.

That natural thing had happened, and that was all.

The air of the coliseum, which had frozen with that terribly cruel despair, was shredded by screams it was hard to believe had come from human throats.

A face the size of an extralarge advertisement on the wall of a movie theater closed in on them: The frozen giant had bent over and brought its fist down on the members. There was a sticky, splattering noise, and then the Summoner was just a stain in the coliseum.

The counting voice that had put Demiquas at ease was gone.

Demiquas roared, charging like a gale at Shiroe—who was just standing there, stunned, eyes wide—and shoved him hard. Shiroe rolled three times, four, before Naotsugu caught him. It put him outside the range of the Frost Giant's twisted club.

"Take that, ya damn coward," Demiquas laughed at him.

In exchange, his left leg had been crushed to a pulp, but he'd gotten to see Shiroe look like an idiot, so he was still ahead.

Kill those cheating raid bosses! Demiquas spat on the ground.

However, neither Demiquas nor Shiroe managed to escape the brutality of Ibra Habra of the Third Garden, the flaming serpent whose writhing body shed a rain of fire. It wasn't just the two of them. Naotsugu, Tetora, and William. The veterans of Silver Shield, who were stronger than Demiquas, and who'd crushed him like a bug no matter how many times he came at them.

All their moisture was gone in an instant, and in the midst of flames that made their bodies twist in agony, the twenty-four members of the conquest unit were annihilated, just like that.

▶ 5

Having just passed through a hut where a foul smell drifted, the line of Krusty's shapely nose warped slightly. The members of his guild called him thick-skinned, but even for him, the stench of the goblin dwelling had taken its toll.

Takayama had accompanied him, and it had been so bad her eyes had begun to smart partway through.

Compared to the hut's interior, with its soiled straw and accumulated filth, it was far better outdoors, even under a freezing winter sky. In any case, Adventurer bodies were sturdy when it came to environmental differences like cold and heat.

This seemed to be true for Krusty as well.

He shrugged his shoulders once, then left the goblin dwelling behind him, as if he had no further use for it.

The dwelling was primitive—just a shallow pit dug in the earth, with a post set in the center and lots of tree branches and grasses piled up around it to act as a roof. There were several like it clustered in the surrounding area.

This was one of the goblin villages in the Silverluck Mountains. This part of the wilderness held countless villages like this one, each with about fifty dwellings. Together, each encampment had probably been home to roughly three hundred goblins.

By now, most of them were deserted.

The Akiba Expedition Army Krusty led had subjugated about 30 percent of them.

They assumed the remaining 70 percent had gathered at Seventh Fall, where the Goblin King reigned.

It had already been a month since the expedition began.

During the interval, Misa Takayama and the rest of the expedition army had explored the surrounding area, confirming the locations of goblin villages and sometimes attacking them. The army's advance had been slow and careful.

From the beginning, the idea that the conquest of Seventh Fall and the defeat of the Goblin King wouldn't be difficult had been common knowledge for the Round Table Council. During the blank period of the Catastrophe, the goblins of Eastal had bred prolifically, and had reached a scale not often seen in history. To the People of the Earth, this was a disaster straight out of their nightmares.

However, to the Adventurers of Akiba—or at least to the combat guild members who'd reached level 90—they weren't a big threat.

Although this was a raid to storm Seventh Fall, according to Krusty, if they went in with a select group of several dozen members, it should be possible to put down the Goblin King inside of two days. Takayama agreed with this prediction.

In the first place, the defeat of the Goblin King wasn't the goal of this operation.

The goal was to secure the safety of the People of the Earth who lived in northeastern Yamato. That meant the problem was the several tens of thousands of goblins themselves. Even if they successfully subjugated the Goblin King and the now-leaderless goblins then overran the Silverluck Mountains, they would have to declare the operation a failure.

With that in mind, the headquarters with which Krusty and Takayama were affiliated was moving with intentional slowness and combing the mountains. At present, there were several dozen Adventurer units deployed in the Silverluck Mountains, scouting and sporadically engaging in combat.

As a result of this maneuver, which was a bit like chasing fish into a net, most of the goblin villagers seemed to have gathered at Seventh Fall. They thought they were mustering forces to begin their opposition to the Adventurers, but to Takayama and the others, it was merely a development that matched their strategy.

Takayama followed Krusty, making for the stream.

Members of D.D.D. were investigating the interior of the village and the area around it. That said, under the circumstances, it wasn't likely that any Goblins had remained behind. They were only confirming the situation, and no one was all that tense.

Krusty and Takayama traveled along a small path, cutting off conspicuous branches as they went.

The well-trodden path was probably an animal track the residents of the village had used when they went to collect water, but Goblins were less than 140 centimeters in height. These two individuals were tall, and as they made their way along the path, the thick branches at face level snagged them and made it hard to walk.

When they emerged on the dry shore at the river's edge, the wind made them narrow their eyes. It carried a chill that swept away the gloomy air, and it felt pleasant to Takayama, but beside her, her guild leader expression wasn't good.

She'd noticed this tendency of Krusty's around the time the Libra Festival had ended, and it seemed as though the anguish was growing more severe. Riezé had been so worried she'd wrung her handkerchief, but up until now, Takayama had left it entirely alone. This was because Krusty was a grown man, and she'd thought it would annoy him to have someone of the opposite sex worrying about him.

Though I suppose being an adult doesn't have much to do with it. Boys are always delicate, at any age.

Takayama's workplace experience made her think this.

Besides, she'd known Krusty for a long time. She knew more or less what that worry was about. That was why she'd thought she'd take this chance, when they'd left the headquarters and gone scouting, to talk with him about it, just a little.

"Milord?"

"Hm? What is it, Ms. Takayama?"

After a time lag so slight it was barely noticeable, Krusty turned a pensive face toward Takayama.

"You don't seem to be feeling well lately. Is something troubling you?"

"Hmm."

Krusty brooded, covering his mouth with his fingertips. He was wearing thin leather gloves today, instead of his usual Adamantite Steel gauntlets. His midweight armor suited his sturdy frame well. He was a good-looking guild master. The series of people who were fooled by this was never-ending, but it was certainly useful as far as administration was concerned. Harboring this impression, she asked straight-out about what she'd felt:

"Are you bored, sir?"

Looking down at Takayama out of the corner of his eye, Krusty thought for a little while. Then, as though ducking the question, he put on a dignified expression, smiled wryly, and raised both hands as if he'd given up.

"…That's a problem. Yes, I'm bored."

"Put up with it, if you would."

"I've put up with a lot of it, and here I am today."

Takayama sighed heavily.

She'd thought this was probably the case, and she'd been right.

Krusty looked intellectual, and it was true that his actions were logical and precise. He had the brains and the charisma to bring people together. He'd launched and managed D.D.D., the largest guild on the Yamato server—truly an achievement to be proud of. D.D.D., which had absorbed 1,700 members, was larger than a midsized corporation in the real world.

However, that public image wasn't all there was to Krusty.

This alabaster young man, who had been placed in charge of running even the Round Table Council, was terribly mischievous and had a fickle personality.

One fact that Takayama and a few of the other veteran members knew was that Krusty had created the enormous organization known as D.D.D. because he'd wanted to see what would happen. In the first place, D.D.D. wasn't a guild. It was part of a personnel exchange system Krusty had thought up, and the guild was just one of its structural elements.

Apparently, one day, Krusty had had a certain thought:

This Elder Tales *game is terribly interesting. However, in order to get absolutely everything interesting out of it, you need lots of acquaintances and friends who'll have fun adventuring with you. The administrators are aware of that, and they actually talk about it. There are all sorts of systems for finding companions built into the game... But if the users created a personnel exchange system that surpassed all that, and if they used that system to conquer end content in the form of raids... Wouldn't that be rather interesting?*

That was why D.D.D. had been formed.

In other words, it hadn't needed to be structured like a guild. The guild system had just happened to exist in *Elder Tales*, and it had been convenient, so they'd used it. Back when *Elder Tales* had been a game, the focus of D.D.D.'s activities had been audio chat and their headquarters' website, and both these systems had been proposed by Krusty. The periodic directors' meetings and the personnel distribution system, which focused on raid unit division, had been his ideas as well.

He seemed to have been interested in constructing an autonomous organization in which the divisions produced results by acting independently, rather than being commanded by him personally. For that very reason, even though D.D.D. had grown so powerful, it had managed to remain a well-ventilated organization.

This had continued even after the Catastrophe. Krusty had seen the establishment of the Round Table Council as a rare, potentially beneficial opportunity, and had sought to expand his organization further and make it more autonomous. As a result, Krusty's curious drive to "see" had been satisfied, but the number of ways were dwindling in which he was required to contribute to the administration.

In short, he'd gotten bored.

Takayama understood her friend's feelings quite well, and she also thought they were troublesome. Although Krusty was bursting with talent, he was the type of man who had so much of it he was hard to associate with. His talent was excess power, and, for better or for worse, it sowed unforeseen trouble and confusion around the area.

When Krusty was bored, nothing good ever came of it.

He certainly wasn't an outlaw, and since he was a rational human being, the final results were often beneficial to those around him. However, the commotion and work that occurred in the process were a pain in the neck for Takayama and the others. It had seemed to her that the boredom had been somewhat alleviated after he'd discovered Raynesia, but she might have been overestimating the girl.

It's unreasonable to push this onto the princess, isn't it…?

When she thought it over carefully, she was filled with remorse.

She had to say a few words, at least. When, thinking this, she caught up to Krusty—who had gone on ahead, strolling down the stream—he was leaning over, inspecting the rocks that were strewn around.

"What is it?"

"Hmm…"

Krusty readjusted his glasses, which had slipped a bit when he bent down, and held the object he'd picked up in front of her eyes. It seemed to be a spearhead.

The mountain stream drew a great arc in that area, and at the inner edge of a deep pool, there was a dry riverbed littered with rocks that were smaller than a child's fist. Patches of lingering snow remained here and there, but in summer, it would have been the sort of cool mountain scenery that invited barbecues.

Krusty kicked several rocks, rolling them away with his toes. He seemed to have found traces of something.

"It looks like this was a training ground."

"A training ground? That's why it's been leveled a bit, then," Takayama responded, accepting the idea.

Now that she was paying attention, she saw that the larger rocks seemed to have been moved all the way over to the thicket of trees. When she looked closely, there were scattered fragments of wood and pieces of battle gear in the gaps between the rocks. This place had probably been used for quite a long time.

The idea of Goblins training themselves had never occurred to her before, but if they were plotting war, it was only to be expected. That said, she couldn't imagine that they'd managed to amplify their military power that way—compared to Adventurers, Goblins' levels were very low.

Having thought that far, Takayama registered Krusty's gaze, wondered at the seriousness in it… And then, in the next instant, she understood:

Goblins. Conducting combat training.

That was a possibility that hadn't existed before. Just as Takayama and the others were attempting to conquer the Seventh Fall raid using a method that was completely different from conventional ones, the Goblins would be able to prepare a return strike using methods that were completely different from anything they'd used before now. This world was not *Elder Tales*. Takayama wondered how often she would have to realize that before it finally sank in. She was filled with the urge to rail at her own incompetence.

"Milord, let's return immediately, report this to the rest of the army and send word."

"We'll have to issue orders to search the training ground and investigate its influence."

"Yes, sir."

After this terse exchange, the pair went back the way they'd come, over the dry riverbed, heading for the village. First, they needed to return to the settlement and meet up with Richou and Kugel from the scouting team. Then they would probably have to travel along the ridge and return to the headquarters.

Takayama was flustered, and it took her longer than it should have to notice that her weapon, a great, folding, military scythe, was vibrating slightly. In the blink of an eye, it emitted a strange, metallic sound and cast a hot red light over the area.

This weapon had been acting strange lately.

It wasn't that its performance had deteriorated. On the contrary: It seemed as though its offensive abilities had increased, so she hadn't sent it out for repairs, but even on this battlefield, it had sometimes begun to vibrate and radiate enough heat to make her writhe.

As a result, with a dubious expression on her face, Takayama drew her weapon from her back, intending to check its condition carefully. It should have been a casual activity, one that required hardly any thought at all.

However, an impact as if a large dump truck had crashed into it ran through Takayama's arm. The shock had been so great she knew the bones of her arm had shattered instantly, and her eyes went wide. Krusty snatched the weapon from her, and then she saw a dark red space envelop him, cutting a sphere out of the world.

Her own weapon flashed red, sending a magnetic field out from the center of the warp, drawing everything into it.

It seemed to be enfolding the guild master of D.D.D. into itself.

Krusty had used his other hand to shove Takayama away, but she didn't recall asking him to do any such thing. Desperately, she reached out for him, thrusting her hand into the warping space.

However, there was a sharp, severing sound, and then the silence of the night left Takayama behind.

Her right arm had disappeared, along with her old friend Krusty and her great scythe, which bore the name "Calamity Hurts."

CHAPTER.

4

GUILD MASTER

► NAME: WILLIAM MASSACHUSETTS

► LEVEL: **95**

► RACE: **ELF**

► CLASS: **ASSASSIN**

► HP: **12040**

► MP: **11890**

► ITEM 1:

[SHOOT THE MOON]
A FANTASY-CLASS LONGBOW SAID
TO FIRE ARROWS THAT CAN HIT
THE MOON. IT HAS A MASSIVELY
LONG RANGE THAT MAKES
IT POSSIBLE TO SNIPE, BUT
WILLIAM PREFERS FIRING
FROM THE FRONT LINE,
AND SO ITS FULL
CAPABILITIES AREN'T
REALLY UTILIZED.

► ITEM 2:

[MAJESTÉ DU GÉVAUDAN]
DURABLE, FLEXIBLE FANTASY-CLASS
LEATHER ARMOR MADE
FROM HIDES OF THE
SHADOW WOLF KING,
A TOUGH RAID BOSS,
REINFORCED WITH FAIRY
SILVER AND EVERLASTING
STONE STEEL THREAD.
PREVENTS BLINDING AND
HAS ASTOUNDING
STRENGTH BUFFS.

► ITEM 3:

[CRYSTAL COMETS]
SPECIAL ARROWS THAT CAN BE BOUGHT, OR
THEIR PRODUCTION RECIPE UNLOCKED, WITH
ENOUGH HONOR IN THE REGION
OF ANCIENT CAPITAL YOSHINO.
SPECIALLY MANUFACTURED
BY CAREFULLY CARVING BLESSED
CRYSTAL. BOTH THEIR THREAT
AND THEIR COST ARE IN A
DIFFERENT LEAGUE, BUT
WILLIAM USES THEM REGULARLY
WITH ZERO HESITATION.

<Soap>
A tool to remove
dirt. Luxury article
that smells good.

He seemed to be on a road, late at night.

However, his surroundings weren't dark. White security lights shone down on the asphalt, throwing black shadows that stretched far away.

Shiroe had determined that it must be late because the shopping district was deserted, its shutters closed, and because everything was deeply, eerily silent.

He passed a McDonald's and a cell phone shop and crossed in front of a florist's sign without looking up. He was used to seeing such sights, and traveling through them. What was weird was that there were no people.

The pedestrian-only shopping corridor down which Shiroe was walking was a bit less than an hour from Ikebukuro, a street built around a station so minor that the local residents were careful to use the term "the Tokyo *metropolitan area*" when referring to their location. Stations with "north" or "south" tacked onto the same place name were scattered nearby. In other words, it was a suburban city that was developing into a bedroom town.

Shiroe had been born and raised here.

However, the town seemed contrived, as if it had been faked, and he felt as though it had always treated him as a stranger.

This town, New Town, had a big population.

It had all the facilities that were required in order to live without inconvenience.

That said, the distance was tricky, and residents who were searching for home appliances or clothes or miscellaneous hobby goods all flowed into the city proper, which meant that the town had no commercial facilities to speak of. This shopping district mirrored the town itself: It wasn't inconvenient, and it had everything. However, if you began to look for something, you generally wouldn't find it.

It was a town that couldn't even be called a small city. It was something like an accessory to Tokyo, and it had no center by which to define itself.

Shiroe's parents had said they'd moved here when they got married. Their two-story house wasn't small, but it wasn't spacious, either, and there were many houses that were exactly the same on its street, like so many identical sisters. That residential district, the station-front area, the few vestigial fields, and the trees that lined the street were commonplace and ordinary, the sort you could find all over Japan, and they flowed past and away.

Because this centerless town had nothing it needed to protect, it changed rapidly. Neither its token station building nor its market street had any stores that could be called long-standing, and their tenants changed regularly. Residents came and went frequently as well.

The same could be said for Shiroe's friendships. Shiroe's elementary school had seemed pointlessly big, and one-third of its classrooms had been empty. He didn't know whether they'd expected that many children when they'd designed it, or if it had had something to do with the city's budget situation. From elementary school through middle and high school, the boys and girls his age had changed at dizzying speed. Now he understood that that had been something like the metabolism of New Town itself. However, as a boy, Shiroe had felt that the world was rather vague and unreliable, and that people and things could disappear at any moment.

Come to think of it...
Remembering abruptly, he looked up.

There had been a local shop on this street, a place that had used eggplant curry, a minor menu item, as its specialty dish. It had been next to the *anmitsu* dessert shop, he thought, after the fruit shop and the bag store. He'd hung out with friends there several times in high school. It had been a cheap-looking place, and a nostalgic one.

However, the sign with the drawing of the shady-looking Indian wasn't there.

For a moment, Shiroe was bewildered, but then he remembered with a twinge of sadness.

It had slipped his mind, but the Indian curry house had gone out of business long ago. A mysterious establishment known as a "beef bowl café" had come in after it, then gone under in a few months, as expected, and had been followed by a ramen chain with a flashy sign that had been expanding its influence in the city center. Shiroe, who came back home from university during the long breaks, remembered it all clearly.

He'd gone to the ramen shop once, but the taste had seemed likely to give him heartburn, so he hadn't gone back.

Although it had gone out of business, what Shiroe kept wanting again was the curry shop. The proprietor, a Muslim who spoke in Yokohama dialect for some reason, had obviously not been Indian, and the curries they served had been less like Indian-style curry than Japanese home cooking (actually, no matter how he thought about it, they'd tasted like that instant brand, Vermont Curry). However, its affordable prices and the astonishing amount of eggplant in the curry had made for the occasional feast to spice up his life.

It's too bad it went under.

When he looked up with a sigh, the store was the ramen chain, with its gaudy sign of dancing black and red letters. Shiroe stopped, observing the shop carefully. The shutter held the words CLOSED WEDNESDAYS. The storefront, which normally had lots of banners hung out, was quiet, and the store name, which should have been written on the projecting awnings, was blurred and illegible.

Shiroe scratched at his cheek with his index finger, then came to a conclusion:

I see. This must be how it goes when you lose your memories.

The name of that ramen chain no longer existed inside Shiroe.

"I suppose that sort of thing happens."

It wasn't much of a shock.

He'd predicted that this would happen, and it didn't strike him as much of a loss. People's memories faded until they no longer remembered where they'd put them, and, like junk inside a treasure chest with a broken lock, they thinned and vanished.

The sight of the Silver Sword members falling in the midst of their attempt came back to him.

He'd known that if he challenged a raid, he would die. In the first place, raids were something you attempted repeatedly, accumulating experience, confirming your capture method, and then broke through. They weren't taking on lower-level enemies, the way they had when they'd gone up against the sahuagins and goblins, and so it was only natural that there would be sacrifices, himself included.

Shiroe felt rather troubled and lonely.

That faint emotion was very nostalgic.

It would have been safe to call it the main hue that had colored the young Shiroe, known as Kei Shirogane.

In elementary school, and in middle school, and afterward.

Abruptly, Shiroe got the feeling he'd been harboring that emotion as he walked through the night.

He couldn't make out even 20 percent of the store names clearly.

…Even though this was the local commercial street of a place where he'd lived from birth through high school. The rapidly changing tenants had touched Shiroe's life briefly and vanished, but it was likely that from their point of view, he'd been the one to disappear. They'd come into contact very briefly, left traces you couldn't even call traces, and evaporated. Before long, even the traces known as memories had vanished.

Considered rationally, Shiroe was the one who'd done the forgetting, and the stores on the street had been forgotten.

However, he felt wounded. It was as if he'd been betrayed.

When he searched for the reason, he was ashamed.

He knew his classmates from elementary and middle school probably didn't remember him.

It was only natural not to remember a classmate who'd tended to miss school, hadn't adapted to the class, and had always stayed in the library until dusk. Shiroe reproached himself, realizing that he'd been superimposing past classmates—people even he didn't remember—on the stores before him.

Venting on others for no good reason. That was awfully selfish.

Even though Shiroe had been the one who'd left nothing in the town where he'd been born, this town which seemed to have everything.

Shiroe walked along the silent street, illuminated by mercury lamps.

At some point, he'd left the business quarters, crossed a bridge that looked modern but was oddly dilapidated, and neared the tree-lined street that led to the elementary school.

He was the only moving thing in this town, but the noise of heavy vehicles passing through echoed from the distant highway. The sound was like the faraway moan of the wind, and with that as background, Shiroe went on, watching his feet.

Reaching a large park, on a whim, he turned slightly and headed into it. The park surfaced palely, illuminated by security lamps, and as he'd anticipated, no one was there.

A pond stood there, covered in tiles with drawings of fish, the whole thing built large enough for children to splash around in. But now it only lay there, the surface of the water reflecting the light. Shiroe and his shadow found a bench from which he could look out over the man-made pond and sat down.

In other words, he concluded, this was probably a type of near-death experience.

Shiroe had died in the middle of the raid with Silver Sword.

In accordance with the rules of this other world, he would probably resurrect at the entrance to that raid zone, but this was a time lag, and the abnormal experience of death was showing Shiroe this dream.

He leaned against the back of the bench, looking up at the sky.

There wasn't a single star to be seen.

…And so here I am again.

He gave a lonely smile.

Shiroe had spent many, many nights on this bench. He'd been raised in a hands-off household where both parents worked, and he'd been a regular guest of this nighttime park since he was young enough to make the staff at the city's welfare center frown when they heard about him.

It wasn't that he'd liked this place. He just hadn't had anywhere else to go. When he stayed at his house alone, even if he crawled into bed, the painful feelings hounded him, and in the business quarter, there were flashily dressed boys and girls who frightened him. As an elementary schooler, the only way Shiroe had been able to forget his unpleasant feelings was to walk around the late-night town until his legs were heavy, then sit down on this park bench.

It wasn't the sort that had made him hold his chest and squeeze his eyes shut when he was a kid, but a faint pain, which unerringly brought a quiet certainty to Shiroe. The certainty that, apparently, he'd failed again.

Shiroe had come to this exact spot many times in the past.

Ever since he was small, he'd grown up hearing people say he was "mature," and it was true that he'd had decent comprehension and good self-control for a child. However, because this was true, children his age had seemed savage and irrational to him, and it had created a distance between them. As a result, he'd made a lot of mistakes.

He'd squandered the consideration of his classmates.

He'd coldly shaken off the hands that had been extended to him.

He'd held kindness in contempt.

He'd abandoned places when he should have stood firm and fought for them.

He hadn't been able to understand his parents' troubles or feelings.

All had been trivial, but they'd all been irreparable failures.

Every time he'd failed, the young Shiroe had cried on this bench, and he'd sworn in his heart to do something about it. Some things had gone well, and he'd managed to think he'd improved a little. Then he'd fail again, somewhere, and he'd sit on this bench, feeling the same way: troubled, or sad, or as if he was defective.

When you die, you understand stuff. All sorts of stuff. Like how you suck at this, or how you're stingy or boring. If you die a hundred times, you see it a hundred times. That hurts, and they can't keep it up.

William's words came back to him.

He could understand wanting to leave the raid team.

This torment was far more acute than losing memories, and it couldn't be ignored.

Shiroe knew what William had meant about this feeling very well.

If they were sent here every time they died, over and over, then Shiroe had died before, on Earth, in that town where he'd grown up.

If this was dying, Shiroe had done it many times already.

The night he'd thrown away the notebook he'd treasured. The night he'd shaken off his friend's hand. The night he'd said "Come back soon" with a faked smile. The night he'd said good-bye to the library…

In short, dying meant feeling as if you wanted to die.

Even if it had been thinly diluted, Shiroe knew what it was like.

That was what was in his heart now. It was the fact that he'd failed at the same thing again and again, not the failure itself, that had gouged open the wound he'd thought he'd gotten rid of. How many times had he felt this emotion? At the very least, he'd been forced to feel it enough that he'd never wanted to feel it again. Still, the next thing he knew, he'd failed and come here. In the end, no matter how many decades he lived, maybe he'd never be able to move a step from this bench. The doubt clung to his back like a shadow, and he couldn't shake it.

Shiroe didn't yet know the future, and to him, it seemed unimaginably long.

"Several decades" was too long for him to understand. Would he live through that time, long beyond comprehension, repeating mistakes over and over?

Shiroe remembered Demiquas, who'd gritted his teeth and shoved him with all his might.

He didn't understand why he'd done that.

He didn't remember having done anything that would warrant getting saved by Demiquas.

William, who'd simply said, "Yeah, sure," and held out his hand.

He didn't know why that young guy had taken his hand, either.

The only thing he remembered doing had made William lose face…

Shiroe couldn't understand any of it. He was so dumb it made him sick.

Naotsugu, too. In the end, Shiroe had come all this way keeping a secret, even from his friend.

Even though Minami wasn't what Shiroe was really concerned about. It wasn't Minami's scouts that had Shiroe on the alert. He already knew about them.

What Shiroe was afraid of was an unknown third party.

He gazed at his fists, which he'd clenched at some point, and carefully relaxed them.

It was very likely that there was something in this world besides Shiroe and the other Adventurers and the People of the Earth. He'd suspected it might be the Kunie clan, but he'd finally realized that it wasn't. However, that meant there must be someone else.

Say for instance that, as Li Gan had said, Shiroe and the others had been summoned to this other world through a world-class spell. The other world just happened to look exactly like the game they'd played. Could anything actually be that convenient? Of course, the possibility of it happening probably wasn't zero, but there had to be a better explanation.

Even on the Earth Shiroe remembered that brain-wave detection technology research had been advanced. They'd been able to extract brain waves and use them to move cursors, to communicate easily with people in vegetative states, and according to recent news, they'd managed to export dreams to external equipment as images. Most of this research was being done in medical fields, and in a few decades, it would probably be applied to the fields of entertainment and space development as well. That cheerful news, the first in a long while, had lit up the Internet.

The latest research tended not to show up on the news. Some national agency might be able to inflict a gamelike virtual experience on test subjects in the course of its secret research. The possibility was definitely there.

However, it had happened to several tens of thousands of Japanese people at the same time, and that was another story entirely; the idea was ridiculous. Shiroe and the others hadn't even been wearing special equipment.

There had to be a slightly better explanation.

Shiroe had endured the eerie feeling he'd had over the past several months, the feeling that seemed to be warning him of something, and he had continued to think on the possibilities. It was the same sensation he'd felt when he'd heard about the Spirit Theory from Li Gan. That explanation had appeared to be the correct answer, and he fumbled roughly through the darkness that lay in its depths, using only the power of his thoughts.

He'd used his Round Table Council connections to commission a variety of investigations.

He'd asked Roderick about the possibilities of flavor text. Soujirou about changes in monster ecology. Michitaka about how the southern plants were flourishing. He'd asked Calasin to collect and organize the folk tales of Eastal, the League of Free Cities.

With each investigation, he'd found multiple items of proof. It was supporting evidence that there was no "third party" in this world. For that very reason, Shiroe's doubt had grown stronger. "Stories someone had just remembered," presented at a convenient time, seemed to be proof from the opposite side.

...But that's no excuse. I was careless. I was afraid, and I stopped trying to know.

There had been more he could have done for Demiquas, and for William.

He should have told Naotsugu everything. Nyanta, too.

Shiroe's efforts to avoid worrying people had probably caused them endless trouble. This was something he should have learned many times over, but his laziness had caused it all to amount to nothing.

Just as they'd waited for him to invite them to a guild on that windy night, the people Shiroe treasured were undoubtedly waiting for him again.

Hadn't they proved to him that his cowardice and laziness had only kept people away?

Shiroe thought about getting up from the bench and starting back to where everyone was.

If he didn't do at least that much, he'd be embarrassed to face them.

He also had to apologize to Kinjo.

In that hut in the snow, Shiroe had doubted him, and he'd been stingy with his words.

He had been stingy. He really should have said everything he could with all the power he had. For the sake of the future Shiroe believed in, he should have persuaded Kinjo. He should have insisted that this was a significant problem for both of them, as fellow inhabitants trying their best to live in this world.

He had no positive proof, but Shiroe felt eyes watching him. It seemed as though it had always been like that, from the beginning, from the very instant of the Catastrophe.

Shiroe stood, using the slight kickback as an assist, and in that instant, he heard a voice he knew from somewhere.

It was like a whisper from someone, foretelling a chance encounter.

▶ **2**

After the lightheaded sensation that always accompanied teleportation, Shiroe was standing on a vast, white, sandy beach.

The clear light of dawn illuminated the waterline.

The slowly repeating waves made faint sounds, trailing lacy patterns of foam.

The borderline between white and blue continued into the distance, as far as he could see.

When he took a step, the noise it made—like crumbling mille-feuille—startled him.

Shiroe began walking, awestruck by the unblemished sand.

There was no point in just standing there, and he felt as if he were being led by something.

When the wind buffeted Shiroe's cheek and he looked up, a great shadow was making for the sky's zenith from behind him.

Did those elegant wings belong to some sort of seabird?

The white shape danced in the dark cobalt sky, as if playing with its fellows.

Its smooth flight rode the wind, and Shiroe remembered a novel by Richard Bach that he'd read a long time ago. Like that seagull, the seabird flew on forever.

Still, what a strange place...

For a near-death experience, it didn't look familiar.

He wondered if it was somewhere he'd visited in early childhood. He remembered reading in an article that people didn't lose memories;

they only stopped being able to retrieve them. *Still*, Shiroe thought perversely, *since human memories are encoded connections between synapses, isn't it all right to consider them lost if you aren't able to decode them?* Regardless, he really didn't remember this place.

That said, even if it wasn't in his memories, it was beautiful.

The perfectly clear winter air seemed to unfold infinitely over the sand dunes.

A pale, unspoiled cream color. An ultramarine so clear it felt wasteful to put it into words. The contrast between the two was so vivid it made his eyes smart.

All alone, Shiroe walked along the water's edge.

His footprints on the ivory sand seemed to be the first in tens of thousands of years. They were a log that traced his path.

Whether it was because he'd left it on that bench in the park or because the silver sands he'd walked over had absorbed it, the sense of helplessness Shiroe had felt was gone.

Only a faint sense of guilt remained. It was a debt he'd have to repay after he resurrected.

Shiroe, who'd walked for a long time, stared out at the ocean as he organized his thoughts.

At his feet, particles of light formed widening ripples.

There was a peculiar crystalline sound, and it triggered a doubt in Shiroe.

The lapis lazuli orb that illuminated the beach was cobalt-marbled with clouds, something he'd seen only in photos. The light in the heavens, which he'd just assumed was the moon, was a blue planet.

—Is this the moon?

When he looked around, that seemed to be the correct answer.

The sand dunes the color of desiccated dinosaur bones and the dreamlike sapphire light that washed over them were a fragile, fantastic sight.

Quickly checking the zone, Shiroe confirmed that this was the fourteenth server, a place he'd heard of only in rumors.

The zone name was Mare Tranquillitatis.

Apparently it hadn't been registered to the automatic translation system yet. If he believed the display, shown in its original language, this was the Sea of Tranquility.

This was probably the test server Atharva Company had packed with content that was currently under development. Shiroe didn't know whether the Catastrophe had brought it to this side of things, or whether there were different circumstances at play.

With no way to investigate, Shiroe searched his memories, grateful for the fact that it was possible to breathe.

Through the Half-Gaia Project, *Elder Tales* had been equipped with a world that approximated Earth, and its territory was divided across thirteen servers. The test server was said to be a fourteenth server not officially included in that number.

However, that didn't mean it was secret.

Users were able to create characters on the test server at will. Characters created on that server couldn't be moved to the regular game server; all they could do was explore an endless labyrinth that spread through a subterranean world.

Even so, this system held benefits both for users and for the developer.

The developer was able to have *Elder Tales* players—outstanding debuggers with basic knowledge—check systems that were currently under development at no cost. The most surefire way to improve quality where the damage balance from special combat skills and weapons was concerned was to ask for input from users who'd actually played the content, instead of simply acquiring the numerical balance through simulations.

To users, this server was a place where they could experience elements that would be introduced to the game in the near future, free of charge. Changes in combat balance and the introduction of new special skills, items, and monsters all changed the game environment. The surest way to get this new information a step ahead of everyone else was to participate in debugging the test server.

These two sets of motives had made it possible to operate the test server.

The server was a system by which Atharva Company, the North American developer of *Elder Tales*, developed common global content and researched system updates in cooperation with beta testers.

Shiroe himself had a subcharacter permanently stationed on this test server.

Considering that the character was a female Summoner, the fact that he'd gotten caught up in the Catastrophe as his main character (Shiroe) was probably all for the best.

However, even though Shiroe had some knowledge of the test server, he hadn't known that that server had a "surface." There hadn't been any data like that on the overseas information sites, either.

As the name indicated, the server was an environment for tests.

When Shiroe thought of it, he pictured a labyrinthine, underground world divided into areas labeled only with numbers and composed of a series of dungeons: some old, some new, and some that had been scrapped.

Although it was only a vague memory, he seemed to recall that, during the week before the new expansion pack had been released, the personnel who operated the test server had been redirected to expansion work as well, which meant it hadn't been possible to log in.

Shiroe mulled over the information he'd acquired, but it didn't yield any new theories.

In the first place, he'd never heard of people coming to the test server during near-death experiences.

Had the other Adventurers not realized this was the test server?

Shiroe thought that was a possibility.

Since the area managed by the test server wasn't in the Half-Gaia Project, the idea that it might be on the moon or something had been debated only on overseas message boards a few times. Among Japanese players, it wasn't anything close to major knowledge.

If Shiroe hadn't known, even he wouldn't have understood that Mare Tranquillitatis was the Sea of Tranquility. He was pretty sure that was Latin.

When he'd thought that far, Shiroe abruptly realized that there was someone very close to him, looking up at him.

The figure was disrupted by digital noise, like falling snow. When Shiroe strained his eyes, it proved to be none other than Akatsuki, the girl he knew well.

She wore a camel-colored duffel coat, and she was looking up at Shiroe with an expression that was wary and slightly troubled, yet pleading.

It made him remember a neighborhood cat that had refused to be friendly, but had always come right up close to him.

When Shiroe nodded, Akatsuki seemed to feel the same sort of relief.

She was looking up through her eyelashes as if she were sulking, but Shiroe knew her expression grew very gentle when she smiled.

A satisfied, cheerful, bashful smile.

As if inviting Akatsuki to follow, Shiroe began to walk down the beach again. After all, there didn't seem to be any information to be gained from staying where he was, and Akatsuki, who was twirling around at the waterline, seemed to want to move forward.

The two of them made their way along the beach, taking their time.

He didn't sense any malice or hostility here at all, but even so, it was an unfamiliar place.

Shiroe kept a careful eye on their surroundings, but Akatsuki seemed to be relaxed.

When he looked back, she was bent over, scrutinizing their tracks in the sand.

When Shiroe noticed this, he turned back and stopped, and she ran up to him with a lightness that made her seem weightless. She spun around him.

Then the two of them began walking again, side by side, and sometimes Akatsuki went on ahead, checking the waterline or pointing at a large bird in flight.

The girl was like a swallow, and her cute camel-colored duffel coat suited her very well.

Possibly because she was a little cold, her cheeks were faintly apple colored, and she sometimes walked ahead of him as if to hurry him along.

This world really must be connected to Elder Tales.

The atmosphere was vast, and the low sound of the wind, unique to the outdoors, showed its slow movement. It harmonized with the sound of the surf, forming the basic background noise for the world. The only other sound was the noise of their footsteps.

Maybe because she was a little frightened of something, Akatsuki's footsteps grew slower, and she started to lag behind.

Shiroe waited for her patiently, taking his time.

Waiting didn't bother him at all.

At some point, pure white phosphorescence had begun to drift down from the sky.

The light was endlessly pearlescent and pale, and it fell equally over the dunes and the wide ocean, Shiroe and Akatsuki.

Startled, Shiroe touched it with a fingertip, and felt his heart ache at its dreamlike fragility.

It was just like the snow he'd touched as a child: Even when he thought he'd caught it, when he looked at the palm of his hand, it was gone.

Akatsuki's eyes were round, and Shiroe nodded to her.

They were both seeing the same wonder.

They were touching the same marvel.

For no reason at all, this brought Shiroe a sense of peaceful satisfaction.

Fear, anger, and regret were all melting into the quiet winter beach. The two stilled in the face of such silence, and its serenity purified them.

"I didn't think it would be such a quiet place," Shiroe murmured, stopping at the edge of a perfectly clear, blue inlet.

"Mm."

From beside him, Akatsuki responded.

The response had been brief, but Shiroe had sensed a feeling of awe in her voice that matched his own.

From far, far beyond the horizon of the ocean, a sound like a church bell echoed faintly.

It seemed almost like an old signal from an unknown species that had lived in isolation since its birth, for tens of thousands of years, and was attempting to communicate its existence to its companions.

Although he had no grounds for thinking so, Shiroe was sure that this inlet was a special place.

Next to him, Akatsuki trembled slightly before she released a heart-rending sigh.

At that, for the first time, Shiroe realized Akatsuki had met with death as well.

Even if it was temporary, death was death. It had passed mercilessly over Akatsuki, and had left its mark. She must have felt grief, as well as humiliation.

However, Akatsuki's eyes at the moment were a little more mature, and far stronger, than the ones Shiroe knew.

If, as William said, death taught you something, then they had a duty not to waste it. Shiroe swore this firmly in his heart, even though he didn't know what the purpose of that duty might be.

If that was why this inlet took memories, then he wanted to offer them himself, as compensation.

That was Shiroe's wish.

This was a necessary ritual, in order to become someone who knew just a little more than he'd known yesterday; in order to overcome his regrets and get closer to something he'd wanted.

Shiroe took a small knife from his pocket and voluntarily cut away a tiny piece of his memories.

Seeing this, Akatsuki cut off the tip of her ponytail as well and let the sea take it.

The snow that fell from the sky, this blue ocean—all of it was made from emotion shards.

As liquid energy, soul fragments created the sound of the surf.

The tears shed by Adventurers who hadn't made it to this inlet were also swallowed by the ocean. This was more a certainty than a guess. Right now, Shiroe was seeing the Spirit Theory with his own eyes.

A small hand gripped his coat.

Without taking his eyes off the ocean, Shiroe whispered, "Amazing."

Akatsuki nodded. Until the throbbing in their chests subsided, they both gazed out over the sea.

"You fell, Akatsuki?"

At Shiroe's words, Akatsuki looked startled, but she nodded.

Gazing desperately up at him, the young woman opened her mouth to speak.

Or rather, *tried* to speak.

It seemed hard for her to do so; she gave it several tries, then shut her mouth tightly in a thin line.

When Akatsuki looked up at him again, she had tears in her eyes, but they seemed to be tears of frustration more than sadness. In the end, she hugged her inner pain to herself, confessing none of it to Shiroe.

Her expression hurt him. To be here in the first place, Akatsuki had to have gone up against a very difficult problem and been defeated. He wished he could have helped, but he hadn't been there.

"I see. That makes two of us, then. I died."

"You, too, my liege?"

"Mm-hmm."

When he closed his eyes, it came back to him—Silver Sword's firm voice:

The ring of clashing swords, of blazing flame and freezing cold spells.

He wasn't frustrated because he'd failed to win.

What frustrated him was the fact that he hadn't done all he could, hadn't accomplished what he'd needed to do.

However, Akatsuki's burning eyes didn't hold the slightest trace of fear.

She might have been defeated, but she hadn't lost.

Shiroe didn't know what had happened, but as he looked at her, he sensed that they were the same. That pain was Akatsuki's treasure. The pride of someone who'd resolved to fight, pride that must be retaken.

That meant there was no need to comfort her.

"I messed up. My predictions were too naïve. —I didn't believe completely."

He'd been reluctant with his words.

He'd been reluctant to take others' hands.

He'd been reluctant to give it his all.

"I don't understand."

The voice seemed to be on the verge of tears, but it was desperately trying to encourage him. Shiroe wanted to tell her, *It's all right. I understand. I know you're working hard, Akatsuki. I know you'll understand someday. Maybe you're a little lost right now, but it's a detour you need to take.*

…But he couldn't say it yet. The petite young woman was fighting. Shiroe was fighting, too. Neither of their raid battles was over.

"It's funny. I never thought I'd get to meet you here, Akatsuki."

"Yes, my liege. It's funny."

So he touched Akatsuki's small, round forehead, praying to the inlet that all the things he couldn't tell her would get through to her somehow.

Mistakes couldn't be erased. However, as Adventurers, they could stand up and try again.

"…And so I'll try one more time."

"I'll try again, too, I suppose— Everyone taught me."

Countless phosphorescent particles drifted down over the two of them.

This world was one horizon leading to eternity, with all emotion etched into it.

That understanding made the world's light even clearer.

From far away, the sound of the surf rolled toward them.

It washed over the shining beach, lapping at Shiroe's and Akatsuki's ankles.

Shiroe smiled at his friend. Their time was ending.

However, it was linked to their reunion.

He moved the hand he'd set on Akatsuki's head slightly, feeling troubled. As a rule, right about now, he could have expected a flying kick from her. *Don't treat me like a child*, et cetera. But because it didn't come, and because Akatsuki's expression was serious, he wasn't sure how to stop.

Akatsuki, looking perplexed, began to say something. The music of the water kept Shiroe from hearing her voice, but he didn't worry over it. The sensation of her hair, like fine, cool silk, remained on his fingertips.

Its softness definitely saved Shiroe.

► 3

When William opened his eyes, he was looking up at a ceiling so high that it blurred in his vision.

A hoarse voice spilled out of his stinging throat.

He knew how pitiful and mangy his face looked, but he couldn't hold back the rumble that seemed to be leaking out of him. In the only resistance he could manage, he rubbed his arm roughly across his eyes. He didn't even have to check to know that they were wet.

He'd been crying like a child. The disgrace of it crushed his chest.

Around him, low, moaning voices rose, one after another.

The members of Silver Sword were automatically resurrecting, one by one.

This was the entrance to Abyssal Shaft, the beginning of the zone.

William's group had been wiped out, brought back to this place, and revived.

It was the sort of annihilation that always accompanied raids, but it was something different as well.

Three raid bosses had appeared and kicked William's unit to pieces.

This informed Silver Sword of two facts:

First, that there was no way they could win this fight.

Second, raids were built on a very delicate balance between being winnable and unwinnable. Guilds that had gotten equipment together and trained repeatedly fought through battles that were like walking a tightrope, and in the end, they won: That was a raid. Therefore, if three large-scale boss battles linked together like that, there was—without exaggeration—absolutely no chance of victory. The more used to raids one was, the better one understood this.

There was no possibility that they could win this fight.

It was despair that painted William's heart pitch-black.

The second news was even worse. No—it was bad beyond comparison. If raid bosses were able to band together now, and if it was happening everywhere, it meant there was no longer a single raid in the world that Silver Sword could win.

Of course, in a raid that players with very low levels—say, level 50—could attempt, if an extra boss appeared, they might be able to deal with it. However, when William's group thought of raids, that wasn't what they pictured. They weren't banding together to seek out weak enemies and torment them.

The raid William and the others wanted was the type where they fought an enemy on their level and their blood seethed in their veins, and that type of raid had just died.

The breath William spat out was stone cold. An indescribable listlessness was torturing him.

The same could be said for his companions. Their low, crushed-sounding voices went on endlessly.

Anything William had been able to understand must have been clear to everyone in Silver Sword as well.

They hadn't even needed to be annihilated: The instant the raid bosses had appeared from the great gates of the coliseum as reinforcements, the raid members had known.

This world had rejected them.

Forcing his limp body to move, William sat up, only to see Silver Sword in the process of being crushed. It wasn't the sort of scene where anyone could have said nonsense like, "I don't want my comrades to see me looking pitiful." Simply being wiped out wouldn't have done this to them. Hearts broken, the members just lay there or curled up, without the energy to stand. They were suffering, all vitality gone.

To Adventurers, physical pain wasn't lethal. What was searing their souls was the brand of having been exiled from the world.

He heard sobbing. Disgraceful weeping, escaping from full-grown adults.

William knew the reason behind it. He'd been in contact with it himself until just a moment ago.

Losing memories was nothing. William could declare this more firmly than D.D.D., who left a safety margin when they acted, or the Knights of the Black Sword, who pressed forward with their captures through strong teamwork, or Honesty, with their damned egalitarian principles. This was something Silver Sword could say precisely because it had, without question, been wiped out more often than any other raid guild on the server.

The instant between death and resurrection when they were shown their own mistakes and imperfections, that soul-chilling torrent of memories, chipped away at raiders' souls. They needed to win only a little. No matter how many mistakes they'd made, they could make a fresh start, saying they'd corrected their errors and had grown... But how could they cancel out a mistake they couldn't fully atone for, or regret they couldn't shake?

Voices reverberated inside him like echoes from the past.

"And? What is that good for?"

"Wow. A game, huh...?"

"On a PC? These days? What's wrong with social network games?"

"You stay home on holidays?"

To hell with that.

William spat the words out.

"Well, sure, you don't look like the type that gets asked to go sing karaoke and stuff."

"You mean you talk to the computer, right? Yikes..."

"Why don't you pick a hobby that could be useful to you someday?"

"Mm, yeah, there are people like that out there, too. Why not?"

To hell with it.

William roughly wiped his face.

He attempted to leap to his feet, but pathetically, his knees were quaking.

He tried to yell, but realized he had no words that would encourage his friends. What was he going to do, inspire them? Tell them they'd win the next one? He couldn't do that. It would be a lie. Then should he tell them to shake it off and invite them to go find a different raid with him? Leave this place and run home... That was impossible.

Could he scowl at them and deliver a parting shot of "Let 'em say what they want," as usual? There was no way he could. His comrades were lying there, prostrate with apathy, and words like those wouldn't reach them.

William's mouth hung open, and his gaze swam.

He saw Dinclon. Touko. Junzou. Eltendiska.

He gazed at his friends, one after another.

Then, before long, he stopped being able to look at anything except his own feet.

William was watching his own guild crumble, and he didn't even have anything to say to them. His heart had been knocked down so many times; every time, it had been shown its own flaws and laziness and had pieces shaved off it, and now there was nothing left in it for him to offer them.

William searched desperately.

He looked for words he could share with his comrades.

However, he found nothing in his frightened, cringing heart.

He heard a voice mutter, "So, what, is this the end?"

He didn't know who it had been, but one of his companions had probably said it. At the words they'd heard from a corner of the sprawling hall, everyone sucked in their breath. After all, it was something that scared everyone here to the point where they'd been trying not to think it.

Those words set a question even William couldn't run from right in front of him.

We'll go back to Susukino and become a good guild that keeps the peace.

The People of the Earth will probably be grateful. This world runs on the law of the jungle, and the Ezzo Empire in particular gets a lot of monster attacks. People are desperate to protect their way of life. That's what Susukino's like, and as long as Adventurers behave themselves, they're popular there. We could even mingle with the People of the Earth, get girlfriends and stuff. We don't have to stick with raids; if we're just conducting defensive quests in the area around the town, Silver Sword's combat abilities are good enough.

It was so utterly ridiculous that William felt as though his insides were on fire.

"Maybe so. Probably so. I think so. But so what? To hell with that."

Surrendering to his frustration, William rebelled, without a thought for the consequences.

That probably wouldn't be a bad way to live.

It was a way of life that skillfully avoided trouble in this other world, purchasing safety.

…But it was also exactly the same as the words of "advice" the adults with know-it-all faces had given William.

"Yeah, we lost. Total annihilation. We might be through. It was probably useless. Like those other guys always say, we're probably just idiots who've been doing stupid stuff this whole time. We're shut-in game junkies. Total rejects. —But who cares? We already knew that. We're doing this with our eyes open. Still, we like games. We chose this."

It would be okay to end it. That was what William had thought.

However, even if they lost, even if they were through, there was something they couldn't ignore.

There was something they absolutely couldn't just leave.

William went on, as if the blazing, roasting heat inside him had given him a shove.

"It's nothing big. We lost in a raid, that's all. This stuff happens all the time. No need to be shocked. All this means is that the wins-and-losses data recorded on the server will go up by one, or it won't. 'Games are just kid stuff. It's about time we grew up and went back to town'—I'm never gonna say that. I won't let any of you say it either. We lost, and maybe we're crap maggots and the lowest of the low, but I won't let even God say it was useless."

To William, raids were something special.

They were the heart of *Elder Tales*, which gave them about the same meaning as "the center of the universe."

"What does the bit data recorded on the server mean, anyway? Is that what you asked? It's got meaning. Because I decided it did. I decided it was something awesome, something fantastic. The lot that believes there's some 'correct value' that the powers that be decided, and that it plays the same way for the entire country… Guys who believe a line like that can't understand this. Guys who say 'The value you people believe in is stupid, and that means you're wrong' won't understand this as long as they live. No matter how dumb we look, no matter what kind of a gilded fake it seems to be, if I—if *we*—think it's awesome, then it's awesome. Isn't that choosing? I'm here because I chose to be!"

To him, this was a sacred oath, and he wouldn't let anyone diss it.

With a chest-searing pain that he couldn't hold back even by gritting his teeth, William harangued them.

At some point, the members of Silver Sword had sat up, or planted themselves on the ground, and they were looking up at their guild master and field battle commander.

"We spent time in *Elder Tales*. We spent a long, long time there. Tough enemies showed up, and we took up our swords and our bows and charged at them. We rushed them, yelling like little kids. Then we either won, or we lost. Yeah, that's right, all of that was just bits on the server turning into ones or zeroes. What about it? We got obsessed over it. That's awesome. If we won, we were flying high, and we'd celebrate the victory. We'd divvy up the fantasy-class stuff equally and drink a toast. If we lost, we'd get frustrated, hold a review meeting and kick up a ruckus until after midnight. If you want to call that pointless, you go right ahead. Maybe it's a toy or a showy trinket, but it doesn't matter. If we think it's awesome, and we decide to sink our time into it, then it's the real thing!"

William howled. He expelled the heat from his lungs, loading it with resentment and bitterness.

But that was as far as it went.

The flames that had pushed him into motion blazed up all at once, burning him to ashes body and soul, and vanished. Victory and defeat belonged to combat; they were a part of it.

Raids were the most sacred of all battles.

They were something that should not be violated.

Making light of them meant showing contempt for the enormous amount of time William and the others had spent striving for them. William's group had lost the match, and now they were broken. There was no way to reverse that.

As a result, there were no more words for him to say.

There wasn't a single thing that could rouse his comrades.

"…I mean, we were like that, you know? That's what we were, right? I dunno about guys who have all sorts of stuff. Guys who can live cleverly and be popular have pretty much everything, so they can just get by on that. Do you have something like that? Anything's fine. Anything that can take you as far as you want and help you make friends with anybody. It could be brains, or looks, or a cheerful personality, or funny jokes. Anything's fine, so do you have something like that, the stuff that makes guys who shine in real life all shiny? Do you? ...I don't. I don't have one single thing."

Even so, still looking down, William went on in a low mutter.

It was no longer a secret that belonged to a sacred battle.

It certainly was true, but compared to the magnificent *Elder Tales*, it was trivial. In short, it was William's small, personal confession.

He no longer had anything that would let him throw out his chest and address the members. Even so, the guild master of Silver Sword continued to face them.

▶4

"Listen. I never said it before, and I couldn't say it before, but you're my friends. Without the game, see, I *can't* make friends. Seriously lame, right? What a loser. But because I had the game, I managed to get by. And because I had the game, I knew what you were thinking. When I game, I think, 'Oh, this guy wants to be recovered,' or 'This one's dropped back, but she really wants to move up,' or 'This one's all hesitant so they can't say it, but they really want this armlet that boosts magic strength.' And that's not all. I think things like, 'This person really thinks about what's best for their friends,' or 'That one's a coward, but they're shouting at the top of their lungs,' or 'He's tired, but he psyched himself up and logged in today.' I can tell stuff like that. I really do understand."

William desperately strung together scraps of words that wouldn't flow smoothly.

It was fragmented sincerity, and not the least bit organized.

It was the last remaining flame, no more than the tip of a fingernail.

Elder Tales had taught William a lot of things. If it hadn't, there was no way a high school kid who was bad at talking and couldn't make friends could have made it as a guild master.

He doesn't understand others' feelings. Self-righteous. Inconsiderate.

Uncooperative. Can't stick with anything. Can't read atmospheres. Doesn't try to be part of the group.

Even an isolated boy who'd been told things like that—who had thought that, if that was how it was, his critics could shove it and he'd have none of it—had been able to make a few connections in *Elder Tales*. He'd treasured those connections and protected them, making sure not to treat them carelessly. As long as William had lent his ear to the very first friend he'd taken into his thin arms, *Elder Tales* revealed many secrets to him.

The first secret he'd learned had been teamwork.

With some players, it went well, and with others, it didn't. Some players were skilled, and some were lousy. Slowly, he'd figured out what he had to do in order to work with them. In short, William just had to match their pace. When he'd thought a player was lousy, he simply hadn't understood what they were trying to do. If he synchronized himself with them, most players' moods got a lot better.

He then began to go on raids.

The required teamwork grew harder and harder, but William didn't let himself fall behind. Little by little, the number of players he could make small talk with increased. Once he tried connecting with them, he found they were all good-natured people.

The second secret: Strangely, on nights when they'd had fun talking about stupid stuff, their win rate rose. He learned that dumb, pointless stories had a mysterious power that brought victory to their efforts.

William learned more and more.

Some of his friends were in good shape, and some were in bad shape. Condition was important. He started taking an interest in how other people lived. Some of his friends played enthusiastically, and some were low-energy. His friends had all sorts of worries. Of course they did. He realized, belatedly, that everyone else was just like he was. Then he started to understand what they wanted. It was simple: They all wanted to go on raids and win.

Who should get recovered this time? Which enemy should they concentrate their attacks on? Should they press forward with their attack, or call in substitutes and build their strength back up? Should they go all out, or keep it to about 70 percent?

Even if they disagreed on what they needed to do in order to win, each of them wished for the best. It just wasn't going well, that was all. They went along resolving those little mistakes and disagreements, one by one. Finally, they won, and even though it was a small victory, William's group was over the moon.

The third secret had been a little painful for William.

He'd learned to ask the people around him questions, and to be open-minded.

It had happened only after his friends had learned to put up with William's short temper, but he'd managed to learn a little. After he'd learned it, he was able to understand that it was necessary.

Many raid guilds were short-lived. Twenty or more members fought harsh battles, winning or losing, over and over. If they were lucky, they could get treasure every time, but even if they were victorious on a raid, there was no guarantee they'd get the fantasy-class items they wanted. Naturally, dissatisfied members cropped up, and strained relationships and calculations about individual interest appeared. In a situation like that, most raid guilds didn't even last half a year before disappearing.

Before Silver Sword had destroyed itself with the strife that always accompanied raid guilds, the people in question had learned enough tolerance to be able to talk with each other. William learned to trust the people around him and speak frankly, and the guild members learned that, although their leader might be short-tempered, he wasn't malicious. For a raid guild, this was a very fortunate thing.

William did sometimes wish he'd picked up on that secret a bit earlier, but on the other hand, it was a secret he'd managed to learn precisely because he'd wanted to protect this guild.

By the time William understood the secret to spending time with others, Silver Sword had begun to develop a reputation as an up-and-coming raid guild.

"So I know now, too... You feel like that was it, don't you? Game Over. It didn't work. You feel like this is the genuine end. It might be. It might be, but..."

For that reason, William understood.

He knew how pitch-black everyone's feelings were right now.

He knew that, with their precious raids taken from them, they were watching him and feeling like abused dogs. Even if he felt so pitiful he couldn't look at his friends, he knew.

"When I came to this world, I'm not gonna lie: I was happy. That must've been true for you guys, too, at least a little. I bet nobody here was one hundred percent against the idea, right? I mean, this is *Elder Tales*. The world we threw ourselves into like idiots. The world of the raids we're better at than anybody. I thought, 'This could work.' But more than that, more than anything, I was glad I was with you. You're just like you were in the game, see. Me, too, but anyway. I guess that doesn't matter. As long as we can go on raids together, I'm good. There's nobody in this world who'll make fun of us, either."

William sniffled.

The veteran field commander, the elf sniper with the byname "Mithril Eyes," was no more.

"Still, that's why even if we lose, we can't run. Listen! Maybe we can't win. Yeah, we probably can't. In fact, we're almost certain to lose. But that's no good; there are some things we absolutely should just not admit. And anyway, if we go home like that, what are we going to do? If you take this away from us, what do we have left?—we played *Elder Tales* so hard we scared other people away! These past two years were solid *Elder Tales* for me. It's all I thought about, morning to night. I ate, slept, and bathed just so I could do this. I even studied for *Elder Tales*. If you want to call me a washed-up loser, do it. I'm such a hardcore gamer no one wants to be around me. I'm such a social misfit that I can be psyched beyond belief, all night, over a single rare item. I played this thing for keeps... So I can't cut and run just because a second or third raid boss showed up. Hell, even if I ran, where would I go?! After I ran, you think I could make fun of games and live like that? Like I could make friends if I stopped raiding? Should I laugh a little and say, 'Boy was *that* a big fat waste of time...'?! Up yours. To hell with that."

It was all mixed up.

Were they supposed to stand their ground and just keep dying? How many more times would they have to feel like that?

They'd been able to suck it up and get through it because they'd had a hope of victory, but that hope was gone now.

What you're doing is just a game, even if the world's changed; it's just a game, you people are parasites, completely worthless, and you can't even win at that game— How were they supposed to face a reality like that?

"I…I've run before. I was confused, but I finally got it. It was in Akiba, at that first Round Table Council. Back then, I'd just gotten started in this world, and I wanted to go raiding so bad I couldn't stand it. That's why I didn't join the RTC: so I could go on raids. That's the truth. I'm not lying. But I also thought, 'These people are doing something really dumb. What a waste of time. I'm surprised the pigs can keep that up when they've got no shot at winning.' I made fun of them. I did something I hate so much I'd deck anyone who did it to me. It cracks me up. I know now. I ran. It looked like it wasn't gonna work, so I just let it go right by me."

Even so, there were players who hadn't run.

That was something William idolized.

The legendary band of players who'd been formidable opponents for the big guilds in tough raids, even though they weren't a guild themselves.

William had still been a new player, and hearing about their exploits had thrilled him.

It had thrilled him so much that he'd resolved that someday, even if he was a loner, he'd get them to let him join that fantastic team.

By the time William had gotten himself leveled up to 90, the group had disbanded. It struck William as an awful betrayal. They hadn't waited for him. Not only that, but its members had gone back to playing solo and scattered, without forming a guild. *Then what was the point of leaving those legends?* he'd thought.

"But Shiroe won. I thought that raid was pointless and impossible and they'd never win it, but he won it, and he made Akiba. It was the raid that made a town. I shouldn't have laughed at that. —I thought he was an awesome raider, and a great commander."

There was a player who'd fought, without running.

The high ranker he'd once looked up to really hadn't been ordinary at all.

"Because when that guy, Shiroe, got down on his knees and asked, I jumped at the chance. 'Of course we don't have a shot at winning. I'd expect nothing less. Machiavelli-with-Glasses brought this one in, so obviously we're all gonna go through hell. You can tell the guy's a damn pain-in-the-butt sadist just by looking at his face!' But...I also thought that it would be fun. I thought it would be great if we could win. Why? Because we're hardcore raiders!"

William could feel the heat gathering in the air. When he looked up, he saw the faces of his guild members. Their expressions held pain like his, pain they were unable to vent.

They might be able to give it just one more try.

The heat that dwelled inside them gave him that impression. William had set his comrades on fire.

However, there was no sense of victory or achievement there. Instead, he felt stifling pressure and responsibility.

William was a guild master, and he was about to lead his comrades into the jaws of death, an unwinnable battle. Neither Krusty nor Isaac would have made that decision. Although they were combat guilds, they'd been smart enough to understand the significance of the Round Table Council and give it their cooperation.

I am a seriously dumb guild master.

William's lips were on the verge of trembling, and he bit them hard.

As he tasted seeping iron, he scrabbled frantically for a plan.

He wanted to win. He wanted to win more than he ever had before, but it wasn't for his own glory. It was from the frenzied desire to give his comrades victory.

▶ 5

Shiroe's consciousness returned in the way dawn gradually began to turn the world blue. Words filtered down to him, like light through water.

It was a mutter like a scream.

A man's halting voice, protesting unfairness.

William's confession was quiet, but Shiroe never lost track of it as he regained consciousness. As if prompted by those words, he began thinking to himself.

Shiroe tended to be isolated, and his normal state was monopolized by pondering, to the point where it was inseparable from his own orientation.

The fact that there was a "self" he could question seemed to be proof that his mind was awake.

The first thing he did was start to confirm the circumstances and examine future developments.

Flatly rejecting the dizzying, drunken feeling and the bewilderment of resurrection, Shiroe began analyzing the raid capture and its peripherals without a moment's delay.

In the first fifteen seconds, he understood that these were seriously difficult circumstances. It would probably have been more accurate to call them impossible. Only twenty-four people could enter this zone, and it wasn't possible to overthrow the enemy's total forces with numbers like that.

If it had been just Ruseato of the Seventh Garden, they could have won.

His grasp of the monster's distinguishing characteristics was complete, more or less. In Black Knight mode, Ruseato gave off single, powerful attacks, reflection of close-range damage, and ranged attacks. In White Knight mode, these switched to self-recovery and kin summoning.

Almost all raid bosses had a variety of distinguishing features. They took special actions and went through transformations depending on elements such as time and remaining HP. It was safe to say that seeing through these features and putting together tactics was the foundation of defeating raid bosses.

He'd finished studying these features for Ruseato of the Seventh Garden. That didn't mean they'd be able to win right away, but he did feel they'd be able to win if they practiced a few more times. They wouldn't have to suffer through hideous consequences like being wiped out in order to practice; even if the front line fell, they'd only have to retreat temporarily. He could say they had a shot at victory.

However, when it came to the frost giant, Tartaulga of the Fourth Garden, and the fiery serpent, Ibra Habra of the Third Garden, things were different. They hadn't even scouted those two yet. He didn't know how far it was safe to use Tartaulga of the Fourth Prison and Ibra Habra of the Third Prison as reference, but it was likely that the two attacks that had annihilated Shiroe's group had been ordinary ranged attacks. They were probably attacks with massive damage and recast times of anywhere between 50 and 150 seconds. They weren't certain-kill attacks, and they weren't "distinguishing features" they'd have to capture. He had absolutely no hope of conquering them.

In addition, those two would attack at the same time. That wasn't all: It was even possible that other bosses in this zone would join the fray. No matter how you looked at it, they were done for. They had no prospect of victory whatsoever.

Shiroe listened to the warning voice inside him: *Don't think about why it's impossible. Think of solutions.* The kind words were entirely correct, but they did make him feel like complaining that the demands were always too hard.

In his mind, a row of blue cards sat before him, to his right. These were the conditions he had. His advantages or, in other words, his weapons: Silver Sword's experience, his friends, support from the Round Table Council, the facts that had been made clear to him up until now, and information.

Farther back on his right were the difficulties he had to overcome, in the shape of phantom cards. Ruseato, Tartaulga, Ibra Habra, and the other bosses they hadn't seen yet. They'd nearly gotten through the dungeon area in this zone. Almost all the map was clear. The only things left were the three, or possibly four, bosses.

He thought up several strategies, then sorted them based on the possibility of making them happen. The odds were so low they didn't really merit discussion, but he tinkered with each strategy, seeing whether he could improve them. They really weren't at a place where they could be put to practical use.

The various reforms in this world were subject to individual limitations. For example, when developing a new dish, the level of the Chef dictated whether or not it would be possible to make it. In combat, this manifested as more severe personalization. Even if you had a lot of powerful weapons, their use was limited by their level. For example, even if he'd had a Gatling gun and trench mortar now, he'd barely have been able to make use of them. More than powerful weapons and spells, they needed to break through the circumstances.

He knew he was asking the impossible, but right now, for Shiroe, the word *retreat* didn't exist.

Next, Shiroe began analyzing not their advantages but the difficulties they'd need to overcome, the weak points in their forces.

There were special capture methods for most raid bosses. Even if they didn't look like obvious shortcomings, it was possible for attacks that seemed powerful at first glance to have vulnerabilities.

Feeling as if he'd just had a sudden flash of inspiration, Shiroe desperately followed the thin thread of his thoughts.

Prisons or gardens, they were the guardians of something. Were they aware of their own roles, especially now that they had wills of their own? They'd cooperated in the battle a short while ago, and when he wondered why reinforcements hadn't made an appearance until Ruseato of the Seventh Garden was obviously losing, he thought the key to a breakthrough might be there. However, he couldn't deny that there were some naïve hopes in there as well.

Temporarily discarding those fond hopes, Shiroe set about constructing and selecting a more realistic capture method. Even after several dozen attempts, though, he hadn't managed to come up with a strategy that seemed any more reliable.

The fantasy that was almost a fault seemed to have the best chance of success.

There was no way to calculate the actual odds, but it seemed to be worth betting on.

"Hey, Shiro. You awake?"
"—Yeah."
Naotsugu had spoken, leaning in to look at him.
Shiroe sat up, stretching his stiff back, and found himself on a marble

bier with a blanket spread over it. There was no telling what the square stone had been originally, but apparently he'd been asleep on top of it.

Naotsugu had been leaning over that stone to look at him, but when Shiroe adjusted his glasses, he seemed relieved. Shiroe turned away, looking back at the open space.

Tetora sat nearby, cross-legged. The two of them were the only ones near him.

He could hear William's thin voice. It was a high voice, trembling but proud; a voice you'd never have imagined belonged to the commander of one of the leading combat guilds on the server. And yet, it couldn't have been more appropriate.

The whole time his eyes had been closed, Shiroe had listened to those words.

He'd listened to the many sobbing voices as well, and the groans that cursed their helplessness.

As a result, Shiroe nodded again. "Yeah."

In the hall, as they watched, the members of Silver Sword slowly got to their feet. They were gazing at their guild master. This probably wasn't something Shiroe and the other non–Silver Sword members were to hear, and for that, Shiroe was grateful to Naotsugu, who must have read the atmosphere and then carried his body to this corner, away from the crowd. At the same time, however, Shiroe needed William's words. The person standing there was just like Shiroe at sixteen.

Elder Tales had caused him a lot of pain.

Being labeled by strangers. Having judgments made about him based solely on what he could do. Never really being seen.

Still, at the same time, it had given him gifts that were much greater.

Captain Nyanta, Nurukan, Aihie. They were all good friends. Kanami had taught him what *easygoing* meant. He'd learned self-control from Kazuhiko, and the strength known as trust from Naotsugu.

As he watched Silver Sword from a distance, Shiroe thought they were a good guild. He also thought William was an excellent guild master. The idea that they had all gone through "that" made his chest feel tight. What if it had been him? He probably would have gotten back up, but he didn't know if he would have been able to encourage his companions with words that genuine.

When Minori and Touya were heartbroken, what could he tell them? What could he do for Isuzu and Rudy? He didn't feel as if there was anything.

He recalled Akatsuki, but in his mind, the small Assassin had just looked angry.

The thought struck Shiroe as a tiny bit funny, and he laughed.

He felt as if he'd been told, I'm *the one who protects* you, *my liege, so mind your own business.*

People were incredibly complicated. Shiroe knew Akatsuki was worried about him; that the friend who shoved him away brusquely with an angry expression actually worried twice as much as most people. He now knew that Akatsuki was worried about him, even as she was fighting somewhere far away.

This was no time to get discouraged in a place like this.

"I want them to win. Don't you, Shiroe?" Tetora murmured as she sat cross-legged, rocking back and forth.

Her back was to Shiroe, and from where he was, he couldn't see her expression. Still, her voice had been strong, and he was able to answer with an honest "Yes." But then, it hit him: He wanted them to win. To have *Silver Sword* win. He wanted to break through this difficulty with this raid team, as one of its members. Tetora's frank words took shape within his emotions and promptly became resolve.

"You say some good stuff sometimes," Naotsugu quipped.

"I am a first-class idol, you know."

As they gazed at William in the distance, Naotsugu and Tetora spoke to each other briefly.

That was all it took: Although the three of them hadn't said anything in particular, their thoughts had overlapped. As a group, they didn't know what form "winning" would take, or what it would feel like. However, whatever they did, they knew that they couldn't let Silver Sword die like this.

That was already a set decision, and the only problem left was how to make it happen.

"And? What do we do? Got any ideas, Counselor?" Naotsugu asked, indifferent and cheerful. He'd phrased it as a question, but he was really just looking for confirmation.

Shiroe's friend had no doubt that there was a way to break through this. He figured that Shiroe was bound to come up with something… And so, Shiroe pushed up his glasses and answered.

"There's something I have to tell you, Naotsugu. You as well, Tetora. And William. The rest of them, too. I should have told you why this raid is necessary, and what's inside this place, and why I want gold. I leaned on you, and I was trying to do it all myself. If you'll forgive me… I have a slightly better strategy. Only slightly better. The odds of winning are fifteen percent."

"Great, bring it on."

"That's perfect."

"I also need to tell Kinjo and the others about our wish, and about the land of Yamato. This time, when we speak, I'll look him in the eye."

CHAPTER. 5

CONSIDERATION OF FRIENDSHIP

► NAME: **SHIROE**

► LEVEL: **93**

► SUBCLASS: **SCRIBE**

► MYSTERY: **CONTRACT TECHNIQUE**

► HP: **11162**

► MP: **12996**

► ITEM 1:
[WHITE STAFF OF RUINED WINGS]

A STAFF THAT WIDENS THE EFFECT RANGE OF ITS BEARER'S SUPPORT SPELLS. IT'S A PERFECTLY ORDINARY STAFF MADE FROM AN OLD TREE, BUT A WING-SHAPED FORCE FIELD CAN BE DEPLOYED FROM ITS TIP. THIS FANTASY-CLASS RAID ITEM IS VERY POWERFUL, BUT IT'S ALSO HARD TO GET, AND THERE AREN'T MANY IN EXISTENCE.

► ITEM 2:
[PHILOSPHER'S COAT]

A REWARD FOR CLEARING THE "WISE BEAST-MAN THAT SLEEPS IN THE DESERT" RAID QUEST ON AN OVERSEAS SERVER. FANTASY-CLASS DEFENSIVE GEAR THAT'S SAID TO GRANT THE PERSON WHO EQUIPS IT DIVINE PROTECTION THAT CORRESPONDS TO THEIR KNOWLEDGE. BOASTS HIGH RESISTANCE TO BAD MENTAL STATUSES.

► ITEM 3:
[MOON KATSURA-FLOWER CHARM]

A FANTASY-CLASS TALISMAN MODELED ON THE LEGENDARY FLOWERS SAID TO BLOOM ON THE MOON. BELIEVED TO BLESS SOUL TRANSITIONS, IT REDUCES THE AMOUNT OF EXP LOST WHEN REVIVING FROM DEATH. IT HAS AN EFFECT THAT STRENGTHENS SPIRIT-ATTRIBUTE ATTACK AND DEFENSE SPELLS.

<Parchment>
One of the basic
mediums of record
keeping in this world

The Abyssal Shaft capture team filled a week with planning.

Reinforcement of their campsite; several dozen recons in force. Elimination of all non-boss-level enemies that could be subjugated. The unit made all the preparations they could think of, then headed into battle again.

Noticing that his breathing was growing shallow, Federico forced himself to draw in air.

The scene that spread before him was almost exactly the same as last week.

It was the overwhelming shape of the huge, dark purple figure enshrined in the center of the enormous coliseum: Ruseato of the Seventh Garden.

The arena that had been the site of the ferocious battle a week before was quiet, and not even clouds of dust were visible.

Keeping his attention on Shiroe, the party leader, Federico waited for the signal.

He thought the taciturn young man had changed quite a bit over this past week.

After that defeat, he'd begun to speak with all the members of the group frequently. He'd known the man was a knowledgeable Enchanter, but over that week, his skills seemed to have grown even sharper. He had a new staff which seemed to have come from storage, and Federico and the others had soon grown used to seeing him equipped with it.

This was no time for grumbling. They'd do whatever it took to boost their chances of victory. Federico and the others thought that in this situation, Shiroe had responded to them very well.

During the week, the raid team's provisions situation had taken a turn for the better. That was thanks to Shiroe's group as well.

They'd donated generously from their Magic Bags, which meant that both the amount and the quality of their meals had improved. Voinen, the amateur Chef in charge of meals for the team, was grateful. Some wondered whether Shiroe's cadre had just been holding back on them until now, but there weren't many such opinions, and they soon disappeared.

It was also true that Silver Sword had been treating the outsiders as guests. It wasn't the sort of thing said outsiders could unilaterally blame them for wondering.

Besides, the annihilation had counted for a lot.

"Death" was horrifying and painful, but sometimes it bound people to each other. It wasn't that they'd gotten along badly with their friends from high school or college, but this raid team was something special. Sharing that bitter experience had been significant, to the point where "friends" seemed like a less accurate description of their relationship than "comrades in arms."

You can't make friends with guys you hate, but...

Federico bit his lip and thought.

You can't keep on hating comrades in arms.

This had been true with regard to Shiroe, and with regard to Demiquas as well.

Azalea, who was sitting with his eyes closed in apparent meditation, lightly raised his right hand.

Using Soul Possession, a Summoner special skill, he'd possessed a summoned servant monster and had gone on reconnaissance in its form. He must have released it: He shook his head two or three times, then delivered a brief report to William: "Still on standby, no change in position. No other enemies sighted."

The result was just what it had been during repeated reconnaissance sessions over the past week.

The raid bosses seemed to have learned to work together, but they each had their own ideas and preferences, and their cooperation wasn't perfect. These were words that Shiroe of Log Horizon had spoken several times over the course of the week. When you talked to him, he seemed to be a mild-mannered, philosophical young man, but if you believed the rumors from Akiba, he was a sinister mastermind who'd control even the armies of hell.

Either way, it's not much of a problem, Federico thought.

It was true that Shiroe was introverted. His cross expression seemed to put up a wall. His explanations were complicated and roundabout. However, these were trivial flaws. The Silver Sword members weren't qualified to talk about other people. They were a group of social rejects, all of them warped to some extent. Shiroe might be an eccentric, but in terms of Federico's friends, he was a sensible sort.

Shiroe chanted keywords briefly, and a spell activated. It was the Elixir spell. This Enchanter support spell raised the base power values of the recovery spells its targets used.

His companion Voinen had turned the palm of his left hand upward and tested Heartbeat Healing. Warmth and a vivid green light showered down on Federico. The recovery amount actually had increased. Shiroe was moving along, casting support spells in sequence, and Federico sent grateful thoughts at his back.

The time for preparation was over. From this point on, it was Silver Sword's time.

This was the continuation of the night when William had yelled as if he were spitting out his words.

A short countdown. Naotsugu launched into a run first, as if stealing time from the "zero." The Second party's guardian outstripped the other members by a wide margin, heading for Ruseato of the Seventh Garden all alone.

Not yet. Not yet…

Keeping their eyes on William's left hand—which he'd stretched out horizontally—and the battlefield, Federico and the others sat tight. Gazing at Naotsugu's back, they waited for the first attack.

"Castle of Stone!!"

Right in front of Ruseato, Naotsugu raised his shield and shouted. It was the absolute special skill of the Guardian, one that negated all damage. Using this ten seconds of bare invincibility, Naotsugu made it through the first big attack Ruseato launched, Hearken to the Moonlit Funeral Bell.

"Now!"

With a yell, William broke into a run.

Federico followed him so fast that they seemed to race.

Hearken to the Moonlit Funeral Bell and Kneel Before the Dark Silver Post were attacks from Ruseato's Black Knight mode that could be described as certain-kill techniques. Unless you were the top tank—Dinclon—and loaded up with support and recovery, it would be tough to defend against those two attacks. Shiroe's friend Naotsugu had gotten through one of them with a single Castle of Stone. In the previous battle, they'd learned that Hearken to the Moonlit Funeral Bell's recast time was ninety seconds. In other words, Ruseato wouldn't be able to use it again for another eighty-seven seconds. Right now, he had no powerful ranged attacks. Kneel Before the Dark Silver Post was a threat, but that targeted single players. Federico and the others could use this opening to move, safely and completely, to their designated locations.

For raiders, this was a natural team play, but the sight of a Guardian from a small guild pulling it off perfectly made the corners of Federico's lips rise.

Even now, death was frightening.

However, their morale was higher than that.

In the instant when he charged shoulder to shoulder with his comrades, and the instant when they pulled off a difficult team play, Federico's heart soared up like a glider riding the wind. It was probably the sort of emotion the world would have ridiculed as childish, but, to borrow the words of the guild master that Federico acknowledged, the world could go to hell.

The yell that night was a letter of challenge, thrown at the world, and just as it said, we're doing this by choice.

Since coming to this other world, Federico had died many times.

Many times, he'd been taken back into those dark memories. He'd experienced his regret and despair all over again.

However, his Silver Sword comrades had never once appeared in those memories. When he'd talked to the companions around him, they'd said the same thing. That made Federico happy. Some people might say that, since it had been a game, that was only natural. Even so, he felt as though it was proof that, to him, Silver Sword was a place to belong and a group of friends he'd never been ashamed of.

…Friends.

It had been a long time since he'd started getting embarrassed about using the word.

At this age, thinking about where the line between "friends" and "acquaintances" fell was a pain in the neck, and even if he'd settled on definitions as far as the words were concerned, human relationships would only be what they were. Federico, a brand-new member of adult society, thought that getting particularly friendly and taking special care to avoid people were equally futile.

When he'd heard the word *friends* from his guild master, a mere high schooler, he'd teared up. The experience had startled him, because his own feelings were a mystery to him.

He might get back to the old world someday.

Maybe he'd return to a life of shuttling back and forth between his house and the office, remember this situation, and think that preparing to die had been ridiculous.

That wouldn't be a bad thing, but if asked whether they could stop in their tracks right now, the answer would have been an emphatic "No." This was a raid zone, and they were raiders.

"Viper Strike!"

Leaping high into the air and using the dark purple gauntlet as a foothold, Federico swung his flamberge sword into Ruseato's arm. Viper Strike didn't inflict much damage, but the "blood loss" icon appeared, and Ruseato's attack hit rate went down. The drop was 4 percent.

Raiders would never say "*only* four percent." That 4 percent might save just as much in recovery spells. It might hold down MP consumption and let them keep fighting, and if Federico let his vanity do the talking, it was a 4 percent that might increase their chances of winning the battle.

Having picked up the role of tank from Naotsugu, Dinclon advanced.

He was one of the mildest-looking guys in Silver Sword, but he was fortified from head to toe in fantasy-class Fantasmal equipment, and his defense was on a level with "Black Sword" Isaac's. In sharp contrast to his usual kind voice, Dinclon was screaming in a way that made Frederico's eardrums tremble. It was War Cry. It had been extended through item effects, and it raised the status abnormality resistance of everyone around him.

Alongside the juddering vibrations, strength infused Federico's body.

Compared to last time, Ruseato seemed almost sluggish. Circling around its back, he kept hitting it with a series of attacks, putting all that strength behind them. Quickly performing special, close-combat skills every which way and piling on damage was an attacker's role. In terms of this particular strategy, the initial sprint was extremely important.

At the western edge of the coliseum, about ten meters away from the battle that surrounded Ruseato of the Seventh Garden, two subdued, metallic sounds rang out.

Ragoumaru, Silver Sword's Samurai, had used Steel-Cutting Sword.

As their advance investigations had shown them, when one of the bars in the gate was severed, it created a gap that a human-sized figure could pass through with relative ease.

Watching this out of the corner of his eye, Federico kept attacking.

Not there yet.

The attackers redoubled their efforts all at once, and their ferocious attacks inflicted considerable damage on Ruseato. There wasn't much Ruseato could do at this point. Naotsugu had negated the badly damaging attack it should have been able to rely on, and it didn't have an attack that could break through Dinclon's formidable defense.

If it asked its friends for help, Federico and the others would be thrashed promptly, but Ruseato hadn't even lost 10 percent of its HP yet. It couldn't possibly call for help yet… But even as he thought this, Federico bit back the fear he held inside.

There were no guarantees. They didn't know when those two raid bosses might force their way in. Or if a different boss might appear, too—there were no guarantees about that, either. All they had were the zone map they'd confirmed through their reconnaissance, and guesses regarding the guardians' system of cooperation.

As time crawled by, Federico and the others attacked and held out, waiting for the operation to begin.

They wanted to win.

Working only from that desire to persevere, they desperately piled on attacks.

Federico's herculean strength swung his beloved sword, Breath of Muspell, like a small typhoon, connecting with Ruseato's armor again and again. Under the red-hot onslaught, the grotesque armor cracked like crystal, and the flying shards of glass cut Federico's bearded face. But that didn't bother him.

Up until now, Federico had never thought of himself as that sort of person, but apparently he liked things to be *fair*.

He'd realized that during this past week.

His desire to win wasn't due to the fact that he wanted to vanquish this tough enemy, or to win glory or treasure. There wasn't a shred of anger or hatred involved.

He only wanted one thing: a just reward.

This was a raid that William wanted to win so badly, his eyes had filled with tears.

It was a battle in which Silver Sword had faced death time after time and pulled through.

He didn't want to think it had all been in vain. He didn't want to think that their attempts had been foolish and pointless. If that were the case, it would be far too tragic.

He bore no grudge against Ruseato. On the contrary: He actually respected it.

All Federico and the rest of Silver Sword wanted was proof, plain and simple.

You aren't wrong. You were right, and you were tough.

That proof was the only thing they wanted.

"Threshold!!"

At William's sharp cry, the buffers and healers started running, detouring. Ruseato of the Seventh Garden was changing. Its cracked armor sloughed off as if it were molting, and its body turned the color of snow: It was transforming into White Knight mode.

The shattered black armor became a shadow-colored swamp and spread, generating countless warriors. The boss's trap zone restricted the movements of all the Adventurers who were inside of it: It was a sticky ranged attack that bound their ankles. Avoiding that area, the raid team changed their formation.

"Hurry! Shiroe's group is the shock team!"

Obeying William's orders, the unit dived into the passage beyond the gate, one after another. At its other end was Ibra Habra of the Third Garden.

Federico's group's counterstrike had begun.

▶ 2

Demiquas was part of the group that had leapt into the western passage first.

The high-ceilinged granite passage, which was decorated with enormous columns, continued in a straight line. Further down, the passage was misty with twilight, but through reconnaissance, they'd learned that the flaming serpent Ibra Habra was in a great cavern at its end.

Demiquas looked around restlessly, but Naotsugu had taken off running straight ahead. Dem followed after, as if chasing him.

As a Guardian, Naotsugu protected his body with metal armor, and to Demiquas, he seemed like a sluggish turtle. He looked like he was hurrying desperately, but his speed was only half Demiquas's, who wore light equipment. If Demiquas got serious and used Phantom Step or Wyvern Kick, he could leave him behind in the space of a breath.

However, if he did that, Dem would end up charging the raid boss first. In order to avoid that, although it was really irritating, he had to stay behind with the turtle.

The party was traveling in a column, with Naotsugu and Demiquas in the lead.

The First party had put Dinclon, the team's main tank, at the back and was retreating, blocking the shadow warriors as it went. They probably couldn't move fast. While the main defensive party was dealing with the enemies that followed them, it was Demiquas's group's job to take the lead in their place.

The beginning of the strategy was simple.

During that hellish annihilation, Ibra Habra of the Third Garden and Tartaulga of the Fourth Garden had *opened* the lattice gates and appeared.

Their sizes wouldn't allow them to pass through a gap in the bars. In addition, those gates, which were like enormous cages, could only be opened from inside the passages.

If this had been ordinary raid content, both gates would probably have been unlocked after they'd defeated Ruseato of the Seventh Garden, but the current situation was different.

This strategy took advantage of the dungeon's construction.

In short, the point of the strategy was to isolate and imprison Ruseato in the coliseum. With the gates down, Ruseato couldn't get into the passages from the coliseum. It couldn't chase the party that had run into the western passage. Of course they couldn't state positively that it wouldn't break the gate down and get in that way, so they'd lured it into White Knight mode, where its offensive abilities were low. They'd taken into account the fact that when in White Knight mode, Ruseato couldn't move unless all the shadow warriors were destroyed.

They'd already scouted the conditions beyond this point, using a stealthy summon beast to sneak in through the gap in the gate. They'd been filled in on the strategy, with explanations tailored for several different situations. In the very luckiest situation, things would go like this:

Practically speaking, since Ruseato couldn't get through the gate or destroy it, it had been rendered powerless. Tartaulga, the frost giant at the end of the eastern passage, might be able to open the east gate and get into the coliseum, but for the same reason as Ruseato, it wouldn't be able to open the west gate. For all intents and purposes, they weren't part of the active forces. Demiquas's group would defeat the fiery serpent Ibra Habra, advance past it to reach the very deepest part of this zone, and conquer the dungeon.

However, none of the raid members thought they'd be able to win that easily.

Even if they defeated Ibra Habra, there was no guarantee that there wouldn't be another raid boss beyond it. According to Shiroe, the dungeon was built in such a way that if you took enough of a detour, it would be possible to get this far from the eastern passage without going through the gates. If the battle got difficult for Ibra Habra, there was no doubt that Tartaulga of the Fourth Garden would come running immediately.

In the first place, the idea that neither Ruseato nor Tartaulga could destroy the iron gates was no more than wishful thinking. They would probably slow them down, but they had to consider the possibility that they'd break through. And, once they had broken through, the gates would have been destroyed, and they wouldn't be able to use this strategy again.

That was right: Demiquas and the other Adventurers might be able to resurrect, but the situation was changing constantly. They'd never get the same opportunity twice. The members of Silver Sword knew this, and as they ran down the passage, there was great tension in the air.

Dammit!

However, that was only natural.

There was no such thing as a stable, perfectly predictable future. That was how the world worked, and even grade school kids knew it. There were unstable elements in every plan, and the danger that someone else would intervene was always there. Wake up on Sunday morning and eat breakfast while watching TV: How many times did even simple things like that go the way you'd planned? As long as you were alive, plans would fall apart; that was just how it went.

Here in *Elder Tales*, they'd forgotten about that entirely. They'd gotten it into their heads that this was a game, and they'd assumed everything would go the way they wanted. Since they *could* do anything, they'd gotten the illusion that it was *okay* to do anything.

And then Shiroe had flattened them.

Demiquas had learned his lesson: This place, where things didn't always go according to plan, was reality, beyond a doubt. However, even after he'd learned that, he'd fallen for the illusion over and over again. He'd been deceived by the world's humble, gamelike surface. That had been the case this time as well. He'd steeled himself over and over, warning himself never to let his guard down, and yet, as if it were a leaky faucet, his caution had drained away, and he'd underestimated things.

In other words, I got careless and lost. I lost because I sold them short… I lost because I treated them lightly.

He remembered a skinny girl looking at him, her hands on her hips.

Her expression was sour. She probably despised Demiquas. That was only natural. Demiquas had done terrible things to the People of the Earth. He hadn't actually killed any of them, but he'd gotten violent and sold them and forced them to work. There was no way they'd like him. The difference in their health was the only reason they never tried to punch him.

She was a girl like chicken bones, not sexy at all. She'd fixed intense, glaring eyes on him, and had smiled sardonically. *If all you're going to do is talk as if you're my master, hurry up and kill me.* She'd said that all the time. *If you're not going to kill me, then get out of my way. I can't clean with you there.* She'd told him that, too.

That time, Demiquas had lost completely.

When People of the Earth died, they died. This was the only life she had, and she knew it, but she risked it anyway. She was betting her entire paltry existence in order to get her own way. Demiquas's cheap life really couldn't hope to equal that.

He'd underestimated this other world.

He'd thought it was just a game and gotten conceited, and that was why he'd lost to Shiroe.

Before he'd managed to straighten out that mistaken impression, he'd lost to this Person of the Earth, who should have been powerless.

He'd lost to Silver Sword, too. They'd rolled him the first time he'd run into them in the tavern, and had made him lick the floor many more times after that. And then the Briganteers had been wiped out.

Then he'd lost to the raid bosses, too, and if that had been all, there might still have been hope, but he'd even lost to William as a guild master. Even after being annihilated like that, that gaming addict still had twenty friends who'd follow him.

Demiquas had been left with nothing.

The passage, which had been pieced together from white stone, abruptly came to an end.

The ceiling, which had been high to begin with, rose to the height of a six-story building: They'd leapt out into a large, round, natural space. It was a huge cavern with a thirty-meter radius, shaped like an upright egg.

The area was made of ochre rock with vivid orange spots. A sloping road several meters wide had been built into the rock wall, making it possible to walk down it in a spiral. There were blue puddles of water in places. The colors in the cave were startlingly bright, and it was illuminated by white light.

"That smell…"

"Yeah, hot-springs city."

Naotsugu answered Shiroe, who was behind them, and Demiquas understand what he meant. It was the smell of sulfur. If these vivid rocks had been colored with sulfur and chemicals, it made sense.

The group ran down the spiral outer gallery. Ibra Habra was lying on the floor of the great cavern; it seemed to be asleep.

That was probably how this raid boss looked when it was on standby.

As they'd discussed in previous meetings, Naotsugu leapt down the last section of slope, heading for the great serpent.

He didn't have much support, but they didn't have enough extra time to make careful preparations, and were acting accordingly.

With Tetora's Reactive Heal and Voinen's Heartbeat Healing at his back, he charged. Even to Demiquas, it was a brilliant rush that betrayed no hesitation.

As if to shake free of the self that seemed liable to cringe back, Demiquas also leapt into the air. The members of Silver Sword followed suit, jumping down one after another and joining the fray.

Immediately, it turned into a melee.

The cave-like road that sloped downhill from a corner of this great cavern was probably what they were after. At its end was the deepest part of this zone, the goal. However, there was no convenient gate at the cave's entrance, and they couldn't split their group up any further. They had to dispose of Ibra Habra here, and they had to do it before Tartaulga showed up as reinforcement.

The long-range attack party loosed ice spells in rapid succession, as if they were impatient.

Demiquas swore, but Naotsugu seemed to have managed to hold the boss.

It was like a firestorm headed straight for him, a scene more like some sort of disaster or accident site than a monster. In the midst of this, the "city" fiend in his metal armor belted out an Anchor Howl, desperately wielding his sword to whip up aggro. Even Demiquas had learned that right now, when the battle had just begun, the aggro the monster directed at the tank was unstable. The attackers wanted to inflict damage as quickly as possible, and he could understand that, but if they got hasty, the target might get switched and they'd have an accident on their hands.

"Fortress Stance! Lemme see what my new shield and armor can do!"

Naotsugu lowered his hips solidly, standing as if he were shouldering a wall. The technique, which made a blue aura erupt from beneath his feet, was a defensive attitude of the sort Guardians—aka "armored scarecrows"—were particularly good at. While he held up his massive shield to restrain the enemy, he paid out attacks from behind it with a longsword. In exchange for taking his mobility, this technique improved his defense, which wasn't something martial artists like Demiquas had.

However, Demiquas also had an ability Naotsugu lacked: the wings known as maneuverability.

"Uoooooooooh! Aura Saber!"

From midair, Demiquas brought down a kick armed with golden light.

The attack drew a large arc like an ax, stabbing into the flaming serpent's blazing outer hide. There was no way it wasn't working. The characteristics of the Aura Saber special skill made it possible to inflict damage that wasn't really affected by defensive power. Besides, thanks to the Druid's Energy Protection, the damage from the flames was considerably reduced. At the very least, he wouldn't end up near death every time he attacked.

Demiquas used Wyvern Step to dodge the compact-bus-sized tail Ibra Habra of the Third Garden swung around at him. He leapt into the air, then unleashed Wyvern Kick, as if trailing an afterimage behind him.

Wyvern Kick.

And another Wyvern Kick.

Heavy impacts that seemed to pierce through his brain traveled up from the soles of his Sturm Assaulter Sabaton Boots, which seemed to have been carved out of lumps of metal. If he'd done this serial strike attack in Susukino, he could have reduced a ruined building to a genuine mountain of rubble. And it wasn't just him. Beside Demiquas, who was punching through with green light, Federico swung his flamberge over and over, and the other close-range attackers from the raid team were holding fast to Ibra Habra. From the monster's perspective, it must have looked like midgets swarming a giant.

Suddenly, Demiquas's feet began to shine silver.

It was Shiroe's reinforcement spell, Keen Edge.

Damn bastard!

Demiquas clicked his tongue in irritation. He would have liked to spit, but the heat from the fiery serpent had left his mouth bone-dry. Instead, since Ibra Habra had come around in front of him, Demiquas slammed his elbow into the underside of its enormous jaw. Tiger Echo Fist. Its hit rate was bad, but when he was up against a huge raid boss, it was possible to use even this technique any way he wanted.

A reptilian eye, white and cloudy as moonstone, looked down at Demiquas, turning inorganic murderous intent on him.

"Wide range, get back!!"

At William's order, the front line backed away all at once, but Demiquas stood tall and crossed his arms in front of his eyes. He was planning to block the flame attack with those arms.

This wasn't out of contempt or carelessness. It was Demiquas's way of showing his resolve.

As he was engulfed by the storm of flames Ibra Habra spat out, Demiquas never even blinked.

In front of Naotsugu, flames roiled. Unlike when viewed on a game screen, the venomous crimson seemed sticky, and it swallowed Naotsugu up like a raging beast.

However, even in the midst of that purgatory, Naotsugu narrowed his eyes and maintained his stance, leaning slightly forward.

True, his entire body was hot. Of course it was: He was being burned by flames. However, on the other hand, that heat was only about what he would have felt if he'd gotten naked on asphalt under a blazing midsummer sky. There was a sizzling sensation on his skin, but it was nothing he couldn't get through.

There were currents and waves in the flames, and Naotsugu observed them calmly. When he spotted a gap, he sucked in a huge lungful of air. He'd been holding his breath, as if he were swimming underwater. He'd done it out of caution, to keep his lungs from burning, but if it was like this, he probably wouldn't be lethally injured even if he did breathe some in.

Besides, that big-headed Monk's pretty awesome.

Tetora's Reactive Heal, Voinen's Pulse Recovery, and Touko's Damage Interception barrier were all currently active on Naotsugu. These pseudorecovery spells were called "class heals." That last range burning attack, Merciless Banquet of Purgatory, had been powerful. The Kannagi's Damage Interception barrier had negated about six thousand of its damage, and he'd regained about nine hundred with the Cleric's Reactive Heal, but even so, with damage on this scale, they weren't enough. It wouldn't have been at all odd for that last attack to put Naotsugu at death's door.

Demiquas had been the one to shoulder that damage for him.

It had probably been Covering, a special technique that took over damage for group members who were a short distance away. Demiquas, a Monk, had more resistance to attribute attacks than Naotsugu did, and the sheer amount of his HP was high. If the damage was spread out like it was now, Naotsugu could stay on the front line. Naotsugu's opinion of Demiquas went up, just a little.

"Awright, one more! Taunting Blow!"

In order to earn more aggro, Naotsugu hit Ibra Habra with a special attack.

This huge, fiery serpent was definitely scary. When its enormous head came at you, it was like facing down a charging dump truck, and its dark red, gaping mouth had the aggressive impact of construction equipment. Since all this came your way at the speed of a train wreck, your legs went weak, and your vision narrowed.

However, as if to shake off that force, Naotsugu drew his lips into the shape of a smile.

It was just bravado. He didn't really have the leeway to smile.

That said, leeway was always vague. If you thought you didn't have it, you didn't; and if you thought you had it, you did. Even when you had all sorts of time on a three-day weekend, you'd never have the leeway to clean and polish the kitchen, and when book-balancing hell meant you had to sleep at the office, you had enough leeway to search convenience stores for their new, private-brand pudding. It was like that.

And so, if he managed to smile, he'd have leeway. Even if he didn't have it, he'd generate it.

Believing this, Naotsugu swung his sword again.

He shouted a taunt, raised his shield, took a defensive stance, and didn't give an inch.

He was smiling fearlessly. To Naotsugu, that was what the first defender in a raid did.

"Okay!"

Naotsugu's short yell must have told William everything. He issued an order from the rear ranks: "Circle around to the left and inflict damage!"

Naotsugu's smile deepened. Just as he'd thought, William understood.

Well, it had been more than three weeks since they'd first invaded Abyssal Shaft. That time had made it possible for them to understand each other. By now, Naotsugu could tell what William was thinking. William must be able to tell what Naotsugu wanted as well.

Recovery spells washed over Naotsugu one after another, and his HP began to rise.

In spite of Demiquas's quick-witted move, his total HP had fallen to 30 percent or so. Unlike Demiquas, who'd stepped in to shield him temporarily, Naotsugu had been targeted by powerful normal attacks without a break. Scales that stood on end like spikes were fired at him over and over. Recovering Naotsugu's HP to reduce the damage from that, and to get him ready for the big next attack, was necessary for the safety of the entire team. Consequently, Naotsugu didn't stand on ceremony, either.

In the midst of the astoundingly fierce battle, Naotsugu was remembering the past.

Of course, compared to this other world, it might have been just a game, but Naotsugu had been the Debauchery Tea Party's main tank. It wasn't that he had no raid experience. On the contrary: The Tea Party had gone on a shocking number of raids. In the first place, when it came to raids, Kanami had tended to disregard even victory and defeat. The woman had considered raid battles to be on the same level as removing obstacles to sightseeing. She'd even meddled in raid captures on an overseas server just "to see new vistas," so there was really nothing to do but laugh.

"Hoh! Hup!"

His new equipment, Armor of Silver Oath, had been reliable. The connections all over his body were smooth, so it felt stable. There were no parts that flapped and bounced up. Guard of Lionheart was brilliant, too. Compared to what they'd been before, the shocks transmitted to his arm had softened remarkably. If things were like this, he thought he could probably keep this fierce battle up for hours. If he guided the points of light that sparkled in his vision to the center of the shield, he could repel even Ibra Habra's tail without backing up. He could feel that his defense had risen considerably.

"I'm nowhere near done yet! Bring-it-on city!" he yelled roughly.

"Yowzers! Naotsugu, you're really into this!"

Tetora, who'd come in close again before he was aware of it, called to him musingly.

Leaning forward even farther to shield Tetora from the flames, Naotsugu yelled back: "Leave it to me! This's nothing!" Tetora set a hand on Naotsugu's shoulder and jumped up, then called to the great hall in a carrying voice.

"Hey, team! Are you into this?"

The fighting was fierce, and no voices responded to Tetora. However, everyone was watching her. Of course they were: Since they were attacking Ibra Habra of the Third Garden, the target they needed to defeat, they were watching Naotsugu, who was taking all of its ferocious attacks by himself, and Tetora was yelling at the battlefield over his shoulder.

A rumbling echo filled the cavern. It was the raid team's will, responding to the little idol's question with desperate effort from each member. Swords and axes were brought down in rapid succession, and ice and lightning attacks battered the enormous monster.

Smiling at the cacophony, Tetora thrust the baton in her right hand high into the air, an expression of defiance on her face.

"Okay, here we go! C'mon, everybody, do your best! You *can* do your best, so do it!"

Tetora's brave voice rang out so well it nearly made them forget they were underground. After rising to the heavens, her voice showered down over her companions.

High in the air, light swelled, and a rainbow-colored aurora appeared. Curtains of light shimmered, holding countless falling stars inside, and gentle music played. Aurora Heal was a special spell. Of the many recovery spells held by the three recovery classes in *Elder Tales*, Aurora Heal was the only spell geared specifically for raids. Its recovery range included every one of their companions that were gathered under the aurora, and even if there were a hundred of them, it administered healing light to all of them.

"That's-real-generous city!"

"Of course it is: I'm an angel!"

Beaming, the Cleric paid out spells in rapid succession, twirling around as she did so. Her speed was even greater than that of the Silver

Sword Recovery classes, who had to be very skilled. She was probably getting support from Shiroe to do it, but it was a magnificent display of raiderly behavior.

As if riding that momentum, Naotsugu also paid out attack after attack.

So far, everything was going without a hitch. Apparently, as Shiroe had anticipated, Ibra Habra of the Third Garden had lower maximum HP than Ruseato of the Seventh. It also couldn't recover by changing its shape. Ibra Habra's specialties were ranged attacks and an area of scorching heat that made you lose health just by getting close to it.

However, since they'd anticipated that, the team had changed into all the fire-resistant equipment they had with them, and they were being supplied with appropriate support spells. Ibra Habra had prodigious HP, but they'd already shaved away half of it. If they kept on inflicting damage this way, they should be able to defeat it.

Not that I'm gonna help it out by getting careless.

Even as Naotsugu kept a close eye on the fiery serpent's movements, he paid attention to the situation around him.

"Great job!"

"Yeppers, just leave it to me!"

He wasn't only talking to Tetora. He was sending a message to everyone around him.

They could trust their shield. The feeling of confidence that he was still fine was necessary for a raid tank.

If it had been possible to solve difficulties with the simple emotions "We can do this" or "We should be able to do this," no one would ever have trouble. They wouldn't need Shiroe's plans. However, on the other hand, one single thought of "We're losing" or "We might lose this one" could lead to actual defeat in raids.

If it was to energize his comrades, he'd raise a shout or even put on an act.

He felt a hand on his shoulder, and a soft warmth that was completely different from the heat of the flames spread through his body. Tetora's Small Recovery was at work. In order to exercise her Cleric's recovery abilities to the greatest extent possible, this little hand had come to the front line, where flames raged, and kept Naotsugu company with her usual cheerful backchat.

Tetora understood, too: This trifling dialogue turned into power for the entire group. Naotsugu knew this, and it put him in a good mood. He managed to give a real smile, instead of one that was just meant to reassure everyone.

"Naotsugu, have you fallen for me?"

"Absolutely *nyet*!"

"Isn't this the scene where we get set up for all sorts of interesting future developments?"

"You-just-shot-the-whole-thing-to-heck-with-that-line city."

The tail was thrust at them like a spear. As Naotsugu used the points of light his shield showed him to deflect its tip to the side, he answered Tetora's playful query in the negative. The question made him worry whether she really understood. Wanting to demand that she give back the warm feelings he'd had up until a minute ago, Naotsugu shot a sidelong glare at Tetora.

"I have a report for you, Naotsugu."

"At a friggin' busy time like this? What is it, huh?"

"Well, if it *wasn't* a time like this, it would be hard to bring up."

Tetora was wriggling restlessly, purposefully saying "Fidget, fidget" out loud, but Naotsugu kept on fighting ferociously. As he used his hands and feet to deflect broken sulfur rocks so that they wouldn't go Tetora's way, he humored her, tentatively: "So? What is it?"

"As a matter of fact, I'm joining Log Horizon."

"Huh?"

Passing the stage where he could get by with looking at her out of the corner of his eye, Naotsugu turned.

There was Tetora, her expression as full of self-confidence as ever and her cheeks flushed red.

"Liar city."

"I'm serious."

"Why?"

"To play with you, Naotsugu." The self-proclaimed idol snickered mischievously while firing off several Heals in a row. She was in an incredibly good mood. Every time she cast a recovery spell, she tapped at the armor over Naotsugu's side in a kittenish gesture, of which he really didn't approve.

"Whose permission did you get to make that happen?!"

"Why, Shiroe's."

"Hey, Shiro! That-was-uncalled-for city!"

…But they couldn't just keep telling funny stories like this.

Ibra Habra had reared upright like a theme park monument and it opened its mouth wide, inhaling. Air and fire were sucked in with a roar. It was the preliminary action necessary for Merciless Banquet of Purgatory, the massively damaging ranged attack that they'd lasted through a short while ago.

"Here it comes!"

"Vanguard, fall back! Federico, stay there and keep debuffing. Cut down the damage!"

Naotsugu and William yelled it almost simultaneously.

Their formation changed yet again. The raid team's close-range attack unit rolled back like the tide.

They were getting out of the firestorm's range of attack to reduce the overall damage. Decreasing the damage meant more than making things easier for the healers; it was also important if they were going to save their MP.

However, the formation shift was disturbed.

Azalea, the Summoner from the Fourth party who'd been conducting long-range attacks, tripped and fell on what looked like open ground, then screamed something, although Naotsugu couldn't make out what it was. At that warning, William snapped out an order: "Dinclon to the rear!!"

With speed that didn't leave time for even a hasty reorganization, a new battle began.

There were two openings in this huge subterranean cavern. One was the white granite corridor up above, through which Naotsugu and the others had entered. The other was the cave passage that extended from the lower part of the cavern.

An enormous savage warrior wearing a coarse pelt, the pale frost giant Tartaulga of the Fourth Garden, had appeared from that cave passage and joined the fight.

4

Saying there was no disturbance in the great hall would have been a lie.

After they'd experienced that devastating annihilation earlier, this was only natural. However, that frozen instant was immediately dissolved by William's exhortation.

The Guardian Dinclon, Silver Sword's pride, leapt forward like a bullet, rushed at the frost giant and used Castle of Stone. A club that seemed as if its diameter alone might be several meters wide swung at him sideways, but the elf warrior slapped it down as if it were a joke and took up a position in the entrance to the passage. As you'd expect from a seasoned raider, there was no wasted motion in his actions.

Pushing up his glasses, which had been jostled out of place by the exercise, Shiroe wiped away the sweat that dripped from his forehead. Now his second prediction had come true.

Apparently Ruseato of the Seventh Garden wasn't able to open the gates in the coliseum. However, Ibra Habra and Tartaulga, who protected their own positions to the far east and west of the coliseum, could enter it, and they could also go through inner passages and reach each other's locations without entering it.

Even if they outwitted Ruseato, they'd have to deal with the fiery serpent Ibra Habra and Tartaulga the frost giant at the same time. That had been within his predictions. Considered in ordinary terms, that would have meant a stalemate. There was no full raid anywhere that could stop attacks from two raid bosses and not be destroyed. Their attacks were far too overwhelming.

But was that really the case?

In the instant when he'd awoken, Shiroe had doubted it, and had hit on this plan.

Part of the reason Silver Sword and Shiroe's group had been annihilated in the coliseum showdown was because they'd been confused by a situation they hadn't anticipated—the raid bosses joining forces—and their teamwork had been disrupted. However, if you looked at the damage on its own, the reason was because they'd taken a wide-range flame attribute attack from Ibra Habra and a wide-range cold attribute attack from the frost giant Tartaulga simultaneously. Either one would have been a lethal attack as far as the rear guard was concerned; if they took both at once, death was their only option.

However, if it had been just one of the two, wouldn't the vanguard have been able to last through it?

Shiroe remembered Ruseato's attacks, and he didn't think a raid boss in the same zone would have attack power that far surpassed that. It might be *more* than that, but it couldn't possibly be double. He concluded that it wouldn't be impossible to last through attacks from either Ibra Habra or Tartaulga.

The conclusion Shiroe had reached was that, *provided the raid bosses' ranges didn't overlap*, it would be possible to bear up under their attacks, and this formed the framework of his strategy.

This vast underground cavern was spacious enough to allow for that. Naotsugu had positioned himself by the southwest wall and was holding back Ibra Habra's attacks, while Dinclon, the Guardian who'd supported Silver Sword, had Tartaulga pinned at the entrance to the corridor in the northeast.

The two shields adjusted their positions, protecting each other from ranged attacks.

This position adjustment was fairly harsh. Each of them had their own dedicated healers, but that wasn't enough. It was necessary for several mobile healers to recover Naotsugu and Dinclon, traveling back and forth as needed, but the distance between the two was too wide, and they tended to be too late. The farther apart they were, the greater their safe zone against ranged attacks, but then the recovery spells wouldn't reach them.

If they tried to keep the distance to a bare minimum, the safe zone that kept them from getting caught up in ranged attacks from either boss in this huge cavern was bound to disappear. For the rear guard spellcasters and archers, it would turn into a touch-and-go battle where they had to make constant, fine position adjustments to keep away from the ranged attacks that both bosses would keep sending at them.

However, on hearing Shiroe's strategy, William had smiled a hero's smile and told him:

I bet we'll win, Shiroe.

Now, as if to prove those words, even as "Mithril Eyes" launched nonstop attacks so rapidly they seemed to be an unbroken line, he was issuing rapid-fire orders.

Shiroe also held nothing back as he fought.

This was no time to stand on ceremony.

True, they'd manage to check the attacks from the two terrible raid bosses. However, it had been done through Dinclon's use of his surefire technique, Castle of Stone. For that reason, in the first battle, they'd gone with a strategy that let him avoid using that technique. In order to stabilize the combat situation, they had to support the two shields with recovery spells; there were only six Recovery classes on the team, and this meant going through their MP at a furious pace. Having anticipated this situation, the members had used their spells in moderation up until now, but if they kept trying to economize from this point on, the vanguards would probably lose their lives. This was a tightrope battle now: If the shields fell, the front line would crumble, and if that happened, they'd be wiped out immediately.

If that happened, their hopes in this zone would be dashed.

"Federico, attack power decrease buff, ranged attack decrease buff."

"On it."

"Miss Tetora, increase your recovery output."

"I can't raise it any higher!"

"I'll support you. —Force Step!"

Shiroe fired a special support spell at Tetora. It accelerated all the recast timers she had. The speed increase was a little under 20 percent, but that certainly wasn't a small number. Aurora Heal's recast time was generally six hundred seconds. If he kept Force Step up without a break, she'd be able to use it again in 480 seconds. This would increase the speed at which her MP was consumed, but Shiroe supplemented this as well, using Mana Siphon. It was an Enchanter special control skill that gave the Enchanter's own MP to a companion.

In a party battle where they were hunting in the ordinary way, MP could be recovered with relative ease by resting. As such, it was easy to disregard Enchanters' ability to control and recover MP.

However, Shiroe loved that rare characteristic, and he'd cultivated it constantly.

In the midst of the dizzying sensation of MP loss, Shiroe kept on attacking, gauging and supplying MP. He provided Recovery classes like Tetora and Voinen with recovery reinforcement, and attackers like Federico and Demiquas with attack reinforcement. Experiencing the battlefield with all of his expanded senses, Shiroe turned his attention to the details.

"Over here!"

Voinen plunged an arm into a puddle that seethed with the smell of sulfur and released a long chant. It was a particularly unique variety of the servant summonings that Druids used. The light that stretched from his fur arm guard spread its branches high into the air, as if seeking the atmosphere, then suddenly turned green and solid. It was Life Sequoia, a summoning technique that Druids—whom nature and the spirits served—could contract with on high-level raids.

"Team Four, close in!"

As if even William's order hadn't come fast enough for them, spellcasters gathered in the shade of the great tree.

This summoning technique, Life Sequoia, manifested as a leaf-covered redwood tree with magic power. Its shade was filled with green light, and it continuously recovered the HP of allies in the area. The amount of recovery was several rungs lower than the Heals the actual Druid used, but it had the supreme advantage of being able to recover all the companions who were close to the tree over the long term.

Shiroe calculated.

The sharp eyes behind his glasses held combat operations beyond what Minori had performed, and his thoughts stretched toward the future.

Twenty-four people was four times as large as the party of six that Minori had handled. However, simply quadrupling the number of people made the combinations of their special skills and actions increase explosively. He examined each of these possibilities, pruned them away, picked them up, or combined and "read" them.

Each single swing in his companions' attacks; each drop of recovery.

The changes in enemy threat level brought about by the surging accumulation of weakening spells, or "debuffs." The invisible remaining aggro, and the flexibility of the action options its leeway gave them.

Inside Shiroe, his companions' constantly changing HP was like an equalizer panel.

Shiroe sensed the currents in the battle's shrinking time line and differentiated them.

"Naotsugu, speed up!"

"Roger that!"

"Voinen, fall back."

"Understood."

Individually, each was only a "sentence."

Strung together, they became "text" that had an objective.

Naotsugu's face rose in the back of Shiroe's mind. Tetora's smile, too, and William's wry, obstinate grin. Federico, Voinen, Demiquas. The members of Silver Sword.

Unconsciously, Shiroe nodded deeply.

He understood what William had said.

The battle had become a "story," and had reached Shiroe.

It was a march to stir up hearts that seemed about to falter and keep them moving forward.

Shiroe had brushed against the thing William had called a secret. It had been made of the same stuff as the old, familiar peace of mind that had surrounded him in the Tea Party.

Shiroe had released all of the calculations he called a full-control encounter, and a humming spell flew from his White Staff of Ruined Wings. Karma Drive split the air like a great bird, striking Ibra Habra and ejecting a burst of countless shining icons.

Fifteen percent...Sixteen percent...Eighteen percent...

Shiroe bit his lip, focusing his mind.

Voinen's Servant Summoning: Life Sequoia had been a good move. With that spell, they could cover more than 30 percent of the HP of a total of ten people.

The fiery serpent's Merciless Banquet of Purgatory ranged attack seemed to come roughly once every 180 seconds. They'd get through the next one with Voinen's Mercy Rain and Life Burst. The next one would be in 360 seconds. They'd negate it with Naotsugu's Castle of Stone, since its recast time would be recovered. For the one after that, in 540 seconds, Tetora's Aurora Heal would have recovered.

In the midst of concentration so deep his field of vision seemed to have lost all color, Shiroe finished his reading.

Before they reached 720 seconds, it would be possible to destroy Ibra Habra of the Third Garden. The effect of Shiroe's Karma Drive would recover the MP of companions who'd landed critical hits on the serpent. If that output shifted the damage, they'd be able to finish off Ibra Habra in seven hundred seconds at the latest.

After that, they'd turn all their fighting power on the frost giant Tartaulga and take it down.

In terms of their remaining MP resources, this was a battle with very little leeway, but they could win by a narrow margin.

It might be thin ice, but it was the possibility of victory.

He'd keep the calculations that could get them there uninterrupted until the very end. Shutting his overheating heart into an icebox, Shiroe made a request:

"Keep the damage output at this level, please."

"You heard Machiavelli, people! Get the lead out, crush 'im! Don't you dare hold back!!"

Just as William issued that order to the group, ominous black clumps dropped into the hall.

Plop.

Plop.

They stuck to the ground, then stood up and, with inhuman movements, leveled their weapons.

An advance party of shadows—warriors born from fragments of Ruseato of the Seventh Garden. Their fighting potential was far below the boss's, but even so, they could take on several Adventurers easily.

Choking back a scream, Shiroe hastily looked up. What he saw was jet-black darkness, seeping out of the gallery that led to the coliseum. The darkness, which had spread across the ceiling, hung down, forming drops like heavy oil, and then released the shadow warriors.

True, Ruseato probably couldn't get through the barred gate.

However, the dark, human-sized soldiers it generated had slipped through the gap in the gate, just as Shiroe and the others had, and had appeared on this battlefield.

▶ **5**

This wasn't a development Shiroe hadn't seen coming.

The shadow warriors were kin produced by Ruseato. Shiroe had anticipated that, and once the battle had begun, they would follow the Adventurer party in here. However, he'd expected a handful of warriors that had escaped defeat. The stain that spread over the ceiling was vast, and there were far too many of the shadows.

The number of shadow warriors generated is equal to the number of people who inflicted damage on Black Ruseato.

Shiroe was the one who'd seen through that.

In this battle, they'd finished subjugating all the shadow warriors who had pursued them out of the coliseum by the time they began their attack on Ibra Habra of the Third Garden. As that was the case, the number of shadow warriors serving Ruseato should have been zero.

Then, since Shiroe and the others had moved on, there shouldn't have been anyone left to inflict damage on Ruseato. Ruseato shouldn't have been able to generate shadow warriors again. There was no reason for this many to exist—

At that point, Shiroe arrived at a single possibility:

Ruseato had run itself through with its own halberd.

Having inflicted damage, it had created one shadow warrior.

Then that warrior and Ruseato itself had inflicted damage on the black armor again, gaining two more kin. Then they'd repeated the process. Ruseato had obtained an army by sacrificing itself—something which hadn't been possible before—and that army was the black shadow that had seeped out of the passage.

"Vanguard!"

That thought left Shiroe in less than a moment, and his mouth screamed instructions.

Just a little longer. He wouldn't ask for seven hundred seconds. If they had six hundred seconds, they could defeat Ibra Habra. Then they'd have excess manpower. They had to buy that time.

How long had it taken them to reach this great cavern? How much time had passed since they'd started fighting? If Ruseato created shadow warriors once every two hundred seconds or so, and their numbers kept doubling, how many were there now? Thirty-one. At most, sixty-three… The answer to his calculations came at once. If it was the latter number, all he had for that was despair, but it it was the former, they probably still had a slim chance. Even as he was embarrassed by that *probably*, Shiroe yelled:

"Charge and kite them—"

This maneuver was the equivalent of a suicide order. Junzou of Silver Sword was on the verge of responding to Shiroe's order—the order to drag shadow warriors along behind him and run—but a powerful raider jumped out and beat him to it.

"Gwaaaaaaaaaaaaah! Move it! Phantom Step! Wyvern Kick! Aaaaaaaah! Taunting Shout!!!!"

Pulling off a two-stage jump as though he'd managed to find a foothold somewhere in midair, Demiquas leapt into space like a rocket, then spun like a top, screaming. It was the howl that the warrior classes used to taunt. Although it was only for an instant, Shiroe saw that Demiquas had captured the attention of all the shadow warriors.

As Shiroe and the other raid members looked up, the long-haired Monk, who'd shifted from his moment of stasis into a fall, seemed to be looking for Shiroe, an expression of rage on his face. He moved so fast that Shiroe lost sight of him, and in that instant, his stance fell apart.

With no idea what had happened, Shiroe rose up, then felt himself yanked backward at overwhelming speed.

"——!!"

He knew Naotsugu was yelling something. However, in the midst of the receding scenery, he couldn't catch the words.

Apparently he was traveling through the enormous cavern at tremendous speed. As if he'd been thrown into a washing machine with a giant drum, Shiroe went through a series of abrupt accelerations and slowdowns.

A shadow warrior suddenly appeared in front of the stunned Shiroe and attempted to bring its great scythe down on him, but his vision rolled sickeningly, and the warrior was blown away. The culprit was a huge greave with a fiendish silhouette.

"Get lost! Phantom Step!!"

Leaving behind a group of enemies that was about to close ranks, Demiquas leapt into the air again.

He had Shiroe by the scruff of the neck and was swinging him around.

"What are you—"

"Shaddup, ya damn four-eyes! Wyvern Kick!"

The hot, stinking blood that splattered across his cheek calmed Shiroe down.

He didn't know whether Demiquas was planning to smash up the raid and get revenge on him this late in the game, or whether he actually had an idea that could help them win. However, it was a fact that Demiquas had grabbed Shiroe by the back of the neck and was treating him like prey he'd bagged.

Still, this situation… This might not be bad…

If you looked at it from another angle, Shiroe was fixed artillery that had been equipped to Demiquas.

Once he'd realized that, there was just one thing to do. Shiroe scattered Enchanter spells, the ones that were ridiculed for being weak, around the area.

Demiquas was probably using Drag Move. It was a special technique meant to be used on one enemy in a group; it made them target you, regardless of aggro, and you dragged them along as you moved. Either that, or he was using his arm strength, which was past level 90, and simply carrying Shiroe like luggage. With Adventurers' extraordinary health, this would be possible. It could be either one.

However, the important thing now was to tear the shadow warriors away from the main raid team.

"Head for the northeastern passage!"

"Shove it! What're you bossing me around for?!"

"Mind Bolt!"

"Damn Enc!"

Still, even as he swore at him, Demiquas seemed to have changed his course.

He kicked the black, smooth, featureless shapes away, bulling through them, and headed for the passage even as countless enemies targeted him. Shiroe put together information from his violently rocking field of vision. He'd managed to confirm about twenty warriors. If he took the ones outside his field of vision into account, there were probably around thirty. If Demiquas stood still, even if he had support from recovery spells, he'd be rendered unable to fight in fifteen seconds. Without support, it would be half that. Shiroe didn't even want to think about what it would be like for him, but the answer to that had been clear ever since he started playing *Elder Tales*: He'd be lucky to last three seconds.

"Shiroe, hey!"

A shadow had been bearing down on him, its attitude low, ready to leap at him, but its head swelled, then burst like a watermelon.

William had sniped it and finished it off.

"You don't need to cover for us. Defeat Ibra Habra, please."

"*Look*, Machiavelli—"

"William! Take down the enemy!"

Shiroe didn't know what his voice had managed to convey to that proud guild master, and he had no confidence in how much emotion he'd managed to load into it. Even so, William squeezed his eyes shut for a moment, his expression anxious, then yelled: "All attack units, concentrate your damage on Ibra Habra! Sorcerers! Don't hold back! Let 'er rip!"

His field of vision flowed as if it were melting, and they dodged past Tartaulga's club.

Ducking his head away from the overwhelming mass that grazed the back of his skull, Shiroe noticed the white film that was approaching their feet.

"That's Tartaulga's Midnight Sun. It's going to disrupt your movement; use fire and—"

"The hell do I care?! Lynx Tumbling!"

Ignoring Shiroe's advice, Demiquas ran as though scoffing at the frozen binding spell. With Lynx Tumbling in him, Demiquas ran up, using the club that had been brought down as a foothold, reached the frost giant's craggy arm, then its shoulder, and kept right on going. Because of the horribly cold air, Tartaulga's breath was always white. Demiquas slammed a foot into its cheek and sped up even further.

This man-powered roller coaster began to run with all the safety devices removed, taking an insane course that would have sent all its opening day riders to the hospital.

Loop, tornado, slalom. Dragging several dozen shadows behind him on invisible threads of aggro, Demiquas launched into a terrifying escape sequence.

Behind them, Shiroe heard a voice scream. He didn't know what it had said. However, he thought it might have been words of encouragement. This was Silver Sword, and the words they'd send at a fellow raider who was leaping into the jaws of death were pretty much a given.

They barreled into the pitch-black passage, and the sounds of the raid battle grew fainter. There were 580 seconds left in the subjugation battle in that big cavern, and it had to go on. Once that ended, they'd need to rescue Dinclon, who was fighting the frost giant.

That meant the two who were racing through the dark passage weren't able to let their guards down for a moment.

For the past little while, Shiroe had been firing the few attack spells he had, one after another.

Astral Bind and Nightmare Sphere. If he hit the shadows with spells that had motion obstruction and petrifying effects, he could delay their pursuit by a few seconds. He couldn't pull in many of them, but his mantle was getting wet and heavy with sweat because of Demiquas, and if he didn't reduce the pressure from their pursuers, Demiquas's HP wouldn't last. Just like his HP, Demiquas's MP was falling rapidly. It was the price of his reckless escape. In any event, it was a stroke of luck that the passage they'd leapt into went downhill. They were both still alive, and the passage went on into darkness.

"Don't use Wyvern Kick for a while, all right?"

Demiquas ignored Shiroe's request.

They could see the first of the shadow warriors, but they seemed to be about thirty meters away. Shiroe abandoned an attack spell he'd started to cast—they were getting out of range—and switched to support spells that focused on transferring MP to Demiquas. In a situation like this, they needed mobility more than attack power. Shiroe concentrated on switching spells, and Demiquas ran flat-out, carrying him away, into the depths of the darkness.

Shiroe didn't know why Demiquas had taken him and run.

As it had turned out, their kiting, which had made good use of restraining spells, was going very well, but he couldn't be sure whether that had been Demiquas's plan or not.

Shiroe didn't understand this outlaw's thoughts in the first place, and he couldn't begin to sympathize with him.

Even now, after they'd lived together on this long raid, although it had faded, stubborn, deep-seated doubt remained.

In ruined Susukino, Demiquas had subjected the People of the Earth to tyranny.

Of course he had no intention of saying that all the blame lay with Demiquas. The confusion and misunderstanding of the Catastrophe had probably given him the impression that this place was just like the world of the game. You could also take the view that he'd been driven by terror, and, to hide that fact, had taken things out on others. He'd heard later that, even when *Elder Tales* had been a game, the Briganteers guild had attracted players with bad manners. Maybe extreme actions stemming from tough talking within the group had become habit.

Shiroe felt a certain persuasiveness in all these circumstances, and he was capable of understanding them. However, even so, deep down, he wasn't convinced.

Demiquas had abused People of the Earth and violated their rights. Shiroe had heard he'd even sold them.

On top of that, he'd stalked Serara and frightened her badly.

Those were tastes Shiroe didn't possess. He couldn't understand them, and he didn't think he could forgive them.

He didn't like this guy. That had always been Shiroe's evaluation of Demiquas.

Apparently, while he'd been thinking these things, quite a lot of time had gone by.

All Shiroe could see was the dark passage that flowed past him. He didn't know how much distance they'd put between themselves and the shadow soldiers, but he didn't think it would be a good idea to widen the gap too much. Demiquas had taunted and attacked them mercilessly. He didn't think that army would forget their aggro, but worst-case scenarios did happen. If the shadows turned back and made for the big cavern again, this raid would fail. Even now, it wasn't clear whether they'd managed to draw out all the soldiers.

"Stop; you're getting too far ahead. Wait a little."

But as if he couldn't hear the words, Demiquas kept running.

Irked, Shiroe had to yell for him to stop over and over before he finally did. Demiquas had rubbed him the wrong way, and Shiroe raised his voice, objecting:

"What are you thinking?! If you keep going this way..."

Before he could get the rest of the words out, Shiroe was thrown into the passage and rolled, coming to a stop when his back struck the wall. As he opened his eyes partway, rubbing his arm by the passage wall, Demiquas spoke to him.

"Hey. Enc. Say my name."

Giving in to his irritation, Shiroe drew a breath, intending to call him "Dental Care"; then he looked up, and chose silence.

Feeling as if he were seeing Demiquas for the first time, Shiroe searched for the continuation of the words he'd lost.

Demiquas was leaning in to look at him, his expression stern and resolute. He'd opened his eyes so wide they looked as if they might pop out, and it was clear he'd spit out those words because he was hanging on to something he could never give up.

Thanks to that expression, the protest *Are you seriously asking stupid questions when we're under this much pressure?* had disappeared from Shiroe's mind.

It was likely that everyone had a wish they couldn't give up, just as William did.

Shiroe had one. If he hadn't, he probably still wouldn't have been affiliated with a guild.

Even Demiquas had one.

In the midst of time that was moving slowly, Shiroe thought, speculated, and discovered that the anger inside him was very similar to self-hatred. During the Catastrophe, Shiroe had felt the helplessness of being unable to do anything, and he'd been so excessively repelled by it that he'd taken it out on Demiquas, who was leaning on the fact that he couldn't do anything and acting like a despot.

Of course Demiquas had done things that couldn't be forgiven. Shiroe had had to rescue Serara. However, did he have the right to judge Demiquas? That was doubtful. Shiroe was Shiroe; he wasn't the law.

Besides, even if I did have the right to judge him…nobody should have the right to steal someone's name.

Shiroe realized he'd been stubbornly refusing to say Demiquas's name.

He wasn't like this outlaw. He wouldn't acknowledge him as a fellow human.

That was the attitude he'd taken.

"Demiquas."
"Yeah."
"—Demiquas, I can't stand you."
"Back at you, Shiroe of Log Horizon."
Shiroe and Demiquas had finally come to an understanding.
They'd reached an understanding about the fact that they couldn't reach an understanding.

And so, Shiroe was about to say, but he wasn't able to continue beyond that.

The outlaw had set the palm of his hand against his chest, and when it moved—slightly, yet brooking no argument—Shiroe's body flew through the air as if it was some kind of joke, then rolled down the passage again. He'd curled himself up, and he rolled like a soccer ball, winding up at a great steel door that was closed, coldly and tightly.

"Shiroe, you die on the other side of that. I'm busy fielding these guys."

Tossing the words over his shoulder as if to shut down Shiroe's argument, Demiquas broke into a run again. Cloaked in green light, at the end of the dark passage, he blinked two or three more times, then drifted, like a comet.

All sorts of feelings he couldn't put into words layered one over another, and Shiroe was left alone in the dark passage.

▶ 6

Beyond the door was a garden that overflowed with dazzling light.

A gear that was easily ten times as tall as Shiroe turned slowly. Wheels that were made of bare framework meshed intricately, interlocking with flywheels and lifts, controlling an immense cycle.

The purpose of this huge space was clear at a glance.

Down a channel that was like something out of Escher's trick drawings flowed an impossible amount of gold coins.

The gears, pistons, and flywheels were an immense mechanism for controlling all that gold.

A gallery of white stone wound its way through the giant machine. A brook flowed in the gallery; it was bursting with greenery, and a riot of flowers bloomed. Shiroe advanced, sometimes crossing small arched bridges or passing ponds which held heavy layers of sunken gold coins.

This garden was the vortex of gold he'd predicted.

There was a noise like a vast number of bells ringing, and he looked in its direction. A huge, iron, box-shaped vessel the size of a bus tipped and leaned, following the motions of complex chains. When it tilted, the countless gold coins inside it spilled onto a round sorting table underneath it. The sound of bells was made by those hundreds of thousands—no, those *millions* of coins.

The only word for the sight was *marvel*.

The channel, which resembled a stairway, moved mechanically. If Shiroe took a single hemp sack of coins from it, he'd probably double his assets. He tried to visualize just how much gold might be in this garden, then realized it couldn't be done and sighed.

The amount of gold coins here was vast beyond imagining.

Even so, the single contract he'd brought along didn't seem insignificant to him.

If he compared the two, it was probably trivial. Up until last year, Shiroe might have gotten discouraged. However, things were different now. When Shiroe had come down the Abyssal Shaft to the very deepest part of the Depths of Palm, he'd been prepared.

"—Welcome. I am not glad to see you, but I suppose I must say it."

The individual who was waiting for Shiroe, there in the avant-garde garden that jutted out of the enormous lake of gold, looked like Kinjo. Shiroe narrowed his eyes, examining him in detail, but he wasn't able to spot any differences. He'd been waiting here for Shiroe, with an angel fashioned from crystal at his back.

The angel was Ur of the Ninth Garden, the final raid boss that guarded Abyssal Shaft. Its height was only about four meters, which meant it was small compared to the previous enemies, but its fighting power was by no means inferior. In short, although it would be one thing if all the members of Silver Sword attacked it, if Shiroe fought it by himself, it would simply be suicide.

Or, no, even if all the members had made it here, the team would have been exhausted by their series of battles, and they might not have been able to win. However, ignoring that threat, Shiroe gazed at the young man in front of him.

The color of his collar badge is different, but that's about it... I really can't tell them apart.

This Kinjo looked like the Kinjo from the snowbound cabin, and he also looked like the Kinjo who'd greeted him at that party in Akiba. He looked like the Kinjo who was in charge of managing the bank services in Susukino as well.

Kinjo was probably that sort of person. The Kunie clan must also be that sort of clan.

Shiroe guessed that the roots of the Kunie clan must have been People of the Earth who had been bank employees and their supervisors, who had had dedicated uniforms and dedicated models, back in the days of *Elder Tales*. He saw fear and wariness in those eyes, and pride.

Well, of course he's scared. Even if he's got Ur of the Ninth Garden with him, an Adventurer has invaded... It looked like a hopeless fight to us, but it must have seemed just as hopeless to him.

Shiroe tried to imagine it.

A squad of more than twenty undying members who simply would not give up, surging into your headquarters.

Once there, they mounted a zombie attack. Even if you wiped them out, they got back up, conquering little by little. Nothing could be scarier. Both the fear and the wariness were only natural. It was probably pride that kept him standing in the way, even now. That pride was the will to protect the People of the Earth and Yamato.

The Kunie clan had adhered to the words of their progenitor and guarded Yamato for a long, long time.

Shiroe, who had been from modern Japan, couldn't begin to fathom their unity and loyalty.

"I came to speak with you, Kinjo."

"Since you've made it this far, it is our duty to hear what you have to say."

"……"

At Kinjo's hard voice, Shiroe froze up.

He'd seen it coming. This was his punishment for having harbored doubts and created unnecessary friction. Shiroe had shut Kinjo into a shell of hostility. For that very reason, the young man in white told himself, remorsefully, he had a duty to give him a thorough explanation.

"Is it all right to assume that this stream of gold coins is what I thought it was?"

"…Yes, that is correct. In accordance with our agreement, we will disclose it to you. All the gold coins in Yamato are produced here and return here. A supremely ancient technology that even we are unable to understand or control circulates the gold. From this vast torrent, coins are distributed to dungeons and monsters. This mechanism is the secret that lies in the darkness of Yamato. It is something unspeakable that the Kunie clan has kept secret for centuries."

At those words, Shiroe noticed something else.

To ordinary People of the Earth and the nobles of the League of Free Cities, the fact that the Kunie clan had managed this mechanism might seem like a betrayal. They might think they'd been providing funds to goblins and orcs.

Shiroe, who knew the *Elder Tales* game, didn't think this. He understood that it was just a system, and that it wasn't good or bad. However, the People of the Earth had fought against the demihumans for a very long time, and he wasn't sure what they'd think. If this fact were to be revealed, a movement to expel the Kunie clan might break out all across Yamato. It might even develop into riots or a massacre.

Kinjo's wariness was only natural. Shiroe hadn't given it enough thought.

"Neither I nor the others have any intention of revealing the truth of this zone or its existence to anyone else."

Even as he wondered uneasily how persuasive his words would be, Shiroe spoke to him.

"—As you have reached this place, in accordance with our progenitor's rules, you may take the gold with you."

However, the things that were going on in Shiroe's heart didn't seem to have gotten through to Kinjo. In a voice that was as hard and wary as ever, he delivered a practiced-sounding statement.

"In the course of our long history, a portion of our progenitor's writings have been lost. Even we no longer know whether you will be able to take one thousand gold coins from this place, or one hundred million. However, the tradition is to communicate our progenitor's words to you."

Kinjo gazed at Shiroe with eyes that seemed to blaze like flames.

No one was swinging a sword, but this was a clash that might surpass, and would certainly not be less than, the battles he'd come through before.

Feeling that gaze with his entire body, Shiroe forced a swallow, although his mouth was dry as dust. It made him aware of his own weakness. He'd managed to behave so nonchalantly during the Round Table Council affair, but now the strength was draining out of his knees, and it felt as if he might sit down right where he was.

However, he remembered William's profile as he'd howled. Akatsuki's worried expression as she looked up at him. Naotsugu's consideration as he joked around, trying to make him smile. Nyanta, who watched over him attentively; Minori and Touya, who trusted him; Isuzu and Rundelhaus.

What he felt now wasn't weakness.

I want them to win, Tetora had murmured.

When you wished for victory for someone else's sake, and you thought of the pain of having failed, you wanted the best so much it hurt. Shiroe the solo player, who'd been able to be irresponsible because it was just him, no longer existed. Shiroe hungered for results more than anyone else. He wasn't able to understand others' feelings well, and this was the only way he could pay them back.

" 'The gold of the Kunie is treasure that brings both fortune and misfortune. Great wealth lies not in wealth. Beware the beast in thy care. It shall destroy the world.' "

Kinjo's words sank into Shiroe. Several interpretations spread like ripples, then grew quiet.

The poem could have been taken as a sinister prophecy, but Shiroe saw it as a benediction.

Deep in his heart, he felt warmth and a gladness that he'd come here.

Shiroe and Kinjo spent long moments surrounded by the distant, ringing sound of countless bells.

Slowly, Shiroe took a single contract from his Magic Bag. Then he ripped it in two. Before Kinjo's wide eyes, the torn contract turned into softly shining flames, then flew away like a flock of butterflies.

Then, from empty space, gold appeared.

"What's—"

"A contract was just established and fulfilled. The Round Table Council does not seek wealth."

As Shiroe spoke to Kinjo, he was smiling faintly.

It was the continuation of what he'd really wanted to say, the talk that had failed at the snowy lodge.

"We don't even need the rights to the guild center. I think we have enough power to live peacefully in Akiba at this point. I'm grateful to the system that gave us that opportunity, but it's time for it to end. The conclusion we reached is that even if more trouble occurs, we should resolve it using different methods. —By being established, then torn up, this Contract Technique is complete."

Kinjo seemed bewildered, unable to grasp his meaning. Shiroe puffed out his chest.

He was proud of the fact that the Round Table Council had been able to agree to this, that it wasn't just something he himself wanted.

"We transfer all rights to the town of Akiba, including the guild halls, Temple and commercial center, to the Yamato server itself. In addition, by destroying the contract, I have made the transfer permanent."

There had been a lot of difficult behind-the-scenes negotiations and long discussions on the way to this point.

Some had held the opinion that cancelling rights they'd purchased was sheer foolishness.

However, after reconciling various merits and demerits, they'd arrived here. The purchase of zones that could be bought and were linked directly to sanction functions could only be described as the seeds of discord.

In the first place, zone purchases themselves yielded no profit. Since there was a possibility that someone would buy them someday and would push disadvantages onto them—in other words, that they would be attacked—*not* buying them wasn't an option. As a result, the Round Table Council had used nearly all of its budget and loans from the major guilds to purchase the Temple, the commercial facilities, and Akiba's aboveground urban zone.

However, now the maintenance fees had become a problem.

It had been one thing when it was just the guild center, but the cost of the Round Table Council's real estate assets—which included the town of Akiba—had swelled to over ten million gold coins per month in maintenance fees alone. This was a big financial burden.

There was an assumption that they would be attacked, and the burden came about as a result of defending against it. That was the structure. A faction centered around Shiroe and Henrietta had explored various possibilities in an attempt to reduce that burden, and had gone through many debates. This expedition had been the result of it all.

"This is… Then you say this money is the cost from when those were purchased?"

"Yes. 'All gold is produced here and returns here,' correct? Since the contract has been fulfilled, the funds used for purchase returned to the ground at my feet, in exchange for the written contract. Just as I expected."

"Did you come here to explain that, Master Shiroe?"

"In a way, yes."

"In that case, the matter of financing—what of that?"

Shiroe's glasses had slipped slightly, and he pushed them back into place with a fingertip.

"That's the main issue. We would like to purchase all the above-ground zones in Yamato: forests, mountains, lakes, adjoining marine areas, et cetera. Then, as I've just done, we would like to immediately destroy the contracts for all of our purchases and transfer them. As I've demonstrated, if we return the ownership rights for the purchased zones to Yamato, the money used for the purchases is returned... The land of Yamato should return to Yamato's hands."

Kinjo clenched his fists so hard they were white. He seemed to be desperately controlling his agitation.

"We can't process all the building-sized zones, and for now, we think they should be fine as they are. However, at the very least, we would like to fix all field zones so that they can never be owned. Besides... The People of the Earth can't purchase zones."

This was a thorn that had been piercing Shiroe's heart for a long time.

"This situation is abnormal. The Round Table Council doesn't want to become the spark that starts a war. We aren't denying the act of owning territory. However, we think contracts between people should be enough. We don't need the zone purchase system now... And so please lend the Council the necessary funds. Loan us money to return to this stream, so that we can get by without destroying ourselves."

▶ **7**

The ground was rough rock that stank of sulfur.

Thinking that only an idiot would lie down in a place like this,

William lay on his back, looking up at the ceiling. When he turned his head to the side, he saw charred arrowheads and rags dyed strange colors on the ground. It might have been somebody's equipment. It was in wretched condition.

He was so tired his whole body felt puffy with heat, and even that small movement seemed to be too much trouble. The great cavern was eerily silent, and the sounds of hissing steam and dripping water echoed loudly.

The present—which was smelly, hot, painful, listless, and disgustingly dull—was a moment of supreme bliss. William knew the liquid flowing down both sides of his nose wasn't blood, but he didn't even think about wiping it away. He'd pulled his bow so much that his arms had gone on strike, and anyway, the companions who were lying on the ground here and there were probably crying, too.

They'd won.

They'd gone through massive amounts of resources, and some comrades had been rendered unable to fight. At times, it had been a cycle of resurrection spells and bouts of unconsciousness. When Demiquas had come back, covered in blood from head to toe and pursued by shadow warriors, a premonition of defeat had crossed his mind. However, the fact that they'd already defeated Ibra Habra of the Third Garden had paid off. At that point, the Second party had plunged into a delayed battle in the passage, and they'd wrenched a high-wire victory out of the coarse melee.

He couldn't do a thing anymore. If black-armored Ruseato had appeared in this great hall now, William knew he'd be beaten with no trouble at all, as easily as an infant. The members were all torn up. They were covered in mud and dirty water, burned with ice and flame, completely exhausted—and they also shone.

Sitting up slowly, William looked around the cavern and laughed.

His laughter was quiet, but before long, it rang out cheerfully.

They'd won.

How awesome is that? he thought.

He was too happy for words. The earlier frustration and self-reproach and unease and even the despair were all being washed away.

"Awesome, that was great!" he yelled in exhilaration. William thought his lack of vocabulary was a bit sad, but that only lasted a moment as well.

"That was totally awesome! My friends are awesome, they're all completely awesome!!"

Federico, who was lying down, was waving at him.

Dinclon had stuck one of his hands into a puddle and was cooling it off. His bangs were all limp and floppy; it wrecked his handsome face.

Odiso was lying facedown, moving a thin rod like a bus guide's flag. A small Alraune abruptly appeared and, after getting scared and dithering a bit, dragged a canteen of water out of Odiso's belongings and passed it around to everyone.

Only a few of the members could move, and even then, shifting positions and sagging limply seemed to be about all they could do. Put without exaggeration, Silver Sword was currently just short of annihilation.

Still, even if they'd been nearly wiped out, a win was a win.

Yeah. Seriously awesome.

All William could do was repeat *awesome, awesome* in his heart, over and over, as if it were the only word he knew. His comrades seemed to sparkle, dazzlingly bright, to the point where it stung his eyes and he couldn't look straight at them. He was absolutely positive it wasn't because he was tearing up.

"We won."

"Yeah."

"We won."

"We actually won, huh?"

Small mutters and responses like these were being repeated around the vast space.

On hearing them, William was so happy he could have burst. He was bad at talking, but his companions' murmurs sounded like they didn't know any other words, either. The thought that there wasn't much difference between them entertained him.

"Hey, guild master."

"What?"

William responded to Federico's hoarse voice. Federico sat up, moving like a semi-invalid. "That. That over there," he said, pointing at a mountain of treasure with his chin. It was the fortunes left by the fiery serpent Ibra Habra and Tartaulga the frost giant. A mountain of gold coins, jewels, and other items that could be traded for cash, several dozen material items, and "phantasmal items"—fantasy-class weapons and defensive gear. Since they'd defeated two bosses, there was quite a lot of it.

Most of the equippable items were nontransferable. William, the raid leader, would have to hold on to them for the moment, then divvy them out among the members.

When it came to dividing up items, there were several methods. You could look at total raid participation up to the present and have members compete with achievement points, or you could decide on a priority order among the members able to equip those items, or you could have the members who wanted them play rock-paper-scissors for them and leave it up to fate. These methods were an issue that all raiding guilds dealt with through repeated trial and error.

Fantasy-class items were powerful, and raids were often conducted specifically to acquire them. Masterpieces with special signatures and abilities that couldn't be obtained any other way commanded respect from the whole server. Sometimes, as with the name "Knights of the Black Sword," they even became a guild's glory.

There were many guilds that had collapsed due to the way they divided rewards. Consequently, all guilds took the greatest possible care regarding management and reward division.

Since the era of the game, Silver Sword had used the point system. This was a method in which members used achievement points from the number of raids in which they had participated to place success-ful bids on items. However, when they'd defeated a boss that was completely unknown and had never been defeated before, the items weren't distributed by points. Instead, that privilege was customarily left to William, the guild master. Distribution according to the points system felt fair, and members found it hard to complain about it. On the other hand, items went to whoever wanted them, provided they spent points, which meant that items could end up with owners who weren't optimal from the perspective of improving fighting power.

Specific distribution by William was an arrangement that gave newly acquired, powerful equipment to apt members, so that they could conduct future captures efficiently.

His body had finally recovered, and William whipped it into action, stood, and approached the mountain of treasure. When he opened multiple layers of acquisition windows and the information was displayed, he saw rows of items that the raid bosses had dropped. Each and every one of them was the sort whose might was apparent in its name.

Well, of course. This was the first time anyone on the Yamato server had tackled a raid that was over level 90 straight on and gotten through it. After having scaled a peak he'd aspired to, William felt surprisingly calm.

Lynkeus's Eye.

Absolute Fire and Ice Blade.

Ouroboros Scale.

All were appealing. Everyone who'd participated in the raid would be able to confirm this information from where they were. Each of them sat up, checking windows that floated in empty space or looking in William's direction. In the midst of their hopeful gazes, the silver-haired young man thought for a while. Then he turned and spoke to his comrades.

"Moon Katsura-Flower Charm. This thing."

It was a charm fashioned from intricately carved metal.

Four stylized flower petals bloomed, rather proudly, in a circular frame.

"I want to give this to Machiavelli-with-Glasses."

Just then, a certain feeling faded rapidly from the area. It was a type of strained hostility, and it was also an edgy tension they'd been feeling ever since they entered the zone.

Federico's nose twitched as if he were sniffing the air. Then he muttered, "It's gotten kinda warm."

The members of the raid team understood, more clearly than if someone had explained it to them, that their capture of this zone was over. Technically, they hadn't subjugated Ruseato of the Seventh Garden yet, but it wasn't necessary anymore. The zone's hostility toward William and the others had vanished, and it had turned into a safe area.

"I guess he did something."

As he spoke, Dinclon raked up his dirty bangs with his fingers.

Just as he'd said, Shiroe seemed to have succeeded in the negotiations he'd predicted. William had thought he'd pull it off, but at the idea that he'd really done it, he felt himself break into a smile again.

"Listen up: This is a good item. Its resistance and ability value boost are both top-class. That's why I'm giving it to Machiavelli. He's not Silver Sword, but he fought alongside us, and he's a comrade."

The answer that echoed in the great cavern was agreement.

As he listened to that proud chorus, William began to hand out the next trophy.

▶ 8

Four days after they'd said good-bye to William's group:

Shiroe and the others alighted on an elevated road that was covered in greenery. As the griffins flew away (they'd exceeded the time limit), Shiroe, Naotsugu, and Tetora waved to them, then slowly began to walk over asphalt from the Age of Myth.

"Honestly! You're so cold, Naotsugu."

"I. Am. *Not!* My armor's heavy, so the griffin doesn't like carrying two riders."

"So you say. Pull the other one. I bet you really have that spot reserved for somebody, don't you?"

"Ow. Ow! What's with that comeback?!"

"Heh-heh-heh! I am an idol, you know!"

As he listened to the two of them cheerfully horsing around, Shiroe looked up at the sky.

It was a bright, peaceful winter sky. Due to the season, it would probably only last another hour or two, but the sunlight poured down on their path.

After that, he'd met up with William and the others, left the Depths of Palm and traveled with them to Susukino. In a complete turnaround from the beginning of their journey, they'd traveled together in an amiable mood.

Demiquas seemed to have undergone some great emotional change. His curt attitude was the same as ever, but he'd stopped flaring up at the Silver Sword members. As before, he didn't talk to Shiroe's group, but Shiroe wasn't bothered by it.

Every night of their return journey, they talked with the Silver Sword members about all sorts of things. Most of the conversations were very practical: They exchanged information about various things that had happened after the Catastrophe.

They hadn't talked about their life stories or discussed their worries. Silver Sword knew most things about Akiba's current situation. For Adventurers in this world, who were able to telechat, as long as you had acquaintances, it wasn't hard to get information about distant places. However, Silver Sword didn't know much of the latest news about production or inventions. Thinking it wasn't the sort of thing to hide, Shiroe made an effort to share their results in those areas. In return, Silver Sword gave him information on things as well, such as new materials they'd seen on their raids in the Ezzo Empire.

What both parties spent the most time talking about was the vast amount of material items they'd obtained on this raid. Shiroe had taken some, but most had remained with Silver Sword. If they wanted, Shopping District 8 and Grandale would probably come up to Ezzo to do business with them. Silver Sword needed to use these trophies as capital to replenish the material they'd used up.

Every night, as they sat around a campfire and ate their provisions— which were nearly gone—they talked about various aspects of their trophies, about equipment that might be possible to manufacture new, and about future courses—in other words, they talked about the exact same things they'd talked about when *Elder Tales* had been a game, and that was all.

However, Shiroe and the other participants felt a deep satisfaction.

They'd won their way through a very painful raid battle.

They didn't need unnecessary conversation. This was fine.

Naotsugu polished a new equipment piece he'd acquired, humming as he worked; Tetora sat on a rock, smiling brightly, legs swinging; and even Demiquas participated, his mouth set in a dissatisfied line, lazily using his elbow as a pillow. Shiroe looked at this, then returned to his discussion with Silver Sword. After all, it was the only souvenir he could leave on this short journey.

Theirs was a fulfilled, triumphant return.

He'd spoken briefly with William, too.

William had said they'd stay in Susukino. Giants appeared in Ezzo as field raids. This was the same as it had been in the *Elder Tales* days, but he said that sometimes new monsters joined them in the attacks. Speaking awkwardly, "Mithril Eyes" told Shiroe that they'd repel these and recover their fighting power, preparing for further raids. William added, at the end, that he was also worried about Susukino.

Shiroe nodded, agreeing with those words. There was nothing about the decision that he could object to. William was a fine guild master, and Shiroe thought the resolution was a good one.

"Add me to your friend list," William said.

Friend lists were one-way streets for both parties. Even if you'd added someone, they might not have added you. If you'd registered someone, you could contact them, so ordinarily, no one asked the other party to register them in return. If you only wanted to contact them, you could just add them to your own list, and that was all it took.

As a result, Shiroe understood that William's words meant, *If anything happens, contact me.*

He was quite possibly feeling self-conscious: William's expression was even sourer than usual.

"You're already on it," Shiroe answered.

"That's fine, then," William responded, and raised a hand.

That had been the end. They'd simply parted ways with Silver Sword, the group William led.

In *Elder Tales*, there weren't many top group players who conducted raid captures. No matter how large the guild, the size of its leading-edge raid capture group was limited. There had been fewer than five hundred of them on the Yamato server. The number wasn't large enough to feel sorry about parting with them. They were always running beside you, and you could fight together again anytime. Shiroe had learned this from William.

This might be another world now, but that probably hadn't changed. When he'd lived on Earth, Shiroe thought, that sort of relationship had been there, too; he simply hadn't known about it. Although he couldn't sense them, he had lots of unknown companions who were fighting the same way he was fighting. To Shiroe, this was no small discovery.

Even now, he had many companions who weren't affiliated with his guild.

Their biggest objective in returning to Susukino had been Li Gan. He'd made himself right at home in an inn, and his attic room had been bursting at the seams with materials. He was surrounded by books that had been brought in from who-knew-where and unintelligible notes he'd probably written himself, and he seemed very excited.

Apparently, he wouldn't be able to leave Susukino for a while longer. He seemed to have made progress in his research on the intercity transport gates. Shiroe and the others said good-bye to him, then left Susukino. Li Gan said he'd need to investigate the other gates soon, and they had plans to meet up in Akiba.

Then they'd traveled through the sky by griffin, and had finally reached Lesswall. If the griffins had been able to hold out for another thirty minutes or an hour, they'd have made it to Akiba easily, but they'd fallen just short. That said, it wasn't far enough that they'd have to set up camp and put it off until tomorrow.

If they walked for a while to stretch their legs, then summoned their horses, they'd reach Akiba after dusk. Naotsugu and Tetora knew this, and they seemed carefree.

"Whoa, hey, hold it, don't climb that!"
"If I wait, then may I climb? Respond, please."
"What-are-you-a-kid city?"
"Children don't smell half this sweet. Heh-heh-heh."
"Where did you learn a line like tha—uh, huh? Ri-right."
Naotsugu abruptly broke off his comedy routine, pushing Tetora away with a "Sorry, my bad!" then took off running, too impatient

even to summon his horse. Tetora, who'd landed bottom first, pouted a bit. Looking dissatisfied, the idol came up beside Shiroe, then twirled around.

"It isn't going well. Maybe I'm not charming enough."

"Don't tease him too much."

"If it wasn't 'too much,' it would be boring."

Chest puffed out, Tetora's face was so proud it nearly shone. Shiroe shrugged his shoulders.

"When are you going to tell him you're a boy?"

"That's a secret until he figures it out for himself. It's more fun that way."

"In that sense, this just might be an important time for Naotsugu..."

With regard to Miss Mari, Shiroe continued silently. The people in question seemed to think they were keeping it under wraps, but the fact that Naotsugu and Marielle's relationship was developing was something Shiroe and Nyanta were tacitly supporting... That said, their support was purely mental: They had no intention of meddling.

"Understood, sir! Just you leave it to me!" Tetora was beaming, and Shiroe sighed, unsure whether Tetora understood or not. He knew the kid was really the type who could read atmospheres, but being able to read them was one thing, and whether or not he acted accordingly was up to him.

It wasn't that momentum hadn't been a factor, but Shiroe was the one who'd let him join the guild. He did think he might have inadvertently made life rougher for Naotsugu.

That said, aside from the way he tended to overdo it, Tetora definitely wasn't the sort of talent who could be turned away because of his personality or ability. He'd really wanted to join, and he'd also come recommended by a friend.

"I wasn't in Susukino because Kazuhiko ordered me to be there, you know."

"I'll trust you on that."

"Besides, I think...you're probably more able to help people than I am, Shiroe."

"Log Horizon isn't a charity."

"But the world isn't hard-boiled enough to let you stay uninvolved, is it? It really is a problem."

You've got that right. Shiroe was forced to agree with Tetora's oddly world-wise opinion.

He'd bought the guild center in order to protect Akiba from a disturbance he couldn't yet see.

But knowing that wasn't enough to resolve the issue, he'd bought up more zones.

However, once he'd done it, he hadn't been able to pay all the maintenance fees, and in that case, he'd thought it would be better to dissolve the contracts and convert them into zones that couldn't be privately owned.

For that to happen, he had to free the rights of ownership to the whole Yamato server from the system, in perpetuity.

His first idea hadn't been that strange.

It had been clear to everyone that the zone ownership system was a potential source of future trouble. Shiroe had thought that since he'd been the first one to use it that way, it was his responsibility to set matters right.

However, it had taken a long time to carry out that plan; he'd had to use a variety of connections, and had ended up going all the way to the Ezzo Empire and the depths of the earth. This world really was difficult to deal with.

Still, it's not as if that's anything new.

Now that he thought about it, things weren't much different from the way they'd been in the days of the Debauchery Tea Party.

Once he started to move, all sorts of unexpected things happened. In the midst of it, he was made conscious of his lack of power. It had been a while, but looking back, he saw that it had happened every time. He remembered KR's irresponsible words: *That's just the stars you were born under. Don't give up!*

"Aaaaah!!"

Once they made a big detour around a crumbling, dangerous section of road shoulder and skirted a mountain of rubble, their view opened up. Tetora pointed down the road, got excited and broke into a run. Ahead of them was a group wearing coats in all sorts of colors, waving at Shiroe. Tetora charged at them at a furious pace, then seemed to have started some sort of ruckus with Naotsugu, who was desperately making excuses.

Smiling wryly but feeling warm inside, Shiroe kept walking slowly.

The Captain, Minori and Touya, Rundelhaus and Isuzu: They had come out just to welcome them back. There were Crescent Moon League members there, too; while Naotsugu, at his wits' end, was being hugged from both sides by Marielle and Tetora. Henrietta bowed to Shiroe silently with a gentle smile. Serara was there, too, standing happily next to Nyanta. Shouryuu and Hien were there as well.

As he began to approach the waving group, Shiroe sensed a presence and turned around.

"Have you grown a little?"
"That's mean, my liege!"

His passing comment seemed to have made Akatsuki mad, but she did look slightly more grown up. She was wearing a shawl over ninja clothes he hadn't seen before, and she really did seem kinder and braver than she had when they'd parted on the shore.

Unable to understand why that was, Shiroe gazed steadily into the small, adorable face, but... "Don't be rude, my liege," Akatsuki said, and circled around behind him.

Shiroe, whose eyes had begun to follow Akatsuki down past his side, abruptly realized that this scene was just like it had been before, and he felt his mood grow gentle.

Akatsuki had fought on a battlefield of her own.

Just as he'd seen on that white shore, Akatsuki must have reclaimed something, too.

She'd gotten just a little stronger.

The world was moving.

While Shiroe had been working hard, his companions had been fighting just as hard in other places. Just as Shiroe had sensed in William, even if he couldn't see them, he had countless companions running beside him. The realization was encouraging, and it made him feel as if he'd been rescued somehow. After a long journey, Shiroe had returned to Akiba and had been reunited with the companions who'd kept up the fight while they waited for him.

Once Shiroe noticed the feeling, he wanted to share it with them; he searched for words, but his quiet happiness kept him from finding the right ones. However, there was no need to hurry. He'd have all sorts of time to tell them.

Akatsuki was gazing up at Shiroe through her eyelashes, as if she was waiting for him to speak.

"I'm home, Akatsuki."

"Welcome back, my liege."

The lost swallow had returned to the branch where it could rest its wings, the treasure it had won through protecting others safe in its breast.

Even if he'd made mistakes, her stubborn guild master had made her wish come true, and had returned.

For now, with the smiles of children showing their trophies to each other, they simply welcomed each other home.

<Log Horizon, Volume 7: The Gold of the Kunie—The End>

RAID Q&A

Q1 What are "raids" in *Elder Tales*?

Q2 Tell me about raid ranks!

▶**A1**: Highly difficult MMORPG battle content in which multiple parties, and sometimes large groups of close to one hundred people, conquer powerful enemies that lone parties wouldn't stand a chance against. These aren't meant for characters who are still leveling up. They're end-game content that lets characters whose growth is (almost) complete enjoy the game even more and have a goal to work toward. Many raids are set as quests.

Because raids are necessary to attain the ultimate special skill level of "Secret," and because there are items which can be acquired only through raids, they're goals people aspire to.

▶**A2** : "Rank" indicates the number of people needed for a subjugation unit.

Half Raid	Subjugation unit / 12 people (smallest)
Full Raid	24 people (basic)
Legion Raid	96 people (largest)

There are many guilds whose main purpose is raiding, but when organizations are able to command legion raid–sized units, that fact alone makes them top-class guilds.

Q3 What are raid organization and basic tactics like?

▶**A3**: Basic combat in *Elder Tales* is based on (six-member) parties, rather than raids. In raids, the whole unit is divided into parties. Since a full raid has twenty-four people, it's composed of four parties.

MAIN SHIELD PARTY

ROLE

Making good use of players with strong armor, vast health, high taunting abilities, and powerful recovery abilities, the main shield party draws all the attacks from a raid enemy with unparalleled strength and aggro-pulling techniques, preventing the target from obstructing other parties. It's the star of the raid, but at the same time, it's the roughest position.

COMPOSITION

Guardian: Required because of its high defensive abilities.

Bard, Enchanter: Strengthen party; perform recovery.

Cleric, Druid, Kannagi: Utilize these three classes at once to maximize healing power.

SUB SHIELD PARTY

ROLE

A second main "shield" to help counter conditions that a lone shield party wouldn't be able to handle, such as increased difficulty of target fixing due to special abilities like Aggro Reset. Also handles simultaneous combat with multiple enemies.

COMPOSITION

As a rule, toughness, endurance, and recovery abilities are emphasized, just as with the main shield party. However, since the main and sub parties monopolize tons of recovery resources when organized exactly the same way, it can be expanded or pared down, depending on the situation. This party emphasizes mobile attacks, and highly maneuverable Monks are sometimes used instead of Guardians.

PHYSICAL FIREPOWER PARTY
MAGICAL FIREPOWER PARTY

ROLE

To attack and wipe out the enemy while the two shield parties draw its attacks. They use high firepower to obliterate raid enemies' vast HP.

COMPOSITION

The main organization method is to focus on Assassins and Sorcerers—the Weapon and Magic Attack classes—and emphasize firepower. However, in order to secure at least minimal defense and recovery, it's common to put one Warrior class and one Recovery class in each party. Samurai are often used because, although they are Warrior classes, their firepower is above a certain level and they can be counted on for high defense, at least for short periods.

This is only one example; there is no "100 percent correct structure." What's important is to grasp the characteristics of each class and participant and find the most appropriate structure for your particular group.

Q4   I want to run a raid guild!

Q5   I'd like to know what rewards you get for participating in a raid.

▶**A4**: When running and maintaining a raiding group, the central figure is the one who proposes raids, the raid host. In a raid guild, the guild master handles this.

Considered mainly in terms of raid battle content, it's popular for the guild master to serve both as raid leader and a member of the main shield party. There's a reason the leaders of famous guilds like D.D.D. and the Knights of the Black Sword are Guardians.

▶**A5**:

COMBAT EXPERIENCE POINTS

Generally, enemies that appear in raids provide higher than normal experience points. That said, most Adventurers who participate in raids have reached the maximum level, so this is a secondary reward.

SPECIAL SKILL REINFORCEMENT

Powerful raid enemies drop Proficiency Scrolls that raise the rank of Adventurers' special skills to Esoteric. It's impossible to raise the special skills of any class to Secret without clearing a specific quest for each class, and those required quests are almost always set as raids.

REWARD SHOWPIECES

A category of items obtained from raid enemies: treasure-class and fantasy-class weapons and defensive gear, as well as material items that have unique effects. Fantasy-class items in particular are powerful articles that can be obtained only on raids, and they're a constant motivation for many Adventurers.

How are you going to fight and win? The biggest reward of raid content is the sense of achievement you get when you feel your way along that line of reasoning, keep trying, and overcome multiple defeats to seize victory together!

Q6 Did anything about raids change after the Catastrophe?

▶**A6**: Due to worsening visibility and the disappearance of the mini-map, raid difficulty increased sharply, and several other important, useful changes are occurring in the environment that surrounds the areas where they take place.

EXTRA-SYSTEM REINFORCEMENTS

By thinking outside the box, D.D.D. was the first guild to defy the common sense mantra that said the maximum number that could participate in full-raid content was twenty-four people. Their idea was to bring separate personnel not part of the actual combat group to observe the battle from a high vantage point and direct the engagement via telechat. This brought about dramatic results and enabled them to clear several raids that were considered impossible in the post-Catastrophe world.

SUPPORT REINFORCE-MENT THROUGH ITEM DEVELOPMENT

Fireman's Hatchet, developed by the Roderick Trading Company, adds powerful fire attribute damage to a Hand Ax, a general-purpose thrown item which has no equip restrictions. By having all raid members throw the item, it's possible to inflict unprecedented fire damage in very little time.

New items are also being created on a daily basis in the field of recovery potions. Great post-Catastrophe discoveries include Rainbow Miracle Elixir, which concentrates the effects of preexisting potions into one, yielding multiple reinforcing effects with just one dose, and Cassowary Blood, which converts all sorts of poison damage into HP recovery.

THE DISCOVERY OF "MYSTERIES"

Unique, powerful techniques known as Mysteries or Over-skills—which don't fit the definition of conventional special skills—began to appear. There are all sorts, from Mysteries that expand conventional special skills in unique ways, to Mysteries that yield effects that have never been seen before, and they provides new options and possible tactics.

However, most Mysteries seem to be the product of individual training. They aren't the sort of thing others can use just by being taught, and currently, they have to be excluded when thinking of team tactics.

The changes to the environment surrounding raid zones haven't settled down yet. This world is still evolving daily. It's very likely that we'll be able to use new workarounds to break through raids that were said to be nearly impossible.

Q7 I want to know about major raid quests!!

▶**A7**:

The Nine Great Gaols of Halos

Mechanism

Famous among the many raids for its outstanding technicality. As the name says, it's large-scale game content in which players must capture one megadungeon composed of nine "gaols" (dungeons). At the starting point, it's possible to challenge eight gaols, including the Sky Prison, the Steel Prison and the Knights' Prison; by capturing all of these, the seal to the ninth gaol—the Final Prison—is released, making it possible to access it.

Characteristics

Gaols one through eight can be captured in any order. The events and mechanisms in multiple gaols work together in a complicated way, and the difficulty level changes drastically depending on the order in which you capture them.

Capture Method

The dungeon's background story is "a magic prison that was created to seal a certain something," and there are a variety of action restrictions (making it impossible to use recovery spells, or negating the effect of everything with a fire attribute, etc.) in each area of the gaols. These can be neutralized by fulfilling certain conditions, so the first stage of the capture depends on how quickly you can find and implement those methods.

However, the prison restrictions apply to all characters within the area. In other words, they restrict the monsters as well as the players. As a result, if you dispel the action restrictions without thinking, the monsters will also begin to use powerful attack methods they weren't able to use before. Consequently, in this dungeon, it's vital to choose whether to restrict or release; to

select appropriate party structure, equipment, and techniques; and to build strategies that are tailored to the restrictions.

Raid Enemies

Ruseato of the Seventh Prison is a raid enemy that appears in the Knights' Prison area of the megadungeon "the Nine Great Gaols of Halos." It's enormous, encased in jet-black knight's armor, and the attacks unleashed by its giant scythe are lethal all by themselves. However, when fighting it, the combat area is even more troublesome. A dungeon gimmick forces you to battle while your Recovery and Magic Attack class Adventurers are rendered unable to move, making the difficulty higher than the stated raid rank.

It's possible to get rid of this gimmick by exploring the Knights' Prison beforehand. In that case, Adventurers will be able to use their full power, but simultaneously, the full power of Ruseato of the Seventh Prison is unsealed. Under these conditions, it switches its form between two modes—White Knight and Black Knight—to suit the battle conditions, and begins to use a variety of powerful spells. When Ruseato is able to fight at its full potential like this, it can also be called Lunatic State, and it's said that during the early days of the capture attempts, a full-raid unit of players at the level maximum who went up against it were annihilated in under fifteen seconds.

Dark Campaign of Heaven and Earth

A series quest set on Spirit Mountain—which towers near the border between Eastal and Westlande—and in the surrounding region. The objective is to subjugate the Undead King, who stole energy from under Spirit Mountain and was reincarnated as a powerful Undead, and it's characterized by being split into roughly two parts.

The difficulty level of the exploration quest known as the Underground Part is set for parties or half raids.

Meanwhile, the Aboveground Part is a raid meant to be a full raid. It begins on the steep mountain fields of Spirit Mountain, and the raid is fought continuously on Sekigahara, transformed into Hades' Breath through the power of the Undead King, and in Undead Town Toyota.

The fierce fighting in the Aboveground Part is incredibly difficult. At the time, D.D.D., the Knights of the Black Sword, Howling, and the Debauchery Tea Party all worked to conquer it before the others, competing in a fierce race that has become legend on the Yamato server.

Tower of the Oracle

On the fifty-eighth floor of the Tower of the Oracle, a gigantic, soaring structure, Wenkamuy Tapisoro—a fallen dragon-god—lies in wait for Adventurers. Shaped like an Asian dragon with a big, long body, it's cloaked in a sinister miasma, and it blocks the path of anyone who's headed for the top floor. The miasma that drifts around its body creates an area of paralyzing poison, and players are continuously subjected to poison and paralysis statuses just by approaching it or being approached by it.

Since its body is so gigantic, "component damage" is set for this enemy. However, if you want to destroy a part, you need to take up a staunch position, and on top of that, battles are inevitably drawn out. It unleashes a powerful, full-body attack with an Aggro Reset effect every time a part is destroyed, so if you do this carelessly, it can lead to annihilation.

ELDER TALES MAP

EAST JAPAN EDITION

The towns and dungeons of *Elder Tales*, revealed! Check the next page for details!

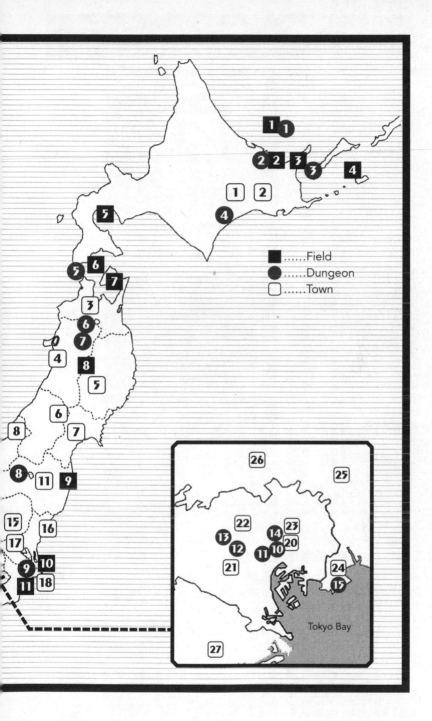

Field
Dungeon
Town

Tokyo Bay

1 Susukino

The capital of the Ezzo Empire, established in the Iskar region in the western part of Ezzo. In addition to being the Adventurer base in Ezzo, it also serves as a fortified city that stems the Giants when they attempt to invade. As one of the centers of the People of the Earth government, it also had political functions that administered the surrounding pioneer villages, but right after the Catastrophe, it was temporarily taken over by a group of outlaw Adventurers. These were subsequently suppressed by Silver Sword, a major combat guild that had relocated its headquarters from Akiba to Susukino. With security activities currently being conducted, the city is in the process of regaining its sense of peace and safety.

The Ezzo sweet potatoes traditionally eaten by the locals have grown popular among the Adventurers as well, especially when baked with butter, made into miso soup, or turned into a variety of other dishes.

2 Shuparo Barrier

A strong stone fortress and long, massive wall that has been constructed to obstruct the Giants when they invade from the North. It has been destroyed several times by attacks from the powerful Giants, and each time, it has been rebuilt.

3 Hirosaki, Town of Cherry Trees

A castle town that spreads out from Castle Blossom, which is located near the Ezzo-Eastal border, all the way to Aomori Harbor. Ships bound for Ezzo depart from here, so the town sees quite a lot of traffic, and Adventurers are sometimes recruited for guard duty.

4 The Town of Ouu

A town located very near the northern edge of Eastal. The town is small compared to the southern domains, but it's surrounded by a sturdy defensive wall that's built to last against severe threats.

5 The Town of Lawaroll

A city on the Takami River. Because it's located beside a great river that runs north to south through the northeastern region of Eastal, it's a town of water transport and commerce that developed as an important relay point for distribution between the inland regions and the South. In this town, you can find a wide variety of People of the Earth merchants, in addition to Adventurers.

6 Fortified City Mogami

A city converted into a fortress that spreads over the highlands overlooking the great Shizukami River. Originally no more than a small town, its lord's power increased due to distribution along the river, and it was expanded into a larger citadel. Now it is the castle residence of the lord who governs nearly the entire river system.

7 Taihaku Cloud Castle and Taihaku Outer Castle

The castle residence of the lord of the Taihaku region, and its castle town. Taihaku Cloud Castle is a sturdy mountain fortress built with actual combat in mind, but it's sometimes ridiculed with the words "What are they planning to fight, exactly?" and "Behind the times." Although a castle town, Taihaku Outer Castle is as solid as any fortress, living up to its name.

8　Free City Iwafune

A town that connects to the maritime trade routes through Sado, heading toward Westlande. Because its lord enthusiastically engages in trade, it's known for its particularly liberal policies, and crowds of minority races—who tend to live in the mountains in the rest of Yamato—come and go here.

9　Marine Town Sado

A port town built on the island of Sado. It is a fishing port, and at the same time it thrives as one of the commercial points of contact between the East and the West. Although it is remote, it's never lacking in physical distribution or information. Because Sado also has abundant mining resources, Adventurers seeking production materials and People of the Earth prospectors are often seen here.

10　Kashiwazaki Thunder Town

A three-level subterranean city, built on a foundation of dwarf ruins. It's called Thunder Town because the weather in the area tends to get rough with many thunderstorms and because the master builder of the dwarves who built the ruins was said to have had a voice as loud as thunder.

11　The Town of Koorima

A town said to be the gateway to northern Eastal. Because the field north of Koorima is an area in which even skilled Adventurers can't let their guards down, people are advised to make careful preparations before leaving. Many structures were built by the ancient dwarves, and some say it's a sister city to Kashiwazaki Thunder Town.

12　Sonohara Floodgate City

A People of the Earth town located on the upper reaches of the Great Zantleaf River, built on the Great Sonohara Floodgate—an Age of Myth relic—and the surrounding ruins. Hot springs well up on its outskirts, and it's possible to relax in them when you've gotten tired from exploring the ruins.

13　The Town of Fourbridge

A fortified city built in a basin in the mountains, at the midpoint of the route from Akiba to Kashiwazaki. There are lots of sour plum trees in the neighboring Haruna Forest, and the fruit liquors and pickles made with the plums are famous specialty products. The blossoms of the sour plum trees are beautiful, too, and many people visit when they're in bloom.

14　Shrine Town Hirose

A town that enshrines the star gods who govern good fortune. The entire town is an enormous ceremonial magic circle, which is used to seal a powerful flame demon. Because the seal weakens in summer, Adventurers are recruited to procure the catalyst needed to maintain the magic circle.

15　The Town of Utsurugi-Shinzen

An "altar-front" town, located to the south of the mausoleum of an ancient sacred king. It is an unusual town whose streets are just as they were in the age of the ancient alv kingdom, and it has an old-fashioned, dignified atmosphere about it. It has a powerful band of priest-warriors, and its defense is solid.

16 The Town of Hitachi

A town that grew up around its metallurgy and shipbuilding industries, thanks to abundant lumber and mineral resources from the nearby mountains. Around the town, entrances to a vast dungeon formed of a complicated web of abandoned mine galleries and shafts yawn here and there. Carelessly wandering into them is terribly dangerous.

17 Magic City Tsukuba

The influence of the academic guilds is strong, and there's an abundance of magic-related quests and items. All Magic-class adventurers visit this town over and over. Its neat streets, the result of organized divisions, are striking, and it's famous for having a griffin-riding guard brigade permanently stationed in it.

18 The Village of Choushi

A port town where the fishing industry thrives, located at the mouth of the Great Zantleaf River. Since it has no lord and isn't fortified, it used to be troubled by monster attacks, but lately, more Adventurers have begun to use it as a casual campground and are there all the time, and a new local specialty has been created: dried sahuagin shavings.

19 Shirahama

The southernmost town in Eastal, it makes use of its warm climate to flourish through fishing and animal husbandry. Many travelers and Adventurers visit just for its beautiful wide sandy beach.

20 Akiba

The first player town in Yamato, and home to many Adventurers. There was great confusion just after the Catastrophe, but since the Adventurers established the Round Table Council, an organization for self-government, public order has recovered quickly, and Akiba has blossomed as a commercial center. Since its streets bustle with facilities that use ruins from the Age of Myth and with fifteen thousand Adventurers as well as the many People of the Earth who do business with them, it's no exaggeration to say that it's the busiest place in Eastal. However, the economic revitalization is creating a disparity between energetic Adventurers and Adventurers who don't have much drive. The Round Table Council seems to have been handed a new problem: how to control the wealth generated by the invention rush from here on out.

21 Shibuya

The fifth player town, added to supplement Akiba's functions. However, as a player town, it's lacking things such as banking functions, and now that the town gate is silent, it's inconvenient. After the Catastrophe, it experienced even greater depopulation, and most of the Adventurers who still live there have a very specific reason for doing so.

22 Ikebukuro

A People of the Earth residential area. The enormous structure known as the Tower of Sunlight is eye-catching. An ancient library dungeon known as the Thorny Hall of Banned Books is located here, and it's visited by magic users seeking forbidden knowledge.

23 Asakusa

A People of the Earth residential area near Akiba. It's characterized by its collection of old temples and the shopping district that surrounds them. There are also lots of restaurants and, since the new cooking method has been popularized, People of the Earth with an enthusiasm for research pursue new flavors day and night.

24 The City of Maihama

The largest city in Eastal, the League of Free Cities, ruled by Sergiad, Duke of Maihama. It's full of impressive structures that use ruins from the Age of Myth, including enormous elevated walkways made of delicately wrought steel hanging gardens and Castle Cinderella, a palace of white stone said to be the most beautiful in Yamato. There are many "living" ruins like these in the area around Maihama as well, and there have been lots of quests for midlevel Adventurers since the days of the game. It also has complete commercial facilities, and it's a very familiar town for Adventurers. At present, Transport Ship *Nereid* has been commissioned to transport materials between Akiba and Maihama. In combination with this, work to expand the port is underway, and they seem to be recruiting lots of engineers.

25 The Village of Matsudo

A People of the Earth village near Maihama. In addition to cultivating medicinal herbs that are used as ingredients in many potions, it has dwarf blacksmith workshops, and it's strategically very important for its size.

26 The Village of Warabi

A village where People of the Earth live. Its specialty product is a fruit known as Maiden Berries. There's a nearby forest where monsters run rampant, and they frequently hire Adventurers to exterminate them.

27 Yokohama

A harbor town that flourishes as Eastal's greatest trading port. It has an area where immigrants from the eastern region of the Eured continent live, and its streets, which are bursting with exotic atmosphere, are popular among Adventurers, too.

28 Gateway City Hakone

A fortified city established on the road that links Eastal and Westlande. A stout checkpoint has been set up, and in an emergency, it serves as a key defensive location. The area is also famous for its hot springs, and lords from all over Eastal visit it in disguise.

29 Suwa Lakeside City

A large-scale peddlers' city that radiates out from the main approach to Suwa Grand Shrine. Under the control of Suwa Grand Shrine, peddlers from the area gather regularly and hold a market. The sight of Adventurers visiting to conduct sales has become a common one, but differences in manners and other types of discord are beginning to surface with the People of the Earth.

① City of Giants

A town of Giants who, according to legend, dammed up the river to create a lake, then built a town beside it. Although it is a town, everyone who lives there is a Giant, and if any of the humanoid races enter, they're instantly surrounded and struck with clubs.

② Samaikuru's Fortress

Samaikuru's Fortress is believed to be in the heart of the Forest of Kamuy, and it's said that no one has ever reached it. Some say that Samaikuru is an ancient hero, while others say he's a spirit, but the details aren't clear.

③ Upepesanke

A field-type dungeon that unfolds in a corner of the Daisetsu Mountains. A tough one, where lots of North-based enemies—including Giants, Ice Fairies, Snow Women, and Snow Wolves—appear in blizzards.

④ Kimun Kamuy's Stronghold

A field dungeon where a band of vicious bear-shaped monsters prowl, led by Kimun Kamuy, an enormous Ezzo brown bear. If you enter recklessly, you'll forfeit your life. Apparently even the Giants have trouble with the bears that live in Ezzo, and they've been spotted fighting each other all over the place.

⑤ Undersea Tunnel

The ruins of an undersea tunnel that links Honshu and the main island of Ezzo. Since it's treated as a dungeon, monsters appear in it. Its structure is simple, but as a result, there aren't many places to run, and if you don't have enough strength, it's hard to get through.

⑥ Seventh Fall

The fortress of the goblin tribe that lies in the deepest part of the Black Forest, deep woods that sprawl over the Ouu region. Lots of goblins appear here, and if underestimated or treated like small fry, it's easy to be flattened by the violence of their overwhelming numbers.

⑦ The Depths of Palm

A complicated structure of ancient mining galleries and tunnels that slumbers deep below the Tearstone Mountains. The upper areas are enormous underground roads that have become a den for ratmen. The area from the middle levels to the lower levels has crumbled in places, and the water there flows in veins. The very deepest part has yet to be implemented as a raid zone.

⑧ Byakko's Grave Marker

An abandoned castle where the ghosts of young warriors who met tragic ends wander. The ghosts still aren't aware that the castle has fallen, and they continue to protect it, mercilessly attacking anyone who enters. Since the Catastrophe, no Adventurer has yet managed to reach the deepest area and put an end to their fight.

⑨ Forest Ragranda

A dungeon distinguished by its two-level structure: a natural cavern with a Burning Dead as boss, and a subterranean shrine where the boss is a Malicious Idol. Many Undead appear, and both areas correspond to different levels. By the time players are able to clear the cavern area, they're probably strong enough to go on to the shrine.

⑩ Kanda Irrigation Canal / Akiba Sewers

An underground sewer dungeon that was implemented in the early days of *Elder Tales* and has expanded several times since. By now, it stretches from beneath Akiba toward Kanda. In terms of difficulty, it's aimed at beginners. All sorts of monsters that seem to have escaped from urban legends appear here. The biggest are giant white sewer crocodiles.

⑪ Heroes' Mausoleum

A cemetery where ancient heroes are enshrined, the stage of the Festival of the New Emperor's Return. The dungeon boss is one of the most powerful, vengeful ghosts in Yamato. Even though it's feared as a god that curses people, it's often worshipped as the guardian deity of the Eastal region.

⑫ Shinjuku Underground Passage

A dungeon zone that runs under Shinjuku. The enemies that appear are weak, and it was often used as an underground road. At present, People of the Earth who fled the aboveground areas of Shinjuku when they were destroyed by the Behemoth attack have set up camps in it, here and there.

⑬ Nakano Mall

A ruin of an enormous building from the Age of Myth. Inside, corridors and small rooms are lined up systematically, and each of the small rooms is a burial chamber. The monsters that appear are weak, and it's used as an income dungeon for beginners, but since the structure makes it easy to get lost if players don't map it properly, they're bound to regret it later.

⑭ Ueno Rogues' Castle

Decaying buildings from the Age of Myth stand like mystical monuments. At night, it's a dangerous place where good-for-nothing People of the Earth and demihuman monsters gather. Since the Catastrophe, it's become a threat to public order in the surrounding area.

⑮ Maihama Underground Passage

A mysterious corridor that lies under the city of Maihama. Its structure is fairly complicated, but apparently once used to it, it's possible to travel to anywhere in Maihama quickly.

⑯ Pied Piper Lair

A city ruled by the clown Mathers Pied Piper. It's treated as an aboveground dungeon, but at the same time, People of the Earth and monsters run shops and other facilities that can actually be used. Other monsters will attack, and the People of the Earth's reactions are rather unnatural. Everything's mixed up, and it gives off a sense of bottomless eeriness.

▶ELDER TALES

A "SWORD AND SORCERY"—THEMED ONLINE GAME AND ONE OF THE LARGEST IN THE WORLD. AN MMORPG FAVORED BY SERIOUS GAMERS, IT BOASTS A TWENTY-YEAR HISTORY.

▶THE CATASTROPHE

A TERM FOR THE INCIDENT IN WHICH USERS WERE TRAPPED INSIDE THE *ELDER TALES* GAME WORLD. IT AFFECTED THE THIRTY THOUSAND JAPANESE USERS WHO WERE ONLINE WHEN *HOMESTEADING THE NOOSPHERE*, THE GAME'S TWELFTH EXPANSION PACK, WAS INTRODUCED.

▶ADVENTURER

THE GENERAL TERM FOR A GAMER WHO IS PLAYING *ELDER TALES*. WHEN BEGINNING THE GAME, PLAYERS SELECT HEIGHT, CLASS, AND RACE FOR THESE IN-GAME DOUBLES. THE TERM IS MAINLY USED BY NON-PLAYER CHARACTERS TO REFER TO PLAYERS.

▶PEOPLE OF THE EARTH

THE NAME NON-PLAYER CHARACTERS USE FOR THEMSELVES. THE CATASTROPHE DRASTICALLY INCREASED THEIR NUMBERS FROM WHAT THEY WERE IN THE GAME. THEY NEED TO SLEEP AND EAT LIKE REGULAR PEOPLE, SO IT'S HARD TO TELL THEM APART FROM PLAYERS WITHOUT CHECKING THE STATUS SCREEN.

▶THE HALF-GAIA PROJECT

A PROJECT TO CREATE A HALF-SIZED EARTH INSIDE *ELDER TALES*. ALTHOUGH IT'S NEARLY THE SAME SHAPE AS EARTH, THE DISTANCES ARE HALVED, AND IT HAS ONLY ONE-FOURTH THE AREA.

▶AGE OF MYTH

A GENERAL TERM FOR THE ERA SAID TO HAVE BEEN DESTROYED IN THE OFFICIAL BACKSTORY OF THE *ELDER TALES* ONLINE GAME. IT WAS BASED ON THE CULTURE AND CIVILIZATION OF THE REAL WORLD. SUBWAYS AND BUILDINGS ARE THE RUINED RELICS OF THIS ERA.

▶THE OLD WORLD

THE WORLD WHERE SHIROE AND THE OTHERS LIVED BEFORE *ELDER TALES* BECAME ANOTHER WORLD AND TRAPPED THEM. A TERM FOR EARTH, THE REAL WORLD, ETC.

▶GUILDS

TEAMS COMPOSED OF MULTIPLE PLAYERS. MANY PLAYERS BELONG TO THEM, BOTH BECAUSE IT'S EASIER TO CONTACT AFFILIATED MEMBERS AND INVITE THEM ON ADVENTURES AND ALSO BECAUSE GUILDS PROVIDE CONVENIENT SERVICES (SUCH AS MAKING IT EASIER TO RECEIVE AND SEND ITEMS).

▶THE ROUND TABLE COUNCIL

THE TOWN OF AKIBA'S SELF-GOVERNMENT ORGANIZATION, FORMED AT SHIROE'S PROPOSAL. COMPOSED OF ELEVEN GUILDS, INCLUDING MAJOR COMBAT AND PRODUCTION GUILDS AND GUILDS THAT COLLECTIVELY REPRESENT SMALL AND MIDSIZE GUILDS, IT'S IN A POSITION TO LEAD THE REFORMATION IN AKIBA.

▶LOG HORIZON

THE NAME OF THE GUILD SHIROE FORMED AFTER THE CATASTROPHE. ITS FOUNDING MEMBERS—AKATSUKI, NAOTSUGU, AND NYANTA—HAVE BEEN JOINED BY THE TWINS MINORI AND TOUYA. THEIR HEADQUARTERS IS IN A RUINED BUILDING PIERCED BY A GIANT ANCIENT TREE ON THE OUTSKIRTS OF AKIBA.

▶THE CRESCENT MOON LEAGUE

THE NAME OF THE GUILD MARI LEADS. ITS PRIMARY PURPOSE IS TO SUPPORT MIDLEVEL PLAYERS. HENRIETTA, MARI'S FRIEND SINCE THEIR DAYS AT A GIRLS' HIGH SCHOOL, ACTS AS ITS ACCOUNTANT.

▶THE DEBAUCHERY TEA PARTY

THE NAME OF A GROUP OF PLAYERS THAT SHIROE, NAOTSUGU, AND NYANTA BELONGED TO AT ONE TIME. IT WAS ACTIVE FOR ABOUT TWO YEARS, AND ALTHOUGH IT WASN'T A GUILD, IT'S STILL REMEMBERED IN *ELDER TALES* AS A LEGENDARY BAND OF PLAYERS.

▶FAIRY RINGS

TRANSPORTATION DEVICES LOCATED IN FIELDS. THE DESTINATIONS ARE TIED TO THE PHASES OF THE MOON, AND IF PLAYERS USE THEM AT THE WRONG TIME, THERE'S NO TELLING WHERE THEY'LL END UP. AFTER THE CATASTROPHE, SINCE STRATEGY WEBSITES ARE INACCESSIBLE, ALMOST NO ONE USES THEM.

▶ZONE

A UNIT THAT DESCRIBES RANGE AND AREA IN *ELDER TALES*. IN ADDITION TO FIELDS, DUNGEONS, AND TOWNS, THERE ARE ZONES AS SMALL AS SINGLE HOTEL ROOMS. DEPENDING ON THE PRICE, IT'S SOMETIMES POSSIBLE TO BUY THEM.

▶THELDESIA

THE NAME FOR THE GAME WORLD CREATED BY THE HALF-GAIA PROJECT. A WORD THAT'S EQUIVALENT TO "EARTH" IN THE REAL WORLD.

▶SPECIAL SKILL

VARIOUS SKILLS USED BY ADVENTURERS. ACQUIRED BY LEVELING UP YOUR MAIN CLASS OR SUBCLASS. EVEN WITHIN THE SAME SKILL, THERE ARE FOUR RANKS— ELEMENTARY, INTERMEDIATE, ESOTERIC, AND SECRET—AND IT'S POSSIBLE TO MAKE SKILLS GROW BY INCREASING YOUR PROFICIENCY.

▶ MAIN CLASS

THESE GOVERN COMBAT ABILITIES IN *ELDER TALES*, AND PLAYERS CHOOSE ONE WHEN BEGINNING THE GAME. THERE ARE TWELVE TYPES, THREE EACH IN FOUR CATEGORIES: WARRIOR, WEAPON ATTACK, RECOVERY, AND MAGIC ATTACK. SEE THE SECTION BELOW FOR DETAILS.

▶ SUBCLASS

ABILITIES THAT AREN'T DIRECTLY INVOLVED IN COMBAT BUT COME IN HANDY DURING GAME PLAY. ALTHOUGH THERE ARE ONLY TWELVE MAIN CLASSES, THERE ARE OVER FIFTY SUBCLASSES, AND THEY'RE A JUMBLED MIX OF EVERYTHING FROM CONVENIENT SKILL SETS TO JOKE ELEMENTS.

▶ MYSTERY

ALSO CALLED OVERSKILL BY SOME PLAYERS. UNIQUE, POWERFUL TECHNIQUES THAT ARE UNLIKE CONVENTIONAL SPECIAL SKILLS. CREATED WHEN INDIVIDUAL PLAYERS EVOLVE AND EXPAND ABILITIES FROM THE DAYS OF THE GAME.

▶ ARC-SHAPED ARCHIPELAGO YAMATO

THE WORLD OF THELDESIA IS DESIGNED BASED ON REAL-WORLD EARTH. THE ARC-SHAPED ARCHIPELAGO YAMATO IS THE REGION THAT MAPS TO JAPAN, AND IT'S DIVIDED INTO FIVE AREAS: THE EZZO EMPIRE; THE DUCHY OF FOURLAND; THE NINE-TAILS DOMINION; EASTAL, THE LEAGUE OF FREE CITIES; AND THE HOLY EMPIRE OF WESTLANDE.

▶ CAST TIME

THE PREPARATION TIME NEEDED WHEN USING A SPECIAL SKILL. THESE ARE SET FOR EACH SEPARATE SKILL, AND MORE POWERFUL SKILLS TEND TO HAVE LONGER CAST TIMES. WITH COMBAT-TYPE SPECIAL SKILLS, IT'S POSSIBLE TO MOVE DURING CAST TIME, BUT WITH MAGIC-BASED SKILLS, SIMPLY MOVING INTERRUPTS CASTING.

▶ MAIN CLASSES

[WARRIOR CLASSES]

GUARDIAN
BOASTS THE HIGHEST DEFENSE. ABLE TO ATTRACT ENEMIES WITH TAUNTS.

SAMURAI
USES JAPANESE EQUIPMENT AND TECHNIQUES WITH POWERFUL EFFECTS.

MONK
A BALANCED TYPE. SHORT ON WEAPONRY, BUT HAS FANTASTIC EVASIVE SKILLS.

[WEAPON ATTACK CLASSES]

ASSASSIN
A FOCUSED ATTACKER. SKILLED WITH A WIDE VARIETY OF WEAPONS.

SWASHBUCKLER
A VERSATILE, MOBILE FIGHTER. USES TWO SWORDS.

BARD
A LIGHTLY EQUIPPED WARRIOR. USES A WIDE RANGE OF "SONGS" WITH MAGICAL EFFECTS.

▶MOTION BIND

REFERS TO THE WAY YOUR BODY FREEZES UP AFTER YOU'VE USED A SPECIAL SKILL. DURING MOTION BIND, ALL ACTIONS ARE IMPOSSIBLE, INCLUDING MOVEMENT.

▶RECAST TIME

THE AMOUNT OF TIME YOU HAVE TO WAIT AFTER YOU'VE USED A SPECIAL SKILL BEFORE YOU CAN USE IT AGAIN. THIS RESTRICTION MAKES IT VERY DIFFICULT TO USE A SPECIFIC SPECIAL SKILL SEVERAL TIMES IN A ROW. SOME SPECIAL SKILLS HAVE SUCH LONG RECAST TIMES THAT THEY CAN BE USED ONLY ONCE PER DAY.

▶CALL OF HOME

A BASIC TYPE OF SPECIAL SKILL THAT ALL ADVENTURERS LEARN. IT INSTANTLY RETURNS YOU TO THE LAST SAFE AREA WITH A TEMPLE THAT YOU VISITED, BUT ONCE YOU USE IT, YOU CAN'T USE IT AGAIN FOR TWENTY-FOUR HOURS.

▶RAID

THE TERM FOR A BATTLE FOUGHT WITH NUMBERS LARGER THAN THE NORMAL SIX-MEMBER PARTIES THAT ADVENTURERS USUALLY FORM. IT CAN ALSO BE USED TO REFER TO A UNIT MADE UP OF MANY PEOPLE. FAMOUS EXAMPLES INCLUDE TWENTY-FOUR-MEMBER FULL RAIDS AND NINETY-SIX-MEMBER LEGION RAIDS.

▶RACE

THERE ARE A VARIETY OF HUMANOID RACES IN THE WORLD OF THELDESIA. ADVENTURERS MAY CHOOSE TO PLAY AS ONE OF EIGHT RACES: HUMAN, ELF, DWARF, HALF ALV, FELINOID, WOLF-FANG, FOXTAIL, AND RITIAN. THESE ARE SOMETIMES CALLED BY THE GENERAL TERM, "THE 'GOOD' HUMAN RACES."

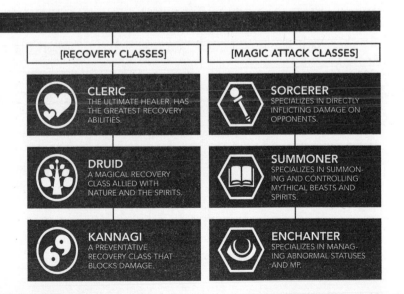

[RECOVERY CLASSES]

CLERIC
THE ULTIMATE HEALER. HAS THE GREATEST RECOVERY ABILITIES.

DRUID
A MAGICAL RECOVERY CLASS ALLIED WITH NATURE AND THE SPIRITS.

KANNAGI
A PREVENTATIVE RECOVERY CLASS THAT BLOCKS DAMAGE.

[MAGIC ATTACK CLASSES]

SORCERER
SPECIALIZES IN DIRECTLY INFLICTING DAMAGE ON OPPONENTS.

SUMMONER
SPECIALIZES IN SUMMONING AND CONTROLLING MYTHICAL BEASTS AND SPIRITS.

ENCHANTER
SPECIALIZES IN MANAGING ABNORMAL STATUSES AND MP.

AFTERWORD

To those I haven't seen for a while, it's been a while. To those I've never met, it's great to meet you. This is Mamare Touno.

Hey, what was *that*, huh? What's with the breezy greeting? Wasn't it supposed to be autumn now, hmmm? (Self-administered comeback.) I'm sorry, I'm really sorry. Apologizing's become a habit for me lately. I'm reaping what I sow, but anyway. When this book hits the shelves, the world will probably be coming up on Christmas (Nostradamus style). I'll corrode your Christmases with what I've sown (Grim Reaper).

If you're wondering why the "great to meet you" greeting is there, it's because—yes, that's right—the *Log Horizon* TV anime has started airing. By the time this book gets to you, it will probably be about half-way through. Thanks to all of you, they've created a very well-made anime. I'm sure there are new people watching it, too.

Thank you for picking up *Log Horizon, Volume 7: The Gold of the Kunie*. Due to the above, I'll be praying that this book makes it into the hands of new readers, too. Or, no, it won't be the power of prayer that gets it to them. It'll be Enterbrain's publishing and Tosho Printing's printing and the distributor's hard work and the bookstores dynamically doing their jobs that get it to them.

Setting that aside, let me talk about the Afterword's Season Two heroine.

In other words, this is about my supervising editor, Ms. F——ta.

Do you know about meetings between authors and editors? They discuss creation theories, sometimes fighting, sometimes acknowledging each other, and it's terribly intense. (Reference material: *Blaze Up, Pen.*) F——ta and I are constantly holding ferocious meetings, too.

"……"

"……"

"It's raining, huh?"

"Yes, what a drag."

"Did you eat already?"

"I could eat."

"You could, hmm?"

"All right, then, let's go."

I was informed that deciding whether it's time to eat, not by the amount of time that's passed since your last meal, but by whether you *could* eat or not, is probably the secret of youth. Not that all we do is skip work or anything.

Come to think of it, when I quoted F——ta's comment that "women are carnivores" in the previous afterword, I got a big response.

I asked about twenty women "Do you like meat?" and all of them answered, "Yes. I like meat."

Is that true?

Are you serious?

I got culture shock. I didn't know women were such meat eaters. I mean, I'm not denying that there are women who like meat. Of course there are. I just didn't think the rate was this high (100 percent, from my observations).When I asked Sister Touno—whose staple food was daikon radishes—just to be on the safe side, she said, "Meat that someone else buys for me is yummy." I'm always treating my sister to things. She's gotten a little sharper again.

Speaking of things F——ta's done lately, she bought a new notebook computer. A MacBook Air. It's a splendid computer. During meetings and whenever she's got free time, she always has her hands on it.

"Ms. F——ta. When you use that computer, you look like a really skilled businesswoman."

"Don't I?! Don't I just?!"

"Yes."

Takka takka takka takka clack!! (Check *that* out!)

"You're very cool."

Takka takka takka takka clack!! (Check *this* out!)

"Very cool."

That pose when she hits the Enter key and the proud look she gets when she's done it (and then glances at me) say "businesswoman" all over. Parenthetically, I've never worked with women in uniforms in an office in my life, so the "businesswoman" that appears in this text is fiction. She likes meat, and she sits on a coffee cup and says "Hisssss!"

Hisssss.

And with that report on the current situation, this has been *Log Horizon*, Volume 7.

Friends are hard. Once you're out in adult society, they're really hard.

It's tough both to make them and to keep them, and it's hard even to admit that friends are friends. When I was in school, if I did something for someone or they did something for me, I thought of that person as a friend. I thought we needed proof, you see.

Once you're an adult, you realize how little you can really do for your friends. You can't take over your friends' problems for them, and when they're worrying about something, you can't draw a conclusion in their place. You feel bad about your powerlessness to do those things, and so you hesitate to call them friends.

Well, Shiroe is bad at making friends, but it isn't that he doesn't treasure them, and I bet he's the type who can. He'll keep making new companions and friends, little by little, along with Naotsugu and the new character Tetora. Guys may be tiresome, but they're simple, and if they kick up a ruckus on a raid together, they're able to make friends with each other.

I think it's okay to be friends even if they don't do anything for you, and you can't do anything for them. As other people, there was never all that much we could shoulder for them in the first place.

About all we can do is go out for dinner together and pay their check.

I can certainly treat them to meat, and I'd be glad to do it.

The items listed on the character status screens at the beginning of each chapter were collected from Twitter in August 2013. I used items from @Dateryu, @IGM_masamune, @RN_oinu, @SakamotoRiji, @ebius1, @haniwatw, @hige_mg, @hpsuke, @iron007dd22, @kane_yon, @kuroyagi6, @makiwasabi, @makotoTRPG, @me_pon, @momon_call, @roqku, @sig_cat, and @yamaneeeeee. Thank you very much!! I can't list all your names here, but I'm grateful to everyone who submitted entries. I actually got submissions from overseas, too. People are supporting *Log Horizon* from all sorts of countries.

For details, and for the latest news, visit http://tounomamare.com. You'll find information about Mamare Touno that isn't *Log Horizon*–related as well. There's also information on the anime. Come to think of it, they're putting out a TRPG, too.

Finally, Shoji Masuda, who produced this volume (and who also attended lots of anime script meetings); Kazuhiro Hara, the illustrator (Tetora's really cute); Tsubakiya Design, who handled the design work; little F——ta of the editorial department! Oha, I'm in your debt yet again! And Kosuda and Nishi from Tosho Printing, of whom I made unreasonable demands right at the end, thank you very much! I'm really sorry to have been late with my delivery.

Now all that's left is for you to savor this book. *Bon appétit!*

Mamare "Dreaming of ordering a new notebook computer and practicing that 'clack'" Touno

GREAT
WORK!!
HARA

▶LOG HORIZON, VOLUME 7
MAMARE TOUNO
ILLUSTRATION BY KAZUHIRO HARA

▶TRANSLATION BY TAYLOR ENGEL
COVER ART BY KAZUHIRO HARA

▶LOG HORIZON, VOLUME 7:
THE GOLD OF THE KUNIE

▶©2014 TOUNO MAMARE
ALL RIGHTS RESERVED.

▶FIRST PUBLISHED IN JAPAN IN 2014 BY KADOKAWA CORPORATION ENTERBRAIN. ENGLISH TRANSLATION RIGHTS ARRANGED WITH KADOKAWA CORPORATION ENTERBRAIN THROUGH TUTTLE-MORI AGENCY, INC., TOKYO.

▶ENGLISH TRANSLATION © 2017 BY YEN PRESS, LLC

▶YEN ON
1290 AVENUE OF THE AMERICAS
NEW YORK, NY 10104

▶VISIT US AT YENPRESS.COM
FACEBOOK.COM/YENPRESS
TWITTER.COM/YENPRESS
YENPRESS.TUMBLR.COM
INSTAGRAM.COM/YENPRESS

▶FIRST YEN ON EDITION: MARCH 2017

▶YEN ON IS AN IMPRINT OF YEN PRESS, LLC.
THE YEN ON NAME AND LOGO ARE TRADEMARKS OF YEN PRESS, LLC.

▶LIBRARY OF CONGRESS CATALOGING-IN-PUBLICATION DATA
NAMES: TOUNO, MAMARE, AUTHOR. | HARA, KAZUHIRO, ILLUSTRATOR. | ENGEL, TAYLOR, TRANSLATOR.
TITLE: LOG HORIZON. VOLUME 7, THE GOLD OF THE KUNIE / MAMARE TOUNO ; ILLUSTRATION BY KAZUHIRO HARA ; TRANSLATION BY TAYLOR ENGEL.
DESCRIPTION: FIRST YEN ON EDITION. | NEW YORK, NY : YEN ON, 2017–
IDENTIFIERS: LCCN 2015038410 | ISBN 9780316383059 (V. 1 : PAPERBACK) | ISBN 9780316263818 (V. 2 : PAPERBACK) | ISBN 9780316263849 (V. 3 : PAPERBACK) | ISBN 9780316263856 (V. 4 : PAPERBACK) | ISBN 9780316263863 (V. 5 : PAPERBACK) | ISBN 9780316263870 (V. 6 : PAPERBACK) | ISBN 9780316263887 (V. 7 : PAPERBACK)
SUBJECTS: | CYAC: SCIENCE FICTION. | BISAC: FICTION / SCIENCE FICTION / ADVENTURE.
CLASSIFICATION: LCC PZ7.1.T67 LOJ 2016 | DDC [FIC]—DC23
LC RECORD AVAILABLE AT HTTPS://LCCN.LOC.GOV/2015038410

ISBN: 978-0-316-26388-7

10 9 8 7 6 5 4 3 2 1

▶LSC-C

▶PRINTED IN THE UNITED STATES OF AMERICA

▶AUTHOR: **MAMARE TOUNO**

▶SUPERVISION: **SHOJI MASUDA**

▶ILLUSTRATION: **KAZUHIRO HARA**

▶ AUTHOR: MAMARE TOUNO

A STRANGE LIFE-FORM THAT INHABITS THE TOKYO BOKUTOU SHITAMACHI AREA. IT'S BEEN TOSSING HALF-BAKED TEXT INTO A CORNER OF THE INTERNET SINCE THE YEAR 2000 OR SO. IT'S A FULLY AUTOMATIC, TEXT-LOVING MACRO THAT EATS AND DISCHARGES TEXT. IT DEBUTED AT THE END OF 2010 WITH *MAOYUU: MAOU YUUSHA (MAOYUU: DEMON KING AND HERO)*. *LOG HORIZON* IS A RESTRUCTURED VERSION OF A NOVEL THAT RAN ON THE WEBSITE *SHOUSETSUKA NI NAROU (SO YOU WANT TO BE A NOVELIST)*.

WEBSITE: HTTP://WWW.MAMARE.NET

▶ SUPERVISION: SHOJI MASUDA

AS A GAME DESIGNER, HE'S WORKED ON *RINDA KYUUBU (RINDA CUBE)* AND *ORE NO SHIKABANE WO KOETE YUKE (STEP OVER MY DEAD BODY)*, AMONG OTHERS. ALSO ACTIVE AS A NOVELIST, HE'S RELEASED THE *ONIGIRI NUEKO (ONI KILLER NUEKO)* SERIES, THE *HARUKA* SERIES, *JOHN & MARY: FUTARI HA SHOUKIN KASEGI (JOHN & MARY: BOUNTY HUNTERS)*, *KIZUDARAKE NO BIINA (BEENA, COVERED IN WOUNDS)*, AND MORE. HIS LATEST EFFORT IS HIS FIRST CHILDREN'S BOOK, *TOUMEI NO NEKO TO TOSHI UE NO IMOUTO (THE TRANSPARENT CAT AND THE OLDER LITTLE SISTER)*. HE HAS ALSO WRITTEN *GEEMU DEZAIN NOU MASUDA SHINJI NO HASSOU TO WAZA (GAME DESIGN BRAIN: SHINJI MASUDA'S IDEAS AND TECHNIQUES)*.

TWITTER ACCOUNT: SHOJIMASUDA

▶ ILLUSTRATION: KAZUHIRO HARA

AN ILLUSTRATOR WHO LIVES IN ZUSHI. ORIGINALLY A HOME GAME DEVELOPER. IN ADDITION TO ILLUSTRATING BOOKS, HE'S ALSO ACTIVE IN MANGA AND DESIGN. LATELY, HE'S BEEN HAVING FUN FLYING A BIOKITE WHEN HE GOES ON WALKS. HE'S BEEN WORKING ON THE *LOG HORIZON* COMICALIZATION PROJECT WITH COMIC CLEAR SINCE 2012.

WEBSITE: HTTP://WWW.NINEFIVE95.COM/IG/

Adventurer, you whose weight is borne by your winged soul! The mystical world of Theldesia is home to dragons and giants, magical beasts, and demihumans. Fragrant green winds blow across this new yet ancient land that opens before you like a blank page. Fill it with your life.

LOG HORIZON